# PROTECTOR

# PROTECTOR

*A Novel of Ancient Greece*

## CONN IGGULDEN

PEGASUS BOOKS

NEW YORK  LONDON

PROTECTOR

Pegasus Books, Ltd.
148 West 37th Street, 13th Floor
New York, NY 10018

Copyright © 2021 by Conn Iggulden

First Pegasus Books cloth edition November 2021

ISBN: 978-1-64313-817-6

10 9 8 7 6 5 4 3 2 1

Printed in the United States of America
Distributed by Simon & Schuster
www.pegasusbooks.com

*To Sr. Andrea MacEachen and*
*Sr. Mauraid Moran – guides in the wilderness.*

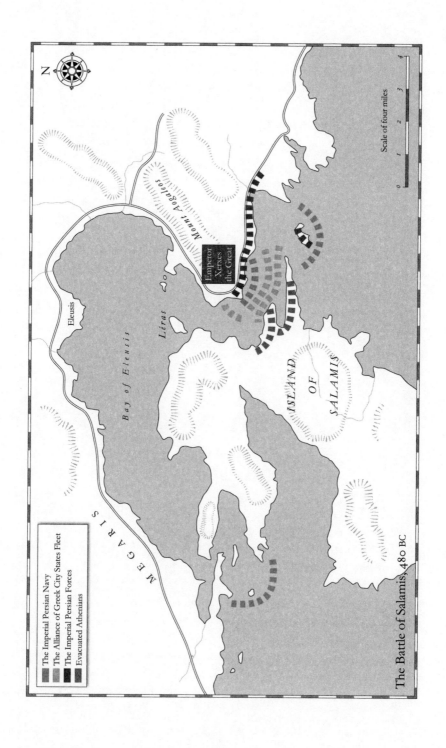

N

Scale of four miles

0   1   2   3   4

MEGARIS

Bay of Eleusis

Eleusis

Léras

Mount Aegáleos

Emperor Xerxes the Great

ISLAND OF SALAMIS

The Imperial Persian Navy
The Alliance of Greek City States Fleet
The Imperial Persian Forces
Evacuated Athenians

The Battle of Salamis, 480 BC

# Pronunciation

## *Military terms*

| | Ancient Greek | Ancient Greek Pronunciation | English Pronunciation | Meaning |
|---|---|---|---|---|
| archon | ἄρχων | ark-own | ark-on | Ruler, leader. |
| epistates | ἐπιστάτης | ep-ist-at-airs | ep-ist-at-eez | Chairman in the Athenian Assembly. |
| keleustes | κελευστής | kel-eu-stairs | kel-you-steez | Trireme officer. |
| lochagos | λοχαγός | lock-a-goss | lock-a-goss | Rank equivalent to captain. |
| phalanx | Φάλαγξ | fal-anks | fal-anks | Body of heavily armed infantry. |
| strategos | στρατηγός | strat-air-goss | strat-egg-oss | General, commander. |
| trierarch | τριήραρχος | tree-air-ark-oss | try-err-ark | Commander of a trireme. |

Underlining indicates stressed syllables.

## Locations

| | | | | |
|---|---|---|---|---|
| Agora | Ἀγορά | ag-or-a | ag-<u>or</u>-a | Open place, market. |
| Areopagus | Ἄρειος πάγος | a-ray-oss pag-oss | a-ree-<u>op</u>-ag-ous (as in danger-ous) | Rock of Ares. Hill in Athens used as a court. |
| Plataea | Πλάταια | plat-eye-a | pla-t<u>ee</u>-a | Greek town in Boeotia. |
| Pnyx | Πνύξ | p-nooks | p-<u>niks</u> | 'Packed in'. Hill. Meeting place of the Assembly in Athens. |
| Salamis | Σαλαμίς | sal-a-miss | <u>sal</u>-a-miss | Island off Athens. |
| Thermopylae | Θερμοπύλαι | therm-opp-ool-eye | therm-<u>op</u>-ill-ay | Coastal pass. Last stand of King Leonidas. |

# Characters

| | | | | |
|---|---|---|---|---|
| Agariste | Ἀγαρίστη | ag-a-rist-air | ag-a-<u>rist</u>-ee | Wife of Xanthippus. |
| Ariphron | Ἀρίφρων | a-ri-frone | <u>a</u>-ri-fron | First son of Xanthippus and Agariste. |
| Aristides | Ἀριστείδης | a-ris-tay-dairs | a-<u>rist</u>-id-eez | Strategos, eponymous archon 489 BC. |
| Cimon | Κίμων | kim-own | <u>ky</u>-mon | Son of Miltiades. |
| Cleisthenes | Κλεισθένης | clay-sthen-airs | <u>cly</u>-sthen-eez | Athenian lawmaker. |
| Eleni (Helen) | Ἑλένη | hell-en-air | e-<u>lay</u>-nee | Daughter of Xanthippus and Agariste. |
| Epikleos | Ἔπικλέος | ep-i-kle-oss | ep-i-<u>klay</u>-oss | Friend of Xanthippus. |
| Leotychides | Λεωτυχίδας | lair-oh-took-i-das | lee-oh-<u>tick</u>-i-dees | Spartan king. |
| Pericles | Περικλῆς | per-ik-lairs | <u>per</u>-ik-leez | Son of Xanthippus and Agariste. |
| Themistocles | Θεμιστοκλῆς | th-mist-o-clairs | th-<u>mist</u>-o-cleez | Eponymous archon 493 BC. |
| Tisamenus | Τισαμενός | tiss-am-en-oss | tiss-a-<u>meen</u>-ous | Soothsayer. |
| Xanthippus | Ξάνθιππος | ksan-thip-oss | <u>zan</u>-thip-ous | Strategos, leader. |
| Xerxes | Ξέρξης | kserk-seez | <u>zerk</u>-seez | King of Persia. |

# Ten tribes of Athens

| | | | |
|---|---|---|---|
| Erechtheis | Ἐρεχθηΐς | e-rek-thair-ees | e-_rek_-thay-iss |
| Aegeis | Αἰγηΐς | eye-gair-ees | a-_jee_-iss |
| Pandionis | Πανδιονίς | pand-ee-on-iss | pand-ee-_own_-iss |
| Leontis | Λεοντίς | le-ont-iss | lee-_ont_-iss |
| Acamantis | Ἀκαμαντίς | ak-am-ant-iss | ak-am-_ant_-iss |
| Oeneis | Οἰνηΐς | oy-nair-ees | ee-_nee_-iss |
| Cecropis | Κεκροπίς | kek-rop-iss | kek-_rop_-iss |
| Hippothontis | Ἱπποθοντίς | hip-oth-ont-iss | hip-oth-_ont_-iss |
| Aeantis | Αἰαντίς | eye-ant-iss | eye-_ant_-iss |
| Antiochis | Ἀντιοχίς | ant-i-ok-iss | ant-ee-_ok_-iss |

# PROTECTOR

PROTECTOR

# PART ONE

'There are no pacts between lions and men, nor do wolves and lambs make peace.'

– Homer, *The Iliad*

# I

The king of Persia looked across the heart of Athens.

The sun was hot on the back of his neck, but a breeze blew, warm and gentle, carrying a smell of sweetness – of rot and the sea. Xerxes closed his eyes and breathed, feeling at peace. The great market, the temples, the streets of households, workshops and taverns – they were all abandoned. It was intimate, somehow. He felt as if he sat at a woman's dressing table, opening every small drawer, learning her secrets.

The soldiers in that place were all his own. They had searched Athens from one end to the other, every store-house, shop and empty home. The only Greeks within the walls had been half a dozen mindless ancients, left behind by their families. Toothless and blind, they had hissed incredu-lous, nervous laughter at the strange voices of Persian soldiers. Xerxes had no need of them. Like stray dogs, they had been killed quickly. It was almost a mercy.

General Mardonius walked three paces behind the Great King, deep in his own reverie. Both he and Xerxes had ex-perienced a strange sort of recognition as they'd entered Athens. Places and natural features surfaced from a hundred old reports, suddenly made real. The Acropolis was one, the cliff of limestone that loomed on their left hand, sentinel for the whole city; or perhaps the pale Areopagus rock, where a council of Athenian noblemen had met for centuries.

Xerxes could see the Pnyx hill ahead, rising with trees like blades and white steps on its flanks. In normal times, the famous Assembly met and argued in that place, acknowledging no king or tyrant. He would have liked to see it, those men so busy with their little laws. Yet only the breeze blew there that day. The people of Athena's city had gone down to the port, to be taken by ship across the deep water. Rather than suffer the predations of his army, rather than learn the consequences of their arrogance, they had *run* from him.

Xerxes walked through streets where doors hung open and every sound echoed. Beyond a few cats warming themselves on roofs, his Immortals were the only living things he could see. They stood in long, panelled coats, ringlet beards oiled to a shine, like statues themselves. The Great King loved them as his father had, like favourite children or beloved hunting dogs, both the shield and ornament of his reign. Half their number had been killed by the red-cloaked butchers of Thermopylae. His Immortals still reeled from that blow, though they had opened the pass in the end! Xerxes had chosen to mark only that final victory, keeping them as his guards, honouring them with his blessing. The five thousand who lived were survivors: battered and bruised, but stronger for having seen the last Spartans cut down. The Immortals had not broken in that pass. Yet they had believed they were unbeatable, without equal in the world. Xerxes had witnessed their shock, their disbelief. The Spartans had made them feel helpless.

Xerxes had even considered resting the regiment, taking them out of his vanguard. Their commander was a great bull of a man – Hydarnes. With his face pressed in the dirt, he had pleaded for the Immortals then, saying they needed to work, that they would fester like a bad wound if they were given too much time to think. Xerxes had agreed. Honour could not be granted. It had to be earned through sacrifice and hard service.

At the end of a street where potters' wheels sat untended,

*Conn Iggulden*

the light changed, brighter and airier than the roads around. Xerxes entered the famous Agora marketplace. There were the statues for the ten tribes, with stone tablets to be read out loud. He did not approach them, but he imagined at least a few warned of his own approach. His pride surged at the thought.

Xerxes looked up as a hawk keened overhead, its cry perfectly clear in the still air. The bird wove huge circles over the city and Xerxes could see the head turning, looking for prey. On any normal day, such a sound would have gone unnoticed, lost in bustle and clatter. Yet here, it was as if he sat on a mountain top and all work had ceased. It was a wonder of war, he realised, something ordinary men and women would never know.

'I swore I would stand here, Mardonius,' Xerxes murmured. His general only nodded, sensing the king needed no response. 'I told my father I would finish his work, that I would bring the army to this very spot. I swore I would punish them for scorning our envoys, for refusing to offer earth and water. My father gave them a dozen chances to bend the knee, and they refused every one. They chose this, not us. Even so, to be in this place . . .' He shook his head in simple pleasure. Mardonius smiled as he walked. Truly, on such a day, nothing was impossible.

High above those streets, the Acropolis filled the gaze wherever it fell. Xerxes could see temples up there, some of them with a wooden scaffold on the walls and unfinished columns, all to honour the deities of the Greeks. His spies had described it, even to the monuments that commemorated the battle of Marathon, ten years before. That Greek victory over the Persians had hurt his father, Xerxes knew. It had damaged his spirit, perhaps even led to the illness that tore him from the world, half his weight and all his strength gone. Xerxes felt a pulse of rage at that thought. He would take down those stones!

He paused then, seeing movement high on the great rock.

'Are . . . people up there still, general?'

Mardonius shaded his eyes to stare up.

'A few dozen, Majesty. Just some priests, as far as I can tell. We'll dig them out.'

He did not tell the king that the skinny old men on the Acropolis had blocked the main route to the top. They had also armed themselves with ancient weapons and armour apparently taken from temple walls. Their presence was no more than a biting fly, but they had not been dislodged by the time the young king insisted on entering the city. Mardonius longed to distract Xerxes from his frowning concentration.

On a sudden whim, the young king glanced at the rock of the Areopagus, not a hundred paces off. Without a word to his general, Xerxes jogged to where it touched the street below and clambered up the steps in a rush of youthful energy. He was still breathing lightly as he reached the huge, flat top.

Athenian noblemen had stood there for hundreds of years. The king rested one foot on the highest point, looking up at the Acropolis as it rose before him. Even the Areopagus was dwarfed by it.

Mardonius was physically fit, hardened by months on the march. He too was breathing lightly as he came alongside. Xerxes nodded to him. The king was in a good mood, able to go anywhere he wanted, in the sacred places of his enemies.

Mardonius narrowed his eyes at movement on the Acropolis, reading the scene. There was not much to trouble him.

'I have sent an entire hazarabam to climb the rear of the great rock, Majesty. There are more men at the foot of the steps

*Conn Iggulden*

there, to distract the Greeks above with arrows. You see them? The rest will overwhelm the defenders when they reach the top.'

'And then make an example of them,' Xerxes said. 'That would please me, general. Make it so. Display the bodies for their gods to see.'

'As you wish, Majesty.'

Mardonius saw the young king turn slowly, enjoying the elevated position. The sea was dark to the south-west and Xerxes squinted into the distance, the Acropolis at his back.

'I will not wait, Mardonius,' he said. 'I want to go down to the sea, to watch my fleet destroy the last of their hopes. Have this city burned. It seems a dry place. I imagine flames will spread well enough.'

Xerxes looked at the canvas-and-wood awnings of the marketplace a couple of streets over. It was much smaller than he had realised. Its dimensions had been made larger in his imagination by the crimes of its inhabitants.

The market would certainly burn, as would streets of brick and plaster, roofs of tile and ancient wood. Xerxes smiled at the thought of embers lofting gently overhead, spreading. He wanted a great conflagration, a city on fire behind him. He wanted the Greeks to see the plume of smoke, to know their precious Athena could not be defended, that she had been plundered and overthrown and raped. It was a good thought.

'Fetch me a brand, Mardonius,' Xerxes said.

He was bright-eyed as the general whistled to waiting servants, never far from their master's whims. When they understood, one of their number climbed the rock, nervous fingers working flint and steel. The fellow was skilled, scratching sparks onto a tuft held in his cupped fingers, then pressing the nascent flame to a club wrapped in oiled cloth, thick with tar. It spat and crackled as it caught, drawing the eye. The servant prostrated himself on the rock, so that dust stuck to his skin.

Mardonius followed the king down, as if Xerxes led a procession. The flame the king bore grew to a sooty ribbon, making trails in the air as the young man jumped from step to step, then halted in the street below.

The summer had been long and the city was dry. Xerxes raised the brand to a roof and the flame bit at laths of wood beneath the tiles. From each touch, it spread, forcing pale smoke out in thin streams as it took hold. Some tiles cracked in the heat, with notes that were almost musical. Xerxes laughed then, striding forward, pressing the flame to every house he passed. At the end of the street, he turned back, standing in the centre of the roadway as trails of smoke joined and rose, already breathing, already beyond any control or curb.

Mardonius had followed the king. The young man's smile was hard to resist, the simple satisfaction at his achievement. When Xerxes tossed the burning brand to him, Mardonius snatched it up.

'Finish what I have begun, general,' Xerxes said. 'I have decreed this city will not stand. It is their reward for defying my father. Burn it all! I am for the ships! I would see the fleet of Athens broken. Give thanks! I have shared this with you. This is a day you will remember for ever.'

Mardonius watched with his head bowed as the king strode off in the direction of the sea. When the general realised Xerxes would not stop, his mouth became a thin line. The general gestured sharply then, sending a dozen of the royal guard and sixty archers running down the road after him. Mardonius whistled for more support, hearing the sound carried back to the main forces. His men had pronounced the city clear of threats, but out beyond the walls? The road to the sea might not be safe. Who knew if any fanatics had remained behind to ambush and kill Persians? It would not do to have Xerxes stabbed by some old man at the moment of his triumph.

Mardonius shifted his grip on the burning brand as the breeze blew flames back on him. If he had ever doubted the blessing of the great god Ahura Mazda on the family of the king, he could not that day. He and Xerxes had marched or sailed for months to reach that place, bringing an army and a fleet so vast there was nothing they could not achieve.

He frowned in memory of that long trudge across the bridge of ships and around the sea of the Greeks. He and his men had endured much to stand in Athens that day. Many would not return home. Mardonius had witnessed extraordinary skill and bravery at Thermopylae. He could admit that in his most private thoughts. Yet even the Spartans had fallen in the end. Xerxes had ordered their king's head removed, the body cut to pieces and thrown into the sea, almost as if he feared the great warrior would rise again. Mardonius shuddered in memory. They had not beaten the Spartans with sword and shield. They could not. In the end, Xerxes had ordered his men to stand back and throw spears, over and over, until the last ones fell.

At sea, the Athenian fleet had been driven back and back, Mardonius reminded himself, putting aside stirrings of superstitious awe. For all their skill and courage, the Greeks had not been able to save Athens, the very heart and wellspring of their power. God was clearly with Persia, and Mardonius dipped his head at the thought. He sent a silent prayer to King Darius, father to nations and companion of his youth, when all the world had been sweet and clean as a new peach. The old man would be watching them, of course, in satisfaction.

The shifting wind brought another flash of heat, the flame

whipping across his arm. Mardonius put aside his reverie, focusing on the work that lay ahead. He was weary, in need of a long rest. He was no longer young! He sighed. The king owned his breath, his sore knees. Xerxes saw no weakness, allowed none. Mardonius would go on.

A few cats still watched from some doorways, curling round the legs of his soldiers and mewing. They would all burn. Perhaps the men would fix brands to their tails and send them off to shriek and spread the flames. Such things had been done in other cities, though Mardonius thought it extravagant. Simple was always better than complicated, in his experience.

He thought of the walls that surrounded Athens. Great gates and towers were as much a symbol as any true protection. Yet whatever they were, they could be broken with hammers and hooked poles. He had an army of more than quarter of a million men, fit as any horse or pack of hounds. They would take down the walls.

High on the Acropolis, Mardonius heard thin shouts and the clash of arms, even as the rising plume of smoke obscured it. He bit his lip. It would not do to trap his own men in streets of flame. No, he had to think like an engineer and set about the task with calm thought. Let the king enjoy his victories! Xerxes had earned them.

Another hazarabam of a thousand men came in quick time down the street, appearing out of smoke that still thickened and spread. Mardonius sent a couple of the lowest ranks back to carry his commands, the rest after Xerxes. The king thought nothing of his own safety. He merely trusted his general to secure it.

Mardonius knew he served his king well. His heart burned at the thought, as fiercely as the roofs around him.

*Conn Iggulden*

# 2

Spray lashed at Themistocles as the galley surged to greater speed. The sea should have been calm in the strait between the island of Salamis and Piraeus, the great port of Athens. Yet their ram crashed through waves broken and boiled by hundreds of ships, thousands of oars.

Themistocles felt a moment of confusion, the product of leaden weariness. He shaded his gaze with a free hand, relying on balance and powerful legs to hold him steady on deck. For just an instant, he had lost the sense of structure, the patterns of ships suddenly chaos all around him. It was still there, if he could just see it! He wiped seawater from his eyes, feeling the stiffness of salt on his skin. He wore no armour. Only his hoplites and helmsmen did, those men the target of every enemy arrow.

Themistocles gripped a hoplon shield on his left arm and watched the enemy ships. Below his feet, three ranks of thirty rowers gripped oars on either side, one hundred and eighty free men of Athens. They were *all* free. Even household slaves had been offered freedom if they agreed to row, so he'd heard. He shook his head. That would surely come back to bite them, if they survived the war.

Below his feet, those oarsmen rowed with eyes screwed shut and every breath like molten iron – but they endured. They could see the ships passing on either side well enough, through gaps in the leather and the oarlocks. Ram and prow were both hidden to their view and they relied on officers and the helmsmen to steer straight and choose targets. Their strength and will was another resource, to be spent well rather than squandered. That they were already exhausted did not need to be said.

In the previous hour, Themistocles had been forced to send two hoplites to replace men who had died in their seats, their hearts giving way. Those bodies had been put overboard, watched by those who remained with a terrible, sick gaze. Yet they were young men, one and all. It would not be them next. It would never be them.

Themistocles was down to just twelve hoplites on deck, ready to leap across if the call came for boarding. Those men watched him for orders, for all the world like his own youth, clad in golden bronze. He jerked his head up in response to their gaze, looking as confident as he could. A couple of them flashed a grin before they turned back to look over the sea. Themistocles the unconquerable. Themistocles the bully, the arrogant, who knew no fear! Themistocles the lucky.

He didn't mind what they called him. It didn't matter how blessed by the gods they thought he was. Nothing he had ever won for himself had come through fortune or fate. He scowled at that foolish thought and touched his tongue to a medallion held in his cheek. His mother had given it to him. It bore the owl of Athena and, though the cord had snapped, he carried it still. He would rather not tempt the gods to punish his pride, not while he rode a fragile shell in the midst of an enemy fleet.

As if in response to his thoughts, a dozen galleys showing banners chosen by Xanthippus began to surge across his path. Themistocles could see the pattern again and he blessed Xanthippus for it. He called half speed to his rowers rather than risk fouling the hunt ahead, though his heart leapt at the thought of joining them. Who had brought Xanthippus back from exile when Athens needed him? *He* had. Noble

*Conn Iggulden*

Themistocles, who had put aside his ambition and personal differences to bring home the talents Athens had to have! Xanthippus could be a cold-hearted bastard, it was true, a man given to looking down his nose and assuming the stern air of a Spartan. Still, he had sharpened the fleet like a sword on a whetstone. Three hundred ships with fit crews, working together for the highest stakes. Themistocles had no difficulty admitting the man's talents. It was the very reason he'd had Xanthippus exiled in the first place. Yet in time of war, strategoi like Xanthippus were invaluable.

Themistocles clenched his fist on the leather grip inside his shield, a spasm of simple savagery, as he might have cheered first blood in a boxing match. Xanthippus and his squadron were tearing into enemy ships. No Persian captain could turn to face two or three galleys coming in hard from different points. As Themistocles watched, he saw one of the enemy approach at full speed, spattering white spray from his oars. Three of the passing squadron turned at the same time, like wolves lunging out of the pack.

The Persian realised his error and heaved his rudder over, but the turn was slow without his oars changing their churn and heave. He only presented his hull, a hunter made prey. Two of the Greek warships hit him then with a great crack of timbers.

As Themistocles passed by, they backed oars, already seeking new targets. Rammed in the heart, with cold sea pouring in, the Persian began to list immediately. Themistocles was close enough to hear a cry of fear go up from the rowers in the hold. Unlike the Greek crews, some of those poor souls were chained to their seats. The ship would take them down as she sank. Themistocles shivered at the thought, though he told himself it was just the sea spray and showed his teeth in a wild grin.

'Shall we board them, kurios?' his captain asked, coming up behind to stare past the prow.

Themistocles shook his head, then spoke when he saw the man's horrified attention was all for the enemy. The sinking galley turned right over. Air bubbled from within and all the screaming choked to silence.

'It is a little late for that,' Themistocles said.

The galleys were fearsome, but they were also unsteady. Low, open sides brought the sea flooding in all too easily. They rarely survived an impact. Instead, Themistocles looked for threats and better chances, resting his rowers. The strait was filled with ships as far as the eye could see. Beyond them, the bulk of the Persian fleet still manoeuvred, seeking the slightest gaps, jammed up hard against one another as the narrowing coast funnelled them into the strait.

Themistocles had honestly lost track of the number of actions he and his crew had fought. Only a splash of watery blood that ran along the planking of the deck showed what they had done. There were a few arrow stubs near one of the helmsmen and some of the men had wounds they could not properly tend in the damp and spray. A knotted strip of cloth was all they had. He had lost another man moments before sighting Xanthippus, a hoplite from his home deme in Athens. The soldier had been made faint by a great gash no one had noticed. Without even a cry, the man had slipped into the ship's wake, snatched down by the weight of his armour.

The crew were all veterans by then, battered and weary. They had fought and they would fight again, but the signs were rubbed away by sea and salt. Themistocles found himself longing for land underfoot, where the dead didn't just vanish as if they had never been.

The thought made him glance over to the strange audi-

*Conn Iggulden*

ence gathered on the shore of the island of Salamis. The entire population of Athens had been brought across the waters, hundreds of galleys rowing back and forth all night to evacuate the city. It had meant men snoring on the rowing benches as the sun rose, licking bowls of stew clean like ravenous wolves – just as the Persian fleet had rounded the tip of the coast.

In the distance, Themistocles saw his people watching, close enough to wave and be seen. Women and children of ten thousand households, more. They gathered on the cliffs like seabirds to watch their fate decided. In that instant, Themistocles did not envy them. He knew he faced death every time a Persian archer bent his bow, or an enemy galley tried to smash their oars and board, with snarling warriors clashing swords and shields. Yet he chose his fate. At least he could die swinging. Those on the shore had no such comfort. The Persians had brought eight hundred ships to that coast. If they triumphed, there would be no second place to run, not for the women and children of Athens. They would have trapped themselves on an island shore, ready to be picked up and herded into slavery.

He looked back to where a great coil of smoke rose above the city. His knuckles whitened on the shield grip in helpless fury. The Acropolis was visible in the distance and Themistocles murmured prayers to Ares, god of war. Though there was no temple there to that bloody god, it was the right time. With a pang of guilt, Themistocles prayed to Athena too. She was a goddess in armour, after all. They were her people. He was hers – and never helpless while she smiled on him.

As he looked towards the city, he saw a marching column appear on the port shore. His soldier's eye knew instantly that they were not hoplites, not Greek. The panelled coats were wrong, the shields a different shape . . . He shaded his eyes again, his sight better at a distance than up close, for which he was grateful that day. At least he could see the enemy, sharp as insects. He bit his lip at the idea of Persian soldiers strolling and laughing in Athens, standing in holy temples unchallenged. It was an abomination, but if a man could not hold what he had won, it would always be taken from him. The gods demanded strength, or gave subjugation and slavery. That was the simple truth that lay beneath all the gardens and gymnasia of Athens. Resist, or be slaves.

'That one!' his captain called. 'Or those two. They look damaged.'

It was a question as much as anything and Themistocles brought his focus back to the ships around him. Xanthippus had passed by and a second wing of ships under Cimon was some way back. Themistocles eyed the possible targets and saw the broken oars and slight list of the closest Persian pair. They had taken a beating from someone. He nodded.

'Ram either of those two. They have hardly anyone on deck. That other doesn't look as if he could outrun a child. We'll take them after. Then, with the blessing of Poseidon and Athena, come back for the third.'

The trierarch captain clapped him on the shoulder, which Themistocles ignored. He heard the order relayed to the keleustes, who stood with only his head showing above the level of the deck. That man ducked to bellow to the rowers, keeping them informed and then raising the pace. The helmsmen gripped the steering rudders and the trierarch went to the prow to gesture left and right, guiding them in. The period at half speed had been a blessing and the galley fairly leaped at the enemy.

The hoplites on deck readied themselves to board or be boarded once again. Themistocles patted his short sword in its scabbard, reassuring himself it was still there. When he

*Conn Iggulden*

held out his hand, a long dory spear was put into it. It was a good weight. He may have been first man in Athens, but Athens was aflame. To save his people, he had made himself navarch of the fleet, over the formal appointment of the Spartan Eurybiades. That too was a good weight. As they closed, Themistocles roared a challenge with the rest, seeing panic in the Persian crew as they tried to escape their fate.

In the moments before the ships crashed together, he could not resist glancing to where he had seen enemy forces gathering in the port. A huge tent was being raised on the beach there, a great white bird pinned in place by bustling soldiers. It looked close enough to reach out and touch. Themistocles felt his stomach tighten. There was surely only one who could demand such a thing in the midst of a battle.

Breath caught in his throat, drawn in and held. The world rocked up and down with the movement of the ship, but on the shore Xerxes was suddenly there, a distant figure who did not labour with the others. The king of Persia stood in a long coat, one hand shading his eyes.

Lost in his own staring, Themistocles almost went over the side when the ram struck, sending a great groan through the whole vessel. That was why they mounted the bronze ship-killers on a keel beam that ran the entire length. It was the only part of the ship strong enough to take the blow.

The Persian captain leaped across, followed by half a dozen men. Themistocles saw desperation in the man's eyes as he was blocked with shields, then stabbed over and over, blades clashing inside his chest. Their bodies were kicked back into the sea, leaving another great slick of red and black for salt water to scrub down to pink threads in the wood.

The cry went up to back oars, tearing the two vessels apart. If they'd had more time, his crew would have loved to search the enemy ship. Persians seemed to wear a great deal of gold and Themistocles had chosen to ignore the jingling trinkets already appearing on his own hoplites. As far as he was concerned, those men could have the whole world if they wanted.

The second Persian crew tried to lose themselves in the chaos of ships. They had managed a turn, though Themistocles could see one side had been oar-stripped already, which explained their slow speed. Some Greek ram had glanced off and slid all the way down, killing every man on one side who held an oar. After that, the ship could only man one seat in two, shifting rowers and oars across. They limped away, too slow to escape. Themistocles found himself grinning as his trierarch turned the ship to follow them. A stern chase was usually a long chase, but perhaps not when the enemy had a hold full of corpses and broken oars.

In the lull, he looked over the battlefield again, just as he might have done on land. When he had fought as a strategos, he had kept a picture of the great action in his mind as best he could. Some men's view of the line shrank to just their place in it, to those who stood on either side and faced them. Yet a leader had to see further – and the same held true at sea.

The Persians had brought a huge fleet to that place. Only the narrow waters of the strait kept Greece in the battle, Themistocles could see that. As things stood, the enemy could simply not bring their overwhelming advantage to bear. The evacuation to Salamis might have bought a respite for the people of Athens, but the enemy were still too many! Ship by ship, the Persians would grind down the allied force. That was the greater picture. The forty brave ships of Corinth had lost half their number. Dozens of Athenian galleys had been sunk or boarded and burned. They had suffered worse and taken down more of the enemy, fighting like madmen

*Conn Iggulden*

while their women and children watched. He wondered if the people of Troy had stared from their battlements with the same fear and helpless wonder. The destruction at Salamis was equally terrible. In places, the water was covered in a slick of splinters and corpses, so that the prow nosed bodies as they rowed through.

In a moment of clarity, Themistocles realised they could not win. Panic surged again at the thought. Then he began to think, to use the mind he had been given, the genius that had made him first in Athens, of a golden generation. The Spartans always complained about Athenian cunning, he reminded himself. Well, he was the greatest Athenian, wasn't he? There had to be a way to turn the battle. As he closed on the hapless Persian ahead, Themistocles looked again to the shore, where Xerxes himself watched two fleets battering one another to the death. Half the Persian fleet had yet to engage, waiting like sharks to ease into the strait and join the battle. Smoke rose from the city he loved. Themistocles saw the end of all he knew, coming down like a hammer blow he could not stop.

# 3

'Don't stand so close to the *edge*, Pericles!' Agariste snapped. 'What will I say to your father if you fall to your death on the rocks?'

Her youngest son looked back at her from under the fringe of thick black hair he preferred to wear right down to the level of his eyes. He stared always in shadow, his resentment palpable. Agariste waited, refusing to look away until he decided he had made his point and shrugged, taking a half-step back. In truth, she had spoken more to relieve her own nerves than out of fear for him. At sixteen, Pericles was like an eel, compact and muscular. She knew he could swim, so had no terror of him falling into deep waters. Yet the rocks were like knives. Agariste was not usually superstitious, but the fate of Athens was being played out on the strait by Salamis. She was afraid to see bright blood that day, not while her husband risked his life against an overwhelming host. They needed the gods to grant them strength and victory. They needed a storm to scatter the Persians.

Xanthippus was out there, perhaps already lost. She could not know, though the possibility gnawed at her. Would she feel his death, sense him breathing his last or sinking away from the light? Xanthippus was both stern and unforgiving, but by all the gods, he had grown into the man she'd once seen in him. Her father had thought him beneath a daughter of the Alcmaeonidae family, but she'd glimpsed something in Xanthippus – personal discipline perhaps, coupled with ambition. She felt a touch of pride at that. She'd taken a man

*Conn Iggulden*

with a little too much kindness in him – and turned him slowly on the coals of their marriage until he had hardened. He had become the husband she knew she needed, her greatest work.

Of course, then Themistocles had intervened, forcing a vote in the Assembly, having Xanthippus banished from his home and family. Agariste set her mouth in hard memory. Those years could not be brought back. Themistocles would never be welcome in her home, not in her lifetime.

Pericles had crept forward to watch the sea battle once more. She understood his restlessness, though there was nothing she could do about it. Her son was shading his eyes against the glare of the morning sun, looking out at an implacable enemy, wishing he was with the fleet. He had tried to stay aboard when Xanthippus brought his ship to the docks for them. His father had knelt by both his sons and told them to protect Agariste and their sister Eleni. Agariste had seen too the knives both boys had accepted from his hand. She wondered if they had thought how they would wield those blades, whether they could truly kill their mother and sister rather than allow them to be made slaves. Agariste tightened her jaw at that. She understood the risks, for herself and Eleni. Yet she would take the knives off them if they tried. Women survived. There was always a path through. Always. She raised a hand in warning as Pericles half-slipped and caught himself, leaning out into space, his arms flung wide to catch his balance.

'Come *here*, Peri,' she said furiously.

He had shocked himself, she saw. The boy was blushing as he stepped back a few paces and sprawled gracelessly on the sand. His brother Ariphron looked away in irritation. Ariphron had no time for the antics of his younger brother and sister. He felt duty as a weight of responsibility. Agariste saw the pain of that in him. He too had wanted to go with their father. At seventeen, Ariphron was on the edge of formal manhood and a vote in the Assembly. Instead, Xanthippus had ordered him to stay. A few others of the same age had been left behind, a scattering of sullen youths in the midst of thousands. All the house guards and male slaves had been sent to the fleet. Agariste had heard Xanthippus promise freedom to anyone who fought or rowed for Athens against the invader. As she and the children had climbed down into the shallows, she'd suddenly seen the longing in the face of old Manias, most senior of the slaves in her household. She did not doubt he loved the girl he had dandled on his knee when she was small. Agariste knew he would have stayed, but in the moments of chaos, she had caught him looking back.

Her husband had been distracted, busy with the ship that was his first concern. Before she could change her mind, Agariste had put out her hand, laying it on top of the tanned and scarred fist of a slave. When she had run around with bare knees, Manias had carried her on his shoulders and snorted like a minotaur. He had told her stories of Homer and showed her how to tie knots. She had owned him all her life.

'Go,' she had said. 'Quickly. Earn your freedom.'

She knew she'd made the right choice when he bent without words and kissed her hand. The old man had wiped tears from his eyes as he'd gone below to take up an oar.

Left behind, the young sons of Athens bore the same look of frustration, she realised. It had been a hard thing to ask of Ariphron and Pericles, but Xanthippus had thought nothing of commanding their obedience. They were his boys! He held them to a higher standard. Until they were eighteen, they were no use to the Assembly. Nor could they fight with the army, unless it was to stand with an older warrior and carry his shield.

*Conn Iggulden*

Agariste reached out at the thought. Her oldest son sat with his hands clasped around his knees, legs bare and patterned with sand. She brushed a lock of hair from his eyes, startling him and making him look at her. Pericles would have jerked out of reach, the little touch-me-not. Ariphron understood, as he always understood.

'Your father wanted me to be safe . . .' she began.

He spoke over her in his frustration.

'I know. He made me give my vow, my oath. I will not leave this place until he returns, or until I know he will not. As if I could, with no ship, no boat.'

'He trusts you,' she said, holding his gaze.

Ariphron nodded without looking away, though she could see the hurt in him.

Agariste saw Pericles was watching, shuffling on his knees towards the rocky edge, when he thought her attention was on the others. As if she would not notice! The boy had never found the right way to deal with his parents, or at least not yet. He always chose mulish and bad-tempered, then sweet as honey. He could not even *see* a right path without turning onto the wrong one.

Her daughter Eleni reached out slyly with one little foot and kicked Pericles in the back, making him curse and leap up.

'Sit *down*, Pericles,' Agariste said again. 'Do I not have enough to worry about with your father out there? How can you be so difficult? Sit, I said!' She spoke the last over his protestations. His sister looked on with a smile of complete innocence.

Bodies were beginning to wash up along the shore. There was not much wind, but the movement of the waters seemed to be bringing them in. Agariste knew, in the instant, that Pericles would want to go down and investigate. She did not relish the battle of wills that would surely follow. Fear had exhausted her, for Xanthippus, for the children, for herself and all the roots of her family. Athens was home. She could not easily imagine starting again somewhere else.

'It will be a long time before we have news,' she said.

She did not have to gesture to the vast Persian fleet that had not yet joined the fighting. For sheer lack of sea room they could not engage, yet they remained, holding place, fresh and savage, while Greeks tired and bled. Of course she was afraid, Agariste told herself. There would be no victory that day. She prayed under her breath for Athena to intervene. Her own city, set aflame! It was an obscenity.

'Ariphron can stay on watch here,' Pericles said. 'I'll go down to the beach. I can see some lads already down there. I'll get news, find out what they know.'

He rose to his feet, shading his eyes. His mother breathed out slowly, trying to keep her temper. It was not his fault, she told herself. He was not made to sit still.

'No. Stay with me, with your sister.'

He began to object, of course. The boy did not listen! Ariphron could write out a thousand lines of Homer, but Pericles would not apply himself long enough to learn a single verse. He hated to write, though he spoke so well; it was hard to doubt the mind behind those dark eyes. His wits were there, but he was like a wild horse, exhausting himself in temper and thrashing.

'Sit!' she said. She held his gaze once more, weary of his stubbornness. 'You think this is the first time our family has been in danger? We've survived worse than this, Pericles. By knowing when to follow orders.'

Anger came off her younger son like a noon heat. In the end, she was an authority he was in the habit of obeying. She wondered how much longer that would last, now he was stronger than his mother. She was thirty-five years old on

*Conn Iggulden*

that day. Her youth and beauty were still there as she gestured to the shoreline and all the people of Athens waiting to learn their fate.

'You see how we sit alone? How there is space between us and the rest? Do you think it was just out of respect?'

Eleni shrugged with the two boys, looking around them with fresh eyes and confusion showing.

Agariste shook her head. She raised one hand and cut the air with it.

'We are not the crowd. We are Alcmaeonidae – an ancient line.' She bowed her head a little, luring her children closer. 'Your father fought at the fennel field, at Marathon – with Themistocles, with Aristides, with Miltiades, father to Cimon. On my side, my uncle revised half the laws of Athens. He enlarged the Assembly, named the ten tribes, a hundred other things. They know they owe their votes to him – to us. Your blood is a golden thread, children. There may be one or two other families who stand as high, but no more. None higher.'

Pericles frowned at the clusters of Athenians all around. They did not seem particularly respectful, at least to his quick glances. Yet they had left space around Agariste and her children. That was true enough. He thought sometimes that his mother put too much trust in the influence or the protection of her family. She had not seen the darker alleys Pericles wandered on his own, away from the crowds. Bodies could be found there sometimes, sprawled in the sun, or tugged by dogs. In his heart, he knew death could take any one of them, no matter where they laid their head. It watched them from the ships in that moment. Yet he did not say so. He had no wish to hurt his mother.

Agariste sat straighter, watching drowned men appear in the frothing surf. She shuddered. Some turned as they rolled, limbs flopping. The sea wore them like a skin, of splinters and broken oars and the dead. Even as she watched, two more ships crashed together, ripping alongside so that oarsmen were crushed and broken deep within. Agariste swallowed.

'Look! Look there!' Pericles said, pointing.

He too had been staring at the dead, of course, fascinated by corpses. Agariste knew he did not see them as men, not really. Boys had to grow into kindness, she thought. Men were built slowly, like towers along the city wall. It did not make her love him less. If anything, it made her love him more, as he needed her. In an instant, Agariste recalled when Pericles had found a dead crow and dissected it on her kitchen table. She had found him staring in awe as he spread the bones of its wing.

She shook away the memory, following his pointing finger to where a dark smudge rolled with the rest.

'It's Conis, I think!' he said. 'I'm sure of it.'

Her husband's dog. Agariste wasn't sure how she felt about that. In his exile, Xanthippus had taken up with a local woman in Corinth. The dog had returned with him, a constant reminder of that part of his life. Agariste had not been too upset when the animal had leaped into the sea to paddle after its master. Her husband had seemed close to weeping, but he hadn't been able to stop and go back, not with a ship crammed with women and children and the Persians coming around the point of the land. Agariste had assumed the mastiff had drowned with so many others that day.

Pericles took advantage of his mother's slight hesitation, her pause for thought. He was climbing down the rocks before she'd raised enough will to stop him. The moment was gone and Agariste was left with both Eleni and Ariphron in wide-eyed pleading.

'Oh, very well,' she said, waving them off. 'Go and see. Come straight back!'

*Conn Iggulden*

In a moment, all her children were racing away. Agariste rose to her feet and brushed sand from her skirts. She sensed every half-glance and head turning to watch her. She was of the Alcmaeonidae family. To see her without trappings of wealth and power, without guards or slaves or high walls, was a little like seeing her naked. Heads bent to whisper and she firmed her jaw. Her children were running across the beach below, heading to one brown mark in a line of dead men. She nodded to herself and saw a path that would take her down to them. Perhaps the dog lived. The children needed something to celebrate. They all did.

Themistocles watched. He had risked his life and his entire crew to land a single lad, the carpenter's boy, fresh and unwounded and full of importance for the task entrusted to him. Without a small boat for the task, they'd considered rowing the galley right onto a beach. By then, though, Persian soldiers swarmed like hornets around their king – and like hornets, they would attack anyone they saw as a threat. The simple problem had seemed impossible for a while, until the carpenter showed Themistocles a slim cedar box that could be sealed in wax, the whole thing heated and smoothed into a shell. The boy could swim and, by Poseidon, they all knew that shore and the best places to land. Themistocles had lowered the lad into the water with a pack roped to one arm so that it bobbed in the waters behind him.

They'd pulled back into the strait then, his rowers still gasping from their labours. Themistocles let the trierarch keep watch for threats. His own attention was on the tiny figure of the running boy, heading towards the most powerful man in the world, as Xerxes sat in his pavilion and Athens burned behind him.

# 4

Xerxes looked down on the bedraggled child. His guards had buffeted the boy cruelly in their search for weapons. With a sea battle going on before their very eyes, the suspicion was that someone amongst the Greeks might have sent poison, or a sliver of concealed blade. The package had been broken apart, all wax stripped away and the cedar box opened and discarded. Even the piece of layered paper, formed from dried rushes in the Egyptian style, would never touch the king's hand.

The boy trembled with a foot upon his back, face down and alone on the sandy shore. The king's herald stood to one side, waiting for Xerxes to nod. He had been summoned for his knowledge of foreign tongues and his eyes were bright with interest as he waited to speak the words of an Athenian.

Xerxes seated himself on a throne of wood and canvas. His pavilion fluttered overhead, the entire front open, so that he could watch the triremes row past. His men fought better in his presence, Mardonius had assured him. They felt his gaze.

'Read it to me,' Xerxes said.

The herald took a moment to prostrate himself alongside the boy, who looked at him in confusion. When the man rose, the urchin began to rise as well. The soldier with a foot on his back had to press down to keep him still.

' "Great King of Persia, Majesty . . ." ' the herald began. He spoke slowly, choosing the best words. Xerxes looked up, his interest sharpening. ' "I, Themistocles, write as friend . . ." no, "ally" is the better word. "It has been my . . . honour to command the fleet for Athens and Greece. I would not see my people destroyed, not if I can save them." '

Xerxes sat forward at that, then left his seat to pace while he listened. The herald raised his voice while the boy squirmed, unaware of the import of the words being read aloud in court Persian.

' "Great Majesty, my authority is limited. Were I to call for surrender, I would simply be replaced and the battle would go on. Many more Persians would then die alongside my people. Instead, I . . . plead with you, I ask, as . . . supplicant. Your family have always shown mercy to those who ask for it. It is that time now. I see smoke rising in the city and I weep." '

Xerxes raised a hand to halt the herald. The king looked out over the strait, wondering if Themistocles was even at that moment watching from one of the ships darting back and forth like stinging insects. He saw too the hulls and oars bobbing on deeper waters beyond, waiting in fresh ranks like reserves. Xerxes understood why a Greek might feel despair at such a sight. Barely a third of his warships had entered the strait. Twice as many remained outside, un-marked, unwearied, a host of swords. With the king's pavilion visible on the shore, Xerxes knew those captains would put themselves in mortal danger to be seen fighting for him. Careers and families were made while the king watched. Even as he had the thought, two of his crews barely avoided crashing into one another, oars sweeping them past at ex-hausting pace.

'Is there more? Go on,' Xerxes said to the herald, waving his hand.

'There are a few lines left, Majesty . . . "The land across

from you, that borders the strait, is a small island named Salamis. If you send half your fleet around it, they can enter the strait at the far end. Faced with your ships on both sides, I would be able to surrender in dignity. I ask for your mercy then. I pray for it and that you and I will meet again, in honour." It is signed "Themistocles", Majesty.'

The herald turned the sheet of papyrus over, looking for any other word or secret symbol. There was none.

'Summon General Mardonius. And fetch a few of my Greek allies to my side. I would have them confirm this Salamis is an island. Someone must know the truth of it.'

One of his guards darted away to carry the king's command. The herald waited for new orders, his head bowed. The ship's boy had given up his resistance and scratched his fingers in the sand, making patterns there.

Xerxes smiled to see that. He had been as young once. Of course, his father would have had him beaten for such a lapse in concentration. Instead, Xerxes had the guard take the lad off to the nearest camp kitchen to be fed. The letter had filled the king with a sense of benign pleasure. His father had understood the Greeks after all! Their leaders could indeed be broken to harness. Gold, and the possibility of mercy, was worth an army.

It was past noon by the time Mardonius appeared, red-faced from running hard and fast. The Thebans with him had all been disarmed, Xerxes noted. His guards were not fool enough to let even trusted allies into his presence with swords and spears.

The king's herald had not been dismissed, so still waited in the same spot, legs trembling with fatigue. His voice was a croak when Xerxes gestured for him to read the letter aloud in Greek, eager to watch their reaction. When he had finished, one of the Thebans asked to see it for himself. It was a rare thing to find a man who could read, but Xerxes allowed it, watching closely while the Theban's lips moved, murmuring slowly through the words as if he tasted them. The fellow shrugged as he handed it back to the herald.

'I do not know Themistocles well, Majesty, except as a name in Athens.' The Theban paused as the herald translated for the king. 'It is true that Salamis is an island. I can confirm that much from my own youth, when I came to this very port.'

'And you would trust his offer to surrender?'

Having his words repeated in Greek gave Xerxes time to watch the response. He noted how the Thebans exchanged glances, seeking some reassurance. Of course, they were Greeks who had decided to take Persian gold rather than raise spears against his army. In his private thoughts, Xerxes considered them less than men. He wondered if such creatures could ever truly judge the motivation of those with more pride who had refused, men who had taken to the sea and marched on land to face an enemy they could not possibly hope to defeat.

'I believe so, Majesty, but it is hard to be certain. The plan he suggests would surely end the battle. No army can fight on two sides.'

Xerxes nodded slowly as the herald repeated all he had heard. With a gesture, the young king allowed the Thebans to make obeisance to him, waiting patiently until all the Greeks had prostrated themselves and prayed aloud for his long life. He wondered if they understood being allowed to do so was an honour in itself, a reward for their service. Subtleties of that sort seemed to be lost on Hellenes, at least those he commanded. When they had been marched away, he addressed Mardonius.

'He promises very little, this Themistocles,' Xerxes said.

'He commands, but claims he cannot surrender. Yet he offers me a way to end the battle quickly. What do you advise?'

'We have the numbers to try it,' Mardonius said. 'If it is successful, it would certainly save the lives of thousands. Perhaps that has value, I do not know. There will have to be plans for Greek prisoners then. Will you allow them to reclaim their city? My men are taking down the walls as we speak.'

'And they will stay down, as a symbol of their surrender,' Xerxes said. 'I do not need to turn the sea red, Mardonius. I came to this place in vengeance, yes, but when the campaign is over, what do I want to leave behind? Just ashes and bones? What would my father say?'

Mardonius thought for a moment, knowing the lives of nations might hang on his words.

'I believe . . . His Majesty King Darius would have desired a show of force and punishment, so that he never had to come so far west again. After that, I believe he would not have thought long on them. With Persian governors to rule in his name, with garrisons to keep the peace, with taxes paid to the royal treasury, I think His Majesty would have been satisfied. Your father conquered many nations. In time, they came to number amongst the most loyal provinces of the greater empire. They send soldiers to fight in our army and they bear the colours and symbols of your house over theirs with pride. Perhaps your father would smile on that course today. Though the decision is yours, Majesty, his judgement lives in you. I know you honour him with every breath.'

Xerxes smiled and gripped his general by the shoulder.

'Very well. Signal to my flagship to put down a boat for new orders. Have Captain Isvant lead . . . three hundred warships around the island of Salamis. It will do them good to row a little after a morning of idleness! They are to enter the strait and approach from the west, but they are not to engage. Wait for this Themistocles to keep his word and surrender. Perhaps I will even meet the man.'

Mardonius dropped to the sandy ground.

'Majesty, what of the women and children on the island itself? Will you show mercy to them?'

Xerxes shrugged. He needed no prisoners and his appetite for personal slaves had grown jaded over years. The wild days were long behind. Still, he knew that was not the case with many of his young officers.

'Take up one in . . . ten. Have them executed, but swiftly.' He smiled and wagged a finger. 'Very well. You may also select the most beautiful to save, Mardonius – as gifts for those who have served well, with courage. Yes, that will do. Make a few of their most comely women and children the reward for unusual service or valour. The rest will be reunited with their husbands and parents – so that they may bless my name in a glad shout. But no walls in Athens. Never again. Let that be the symbol of my victory.'

Mardonius deliberately prostrated himself again, tears showing under his lashes, his face shining with new purpose. The son was his father reborn. At the very moment of victory, Xerxes had rediscovered the mercy of his line.

'Majesty, you have turned the day to gold. I will have the scribes record every detail.'

Straining joint and sinew, Pericles dragged the huge dog out of the surf. Further along the beach, Agariste half-raised her hand to stop him, but refrained. She did not think he would have listened anyway. Her husband's mastiff was clearly dead. The beast's entire head had been underwater. Even so, Pericles heaved it out, pulling on flopping limbs in desperation.

With his brother and sister gripping folds of wet flesh, they lifted Conis onto dry sand. Eleni was weeping as she stroked the animal's side.

Agariste looked beyond them, to where ships moved and fought. Some of them passed so close she could see the individual expressions of men at the oars and on deck. She saw archers among them and wondered if they would bend their bows for sport or cruelty. To have the thought was to fear it, with her children so exposed. There was already too much death in that place. Agariste tried not to look at the bodies in their horrible mockery of life, seawater spilling from their open mouths. Some of them wore Greek tunics, while others had Persian beards curled and dark, oiled locks proof even against the salt sea.

'I think we should come away from here,' Agariste said. 'The Persians have archers on those ships. I do not want them seeing you down on the shore and trying to hit you – or rushing in under oars to land on the beach.'

That was a new thought and one to send a thrill of fear through her. Xanthippus had left a small force of hoplites behind on Salamis, men he could hardly spare. She did not know if they would be enough if one of the Persian crews landed.

Pericles was peering into the dog's eyes, ignoring his mother and her worries.

'Come away, Pericles. *Now!*'

He always ignored the first calls, as if it took a few repetitions for his ears to open. Honestly, the boy was infuriating.

'Come on, Peri,' Ariphron said.

Pericles muttered something back that made Ariphron flush in anger. No one else in the world could annoy her oldest son as easily as Pericles, when he was of a mind. His lack of courtesy to their mother seemed to offend Ariphron on her behalf, as if he was another parent, almost. Agariste spoke to head off another argument, or worse, a fight between them, with the women of Athens watching from the dunes and cliffs.

'Conis is dead, Pericles. I'm sorry. Come away, before you tempt one of those ships to land.'

Her son looked balefully up at that, his gaze utterly feral.

'I wanted to stop. I *told* you he would drown. I told Dad! Conis didn't give up and now . . .'

To her surprise, her son suddenly sobbed, burying his face in the wet folds of flesh around the dog's muzzle. Agariste had not understood how much he had loved the animal.

'I am sorry,' Agariste said more gently. 'But there's nothing we can do for him now. I don't like all these bodies, Pericles. Come away now.'

He rose to his feet, looking down on the slumped figure of the drowned dog. Conis had got himself lost on the quayside crowds in the midst of the evacuation, then leaped into the sea to follow his master's ship. For the first time, Agariste felt a pang of sadness at the thought of telling her husband his dog was dead. It seemed trivial in the midst of death and destruction, with everything they knew as the stake, yet she felt tears springing to her own eyes, beyond explanation.

Strangely, the sight of her weeping seemed to calm Pericles. He took her hand and they walked back to their place on the dunes, climbing up as a family. No one else had claimed that spot, Agariste noticed. She had status, still, even with sand clinging to her dress and her stomach empty.

When they were settled, Pericles stood once again on the edge, though she did not rebuke him for it. The air was clean and tasted of salt. They could all see the brown smudge of the dog, drawn up from the rest of the dead like driftwood below.

Her gaze drifted to the column of smoke, where Athens still burned. 'Perhaps it all ends here,' she whispered to herself. She did not mean to be overheard, but somehow Pericles caught her words. He shook his head.

'No,' he said. 'Our crews and hoplites will break the Persians. They will not fail. They are Athenian.'

He stared at her, daring her to disagree. In response, Agariste only nodded once.

In the distance, Persian ship formations began to change subtly. The movement was different from the tides of war and it was hard to understand at first. Galleys that had been ready to join the fight suddenly rowed away, after a long time in one place. From so far off, it looked like a drift of sand washed by the sea, or a colony of bees breaking apart.

Agariste fell silent, wondering what it could mean. Slowly, she rose to her feet with the women and children of Athens, watching ships row clear of the strait, beating the waves white. Eleni and Pericles looked to her for answers, but she had none. Agariste could only shake her head and bite her lip as almost half the Persian fleet broke off and headed around the island of Salamis.

*Conn Iggulden*

## 5

Passing on orders in the midst of a raging sea battle would have been impossible if not for the reforms introduced by Xanthippus. From the moment the man had returned from exile, Xanthippus had understood the fleet of allies was just too big, too cumbersome to command from any single vessel. The Spartan commander, Eurybiades, may have called himself the fleet navarch, but the truth was, his orders were answered only by his Spartan galleys and then usually lost in the constant shifting of individual captains. It had been Xanthippus who'd introduced flag signals and squadron commanders. Even then, they had endured the fiction that the Spartan was still in command, at least until Eurybiades had given an order for the fleet to abandon Athens and pull back to the Peloponnese.

On that night a week before, with visible reluctance, Themistocles had told the gathering of captains that he would not be obeying that order. Instead, Athens would be evacuated and the strait defended. Themistocles had informed a furious Eurybiades that his Spartan ships were free to leave, but if the Persians were not stopped by Salamis, they had open sea to the Peloponnese peninsula – home to Sparta and Corinth. A dozen Spartan ships could not stop eight hundred – unless they fought as part of the main fleet.

Themistocles had made his disobedience as gentle as possible, but there had been no room for misunderstanding. Athens had provided two hundred triremes and crews, freemen and freed slaves, anyone who could sit on a bench and row till his heart broke. Compared to the ships of Sparta, even the forty crews Corinth had provided, men of Athens *were* the fleet.

Themistocles watched a black banner raised above the deck, a long strip of cloth held on two dory spears lashed together. Word would spread as it was sighted. He and Xanthippus had agreed the signal, though only when there was no other option. He waited then, while the officers of his galley sought to avoid the fighting for a time. That was no small task, with so many Persian crews bent on their destruction. Before raising the flag, Themistocles had called six Athenian ships to his side, working them in the sort of small squadron formation Xanthippus had described. Whenever an enemy galley came too close, they attacked as a group. It was a successful tactic and Themistocles saw two more Persian ships rammed while he waited for a response. No one surfaced when Persian galleys rolled, showing their hulls to the sky. The oarsmen were chained in and the soldiers wore too much armour to struggle back to the surface.

Themistocles felt his heart thumping as time passed. War at sea was much slower than war on land. Below his feet, Athenian rowers leaned back, or slept, or slurped bean stew from bowls and drank heavily watered wine as a skin was brought round.

Themistocles was beginning to fret when he saw a shift in patterns ahead. Xanthippus was no friend of his, not after the banishment. Yet both men trusted one another, at least against this enemy. While Athens burned, they could both put aside petty differences. Still, Xanthippus was not the first commander to answer the flag.

Themistocles saw a group of ships approach, swimming as one, for all the world like a shark drifting through bodies and debris. He recognised the young man on the foremost

*Conn Iggulden*

deck. Cimon stood by the high prow, moving well with the rise and fall of the ship, legs slightly apart, hands clasped lightly behind his back. The strategos had inherited his father's ability to lead, or perhaps just his family wealth and name. No, that was unworthy, Themistocles thought. Cimon moved well, stood well, weighed his words before he spoke. It was not important which quality gave him authority. If men obeyed, the result was much the same.

In truth, it did not matter what Themistocles thought of any of his colleagues, not while they fought to survive – not while their people watched on a bare island. Themistocles bit his lip at the thought. Was there even water on Salamis? Food? He did not think he had ever landed there, though he'd rowed and fished for squid around it a hundred times. Just across the strait from Athens, it had been the only possible refuge for their people as the Persian fleet rushed down the coast after them. He and the other captains had saved their loved ones, but perhaps only for a day. Themistocles wished there was a chance for them to run, instead of an island that might as well have been a prison . . .

As Cimon drew alongside, they both saw the galley of Xanthippus approaching. Together, the three Athenians formed a raft of ships, close-packed in the centre of the strait, with trusted crews on all sides to see off any sudden surge of the enemy. Around them, the battle went on – and allied ships were suffering with three of their commanders out of the fight.

Themistocles felt strain grow in him as Xanthippus came to the edge of his deck. Ropes were thrown and those below dragged in oars so the ships could ease together. Themistocles wondered if the famous bridge of ships Xerxes had built for his army to cross the Hellespont had been formed in the same way. He could imagine a snake of hundreds of galleys, their entire decks boarded over. On that wide causeway, the army of Persia had marched into the west.

Cimon's helmsmen brought him in on the other side, with Themistocles pinched in the middle. Without warning, Cimon jumped across to the open deck. He landed close by Themistocles, making the perilous manoeuvre look easy.

Xanthippus did not step over. With grey at his temples and a character steadied by bitter experience, he would not take a wild risk just for the joy of youth. Themistocles saw the man's arm had been wrapped. Worse, a great swollen knot showed on his forehead, where something had struck him. Arrows too had been snapped off on his deck, standing up like stems of some strange weed. Still, he returned Xanthippus' gaze without shame or apology. They had all been in the fighting that day, killing other men, boarding or butchering Persians intent on the same.

There was no patience in Xanthippus. He had come in answer to the signal flag. He jerked his head up in question, wanting to be away and back to the battle.

'Well, father, I came,' Cimon said, standing at his side.

Themistocles eyed the younger man, irritated at the term. He was not that old! Though he had known Cimon's father. In reply, Themistocles took a breath to carry his voice to Xanthippus, all while the waves lifted and dropped him down, a beat later than the deck under Themistocles.

Themistocles swallowed, hesitating. The words were harder to say than he had thought.

'I sent a message to the Persian king, to Xerxes,' he called out.

Xanthippus had been looking stern before. His brows tightened in thunderous astonishment at that.

'You did *what*? Without asking me?'

'What was the message, old man?' Cimon said.

There was a sort of bleakness in his tone and Themistocles saw his hand was on the hilt of a short sword worn at his waist. Themistocles rolled his shoulders and took a subtly different stance, his feet planted firmly on the deck. He had boxed and wrestled from his earliest youth. No matter how young Cimon was, or how valuable as a commander, if he drew that blade, Themistocles knew he would pitch him into the sea.

More ropes slapped against the deck at his feet. His own hoplites drew the galley that carried Xanthippus closer, decks rubbing strips of lighter wood alongside, until the man could take a single long step across. Themistocles felt himself bristling at being crowded on his own ship.

'Well, Themistocles?' Xanthippus demanded. 'What have you done?'

He and Cimon stood almost on either side of him, as if they confronted an enemy. Themistocles wondered if his crew would defend him if he came under attack.

'I sent a boy to him, there – on the beach where Xerxes came to watch us fight, as if we are all athletes at the Olympics. I told him we would surrender . . .'

He broke off as Cimon made a sound of rage and began to reach for him with one hand while pulling his sword clear. Themistocles turned his back on Xanthippus, trusting in the man's maturity and the years they had known one another. He grabbed Cimon by the wrist and matched his strength. The chance to hook his leg and heave him into the sea had vanished as Xanthippus brought his ship close enough to rub and creak. To his dismay, Themistocles felt the young man only seem to get stronger. He could not hold him and he spoke quickly.

'I told Xerxes to split his fleet and take them round the island of Salamis, that if he did it, we would be forced to surrender.'

'*Traitor*,' Cimon said. 'With all our people looking on? I will put your head on my prow.'

'Be silent, pup!' Themistocles snarled at him. 'If Xerxes does as I have asked, he will split his fleet, do you understand? Use the wits you inherited from your actual father, would you? We cannot win against so many, not as things stand. They have been grinding us like a stone on iron, until all the iron is gone! Xanthippus, tell him, before this boy kills me in his temper.'

Themistocles was forced to let go as Cimon's sword came free of the scabbard. Yet the young man was the son of Miltiades, who had fought at Marathon alongside both Xanthippus and Themistocles. Cimon did not run mad in that moment. Instead, he looked to Xanthippus.

Themistocles stood back, surreptitiously rubbing his fingers where they had been wrenched.

'Themistocles is many things, Cimon,' Xanthippus said. 'I do not believe he is a traitor, however.' He took a moment to glance across the strait, to where at least half the Persian fleet still waited to engage. He glanced at Themistocles then. 'Though I do wonder if he is a man who might secure his own future, even in the middle of a war. If Xerxes does as you have asked and wins, will he look favourably on you, Themistocles? I imagine he will.'

'If he accepts my offer, he will split the fleet,' Themistocles snapped. 'That is what matters. You and I have tested new ships in the waters around Salamis, Xan. It took us almost a whole day to row and sail around it, as I recall. Eight or ten hours. That much time would give us a chance . . . and *you* will owe me then, Xanthippus.'

'*I* will owe you?' Xanthippus said softly. 'The man who had me ostracised from Athens?'

'The man who brought you back, though I had to bend

*Conn Iggulden*

the Assembly almost in half to do it!' Themistocles said, his jaw jutting.

Cimon's eyes were sharpest over distance. While the other two growled at one another, he stiffened suddenly. To the surprise of the older men, Cimon grabbed Themistocles by the shoulder, turning him, pointing with his free hand.

'Look there!' he said. 'They have taken your bait, Themistocles.' Cimon looked on him in awe then, with no more of the mocking 'father' or 'old man'.

Out beyond the tumult of the battle, hundreds of ships had broken free of the main group and begun to row, moving south. Themistocles watched them like a man in a fever dream, hardly daring to believe they would not yet stop and dash his hopes. All three Athenians waited until the Persian galleys were clearly heading right around Salamis, until there was no doubt the Persians had committed to the manoeuvre.

'We could not hope to defeat so many before, Xan!' Themistocles said. 'But now? We have eight or ten hours – with luck, until tomorrow's dawn. In this moment, if we commit everything we have, perhaps we can break through those who remain. Athena and Poseidon watch what we do.'

'I hope so,' Xanthippus said. 'Very well.'

He nodded as he considered the opportunity the ruse had won for them. Xerxes had sent fresh ships away from the battle. If it could be won before they returned to the fight, perhaps it would not matter which direction they came from. It was a narrow advantage and he understood it had been Themistocles who had won it for them.

For the briefest of moments, Xanthippus clasped hands with the other two. None of them needed speeches, or to be reminded of the stakes. Their people watched and the ships of Persia still swarmed like shrimp in the strait.

Xanthippus turned and took a long step back across,

steadied in the arms of his own hoplites. The keleustai on both ships had heard every word. As soon as Xanthippus took command of his galley once more, that deck officer was yelling for rowers to make ready. A great rattle of timbers began to sound below.

'Loose those ropes!' Themistocles roared. 'The order is to attack! Pass the word. Every group, every ship. No rest! No one stops until it is over. Follow orders! No quarter, no mercy. No end, until we are victorious.'

Cimon leaped across to his own galley, his men easing the ships apart with spears while ropes were gathered in great loops. Dark water showed between the three ships and oars rattled out again like bristles, the crews eyeing one another in grim concentration. The enemy still clustered at the mouth of the strait. With clear orders, three squadrons formed to face them, gathering stray ships as they went. Themistocles and the Spartans formed the right wing with sixty galleys. Xanthippus made the centre with at least as many. Cimon gathered in the battered Corinthians with twenty more of his own on the left, in massed lines of ships.

They swept up all those that still swam in their battered alliance of thirty small states, reduced and wearied as they were. Orders were spread in shouts from passing crews, but it was simple enough – attack in formation, before the rest of the Persian fleet could row around Salamis. It was a race against time and the Greeks muttered prayers as they rowed or leaned into the wind.

On shore, Xerxes watched the shifting masses of ships with mounting alarm. He rose from his seat and stood as the entire Greek fleet swung in close, working in visible formation. They sprang forward in white spray, leaving a wake of hulls and dead men. He saw some of his captains try and turn

Conn Iggulden

from that massed line. Others tried to break through it, though that meant they presented vulnerable flanks to the Greek squadrons. Persian ships moved in nervous darts and lunges, unable to respond to the formations, lacking the orders to know what to do.

The king watched in horror as his fleet was broken by an enemy no more than its equal, but somehow driven to extraordinary feats. By some madness of their gods? By the smoke that stained the air over Athens? Perhaps it was the sight of their own people waiting on the island across the strait. He did not know. The Greeks had fought in helpless desperation before. In an hour, something had changed.

Xerxes looked to the west, in wild hope that he might see a miracle and three hundred warships coming hard up the strait. The sun was low in the west, so that he shaded his eyes against a sky of red and gold. The waters were clear, of all but the dead. He collapsed into his seat, his legs suddenly weak.

Themistocles howled in delight as splinters filled the air around him. The noise was a thunder and he could see Persians racing in panic this way and that on deck. Some of them tried to leap the space between while the ships ripped past one another. They were killed by battle-hardened hoplites, or knocked back onto broken oars by shields. Sea spray lashed them all in the collision. A cold hell of sharp stubs and cracking timbers churned like teeth amidst the Persian rowers.

Themistocles batted a shard of wood away as it leaped, whirring like a sparrow at him. In the time it took to pass the Persian vessel, the bronze ram on his keel smashed banks of oarsmen, snapping bones, leaving them helpless. Themistocles could hear their cries over the breaking wood and rush of waves – and he exulted in it. The triple formation had done horrible damage, sending dozens to the bottom. He'd seen one Persian craft roll and show its hull when its captain turned too sharply from the Greeks. The oars on one side had bitten deep and the entire vessel had gone down without a single blow being struck. It didn't matter how it came about. Those within drowned just the same.

The battle had turned and the results were still unfolding. Themistocles could hardly believe the chaos they had wreaked in the Persian lines, nor how well he, Cimon and Xanthippus worked together, once they had a simple order and a clear strategy. Themistocles felt a sort of wild joy as he left another oar-stripped Persian to be sunk by the rank behind. Eight Spartan ships had eased into his wake and he hoped one of them carried Eurybiades himself under those red sails, watching the results of Athenian command, Athenian silver, Athenian cunning!

Themistocles looked to the shore, seeing clearly that the young king had risen from his seat and come right out of the pavilion his people had erected for him. By Ares, Themistocles thought, if they had an archer worth his pay, could he swing an Athenian ship close enough? Surely Xerxes would withdraw as soon as the threat was seen, but could he make a single shot first? The idea was tempting, but Themistocles shook his head, chuckling at his own madness and exhaustion. He was giddy with it, so that he wanted to shout or laugh or weep.

The sound died in his throat then as he considered a different plan. He and his fleet had broken the back of the enemy over hours. The sun showed as a gleam of gold on the western horizon, light already shading purple and grey, sending shadows ahead. Yet there were still around a hundred Persian warships left – and in truth the pace was slowing.

They were only men, at his oars. No matter how important

it was, no matter how their officers called on them to give everything they had, they had to rest or die. Some of them were already shadows of their former selves, rowing listlessly and sunken-eyed. No, Themistocles needed something else, something to grant them a respite before the second half of the Great King's fleet came surging up the strait with blood in their eye, ready for vengeance at the way they had been used.

He rubbed his jaw, feeling the stubble that had grown there. He could not remember the last time he'd eaten. Before that dawn, with the rowers? He needed to order another break, for bowls of food to be passed out . . . He smiled then, at his own audacity, understanding what he had to do.

Themistocles looked to the stern, where signal flags were rolled and ready for use. No, there was no time to summon Xanthippus and Cimon, even if they would have come at such a critical point, just when the enemy were ready to break. After so long in battle, the Greeks finally had the numbers. Every moment increased their advantage, pinning Persian ships from both sides, released only to drown. Yet the pace had fallen off. As he looked with fresh eyes, he saw the way oars fouled one another and dug weakly at the sea. It was as if he stood once more at Marathon, watching an enemy line shudder and flicker, the day hanging in the balance.

Themistocles firmed his jaw. This was something he had to do himself, to save them whether they appreciated it or not. He looked for the boy he'd used before, then grimaced as he realised the Persians had not returned him. Themistocles sent a brief prayer for the lad, hoping he had at least been set free.

'Fetch me one of the rowers, someone who can swim. And get the brazier lit once more – and some wax and papyrus. I have a second message to send.'

Some of his crew had heard every word of the conversations with Xanthippus and Cimon. They knew exactly what he had done and the risks he had taken to achieve the victory to that point. To his surprise, Themistocles heard them chuckling and muttering that he had another one of his plans. They were like children on a feast day as they clapped one another on the back and called for an oarsman. Themistocles took a slow breath, calming himself. The first letter had sent half a fleet away. The second needed to be a masterpiece of persuasion, if it was to work at all.

# 6

Darkness brought fear, as it often had in childhood. Xerxes paced up and down in front of his pavilion, sand crunching beneath his feet. There was a distant glow at his back from districts of Athens that still burned. The moon too cast a gleam across the strait. Even so, his previous mood of peace and calm had vanished. In the night, he fretted, twisting a fold of cloak in one hand.

There was no sign yet of the ships he had sent round Salamis. Before the last light had gone, he'd ordered men to run down the coast to look for them. They had reported no sails, no sighting of oars sweeping back. Xerxes blessed the name of Themistocles for trying to end the battle quickly, but the cost was too high.

Out on the waters, the hiss and race of battle had slowed almost to nothing. Even with the moon, no one could row full speed at another ship to ram, at least until they were certain the dark shape was not one of their own. Neither could they truly rest, for fear of enemies leaping onto their exposed decks, murdering them while they slept. It was not a truce for the hours of the night. Screams and distant clashes could be heard, with sudden angry yells or calls in the tongues of Greeks or Persians. There was fear out on the deep waters. More times than not, it was easier to decline battle simply by backing oars and disappearing in the dark.

Many ships had dropped anchor close to Salamis, to lose themselves against the black landscape. Men snored on those, with just a few left on watch. The crowds still huddled like gulls across the dunes. They slept, some of them, exhausted by their vigil.

On the shore by the port of Piraeus, with Athens a dim coal, Xerxes could not rest. His Immortals waited on the quays and sloping sand, staring across the strait. The rest of his army slept in peace, after days of hard marching and breaking walls.

Xerxes clasped both hands behind his back, rocking back and forth on his heels, unconsciously resembling his father. He had seen too many of his galleys sunk to feel any satisfaction. Fewer than a hundred remained by Salamis, the losses of men and wealth almost unimaginable. The Greeks had proved a terrible adversary at sea, as if they had salt water in their veins. He shook his head in the darkness, unseen, as if to fend off evil. He could not number the thousands who had drowned or been cut down that day, men who had taken up arms in his name. Their loyalty filled him with pride. He only wished his father could have lived to see their sacrifice. Xerxes had learned a great deal – that a fleet was far more than just a means to carry men and horses. A fleet could fight like a school of fish, darting and spearing and pulling back.

The Greeks had tactics and strategies he had never seen before. None of his captains had. Strange flag signals that worked almost like a field of battle, calling ships in, even sending them away to some far quarter. Xerxes gestured suddenly, his hand cutting the air as his mind picked and worried at humiliations. He groaned aloud. He was not his father! There would be no sleep for him that night. He would not find peace.

Surely the Greeks had rowed and fought to complete exhaustion. It had been hard to see if they suffered as much as his own captains. When they'd formed up in three great spears, the battle had grown ugly, like fishermen drawing a

*Conn Iggulden*

trident through the waters. They'd become more skilful and more sure before his very eyes, scattering his fleet in blood and scales. He owed them vengeance, by the grace of Ahura Mazda, by the love of angels, he did.

It was not over, he told himself, though terrible despair gnawed at him. If dawn brought the second part of his fleet coming up the strait, the Greeks might still surrender. Xerxes had imagined mercy for them then, when he had discussed it with Mardonius. Perhaps they had fought too hard against the collar for that. When a dog bites the hand that grips it by the neck, it is hard not to batter down its resistance, with force and rage so great it either dies or submits. Xerxes felt the need for that, a fantasy of vengeance growing in him like tendrils unfurling. He would certainly burn their ships and the crews on them. Once they had surrendered. He would do it for the education of those who watched from the hills and sandbanks of Salamis. The king had seen them all day across the strait, waving their arms in support, urging their men on. It had been an unforgivable display, without dignity. He thought of making an example of their women and, to his surprise, felt arousal stir. The sensation faded as quickly as it had come, leaving him cold and numb.

Like a child gorged on honey, Xerxes had grown sick of sweetness. Only the thought of seeing his enemies crushed could intoxicate him now, dreams so vivid they might even banish the real world.

He paused in his thoughts, though it was like throwing a rein on a wild horse. He scowled at the sight of Mardonius approaching. Under moonlight, his general marched along the sand with two of the king's guards and the slender figure of the herald flanking him. The small group prostrated themselves as if they had been struck dead. Xerxes waited just a beat, then bade them rise.

'Our ally in the fleet has sent another letter, Majesty,' Mardonius said. 'I'm afraid your guards killed the messenger, thinking him a spy or an assassin. They brought me the package he carried, however. I am sorry, Highness, Great King. I have had the men responsible taken to be whipped.'

Whatever irritation Xerxes might have felt vanished at the news.

'Don't be too hard on them,' he said expansively. 'My safety is their first duty. I would rather they reacted with too much vigour than too little.'

'Your mercy is infinite, Majesty. Thank you.'

'And the package? From our ally, Themistocles?' Xerxes asked. The king could hardly contain his hope, no matter how illogical. He had felt a terrible vice closing on his head. He longed for deliverance from that pressure, for a clear path to follow.

'It is, Majesty,' Mardonius replied, his tone colourless as the night. The general handed a single sheet of papyrus to the king's herald. Without being asked, one of the guards fetched a torch and held it at a careful distance so that light fell on the page. The translator's fingers trembled as he began to speak.

' "To His Majesty, Great King of Persia, Xerxes, ruler of all . . . know that my fleet captains have grown bold with successes today. I had hoped to see your ships block the strait before dark, so that I could ask for surrender and be honoured for my service. Instead, my people are talking of cutting off your retreat, of holding you here. They describe a great bridge of ships and say how easy it would be to . . ." ' the herald wiped sweat from his forehead as he peered at the page, ' "to destroy such a thing and strand your army in Greece without supply. Perhaps a hundred captains wish to break out this very night and head east to that end. Majesty,

*Conn Iggulden*

I speak as your most loyal servant. My life is forfeit if they know I warned you. It is my hope that you will use what I have said to bring peace. I hope then you will remember who stood as a friend of your noble house and the empire. Themistocles." '

Xerxes felt his stomach flutter as the translator read. At the end, the silence was profound.

'Can they do it?' he demanded. 'Can they break my bridge of ships?'

Mardonius considered only for a moment. It was a bold move, like locking a door behind a violent man, trapping him in the room with you. It seemed the Greeks were more confident than he had understood. Mardonius closed his eyes briefly before speaking, feeling ill.

'It is, Majesty. We left a baivarabam of ten thousand men to guard the bridge – but yes, if the Greeks took a hundred of their galleys, they could break it. We saw once before what happens when a storm lashes the bound ships. If just one comes apart, the rest flail like a whip. It would not take much to smash the sea-road.'

Xerxes felt cold, though he was sweating and a bead trickled down his cheek. He had brought an army and a fleet greater than any the world had known before, but the Greeks had not given way. They had stood in the pass at Thermopylae, with the sea crashing against the shore – and they had refused to surrender. At sea, they had only grown stronger with every ship they sank, working together, forming great spears and drowning his men . . . For the first time, he considered the idea that he might *not* break them, that he might not win. The horror of it sat before him like a chasm and he trembled over its depths. He turned his face to the darkness, ashamed.

Mardonius did not speak again. They waited for the king's

word, his order. That was both the glory and the curse of royal blood. Whatever Xerxes decided, they would do. If he asked Mardonius to take his own life, the general would draw a blade and do as he was told without demur. Their fate was his to command, but Xerxes had not expected his own to be threatened. The idea of Greeks conspiring to keep him *in their reach* was an axe thumping into his roots, disturbing, frightening. He could only bless the name of Themistocles, who had warned him, honoured him even above his own people. He made his decision.

'General Mardonius, you have an army of the forty nations: my Immortals, regiments of Lydians, Medes, Egyptians, Assyrians, Persian truebloods . . . all the peoples of the empire. My elite. Your own sons ride with them. You and they . . . have earned my trust, in all things.'

Mardonius chose to prostrate himself again, hiding the anguish he felt at the strange tone. He did not know where the young king was heading in that moment, though he feared it. Xerxes spoke almost dreamily. The Greeks had undermined his confidence and it broke the general's heart, for all he understood it. Mardonius too had witnessed the Spartan last stand at Thermopylae. Until that moment, they had not believed Persian warriors had an equal. What he and Xerxes had witnessed over those few days had shaken them both.

'Rise up, Mardonius,' Xerxes commanded. His certainty had returned. 'I cannot let them break that bridge. So, here is my order. You are in command – of all the army and the fleet. The winter storms will make passage home impossible in just a month. Better for me to go now rather than be . . . trapped here. Yes, that is my decree. I will return home, to guard the bridge of ships and our peoples there. I will be the royal shield. And when it is over, I will honour

*Conn Iggulden*

you and your sons above all others. Speak with my voice. Bring me victory – and I will give you a city as your own, Mardonius. On my oath, before these witnesses, I will.'

Mardonius was speechless. He knew better than to argue with the most beloved representative of God on earth. Xerxes reeked of fear, trembling under moonlight like a young girl on her wedding eve. His father Darius would never have run, no matter the threat! It felt as if some great weakness had been revealed by the first setbacks of a campaign.

The sons of strong men could sometimes be hollow things, Mardonius knew. At least one of his own lads was not the man Mardonius wished him to be, relying too much on his father's position and authority rather than his own. He had thought more of Xerxes, however. Mardonius wondered if he could have been blinded by the son's manner and confidence at home. Perhaps Xerxes had always been weak. War revealed men. It rarely made them.

Silence stretched for what seemed an age. The young king frowned, looking at his general almost in challenge. Mardonius longed to speak. Yet he could only gape, his mouth opening and closing as words came and went like breath in him.

'Majesty, I obey,' he said at last. In the end, those were the only words demanded of him. Yet in a rush, he went on, driven to wild incaution.

'Th-though we have burned Athens, Majesty. It is a great triumph! Our army has not been bested. We lost no more than twenty thousand at the pass. Please. Let me send back my second in command, Artabazus! Let *him* secure the bridge of ships. I beg you not to remove your light from us, Majesty. If you stay, I will deliver you victory, I swear it.'

The king did not reply and Mardonius felt cold as he

sensed he had gone too far. Whatever weakness or cowardice had been exposed by the Greeks, Xerxes was still the Great King, ruler of forty nations, to the very edges of the world. He could not be gainsaid and Mardonius knew his life hung in the balance. He prostrated himself and waited, hands touching both sides of his head as he breathed against sand. After long enough to know he had displeased the young man who ruled an empire, Xerxes bade him rise.

'Do you have anything more to say, general?' Xerxes asked.

Mardonius shook his head.

'No, Majesty. I obey. As you speak, I obey. Whatever I must do, I will not rest until the Greeks beg to surrender.'

'How blessed I am to have you in my service!' Xerxes said softly, dangerously. His mouth twisted in petty anger. 'My decision is made. A king . . . orders the world as he sees fit. I do not need to watch as you carry out my commands. I brought you here. Complete my task! Bring them to heel, Mardonius. I want them to remember me.'

The king turned away, walking up to the road that led back to the city, still burning in the night. His Immortals fell in beside him in a white-armoured column, their steps tramping together without an echo in that open place. Mardonius was left staring, his entire world falling down around his ears.

Dawn was later than in summer, though the sky remained clear and the air was warm, the breezes soft. Ships rocked gently at anchor or out on the strait. The light began as soft greyness, with men yawning and peeing over the side, dozens at a time. They emptied their bowels off the stern in sleepy distaste. At the same time, the carpenter and his boy heated slabs of stew, unwrapping cloth from something pale brown and filled with beans, more like a stone than food. With fresh water and salt, the result was stirred over a small brazier. There was never enough. Rowers ate like hounds, in great gulps that caused some of them to cough and go red. They were still leaner than they had been, with muscles like cords beneath sagging skin.

The last water casks were broached on deck, the precious stuff within tasted. One had spoiled and was full of thread-like worms. Though men watched and licked dry lips, it went over the side. The rest was given out mixed in wine. Each man was allowed two full ladles before the heat rose. By the time they had all had a turn, the barrels were almost empty. No one had expected to remain at sea for so many days. In normal times, they would have sought out natural springs as they came down the coast, even the ones that joined the sea invisibly under the surface, so that fresh water could be brought up from the brine with buckets and ropes. Local boys always found those spots when they swam through the rushing coldness as children.

Stiff and aching, men groaned as they took places on the oar seats, crammed in like a meeting of the Assembly. Sores from the day before cracked and wept as oars were manhandled into place, resting on the pivots. Fresh oil was rubbed on scabs and wounds, but it was not much comfort. Joints protested as they readied themselves, settling into position with dark eyes as they looked into a day ahead and could not see how to survive.

On deck, Themistocles stood with the sun rising before him. The light spread quickly once it sprang gold, but he could not quite believe what his eyes were telling him. He had slept fitfully and dreamed. This seemed an echo of something glimpsed in the night.

His fleet and his trierarch captains had worked wonders

the day before. They had fought like lions for him – and for those they loved, who watched. He could not have found a single man who had not given his all – and the result had been the destruction of Persian hopes. He felt a warmth begin in his chest and his bladder tightened, reminding him he had not emptied it yet. He'd been too concerned with what dawn might reveal, hoping against hope that his letter to the king had brought about some effect.

He had not dared dream so much. His idea had been to persuade the king of Persia to pull back a dozen ships, two dozen – men sent away who might have sent Greek ships to the bottom. Instead, the sea was empty. Themistocles looked around in wonder as his officers came on deck. The news was spreading already. Cheering began below, swelling in a great wave as fleet crews heard and understood.

The king's pavilion had been taken down on the beach. Xerxes and his guards had gone, his hundred ships vanished, rowed away in the small hours. Themistocles raised both arms suddenly, like a victorious boxer. He had done this! He had played his man and judged it to perfection.

Another cry went up to drown the first, a great howl that was different from the exultation of sailors. In response, their cheering died away as if it had been choked. Themistocles followed pointing hands on a dozen ships, looking west, away from the rising sun, to where his own shadow fell. His people called in warning, standing on the dunes of Salamis. They shouted and whistled to husbands and brothers and sons.

The second half of the Persian fleet was in the strait. Those men had rowed through unknown waters, risking rocks and hidden banks. Themistocles felt his lips ease away from his teeth as he snarled at them. Three hundred ships – more than sixty thousand men rowing up the strait to attack them. Yet inexperienced, untested.

*Conn Iggulden*

His expression became a fierce grin, a smile of savage confidence. Those ships had left a fleet beleaguered and ground down. They had returned to one battered, yes, and weary, yes, but a fleet that had learned how to fight.

'Put up the signal for my group to assemble on me. Every ship, every captain to engage and attack – in formation. On Xanthippus, on Cimon, on Eurybiades. On me. They came for war. Give them what they want.'

His order was echoed in joyous, roaring voices. Men grinned as they understood, looking on him in a kind of awe. His crew knew what he had achieved, though no one else did, not then. Themistocles felt light as he took up spear and shield, rubbing the bristles on his face that had come in white. The labours of the day before made him feel twenty years older than he was. Yet he had given his people the chance they needed. The Spartans would call it Athenian cunning when they heard about the two letters, but they would not refuse the opportunity he had won for them.

On impulse, Themistocles knelt on the deck and bowed his head. He heard a dozen men stop their preparations and do the same, touching a knee to the planking.

'Athena, you have kept us safe. Allow us the vengeance they have surely earned. I ask your blessing on this ship, this loyal crew. Give us the strength we need to finish the work, to save our women and children. I ask in your name. I ask the blessing of Ares and mighty Poseidon. Let us be your sword, your spear. Let us be your *answer.*'

He rose and opened his eyes, aware of soldiers and oarsmen below with bowed heads, making their own prayers or repeating his words. He saw determination in them. They were his people. Battered as they were, weary as they were, they would not fail, not that day.

# 7

Aristides hid any sign of irritation as he walked the main street of Eleusis. The Spartan regent walked at his side, red cloak flicking back and forth in the breeze, hands clasped behind his back. Pausanias was in the first bloom of his youth and health. He seemed always to have one eyebrow raised, which gave him a constantly sardonic expression. It was as if he found something to displease him wherever he looked.

On the Athenian's other shoulder, Pausanias' soothsayer walked in a belted robe and sandals, arms left bare and tanned. They walked like young lions, the pair of them, Aristides thought. Never injured, never broken. Certain of their own value and place in the world. Aristides showed no sign of the dismay he felt at dealing with men of their relative youth. Athens would never have appointed a regent below the age of thirty.

'I must say, I am disappointed not to have witnessed the Mysteries,' Pausanias said. 'My uncle and father spoke highly of the services here. Yet I have never been invited, not into the inner sanctums.'

To Aristides, the regent's voice had a sharp tone, always on the edge of complaint. He wanted to ask if Pausanias thought a sacred festival should be begun again at his whim. The goddesses would surely not mind too much, or see it as mockery. Yet he remained silent. He had already brought up the reason they were all in Eleusis – and been rebuffed as if he had broken some rule of good manners. Aristides needed to persuade a man whose support he had to have. So, if Pausanias appeared brash, or a fool, it did not matter. Aristides would flatter and compliment, do whatever he had to, to gain the Spartan's goodwill. He counselled himself to be cautious. Pausanias seemed somehow distant, oblivious in the manner of certain noblemen Aristides had known, as if only his own needs and interests mattered. Yet if Pausanias was truly unaware, Aristides suspected the man's soothsayer was as sharp as obsidian. There was intelligence in that one, in every shadowed glance and half-smile.

The news of the death of King Leonidas was still spreading through the cities and towns of the Hellenes. For Aristides, for any citizen of Athens, the action at Thermopylae was relatively trivial. He knew the Spartans had lost their battle king. Pausanias had lost his uncle! It was only right to show respect for such a recent grief. Yet what was that loss against the horror of a Persian army trampling sacred places in Athens, pulling down walls and desecrating tombs? Aristides felt their presence in his city like a weight on his shoulders, a cloak he could not throw off no matter how it bore him down. He reminded himself the *people* had been saved and taken to Salamis. He could see the island across the bay from Eleusis, the sea glittering between. At that very moment, the Athenian Assembly rowed and fought. Xanthippus was out there somewhere among them, with Themistocles and Cimon. Their wives and mothers and sisters watched and prayed. Aristides clenched his jaw. While the fate of his city was being decided, he had to play politics with Spartans.

He knew a city was more than streets and a market. Athens lay in the memories of those who actually lived in her. Walls could be rebuilt, even temples raised again. Aristides still felt like a husband whose wife had been ravished, enraged and helpless. Persian soldiers walked and urinated in the dust of his city – and all he had been able to do was wait on neutral ground for Pausanias to agree to meet him.

Aristides felt the strain like a hand gripping his neck, a growing pressure. He'd expected to deal with Leonidas, a man of vast experience, renowned for his wisdom. The king's brother too had been such a man, though it seemed Cleombrotus was too old or perhaps too ill to become regent. Pausanias had just waved that question away like an impertinence.

As they walked down the hill, the young regent frowned, gazing out to sea, shading his eyes to catch a glimpse of the fleets. Salamis was a blur of hills at that distance, but the detritus of fighting was already washing up along the shore. Like kohl painted on a woman's eye, it thickened – a line of dead men and broken timbers. The sight cried out for an answer, but Aristides could not shake the Spartan from his complacency. He could not take Pausanias by the shoulder and force him to really look, to understand! Once again, Aristides sensed the lowered glance from the soothsayer, Tisamenus. The man went unarmed, though with Pausanias bristling with weapons and half a dozen Spartan guards in their wake, perhaps that was not important.

Another day was being lost, allowed to slip away. Aristides strangled desperation as it swelled in him. One thing was certain – he could not beg the Spartan for help. He had sensed that from the first moments. Pausanias was one of those who would take smirking delight in turning his face from the needs of Athens. No, he had to be persuaded, *managed*, if Aristides could summon the patience. He breathed out. For his people, he could.

The festival of the goddesses had come to an end just a day before, after a full month of services and sacrifices for

Demeter and her daughter Persephone. Aristides had actually taken part in some of the processions, while he waited for the delegation from Sparta. Eleusis had become very familiar in the weeks since setting out from Athens with eight thousand hoplites. He and his men had doubled the local population overnight, at least until the festival of autumn had begun. The Eleusinian Mysteries had not changed, though years had flown since he'd last graced those streets and simple temples. Aristides had whispered the sacred words given only to those who had been admitted to the inner sanctum of the temple. Other worshippers had looked on with envy as he'd been waved through.

The small city still carried odours of narcissus and pomegranate on the sea air. Flower petals had been carried by the wind into drifts, browning as life fled. The crowds too were thinning as men and women made their way home, leaving behind the experiences of converts and whatever secrets they had gleaned. They hurried along, casting worried glances at Spartans marching along their streets. War was in the air, along with rumours and fear. Mendicants stood on street corners and warned of the world's ending, calling out to the gods with eyes closed and hands outstretched, emaciated and unwashed.

Aristides sensed disapproval in the two Spartans walking at his side. No, he recalled. Only Pausanias was a Spartiate by blood. Tisamenus was something stranger. It was hard to deny the power to know the future. The gods granted it to a few men or women each generation. Aristides had seen the prophecies of Delphi entwined with his own life – and the lives of his people. What was the fleet, if not the 'wooden walls' the oracle had once said would save his city? Yet this Tisamenus seemed clear-eyed and fit, more like a warrior than any holy man or wild cave-dweller. There seemed to be a humour and understanding in him that was oddly discomforting. No man enjoys the company of one who truly sees through artifice. With a gleam in his eyes and a slight twist to his mouth, Tisamenus gave that impression. He also spent words like a hermit, apparently willing to let Pausanias speak for them both. Aristides knew he was being judged by the younger man, but there was little he could do about it.

Together, they reached the great temple of Demeter at the bottom of the hill. The columns were as wide as a cart at the base, stretching up in cream stone. Four men could not have joined arms around them. The priestesses were still singing within, Aristides could hear. Yet the great doors remained closed.

Pausanias reached out and rested his palm on the wood. The day had turned cold, though of course the Spartan showed no awareness of that. He knew very well that Aristides waited on his answer. Aristides feared Pausanias was a man who would make him plead in the end – and then still refuse. He prayed he was not correct. Athens needed the Spartan army.

'I was told that some sort of drink is offered to those who are accepted into the inner sanctum,' Pausanias said, 'that it . . . sweeps men away, more powerfully than wine.'

He spoke almost idly, though his artifice was clear. Aristides felt his spirits sink further. There were some things he could not procure, even for a Spartan regent.

'To enter,' Aristides replied, 'to be allowed to enter, a supplicant must spend a full winter in prayers to the goddess, arriving each day before dawn. He must learn the chant of the lesser mysteries and repeat it each morning as the sun rises, without flaw. If he – or she – misses a single day, they are not allowed to go further.'

'You have gone in?' Pausanias said.

He glanced once at Aristides, a flicker of the eyes, fully aware that the Athenian needed an answer of his own. Yes, Aristides thought, there was cruelty in the young man. The gods were capricious to have raised Pausanias, just when his need was greatest.

'I have,' Aristides said, 'when I was young. A few times since. There is a drink, yes, though some refuse it. I do not trust my memories from that first time, though they were . . . vivid. But, Regent Pausanias, I would . . .'

'And they teach you a phrase, do they not? I have seen men bend close to the ears of priestesses. They are then let through, into the temple beyond.'

'That is . . . true,' Aristides said. He was afraid the regent might try to demand those words from him, in exchange for what he needed. Was it all just a game to him, while men fought and died? While statues of Athena were being smashed by hammers?

Pausanias saw his concern and chuckled, waving a hand.

'Oh, don't worry, Aristides. I will earn the words myself, or not at all. I would not make you tell me. What value would they have then?'

He ran his hand over the wooden door, twice as tall as he was. Aristides felt a flush come to his face at the assumption that he could have been made to give up the secrets of Demeter. With the survival of Athens as the stake, he was not certain he would have refused.

'I have seen enough of this place,' Pausanias said. 'Unless you would like me to rouse up the priestesses, Tisamenus? If you have questions for them, I'm sure they would be willing to answer.'

'I have been here before,' Tisamenus said. Aristides saw he did not bow, but answered as one of high status. 'I completed the dawn chant and gained the greater mysteries. I am forbidden to speak of them, on peril of my immortal soul. It was . . . glorious.'

Pausanias did not seem pleased at the news that his soothsayer had also entered the temple. The doors were still closed to him, and Aristides watched the regent rap the heel of his hand against the wood, almost in rebuke as he turned away.

The man's guards stood to one side as Pausanias began to walk back along the main street, the sea on his left shoulder. Aristides considered himself a patient man, but he had waited an age for Pausanias to arrive and now the regent seemed blithely unconcerned by his reasons for being there.

'Regent, have you considered your support?' he asked.

Pausanias did not reply, merely walking on, his head nodding as if in deep thought. Why did some men make everything a contest of wills? Aristides hated coming to another as a beggar. Having power over him clearly pleased the Spartan.

'What you must understand, Aristides,' Pausanias said at last, 'is that the people of the Peloponnese are not threatened by Persia. Our wall across the isthmus is complete – a man can walk an hour from one end to the other and find no way past a fortification of stone, three times the height of a man. Gates of iron and Spartan soldiers guard that wall – and the only way in. My own father, Cleombrotus, has overseen the work and deployed the garrison there.'

'It was Cleombrotus who pledged the support of Sparta against the Persian invasion,' Aristides said quickly. 'Your father is a man of honour.'

Pausanias stopped suddenly in the road. His eyes hardened and, for the first time, Aristides thought he was encountering the true man. He held the steady gaze and waited.

'That oath . . . was given before the death of my uncle and his personal guard at Thermopylae.'

Aristides knew enough of Spartans to say nothing. He was rewarded by a flush spreading on the regent's face and neck.

'Yes, Athenian,' Pausanias said, inclining his head in mock acceptance. 'An oath is an oath. We are a pious people.'

'I have been told so, yes. Then you will be coming out from behind your wall? Winter is not far off, Pausanias. An army the size of the one Xerxes brought will starve unless they gather supplies. There is a moment coming, soon, when they will be low on food. We can bring them to battle then, if you honour the oath your father gave. Will you join us in the field before winter? Will you bring your army out, as was promised?'

'We did not build a wall just to leave it behind us, Archon Aristides,' Pausanias replied sharply. He saw Aristides open his mouth to speak and went on. 'I have not said we will not come. Yet it will not be at the pleading of Athenians, but at the right moment, when we are ready.'

It took the discipline of a lifetime for Aristides not to snap a sharp answer of his own. He bowed his head.

'I pray it is soon, Regent Pausanias. Not for Athenians, though our need is great, but for all Greece.'

Pausanias waved a hand in the air, as if he brushed away a fly.

'There is no Greece. There are only cities, like Sparta – and Athens, though I understand it is much reduced.'

There was a spiteful pleasure there and Aristides stood very still.

'We too swore an oath, Pausanias. To defend the land against a foreign king. We took to the sea – and I have marched eight thousand men to this place in the knowledge that Sparta's word, once given, would be iron.'

Aristides paused. He hardly needed to say his fear out

loud. The leaders of Sparta were famously reticent on the subject of their own internal politics and divisions. For all Aristides knew, the ephors of Sparta were engaged in a civil war. Pausanias would tell him nothing – and he would not know whether their army would march until they did. Or until the forces of Persia slaughtered the last man of the Assembly and all was lost.

'I have heard you, Aristides,' Pausanias said. 'And I have answered. When the moment is right, we will be there. Not before.'

The Spartan regent gestured to Tisamenus, so that the soothsayer halted. Pausanias walked on, leaving them both behind. Aristides watched the Spartans march away, just seven men, but in that place, unstoppable. He could not make them listen, or understand. He found himself trembling with the frustration of it.

'He is a good man,' Tisamenus said. There was affection in his voice and Aristides wondered if they were lovers.

'Will he bring his people out? That is all that matters.'

'There are . . . difficulties at home. I fear I would betray a trust to discuss them. I'm sure Pausanias will find a way through. He wants to honour his father's word, be sure of that.'

Aristides turned to the young man, his patience unravelling.

'Who *are* you, really? Tisamenus is not a Spartan name.'

'No, that is true. I am a Greek, however. That is all that matters.'

Aristides chuckled.

'You don't agree with Pausanias, then? He sees only Sparta – and all the rest as slaves or enemies. In Athens, we see Greeks – people who know the same gods, who speak with one language! I have more in common with the meanest Spartan than a Persian king.'

'It is a fine dream, I think,' Tisamenus said, inclining his head.

'And you can tell the future?' Aristides asked. 'Can you say then whether we will win, or be destroyed?'

'I am not an oracle . . .' Tisamenus said with a sigh. 'Though . . .' He paused, clearly deciding whether to go on or not. After a moment, he nodded. 'When I was still a boy, I went to Delphi, to ask the Pythia what my life would hold. She told me I would win five contests. In my youth, I thought she meant the Olympics – the pentathlon. So I began to train, to run, jump and wrestle, to throw shield and spear.'

'I . . . remember you!' Aristides said in dawning amazement. 'I was there, that day. By Athena, you were . . . you are, a fine athlete. But you did not win, did you? Unless my memory has failed me.'

'No. I came second, to a Spartan. My entire life had been devoted to that single moment and I . . . lost. He saw my dismay and as he was a fine man, he took me to get drunk. I told him about the oracle . . .'

Tisamenus looked away, staring into his own memories. Aristides felt the breeze pick up from the sea, bringing a winter's chill to Eleusis.

'In Sparta, they call their battles "contests", did you know that? My new friend became very excited when he heard my prophecy. He believed – he still believes – that I am destined to win five great battles in my life.'

'It was Pausanias?' Aristides asked. 'The Spartan who won?'

Tisamenus nodded.

'It was. The nephew of the battle king of Sparta. He believes I am a sort of talisman, that I will bring him victory five times. I have visited the ephors in Sparta and they confirmed it. He gave me back my life's purpose.'

The young soothsayer reached out and gripped Aristides by the upper arm, close enough to speak in a low voice.

'Don't judge him too harshly, kurios. His uncle's death changed his life, just as mine changed on that day at the Olympics. It takes a little time to adjust.'

'You think he will honour his father's oath?'

'He is the battle king of Sparta, at least until his cousin comes of age. And Pausanias wants to win in battle, with me at his side. Trust in that. He wants to win.'

Aristides replied with his voice unstrained, teasing the younger man out.

'And these "difficulties" at home? They will not stop him?'

'Pausanias is a man of honour, Aristides. Believe in that. The helots are . . .' Tisamenus paused and chuckled. 'I do not think Pausanias would want me to discuss such things with an Athenian.'

'Son, this Athenian will stand as strategos on the field when the army of Persia marches into view. I have seen them. There will be no distinctions then, not between us. If we stand as Spartan, Plataean, Athenian, Corinthian . . . we will be destroyed. If we are Greeks, together on that day, one culture, one language, we have a chance to win. If you know something that will keep Sparta behind their wall, you should trust a man who has already lost everything. My city *burns* this evening, Tisamenus. My commitment to this cause is beyond doubt. If you need advice, ask. We are on the same side.'

They stood alone on the main street of Eleusis. Aristides let his expression remain still as he waited. He had done his best. The young man wanted to speak, he could feel it.

'Very well,' Tisamenus said. He glanced over his shoulder to where the Spartans had vanished, returning to their camp for the night, or perhaps already heading back to the isthmus that guarded the Peloponnese, just a day or two's march to the south-west.

'In Sparta, the helots are many. They are slaves, though the word means "captives". Men like Pausanias hardly ever think of them. They are just goats or oxen, there to draw water and till the fields.'

'I am familiar with slaves,' Aristides said. He was impatient, nervous Pausanias would send a man back for the soothsayer. If that was even a term he could use after what he had heard.

'Not like these,' Tisamenus said, shaking his head. 'Slaves are bought and sold everywhere, yes, for debts, for work – sometimes for pleasure. The helots inherit their condition. They are born slaves, generation on generation. And there are some who resent it bitterly. They watch their daughters and sons grow and understand they will never be free . . . There is great anger there. I have seen it.'

'I don't understand . . .' Aristides said. He saw a flicker of red in the distance. No doubt Pausanias was wondering why his talisman had not reappeared.

'The Spartan army does not like to go far from home – ever. They know the helots could revolt and slaughter their women and children. It is as if everyone in Sparta stands with a knife at their throat!'

Unless he looked over his shoulder, Tisamenus could not see the single Spartan soldier making his way back down the hill. Aristides had never heard so much about the politics of Sparta in all his years. He struggled for the right question to ask.

'They have come out before, though! Leonidas himself, or the two thousand who came to relieve Athens from a tyrant in a previous generation. How is that possible, if the situation is as you describe?'

'They always leave a force of warriors great enough to keep the helots submissive,' Tisamenus said. 'But this time . . . if they send every Spartiate, every one of the perioikoi . . . ? Against the army of Persia, they will need every soldier. But who will protect their families then, when the helots see all the masters have gone? They would come back to ashes and bones.'

The Spartan who approached was frowning at the earnest conversation going on between them. Tisamenus understood the import of the footsteps and Aristides' expression. He closed his mouth.

'The answer is obvious enough,' Aristides murmured.

Tisamenus paused in the act of turning away.

'What is it?'

'Bring the helots out with you. All of them.'

Tisamenus opened and closed his mouth like a fish.

'But . . .'

Aristides shrugged.

'You are the soothsayer. Persuade Pausanias.'

The soldier halted, suspicion writ clear on his face.

'Regent Pausanias sent me to check you had not been delayed by idle talk,' he said.

Aristides hid his frustration and smiled.

'I apologise. I have kept him here. It is a fault of my people.'

The Spartan nodded, sarcasm in his expression. Tisamenus went with him without looking back.

# 8

Themistocles longed for rest. His body craved it, so that he wanted nothing more than to lie on the deck and look up at the sky and just sleep. He could hear cheering across the strait and he closed his eyes for a time, then opened them as the galley lurched, the prow striking some heavy piece of debris. It would not do to be thrown overboard at the greatest moment of his life.

He, Xanthippus and Cimon had worked like dogs or rowers, from the first moments of dawn till the sun reached the west, turning the sky to fire. The squadron formations and tactics they had created had proved their worth. At least a third of the Persian ships that had rowed around Salamis would remain in that strait for ever. Some burned with the oily smoke of a funeral pyre, hissing as cold sea flooded in. Others floated just beneath the surface, a danger to ships passing above. Dead men stared up from those, slipping into the wake.

Themistocles shuddered. Someone came and hugged him, another pounded him on the back, though he was badly bruised there. Slowly, he went down onto one knee and rested his forearms on it. He made a noise as he panted, past mere exhaustion. He just needed to breathe, in and out, to fill himself with clean air and something more than dazed emptiness.

He thought he had become immune to corpses, over the years. He had killed men before with sword and spear. Not one of them had mattered, not a single straw, because they had tried to take all he was, all he had. There was no simpler cause than Salamis – to resist an invasion, while his wife and daughters sat and prayed! Yet even as he had the thought, he saw another drift of bodies passing under the keel, rolled down into the deep. It made bile rise in his throat. He had witnessed men drawn pale by the sea, their hair swirling grass. Many more struggled and yelled on the surface, churning it with their hands. They were all dragged under by their armour in the end, breathing out silver.

He shuddered. That was one death he feared, that he would be sent down and down, made to vanish with no tomb, no light, no coin for the ferryman or prayers said. He had endured that thought for days at sea – he could no longer be sure how many! His knees hurt, his joints had sand in them, his arms were too heavy to move. Slowly, his great head sagged. He closed his eyes once more, ignoring the sounds of the ship and the fleet. He just needed a moment and then he would be striding among them once again, laughing and congratulating and reminding them what Athenian heroes looked like.

Though his eyes were shut and his head dipped low, he smiled at that. He had brought back Xanthippus and Aristides. He had mentored Cimon in politics and restraint, making him the man he should have been and not just a weeping drunk. More than any of them, Themistocles had played his enemy well. Xerxes had split a huge fleet into two halves they could beat. He had abandoned an unassailable position on the word of an Athenian! Themistocles began to chuckle. That was what he had seen in the chaos of the battle. A king with Greek allies had to accept that *any* Greek might choose to follow him. It was the greatest strength of the Persian force, that no man standing against them could ever trust his brothers. Yet it meant Xerxes had listened, and believed, even as their fleets clashed. Themistocles opened his eyes, though they stung with salt. He looked out, in pride, upon the strait.

His crew had lined up on deck. He understood the small noises had been them shuffling into place, standing to ragged attention despite all their wounds and battered equipment. Themistocles cleared his throat then, like a growl. The sound covered his body's protest well enough. Slowly, he rose, feeling very much the old lion. His blond hair hung in a great mass of dried salt, sweat and blood. He tried to run a hand through it, but it was impossible. His fingers tapped each wrist, a habit of old as he looked for a thread or leather thong to tie it back.

Only eight hoplites remained of his command. One of the helmsmen had taken an arrow in the eye. The other gripped both steering oars, standing in the centre point. Beneath their feet, the rowers were quiet. It would be some time before they were able to do more than pant and stare. They had rowed and rested and rowed again for days, a thousand wild turns and lunges, all on little food, trapped and cramped, with death stalking them. Their world had become the oar in their hands, a drumbeat and the calls of the keleustes.

That man too had lived, Themistocles saw. The fellow had come to stand on the deck, abandoning his usual place in the great open trench that ran down the middle. There were tears streaming down his face and Themistocles could not think of anything to say to him. Instead, he just nodded and gripped the back of his neck, squeezing. A father might have done the same with a son he loved. The man's face crumpled, eyes vanishing into folds at that simple mark of thanks and praise.

Themistocles began to inspect his men, stepping in close to rub away a smear of oil or blood, tapping them on the stomach or shoulders so that they stood straighter. It made the hoplites smile, through all their pain and weariness. In just a moment, Themistocles was chuckling along with them, sound without words. Not one of that small group could have said exactly why they laughed, but it was right.

When the sound died away, Themistocles had reached the end of the line. He turned back to them.

'Gentlemen, it has been my privilege to serve with you. We have all lost friends who stood with us. They know we did not give way. We continued to fight – and we won. Their lives were not wasted. Tell that to the women and children on Salamis! When they ask how fathers and brothers and sons died, tell them they went with honour, to save us all. That if they had the chance, they would do it again. Tell them there was never a cause so clean, so noble as this. We offered all we have – and we are here still. Give thanks for that, to Poseidon who kept us safe, to Ares who guided our hand, to Athena, who brought us through. In her name, in the name of all the gods . . . in the name of all those who no longer stand with us, thank you.'

He looked at them and felt tears come to his own eyes. There was no shame in it, not for an Athenian. Not that day.

'I stood at Marathon, lads. I thought I would never see its like again, nor know men as brave. I can't say that now. I have known you. I am proud of you all.'

Some of the Persian fleet had escaped the net of galleys thrown across the strait. Xanthippus had left them a breach, preferring to let them run rather than fight to the last ship and last man. Themistocles had witnessed over a hundred Persian captains decline battle at the last, just going flat out to reach open sea and leave their tormentors behind. One or two had been marked by splashes as they threw protesting officers overboard.

*Conn Iggulden*

Lost in the desire to punish them, Themistocles had almost manoeuvred his smaller group into their path, but held back. There was an hour in every conflict when both sides came close to breaking. Exhaustion can ruin an army, no matter how well trained, no matter how committed. Themistocles had sensed in time how near his people were to being overwhelmed. He wondered if the choice to hold back counted as another moment of genius from him. He decided it probably didn't, not in comparison to the rest.

'Now, smarten yourselves up, would you?' he said, his tone suddenly brisk. 'We are heading to Salamis, to collect our people. So try to look less like we lost! Get a bucket and sluice the deck clean. Run a hand through your hair. We'll have strangers on this deck before nightfall.'

His words served to snap them back to bustling action, heading this way and that as they began to remember a life before constant danger. It was as if they were waking, slowly, in joyous disbelief. Themistocles grunted. In such times, it was good to keep men busy. He could see ships already heading towards Salamis. The sea was clear of the enemy and cheering rang out across the strait. He shook his head as exhaustion threatened once more, like a weight on his eyes. Athena alone knew where they would take the women and children. Smoke continued to rise over the city and the Persian army was still there, somewhere, untested, unbeaten.

One of his men came jogging past with a bucket of seawater. Themistocles stopped him and dipped both hands in, running them through his mane of hair and slapping both cheeks. The cold helped a little. The ship rolled in the swell ... He blinked. The rowers! Stiffly, Themistocles climbed down into the trench, ducking his head into the gloom and stench of the hold.

They reeked of sweat and urine, those men, of bowels

made loose by poor food and constant labour. The oarsmen had lost weight alarmingly. Wherever he looked, eyes seemed too large in their heads. Ribs showed on them all, but also pride. What had been asked of them had been brutal, but there they were, alive. The gaze of the rowers was a steady one, with humour already glimmering in it. Themistocles grinned, responding to what he saw in them.

'Gentlemen,' he began again, 'it has been my privilege to serve with you . . .'

Mardonius reined in and dismounted. He had cantered from one end of the marching column to the first stopping place, where a stream crossed a land much drier than home. Entire regiments were already busy along the banks, refilling skins and casks with water, quenching their own thirst until they were drenched and laughing. His men preferred to be clean, he knew. He envied them their freedom from care when he saw them blow and spit, flinging unbound hair from one side to the other. There had been that sense of authority loosed, ever since news had spread of the king's departure. Some of the men clearly felt as children whose tutors have been delayed or fallen ill. Whatever dark clouds lay in the future, they were a little giddy for a time. Mardonius frowned at the thought. The quickest way back to discipline would be to flog a few. Yet perhaps his irritation sprang from the same source. He too felt abandoned, though it was without any sort of joy. The thoughts that whispered in the vaults of his mind were close to treason.

Everything had changed and nothing had changed. Mardonius told himself he still had the army. Xerxes had sent some regiments home by land and taken others on board the ships, heading home with forty thousand men. At least he had left the Immortals, reduced though they were. No excuse would matter to the young king, if Mardonius returned without a victory. The Greeks had to be made vassals, or his life – and the lives of his sons and daughters and wives – would all be ashes on the breeze. The king had hostages in the families of all his men, Mardonius thought. They were loyal enough, of course they were! Still, it was a consideration.

He dismounted and passed his reins to an attendant. In the absence of Xerxes, the servants and camp followers had raised the great pavilion once again, for the general to meet his subordinates. Incense burned in golden braziers, sweetening the air. A pot of mint tisane seethed on a tiny flame, ready to be served. Mardonius greeted Artabazus with stiff courtesy, kissing him on both cheeks.

'Brother, you are welcome,' he said. 'Will you eat? I find a little mint and a sweet cake ease my weariness at this time of day.'

The sun was setting and Mardonius knew half his men had still not set up to cook a meal, or even laid out their sleeping blankets. The ground was stony there and the nights were surprisingly cold. Yet at least it was dry.

'You are too generous, general. It gives me pain to refuse you, but I must. I have Hydarnes of the Immortals and Masistius, master of horse, both doing nothing of use while they look to me to tell them where to place their regiments, where to corral their carts and animals! I think sometimes you and I are fathers to children.'

Mardonius said nothing, though he felt his eyebrow rise almost on its own. Artabazus was a fat little man, a head shorter than either the general of the Immortals or the commander of horse for the Persian king. Mardonius wondered if Artabazus would speak so irritably if either Hydarnes or Masistius had been there to hear. He thought not, on the whole.

*Protector*

'It would please me if you shared what little I have, Arta-bazus. I value your opinion.'

It was all simply the ritual of good manners, of course. The first offer was always refused, the second accepted. Mar-donius had seen from the first moment how Artabazus' gaze lingered on the plate of honey cakes. He had a weakness for such things, which was why Mardonius had displayed them on a plate of gold.

'If you wish, I will try a small one,' Artabazus said. 'You do me a great honour, general. All I ask is to serve.'

In moments, they were both seated cross-legged on a rug of silk weave, enjoying the soft cakes and accepting wine. Neither man did more than compliment the food until it was all gone. Artabazus managed a surprising number of the little cakes, though he expressed regret as they vanished and sighed when the last crumb had gone.

'I was once as slender as a youth, can you believe it?' he said.

The man produced a needle of ivory to work between his teeth. Mardonius smiled to see him relax, though he won-dered if it might all be an act for his benefit. Certainly Artabazus was wondering what he would say.

'I know I can trust you, Artabazus,' Mardonius said at last.

'It is beyond doubt,' the man replied, bowing his head.

'I will speak to Hydarnes and Masistius. You three are my most trusted officers, along with my sons. I must rely on you all now, to bear weight and responsibility – to pass on my orders to each regiment, to see them carried out. I have been entrusted with a task, Artabazus. I need to know you under-stand its importance. There will be no disobedience, no interpretation, is that understood?'

'Of course!' Artabazus replied. He rocked forward, so that the swell of his belly hid the hands he crossed over his waist. 'I came to this place to serve the royal house of Persia, general. That has not changed. Nothing has changed! Only the worst workman needs an overseer to watch he does not sleep the day away. We know what we must do.'

Mardonius nodded, pleased.

'Good. His Majesty entrusted to me the task of bringing the Greeks to heel, Artabazus. He wants them as loyal vassals of the Persian court.'

He watched as a slight frown line appeared between the man's eyes. Artabazus blinked slowly as he listened.

'I . . . believe I understand, general. The authority is yours, to destroy, to enslave . . . Merely order me and I will obey, of course.'

Mardonius looked away for a time. The silence was in part for him to gather his thoughts, but also to remind the little man facing him that Artabazus truly waited on his whim. Mardonius had spent the previous day watching Greeks smash a Persian fleet, growing stronger and more skilled with every hour that passed. He had looked around at a city in ruins, its walls pulled down, some streets still burning – and in that grim hour, he had sent men for a tally of their supplies.

The figures that had been brought to him had not been pleasing. The army of Persia had marched for months, each man needing to be fed twice or three times a day. The sheer volumes were beyond imagination, but despite all their planning and all the caches they had left along the route, they were running dangerously low – with cold months coming. Mardonius sensed the poorly hidden worry in his second in command. He too had felt adrift ever since Xerxes had panicked, his nerve deserting him. There was anger there too, words that Mardonius would never dare say aloud. They had been abandoned in a foreign field, with food running low and two hundred thousand hungry men to keep alive. No one fought in winter! It was impossible. Men went home and hung their sword above the door, eating wizened apples and the grain their families had dried and kept. An army had to carry its food or take it from the land. When the cold came, starvation and death threatened anyone fool enough to remain in the field. Yet there he was, with barely enough left to feed the men for another month.

'I am going to head north,' Mardonius said, 'into the region of Thessaly. It is a rich, flat land, with flocks of sheep and golden crops. It is known as the breadbasket of the Hellenes, so I am told.' The general reached past the edge of the rug on which he sat, picking up a handful of dust. 'Not like this poor stuff. If we remain in Attica, we'll starve before spring.'

Artabazus digested this, his head slightly lowered so that his eyes were hooded and hidden. After a time, he nodded.

'As you say, general. I obey. His Majesty trusted you with the campaign. You are responsible.'

Was there a knife-edge in that choice of words? Mardonius wasn't sure. Artabazus was not above considering his own future, perhaps his own promotion if Mardonius failed to bring about victory. The general allowed himself a tight smile, inclining his head to a competitor. The responsibility was indeed his. Yet he was not one of those who feared authority. Mardonius enjoyed the exercise of power, and all that came with it. It was always more satisfying to lean on others than to be leaned upon. That thought guided his reply.

'I know you will be my right hand, Artabazus, that whatever orders I give will be carried out quickly and well. I thank God and the angels to have such men as you, Hydarnes and Masistius. Give me your best and I will raise you all.'

For one with ears to hear, it was not a particularly reassuring message. Mardonius was making it clear he would lay responsibility – or blame – on the necks of his subordinates. It was always that way and Artabazus was not surprised. His mouth twisted as he uncurled and lay flat, making obeisance with his hands up about his head.

'I am honoured indeed, general,' he said as Mardonius bade him rise. 'In truth, I think there is no other choice. There is nothing left in the city we burned. Whoever lives there will surely starve this winter. I will tell Masistius we are headed for the plains of Thessaly. Our master of horse thinks more of those animals than his men, so he will be pleased.'

For a moment, the same hooded look returned, the political consideration surfacing. Mardonius watched the change of expression with a sigh. All men in authority had to appease those above, while intimidating the ones below. Artabazus was obsequious and willing in his presence, but a cruel tyrant with those he commanded. It introduced an element of deceit into every level of authority, as each officer chose the path that best maintained his status. Still, it was important to be clear. Mardonius waited for the question he saw bubbling to the surface.

'General . . . our march north . . . will it not take us past the Spartans? I recall I saw a map that puts them to the west of such a route, but not so far they could not come out.'

Thermopylae had wormed its way into the fears of his entire army, Mardonius knew, not just his own. None of them had ever seen a fighting force like those red-cloaked maniacs. The death toll alone had been horrific. The thought of facing thousands of them was enough to put a cold clench into the bravest of men.

'According to our tame Greeks, the Spartans have built a wall and cower behind it. They will not come out – and if they do, we will overwhelm them.' Mardonius waved a hand, directing the attention of his second in command to the landscape and hills around them, marked in scattered regiments as far as either of them could see. 'There has never been a host like this in the world, Artabazus. I do not fear the few Sparta can put in the field, not against these.'

It was said with a fine confidence. Artabazus bowed his head once more, choosing to dip down and kiss the general's sandal rather than speak. It was only when he had left that Mardonius wondered if that meant he agreed, or not.

# 9

An easterly wind had risen in the strait by Salamis. Out on deep waters, galley crews raised masts up from the hold and rigged sails. Others rowed, driving hard at the beaches, their long keels grinding trenches in the sand.

The hungry crowds on Salamis were not triumphant. A thin plume of smoke could still be seen over Athens and for most it meant the loss of everything. There could be no going home, because home had gone, along with the lives they had known before the invasion. They trooped on board even so, cramming themselves onto open decks, waiting miserably to be taken away.

Out at sea, Themistocles had summoned the strategoi with the black flag. There was no better word for the role, he thought. As on the battlefield at Marathon, Xanthippus and Cimon had both acted as good senior officers, commanding formations of ships. Neither had followed in blind obedience, Themistocles thought with pride. The Assembly of Athens raised thinkers, not slaves. The council of five hundred men began each monthly term with a solemn oath: to 'advise according to the law, all that is best for the people of Athens'. That vow was a simple thing, even when the result was war and evacuation.

As Xanthippus and Cimon lashed their galleys to his and stepped on board, Themistocles could see wariness and suspicion, rather than congratulation. He stifled a yawn, feeling his jaw crack. There was still so much that needed to be done.

Another galley rowed close enough for rowers on both sides to grasp oars and heave them in. Themistocles was not surprised to see Eurybiades of Sparta. He gestured for him to come across, the man using the galley of Cimon like a bridge. Themistocles watched the Spartan do it with neat precision, though the swell made the ships rise and fall, grinding against one another. It was much the same with Spartans themselves, Themistocles thought. They roughened his skin.

As Cimon and Xanthippus greeted the Spartan navarch, Themistocles saw others coming in. The leaders of the Corinthians, the Megarans, the Aeginetans – half a dozen others were making their way to that flotilla, some of them limping and baling water as they came. Themistocles had not expected a conference of all the allies. He'd called the leaders of Athens, but it seemed that was an oversight. These were all men who had fought. They had ferried Athenian women and children, and risked their lives over days of exhaustion and pain. Themistocles nodded, to himself as much as Xanthippus and Cimon. His people were Athenians first, yes, but if there was any truth in that great fleet, they were all Greeks as well. Even so, he felt too weary to welcome so many, to be the easing oil between them, the salt to lend flavour! He thought he might never enjoy salt again, he had swallowed so much of it over the previous days. It coated his skin as well as the deck and rimed oars like a winter frost. As each of them came on board, Themistocles pasted on a smile. He accepted every outstretched hand, gripping arm to arm.

'I give thanks to Athena and to Poseidon – and to you all,' Themistocles said. They had come to his ship, after all. He was the host and they would hear him speak. 'We fought well together – and those of us who were here will always remember how it was done. The formations, the spear tactic. I give thanks for Xanthippus – a man I brought home, whose value was clear to me.' He ignored the spasm of irritation that crossed Xanthippus' face at that. 'I give honour to the men of Corinth, who fought like wolves and did not give way. I give honour to the trierarchs of Sparta, who lost half their ships in savage fighting and yet did not break.'

Eurybiades bowed his head, his lips moving in silent prayer. Themistocles paused. There was a time for politics, for subtle persuasion and pressure. A true leader would name each man, each contingent. He would record all their victories and raise them up with praise. On that day, he was damned if he could bring himself to do it.

'I sent two letters to the Persian king,' Themistocles said.

Eurybiades blinked at the sudden change of subject. He too knew the rituals after a battle.

Themistocles looked at their frowning faces. They were so serious!

'The first went with my carpenter's boy. I asked Xerxes to send half his fleet around Salamis. I told him we would surrender if he did, that we could not defend both ends of the strait. As a result, he split his fleet. Acting on my instruction, he made them into two halves we could destroy, instead of one great formation we could not. That single decision saved us all, but even then, while Athens burned, the future of Greece hung in the balance. Last night, I sent a second letter, saying some of my most warlike captains were intent on sailing back to his famous bridge of ships, to destroy it. To prevent that, Xerxes stole away in the night – taking another hundred ships with him! So when you drink to our victory, be sure to raise a cup or two to luck – and to Athenian cunning. Or, why not? To Themistocles!'

He said the last while raising a hand, as if he made the toast himself. The Spartan leader blinked. He did not echo the words. Cimon laughed though, leaning back slightly as if blown by a wind.

'To Themistocles!' he said.

Themistocles bowed his head in thanks.

Xanthippus scowled at them both.

'Gentlemen, I did not come here to praise, or be praised. Perhaps it has escaped your notice, but we have the people of Salamis already going on board our ships. We must have a destination! My crews have no water left, no food on board. They are in desperate need. I came here to see if anyone has stores we can share out, fresh water in particular. I came to find out if anyone knows a safe place we can take our women and children, before the rowers collapse. Even if Themistocles is right . . .' He paused to glare at his countryman, still standing with an eyebrow raised, as if surprised to be interrupted. 'If he is right about the Persian king, there is still an army in Attica. I assume they left when they torched the city, but can it be safe to land at the Piraeus? I don't want to have won the war at sea, only to deliver our people into their hands!'

Xanthippus was low-voiced and serious. In just a few words, he had turned the mood from giddiness and exultation to grim purpose. Though his words made perfect sense, Themistocles had never liked him less.

'I came to say farewell,' the Spartan Eurybiades said suddenly. 'As you say, half of my sixteen ships were sunk, their crews lost. It is my duty now to return to the Peloponnese, to take this news and patrol the coasts there.'

'And to summon out the army of Sparta,' Xanthippus added.

Eurybiades seemed to hear criticism in the tone. It may have been there.

'That is the decision of the regent and the ephors. Be

*Conn Iggulden*

careful, Athenian. My people have already given King Leo-nidas to this cause, as well as half the Spartan fleet. You will not question our oath.'

Xanthippus stood with Athens at his back, across the strait. Smoke still rose there, though it was a hundred pale threads compared to the stream of soot and fire it had been, visible all the previous night. Still, the Spartan seemed to understand he could not win in comparing losses or commitment.

Instead, Eurybiades turned to Themistocles.

'I said before that I would call on you when this is all done.'

'It is not done,' Themistocles said with a shrug. 'But if you wish, I will meet you. Boxing. The Academy ground on the Ilissus, assuming they have left anything more than ashes of my gymnasium there. Name a day and I will attend.'

To the surprise of all the other strategoi, the Spartan chuckled.

'I merely wished to remind you. The time is not right. Sword and shield are my weapons of choice, however. When this is over, I will come to you.'

Themistocles bristled, weariness falling away as his anger surged.

'I'd bring some friends, if I were you. One of you doesn't seem quite enough.'

'I do not need friends . . .'

'Oh, you don't have any?'

The Spartan was growing red in the face and it was Xan-thippus who spoke over them both.

'Gentlemen, if I may interrupt, we have not yet addressed our real needs. Navarch Eurybiades? I would ask that you lend your ships to us for another day, to help carry women and children.'

'No, Xanthippus,' Eurybiades said, still glaring at Themistocles. 'Duty calls me home.' He seemed to understand his response had been too curt. His face darkened. 'I know you for an honourable man, Xanthippus of Athens. My captains speak well of your leadership. You have my thanks.' There was a subtle emphasis on the 'you', to leave Themistocles out.

'Captains you would not have if not for me,' Themistocles said. 'Perhaps you should bend the knee and give thanks to Athena, Eurybiades.'

'Enough!' Xanthippus snapped, surprising them both before Eurybiades could reply. 'If you cannot keep a civil tongue for your allies, Themistocles, why did you summon us here? Navarch Eurybiades knows the stakes. The Spartans will come out. Aristides will join our hoplites to them, with all the forces of our alliance! We know the enemy – and we cannot beat that army alone, any more than we could their fleet. There is no need for petty rivalry.'

'You are correct, Xanthippus, of course,' Themistocles said stiffly. 'Very well. On your way, Navarch Eurybiades. And thank you.' The title of 'navarch' was a subtle insult, given that Themistocles had overridden the man's command and made it worthless. Even so, a flush spread on the Spartan's face, down to his neck.

'Another *word*, Themistocles,' Xanthippus said, 'and I will bring a case against you, in front of the Assembly.'

He felt Cimon's gaze grow cold at that, but there was no help for it. It had been Xanthippus who had brought down Cimon's father, in exactly that way. It was not an idle threat and Themistocles turned on him in shock. Yet through some wild incaution, from weariness or hunger, Themistocles was endangering them all. They needed to go their separate ways, to rest, eat, drink and rest again. Whether any of them would get the chance, Xanthippus did not know.

*Conn Iggulden*

When Themistocles remained silent, the Spartan nodded to Xanthippus. Eurybiades wished to support a man who could silence Themistocles.

'I can wait another day, Xanthippus. I'll lend my ships for the work. But where will you land your people?'

Xanthippus looked at the island of Salamis. Eleusis lay on the coast beyond it, where Aristides had encamped the hoplites of Athens. Yet with the army of Persia out and roaming, that sea town was as vulnerable as anywhere else in Attica. He felt tiredness sap his thoughts. After a moment, it was the Corinthian strategos who cleared his throat.

'I think ... gentlemen, that nowhere is truly safe, not while Persians remain. They could march on any city and destroy it, as thoroughly as Athens. Until they have been broken, or made to run, there is no refuge.'

It was true, but so bleak it made them all pause.

Reluctantly, Eurybiades spoke.

'Your people could come to the Peloponnese. The wall across the isthmus keeps Corinth and Sparta safe. They can rest and grow strong there, as refugees.'

The word made both Themistocles and Xanthippus wince. The thought of hiding behind a wall was bad enough. Being indebted to Sparta was worse.

'Thank you, navarch,' Xanthippus said formally, without any of the sting Themistocles had managed to bring to the rank. 'However, before we make that decision, I will send men back to Athens, to be certain the Persians have not left soldiers there.'

'Unless they can breathe flame, they have not,' Themistocles muttered.

He was dull-eyed again, the last of his energy draining away. For that, Xanthippus was thankful. The Spartan had come very close to drawing a weapon on the man needling him. Had he done so, the Athenian crew would not have stood for seeing a Spartan attack Themistocles. It would have gone bad very quickly indeed.

'According to my men, the Persians pulled down the walls of Athens,' Eurybiades said.

Xanthippus smiled, though there was a great deal of bitterness in it.

'You have no walls in Sparta,' he reminded.

Eurybiades blinked.

'Well, no. *We* are the walls . . .' He trailed off, understanding the point Xanthippus was making.

'These ships are ours,' Themistocles said. 'If the Persians threaten our city, we can take to these wooden walls to escape them! We did it before. It's not as if they have a fleet of their own now, is it?'

The idea seemed to liven him up once more. He put Xanthippus in mind of a guttering wick on its last drops of oil, flaring back to life at intervals.

Xanthippus nodded. Perhaps because Themistocles was almost out on his feet, he saw they were all looking to him to make the decision. Some men had authority running in them, deep in the bone. For some, it came from a family name or bloodline. Others built it through hard work, age and experience, but also through being right when it mattered, a few more times than they were wrong. However it had come, the fleet strategoi all looked to him.

'We'll take the people home,' Xanthippus said. 'As soon as I have checked the city is safe, the ships should return our people to the Piraeus. The city is not walls, or even temples. The city is in the lives we saved. They will rebuild – and we still have ships to take them clear if the Persians return. I will not forget what you have done, all of you.'

One by one, he took the hands of each of the others, even

*Conn Iggulden*

going so far as to drag Themistocles two steps by the arm so that he and Eurybiades shook hands once more. It was not done in friendship, however.

'Don't forget our little discussion,' Themistocles said.

'I won't,' Eurybiades replied, showing his teeth. 'I look forward to continuing it.'

## 10

From the moment Xerxes had left, Mardonius had known the year was over, as far as campaigning went. Neither he nor the Great King had expected to end the conflict in a single season. He reminded himself of that as he rode north, heading into lands his Greek allies swore were rich and fertile, with fields of wheat and herds of goats and sheep. He hoped it was so. His army remained on half-rations, with sour looks and grumbling bellies. Though his men had slaughtered every living thing for a day's march, it was barely enough for one meal a day, never mind three. As importantly, two hundred thousand soldiers needed cooks, smiths and leatherworkers just to remain in the field. Kit wore out and horses grew thin, in just a few days of hard labour and poor food. The army of Persia had descended on Attica like locusts, snatching at all that moved or grew until there was nothing left. Mardonius had hopes of the plains of Thessaly, not least for the animals. The general reached forward and patted his own gelding on the neck. It was a fine and sturdy mount, yet one that needed to crop sweet grass each morning, or better still, grain, if he wished to ride all day.

While he remained at the halt, his regiments trudged past. They did their best to appear ready for battle, but he saw weariness in them, even fear. As the days went by, they had begun to feel the loss of the king's eye on them. They wondered what it meant for them that Xerxes had gone home. Still Mardonius smiled like a proud father, nodding to his favoured generals as they rode past, each one bowing in the saddle. He had a special wink and tilt of his head for his four sons, but in truth he could not complain about the men Xerxes had brought to those dusty hills. The Great King had left the training and composition of the army to Mardonius and his senior officers. As a result, they were hardened and enduring. It turned out the only real weakness had been the king himself.

Mardonius still shied away from that in his thoughts, as a horse will jerk back from a darting shadow. From long habit, it was hard for the general even to criticise a member of the royal family. They were a different breed, more akin to angels than men, certainly beyond dispute or question. Yet the mornings were quiet as the army marched away from Athens, crossing hill after hill. An army of that size did almost nothing quickly. Days passed, simply in movement – and reflection.

In his most private thoughts, Mardonius kept returning to the failure of Xerxes, a young man he had revered. His tongue touched a cracked tooth in the same way. He knew he would have to get one of the blacksmiths to pull it for him. Pain could make a child of any man in the end; he had witnessed it. The will slowly wore away, sanded down by fear and suffering . . . Mardonius was furious at being abandoned, but he would not spit a single syllable of that aloud. Not for fear of whispers that might be carried home, but out of loyalty – to Xerxes, and most of all to the memory of his father. Mardonius was a loyal man. That alone would sustain him when the wine ran dry and the last of the bread was furred with mould. He hoped so.

In the distance, two scout riders appeared on a hilltop. They carried no shields or spears that he could see. They were clearly watching the passage of the Persian force, no doubt reporting back to the leaders of Athens, or Sparta – or any of the other small states. Mardonius ignored them. If they came closer, he might send a few horsemen to run them off. He shook his head, turning his thoughts again to what he had to do to finally go home. When he closed his eyes, he could see his garden, with all the flowers filling the air with scent. Persia in the spring! Yet when he opened them again, the ground was just dust, with olive trees twisted like old men.

Xerxes had told him to bring the Greeks to heel, to make them bend the knee and acknowledge the empire. Mardonius set his mind to fulfilling the task he had been given. After a time, he found he was enjoying himself. It felt like a weight lifting, to have a problem that needed his wit and experience to solve. No, it was more even than that. He had been so long under the gaze of Xerxes that Mardonius had almost forgotten the simplest reward of authority. As a breeze blew across his face, he let peace flood through him. He was in command, of all the forces in Greece. He was free – free to fail and starve, yes, but also to triumph and know the achievement was all his own. Mardonius was on campaign, with strong sons and trusted men! For an old warhorse like himself, it was not too great a burden.

A few of his horsemen blew horns ahead, dragging his thoughts back to the present. Over to the west, Mardonius squinted into the distance, seeing a haze of dark blue, but also a dun line – the wall across the famous isthmus. Mardonius tasted acid when he understood the dots of colour were red-cloaked Spartans, watching his people. He muttered a curse at them and spat on the ground.

He had not realised his regiments would pass quite so close to the neck of land that separated the Peloponnese from the rest of Greece. He recalled Artabazus had said something along those lines, but the reality was still surprising. All the Persian officers had heard of the wall the Spartans had built. Mardonius scowled, recalling how he'd

*Conn Iggulden*

laughed on first hearing of it. It would have availed them little when a Persian fleet could land anywhere on their rocky coast! Of course, that fleet lay at the bottom of the strait at Salamis, or as driftwood still appearing on every beach of the Aegean. The Spartans had made a poor choice with their wall, only to have it become a stroke of genius. It was enough to make a man believe in their gods . . .

With his enemy watching, Mardonius felt a pang of regret at his marching formation. He had the men in over two thousand ranks, each eighty or a hundred deep. It made a great snake of a column when crossing unknown land, but it would not look quite as intimidating as he might have wished. Still, it took hours for them all to pass the distant Spartan line. Let them observe that! Regiments of Persian horsemen swirled around the edges and thick dust hung in the air for half a day.

No one moved on the wall, Mardonius noted. After what he had witnessed at close hand in the pass of Thermopylae, he'd half-expected the gates to be thrown open and the Spartans to come charging out. He spat again in the dust, disgusted at the relief washing through him. Damn them for the damage they had done! He wondered if he would ever be able to face those red-cloaked warriors without his stomach creeping up behind his ribs.

He reminded himself of what the Thebans had sworn was true. The Spartans had no more than ten thousand – at the very most. As Xerxes had ordered with Leonidas, Mardonius could surround them, bring them down with spears and arrows and sling-stones. They were just men. Their gods were false. He told himself that, though his stomach croaked, for all the world like a warning voice.

Agariste stepped down once again onto the port of Piraeus. She knew well enough that Athens would not be the same, but it was hard to comprehend the reality. The shore was littered with broken beams and curved ship strakes like the carcasses of whales. Bodies still bumped every hull afloat, some shuddering as if alive. Fish bit at them, she knew, nipping at flesh unseen. She had seen one poor fellow dragged out with great pale parts missing from his face. The rest were left where they lay for the moment. Real life – ordinary life – had not returned.

She stood, with her three children, on a stone dock. The horses she had brought down from the estate had long vanished, of course, either stolen or run off. Agariste understood she would have to walk. She looked round as another of the young women in her household came running up, head down and wild-haired. Two others had found their mistress, full of apologies for their absence. Agariste had caught glimpses of them in their brief exile across the water. She was certain one of them had also seen her, but Agariste had not called her over, for fear she might not come. Yet with every passing hour, the laws and certainties of life were being asserted once more. The slaves of her house had nowhere else to go, after all. If there was a moment of resentment or resignation in them, it was quickly hidden.

Agariste felt her heart leap when she saw another face she knew in the passing crowd. The entire city was flooding through that port, trudging home to whatever they would find in Athens. The Acropolis was visible in the distance, as if nothing had changed. If not for the smell of smoke and bodies turning in the surf, it might almost have been an ordinary day.

'Manias!' she called.

It was as if her voice was a hook, pulling one fish out of a shoal. Relief swept over her as Manias came to her side. She saw he wore an odd expression of discomfort, but the reason for it was lost in her joy at finding him.

*Conn Iggulden*

'I'm so pleased to see you alive!' she said.

Manias looked weary, though he took a moment to clap Pericles on the shoulder.

'We lost . . . many,' he said. His mouth was pale as he added a term from one of low estate to a superior: '. . . kuria.'

In that strained word, Agariste understood. Her hand flew to her mouth, covering her shock.

'Oh! You are free, Manias! By my husband's word.'

'If that word is honoured,' he said, looking past her to the throng still coming off the galleys.

There was little chaos there, nor celebration. The strategoi had declared the city safe and free of enemy soldiers, at least that day. Every family back from Salamis just wanted to get into Athens and see what could be salvaged – ideally before their neighbours had a chance to sift through the rubble first.

Manias had rowed for Athens, but also for a promise of freedom. In that moment, Agariste could not be certain her husband's authority truly stretched so far. It would be a matter for the Assembly to discuss and make a formal judgement . . . Her thoughts trailed away. Was there still an Assembly of Athens? A council? Her uncle Cleisthenes had never imagined a foreign army actually invading and burning the city. Yet Xanthippus said the people were the Assembly – all around her, heading away from the port in determined groups. Families were reuniting on the quayside, while thousands more drifted back to all they knew, away from memories of fear and desperation.

'Manias, you know my husband's word. You are free. Yet I would feel safer if you remained with me, at least until we have returned to the estate, or my husband's house . . .'

She halted again, suddenly aware that those places would be ashes and charred beams. She felt out of place, lost, with tears stinging her eyes. Manias saw and yet he did not speak immediately. He bit his lip after a time. He had been free for a day, but it had been hard-won and he would not give it up.

'A free man works for pay, kuria . . .' he said, blushing.

Agariste nodded and brought out a pouch, fishing two silver coins from the depths.

'A day's wage for a free man, Manias. Is it enough?'

He chuckled then, his own eyes gleaming with strong emotion.

'It is, kuria. Thank you.' He accepted the coins almost with reverence, the very first he had earned in his new estate.

It was his voice that rang out a few moments later, gathering in a few more of the errant female servants, herding the group together and leading the way. Agariste looked to her two sons and her daughter. They still thought of it as a great adventure, of course. Journeys on a galley's deck, a sea battle played out before their very eyes. Agariste hid her own fear from them. There was a Persian army still in Greece, a host larger than all the cities could muster. She hid her terror from them. Daughters and sons faced different fates, when Persia made war. Despair flickered in her, like the dying light of a fire. It would be too cruel to watch the impossible victory at Salamis and *still* lose.

There was always hope, she reminded herself. Xanthippus and Themistocles and Cimon had triumphed against a huge, royal fleet. She began to hum an old prayer to Athena, something Xanthippus had taught her. He said it had been sung at Marathon and it gave her comfort. She looked up when she heard the tune echoed in the crowd walking back to the city. More and more began to sing, the sound spreading throat to throat. They knew the words because they were Athenian. She felt her heart lift as Pericles and Eleni and Ariphron joined in. It was not a joyous tune, but she felt her heart swell nonetheless.

*Conn Iggulden*

They entered Athens in song, though the sight of burned streets and rubble choked the hymn back to shocked murmurs. As the stream of men, women and children passed the broken stones that had been walls and a gate, many wept or called aloud in grief. For most of them, it had not been real before. The men had rowed in a private hell, or fought on deck, their world reduced to whosoever stood against them. Their families had waited on a sandy shore, enduring.

The reality was a blow to the heart, with each corner revealing more destruction. Ash coated *everything*, so that those first through the gates were soon made black by whatever they touched or picked up. As Agariste and her family went further, they reached places where families huddled in the ruins of their old homes. Mothers and fathers were already seeking whole tiles they could salvage, though tears ran in soot and muck down their cheeks. To Agariste's surprise, she saw children chasing one another through gaps, scrambling along charred beams and laughing. It made her smile as she passed by, heading to her husband's town-house.

The Persians had been thorough. Everything had been set alight, or pulled down with ropes and hooks. Only the streets themselves remained open, though the sewage trenches had been baked by fires roaring overhead. For once, the smell of the city was smothered by charcoal and the peppery taint of stones heated until they cracked.

Agariste was glad Manias was with her when she came across groups of young men, shouting and arguing. Order would soon be restored, she knew. Her husband would organise them and have them work until they were exhausted. Xanthippus knew how to apply force and how to bend men to his will. It was his talent, the reason Themistocles had called him home.

When they reached the site of her husband's town-house,

it had been consumed. Somehow, Agariste had hoped for more than a few charred beams and a broken column. The door was still discernible, but made into a shiny black plate that broke under the pressure of a hand.

'We'll need new wood – and tools,' she said. 'I shouldn't think iron tools would have burned. Manias? Will the road be safe, do you think? We could fell trees out at the estate, if they are still there. Surely not all will have burned. We'll need as many men as you can find to work. Can you gather them?'

'I think so,' Manias said.

He had been a slave to her house for over thirty years, serving her own father and uncle before her. Though the hair on his forearms and chest was white, he was still strong and somehow relieved to have a purpose. His freedom remained, as a hard seed in him. He felt it there. Yet when he heard Agariste rattling off instructions, it brought a sort of comfort amidst all the strangeness of the new world.

'We'll rebuild, Manias,' she said. 'Take Ariphron out to the estate. Pericles will keep me safe until you return. Eleni and I will clear the site and gather whatever might be reused. I think this would be a good time to buy the plots on either side, if we can make the owners a good offer.'

Manias blinked at that. She was looking around her, like everyone else, but somehow seeing the future. He nodded to her. A fleeting thought had him wondering how she would find silver even to pay for workers, when all Athens wanted the same. Yet somehow, he knew she would do it. Or her husband would. For some of the families wandering through what had been their home, broken walls and burned streets would be the end of the world. Yet they were Athenian – and he saw what that meant in Agariste. The world owed them nothing, but that did not matter. They would rebuild. Better and more splendid than before.

*Conn Iggulden*

# PART TWO

'No one escapes his fate, whether brave or coward,
not from the moment he is born.'

– Homer, *The Iliad*

## II

The sun stood low in the sky, though it was noon. Athens rang with the sounds of hammers and saws, the music of regeneration and life flooding back in. Barely three weeks had passed since the last Persian soldier had left to march into the north, but the city had already lost the stunned calm of a funeral pyre.

From the height of the Pnyx hill, Themistocles could see entire new streets under construction. It was astonishing what a people bent to a single task could accomplish. The kilns in the pottery district had been the first things repaired. The enemy had left many of them intact or simply kicked apart. Those glazed bricks had been reassembled by hand. It hadn't been long before they were back up to firing heat, running night and day, turning out tiles before the winter rains came. New roofs began to appear by the hundred, raised on fresh-cut beams and planking. All the carpenters knew green wood would warp and twist, but that was a problem for another month. Once they had put new handles on axe heads and saws, teams had gone out into the hills, cutting down firs, poplars, oaks, anything they could find. The results brought a smell of sap and sawdust overlaid on the sour reek of char. It was the smell of industry – and hope.

The Assembly had gathered up on the Pnyx to hear the latest reports – a daily event during the period of emergency. Themistocles found it oddly comforting to traipse up the hill each noon, to sit quietly and listen to merchants from the port, or the mine master in from Laurium, come to beg for more men. That last was perhaps the most important. They had the people of Athens, even the raw materials to rebuild a city. What they lacked was silver to pay them and food for them to buy. It had not been lost on Themistocles that Xanthippus had freed thousands of slaves. Perhaps that oath had helped to win the battle; Themistocles could not judge every small contribution. Nor could he gainsay Xanthippus' authority to make such an offer. In that moment, in the middle of the evacuation, Xanthippus had *been* the Assembly, a tyrant in all but title. If it had been a plague, say, or a great storm, Themistocles might have considered calling an emergency meeting to debate the decision. As things stood, they were still at war – and he did not think ten thousand slaves would return to their previous owners without a struggle no one could win. Themistocles frowned, gripping the bridge of his nose between two fingers. He had brought Xanthippus home for exactly that sort of decision under pressure. It was done.

Over the previous week, the Athenian fleet had gone out in armed squadrons, with orders to bring back grain or any live thing. The Persians had stripped their city, though some stores had been missed in their eagerness. Themistocles had put guards on a basement still filled with sacks of wheat. It had been toasted a dark brown and the bread made from that flour was very bitter. There were still mouths to feed, however.

The sheer complexity of a city was something few of them had considered before. Athens had grown up over centuries, street by street. If enough people needed shoes, a cobbler opened a little shop. It was a hard thing to get started, however, like a great stone rolling downhill.

The thought made Themistocles look across to where

Aristides was waiting to speak. The man had brought his hoplites back to keep order in Athens. Themistocles suspected Aristides had no choice in that, with the Persians gone and winter upon them. The people of the city were in desperate need. Those who had taken up shield and spear would have wanted to return to their families, while Aristides rejoined the Assembly.

Themistocles forced his smile a touch wider as the rest of them fell silent. Aristides had never been liked exactly, but he was certainly respected. It had been hard enough having him banished the first time. That would not work again. Themistocles was stuck with the man, at least for the duration.

'Speaker here!' someone called by Aristides.

The epistates for the day beckoned him up and stood back, awed in the presence of a banished man returned. Aristides had not shared in the naval victory at Salamis, Themistocles reminded himself. The Assembly had no reason to look on him with such reverence.

'Thank you,' Aristides said.

He wore no armour in that place, choosing instead his habitual robe, a ragged old thing that looked as if it might be the one he'd owned from before his banishment. Themistocles raised his eyes to heaven or the Acropolis as Aristides began to speak.

'I cannot report any progress with the Spartans,' he said. 'Their regent knew of his father's oath. He did not seem . . . particularly bound by it. They feel too secure, the men of Sparta and Corinth, safe behind that fortress wall they have built, as if armies of Persia are no concern of theirs. I have not found a way to shake that misplaced confidence, not yet.'

'Will they take the field in spring?' someone called.

Aristides paused, stroking his upper lip with the pads of his fingers.

'I cannot say,' he replied.

He waited while a rumble of anger rippled across the thousands present. They were sweating and dirty, most of them. They had worked hard all morning, with lunch waiting. They were desperate for news. Aristides regarded his people, gathered in that place. His gaze fell across Cimon, standing with his friends, his young wolves; then briefly, Themistocles, registering his presence there.

'Sparta will do what is best for Sparta,' Aristides said. 'Our task is to make sure it is also what is best for us. We need them. Understand that. Without the Spartan ten thousand, we cannot stand against the Persian host. I have watched them pass and I can say there is no army like it in the world. I do not think there ever has been. It is an army of *forty* nations like ours, a force so vast, it will take all we have to send them home. Do not think I am complacent, gentlemen. Even if Sparta comes out, if we take the field, it will be a straw in the wind how many of us come home again. They have cavalry armed with spear and bow, archers of great skill, regiment after regiment of foot soldiers. I stood at Marathon! I saw how good Athenian hoplites could beat two or three times as many – with formation discipline, with a spear-thrust and a good shield. Yet these are four or five times the number we might bring to the field, perhaps more. I have eyes on them in the north, with relays of fast horses on the hills between. If they move, we will know. *When* they move, I believe we will triumph – Athena stands with us – but it will be hard. There will be sorrow in the spring, amidst the horns of victory.'

The crowd were silent, though a breeze arose, flapping robes and cloaks. Themistocles turned at a disturbance fur-

*Conn Iggulden*

ther down the hill. He watched Xanthippus come up the last steps, the crowd parting for him. Some of the men patted him on the back as he came, so that he smiled. Themistocles nodded, feeling a sourness in his stomach he knew was petty and vain. Was the world so small that he had to begrudge another man the crowd's acclaim? Or was it that they seemed to lionise Xanthippus more than the one who had actually saved them all?

'Speaker here,' Aristides said. He stepped back.

The epistates beckoned, bowing his head to Xanthippus as the call was seconded. The strategos rose like a stone from the sea of heads, coming to stand above them. Themistocles found himself glowering and forced a more benign countenance.

'Assembly, thank you for hearing me,' Xanthippus said.

He smiled at them and Themistocles thought how tanned and fit he looked. It could hardly have been more irritating.

'I can confirm three more ships are back, filled with grain and cured hams. The fishing fleet report great shoals, so many they are in danger of tearing their nets. It is a start, but I can confirm supplies for another week. With discipline and restraint, there will be food enough for all. Be assured, we will continue to fish and seek out provisions. No one will starve.'

They cheered at that, revealing more worry than they had known themselves. Xanthippus raised an arm to include Aristides.

'If you would honour anyone, it should be Aristides, who organised the crews and, more importantly, allocated their catch fairly.'

There was another cheer, though it was more muted. There had been riots in the first few days, with fishing crews overwhelmed and six men stabbed to death. Aristides had restored order with brutal efficiency and set his hoplites to oversee every part of the process. It was all new to them, but they had learned quickly.

'What about the Persians?' a voice called out from the midst.

Xanthippus might have ignored it, but it was echoed by a dozen more, growing louder as he hesitated. He was not a man who enjoyed being harangued by the crowd. He could not raise their spirits or make them laugh the way Themistocles could. Yet the noise did not die down. Of course they were worried, he reminded himself. They had been forced to run once. The army of Persia was still in Greece and could appear over the hills at any moment. Xanthippus had endured the same questions from his children and wife, from his friend Epikleos and a hundred other voices. It was the weight that pressed them all down, the not knowing. He wondered what they thought he could possibly add. Themistocles said they just needed to see confidence at such times, that men were not so very different from children, at least when they were afraid. Xanthippus blew air out and nodded, looking across the heads of the Assembly. They *were* afraid. It would have been madness not to be.

'The Persians have made a camp for themselves in Thessaly. They have organised patrols, felled trees for wood, piled up ramps of earth and stone as a boundary. Our scouts say it all looks . . . solid. I imagine they have settled in for winter.' Someone else began to call out and Xanthippus snapped an answer over him. 'If they *do* come before then, perhaps with supplies stripped from the orchards and flocks of Thessaly, we will either meet them in the field with our allies – or if Sparta still refuses to come, we can abandon Athens a second time.'

He raised his voice then over the babble of fear and anger.

*Conn Iggulden*

'*To that end . . . !* To that end, I have prepared landing spots on Salamis, with supplies of food and water. We did the best we could once, with no warning. We will do better if we have to decamp again. I pray it will not happen, but you would call me remiss if I did not consider every possibility.'

He pursed his lips as he stood there, glaring at the Assembly as if they had offended him. Themistocles cleared his throat. He had waited for his moment and saw that it had come. Xanthippus glanced over as he stood up, looking relieved as much as anything.

'Speaker here,' Xanthippus murmured.

Others in the crowd called out support, so that the name of Themistocles sounded amongst them like a breeze. It was not quite the shout of acclaim Themistocles would have liked, but good enough. He mounted the steps and stood with Xanthippus and Aristides. He felt the lift in his own spirits, the quickening of his heart that came whenever he had to speak to a crowd. He loved it, or he loved them, it was hard to say which was most true in that moment.

'Step by step, gentlemen,' Themistocles said. 'Step by step, we walk the path before us. Temples on the Acropolis are rising again; homes spring from the ground! Children laugh and play in the ashes, black as wolves or Ethiops. I see the spirit of Athena in them – and in us, as we gather here. Food? It is coming in, distributed fairly so that everyone may eat. Shelter? We sleep under the roofs of neighbours, or they under ours. We are Athens! When I told Eurybiades of Sparta that we would not abandon you, that it was possible to use the fleet to save a city, he was so angry he challenged me to dispute with him over sword and shield! When the war is over, I will have to meet him on the field, to show him Athenian cunning.' He chuckled. 'I wonder if I should pray he dies first. A Spartan is a fearsome opponent.'

Laughter swirled through the crowd, his words repeated for those who had not heard.

'You and I have learned of the Persian forces from Aristides and Xanthippus. I don't think they will move before spring, but if they do, we'll meet them.'

Heads nodded at that, while eyes gleamed. Themistocles decided not to repeat the possibility of evacuating a second time. It was just too painful to consider.

'The weakness in our plan is Sparta. I cannot say I understand them, not while a Persian army camps in Greece. Oh, they have built their wall, but it confines more than just the warriors of Sparta. Men of Corinth, a dozen towns in Arcadia, all lie behind it. I wonder if the Spartans might be persuaded to come out if they saw those others marching past. I took their oaths myself, gentlemen! That if the Persians came, they would stand with us. Perhaps it is time to remind our allies of that.'

The crowd growled assent. Themistocles nodded.

'We should send a senior man, someone they will respect.' He shook his head when someone called his name. 'Not I, not today. I must oversee reopening the mines at Laurium, so that silver flows once more through this city, in the flood we desperately need. No, I propose Xanthippus for the role. His judgement is sound. He lived in Corinth for a time and he is known there.'

As the crowd murmured, Themistocles added under his breath, 'And some say he is more Spartan than Athenian anyway.'

He saw from the stiffness in Xanthippus that the words had found their mark. It was not a plan they had discussed before. Sometimes, a man had to be pushed.

'With the permission of the Assembly, I would like to go with him,' a voice said from the left.

Themistocles turned to see Cimon standing with his hand raised. He shrugged, glancing at Xanthippus to see if the idea met with approval. Xanthippus was looking wary, as well he might with one who still blamed him for the death of his father.

'He is a fine young man,' Aristides murmured.

His approval was enough to make Xanthippus nod, putting aside his worries.

'It would be my honour, Cimon,' he said.

He turned to Themistocles then.

'Why not simply ask me?' he said softly. 'Why must you always arrange us, like clay soldiers all in a row?'

'*Ask* you? Where is the joy in that?' Themistocles replied. He nodded to the epistates. 'Young man? Call for a vote. Though I think there will be no dissent. My friends are going to Sparta!'

The weather had turned. Day after day was overcast and rains had drenched the land. It was a bleak time and about as far from the memory of Persian heat as it was possible to be. Mardonius found himself shivering as he warmed his hands before a brazier of black iron. At least olive wood burned well, with great heat.

One reason for a proper camp was to protect the men from the scouring winds that howled over the plains of Thessaly. No one fought in winter. Leaving aside the difficulties of supplying food, it was a time for men to return home, to father children on their wives, to sleep and heal. The blood grew thick and full of torpor in cold months, like bears or dormice. In summer and autumn, they worked, tending their lands. In spring, as the blood rose, they went to war. Mardonius yawned, feeling stiff in every joint. Spring seemed a long way off that day.

The sound of hooves and jingling iron jerked him from his reverie. Horsemen coming in. The camp was always busy around him, a true city in the wilderness, created from earth and wood. He heard them even so, looking over in anticipation. Mardonius hoped it was the ones he had summoned in the king's name. He had expected them for weeks.

The party of riders had to duck to come in under the camp gate – three men in furs and cloaks, one clearly the leader. Mardonius nodded to himself, pleased. They were not Persian. Despite the cold, their legs were bare in the Greek style, legs hanging low, using heels and reins to control their mounts. Yet their horses were bloodlines of Persia, magnificent beasts both stronger and taller than the mounts of Thessaly. The Greeks did not seem to understand the power of horsemen, Mardonius thought sourly. Only foul luck had taken the cavalry from the field at Marathon, or they would have learned very swiftly. He still hoped to teach that lesson before he went home, though as he told his sons, a perfect campaign was one where victory came *without* a pile of corpses. Not that he minded either way.

Mardonius could almost feel his Immortals bristle as the strangers approached. A hundred bustled up in white coats, halting with their red-faced officer, all too aware of the eye of Mardonius on him. The general hid his sigh. Youngest sons always tried too hard. It was their nature. In response, he praised only sparingly, when the lad really did well.

By the time the Macedonians dismounted, two curved lines of white-coated warriors watched, with Mardonius at the deepest point of the cup. The general made a snap decision. Though he did not know them well, they had proved themselves as friends, both in allowing the passage of the Persian army through their land and in answering his personal call. Mardonius knew he could insist on proper

*Conn Iggulden*

obeisance – on them lying face down before him in the mud. He was, after all, the representative of the imperial throne. Yet his Greek allies always seemed to resent being made to show proper respect. He needed them to work for him, or at least their leader.

On a wild impulse, Mardonius held out his hand as if to an equal. He felt the strength of the younger man's grip as he took it, like jaws closing on his hand. The Macedonian king was tall and dark-eyed, with a spring in his step that spoke threat into every movement. Though he had ridden three or four days southward, from his capital down to Thessaly, he gleamed with health. His hair was blond and very thick, reminding Mardonius of a lion's mane.

'You are welcome in my camp,' Mardonius said. 'I have food prepared – and quarters for you to rest and bathe. Your Majesty, I am grateful you came.'

'I gave my word,' the man replied. 'And I am a friend to Persia.' He smiled then. 'I am pleased to finally meet you, Mardonius. You were out with your men when I greeted your king, when I opened my land to your army.'

Mardonius saw the king's cloak was held by a large clasp in the shape of a lion's head, the gold a statement both of wealth and power. He smiled. In the Persian court, it might have graced the shoulder of an attendant, or a child's tutor. Here, it marked Alexander of Macedon as a king.

'It is my honour,' Mardonius said. 'Please, I will show you where you will sleep tonight. There are slaves and clean robes, whatever you need. I hope you and your companions will break bread with me.'

Mardonius would not usually have said more until the rituals of welcome were complete, later that evening. Yet he could see the little group already frowning to one another, more suspicious with every passing moment. They saw the

Persian strength of arms in the camp, in tents and lanes stretching into the distance. It did not mean they understood Persian hospitality. Mardonius said a silent prayer and forgave himself. The big Macedonian was little more than a shepherd with a palace, after all.

'Your Majesty, I asked you here . . . as a favour to me – and through me, to Xerxes, king of kings. The Athenians count my Greek allies as traitors, to be killed on sight. Macedon, however, is another matter. I believe they will listen to you – and I have words I wish them to hear.'

# 12

Though Themistocles could be irritating, Xanthippus could not argue with this particular task. Perhaps Aristides might have gone in his place to Sparta, but it was hard to think of another. It certainly could not be Themistocles himself, not after the way he had fallen out with the Spartan navarch.

In negotiations with Sparta, everything had to be finely judged. They cared nothing for wealth or trappings of power. Worse, they often scorned such things and considered them effete. Xanthippus rode with Cimon at his side and just two servants riding behind, Relas and Onesimos, both men in their early thirties and veterans of Salamis. All four carried swords and Relas had a bow case on his back, hard-shelled and well worn. Together, they made a fearsome enough group to warn off thieves or vagabonds, or so Xanthippus hoped. Rumours were that the roads were quiet that year. Criminals who scraped a living by robbing or murdering travellers had retreated before the movement of armies. He imagined they would be back when their starvation was greater than their fear.

Xanthippus had seen no sign of anyone watching his progress as he and Cimon left the broken walls of Athens behind. The countryside seemed deserted, entire demes of a dozen houses or more left empty and echoing. Some of them would have lost their men to the sea, he had realised, others to Persian outriders. It was a grim thought.

Xanthippus had paused briefly at his own estate on the road north-west. Whoever had torched and looted the place had been thorough. Even his horses had been butchered to feed the enemy. Xanthippus had found the heads and hooves piled in his yard, white tendons showing. The mounts the Assembly had rounded up for their party were skittish things in comparison – the sort of animals that survived an invasion by spooking and galloping away at the first threat. Cimon cursed the one he rode, keeping the rein tight so that the beast nodded and pranced in circles, clearly in distress. The young man may have been the future of Athens, Xanthippus considered, but he was a terrible horseman.

'Ease the bit a little,' Xanthippus called. 'He's fighting you because it's pinching his tongue.'

He looked away as Cimon glared at him, but the horse quieted a while later. Xanthippus could not say he enjoyed the younger man's company. The thought of spending days with Cimon was wearing. Yet his father, Miltiades, had commanded at Marathon – a vital victory against the Persians ten years before. Having Cimon there was a reminder to Sparta of Athenian strength. Or so Xanthippus assumed. He suspected Themistocles had arranged it, all to some plan or design of his own. The man was determined to make them dance. Xanthippus shook his head. The day was getting late and he knew he should look out for a good spot to hobble the horses, sleep and eat. The road was no place to let his guard down.

'Do you want to take first watch tonight?' he asked Cimon.

The young man considered.

'I don't sleep much. Not unless I'm behind a good wall. Out here, I doubt I'll get my head down at all. It doesn't matter. I can stay up.'

Xanthippus hid his irritation.

'You go first then. I can sleep anywhere. We'll make camp, but without a fire. I have a little meat and bread in the pack, enough to tide us over. We should reach the Spartan wall around noon tomorrow. After that, it will be their rations.'

The prospect didn't delight any of them. Xanthippus saw the young man was licking his lips, as if they were sore. He had heard rumours Cimon drank more than any three men, without much effect. Xanthippus shook his head. It was not his concern, though he wondered how much a hold it had on him.

As they crested a hill and looked down into a shallow valley, their spirits rose at a stream running through the land below. There were some fields and a tiny home there, though the fences lay flat in places, clearly broken. That was not a good sign. Xanthippus grimaced as they guided the horses down. Persian scouts had come through there, looking for anything they could take. There was no law at such times. Some men revealed a noble spirit. Others became little better than wolves.

With Relas and Onesimos keeping an eye out for ambush, Xanthippus and Cimon reined in and dismounted. Xanthippus gestured silently, drawing his sword. To his irritation, Cimon left his in the scabbard and just shrugged, looking around.

They stood in the yard of what had once been a small-holding, a family farm scratching a living out of the dry earth. Xanthippus saw the door hung open on one leather hinge. He had barely ducked under the lintel before the smell told him all he needed to know. Three bodies lay inside, close to the door, each torn and broken in different ways. There was no second floor or second room, just a simple hearth and a curtain where the father and mother must have slept in happier times. Flies crawled everywhere and the smell was so thick it seemed to cling to his skin. It brought back every battlefield he had known, as well as a memory of his childhood, when he had discovered a rotting badger under a barn, a reek he associated with death ever after.

'No one alive in there,' Xanthippus called back to the others.

He wondered if he should bury them. As soon as he had the thought he regretted it, but they were his people, after all. Xanthippus cursed under his breath. When he turned, it was to see Cimon staring at a lone chicken, scratching in the yard. The fate of a young family had not concerned him at all, but this had his full concentration. Whoever had murdered the farmer had missed it, one single brown fowl.

Xanthippus stood still as Cimon slowly reached out his hand. One of the two hoplites had been his choice, Xanthippus recalled, a burly hoplite he had introduced as Relas of Hippothontis, who wore a thick black beard and smelled of olive oil and sour wine. With infinite care, Relas removed a bow from the case on his back, sliding it out without sudden movement, then handing it to Cimon. Xanthippus just breathed and waited. The sun was low on the horizon, a chill already in the air. It took time to dig even a shallow grave. If they buried the bodies, perhaps the air would be clear enough for them to sleep in the house. Otherwise, he could wrap himself in a blanket under the stars. At least it didn't look like rain.

With perfect control, Cimon strung the bow and placed an arrow, bending the weapon into a curve without a tremor. Xanthippus noted the power in his arms. His father's son. In the silence, the chicken scratched and pecked at something, accompanied by a soft clucking sound. It froze, turning its head this way and that, sensing danger.

The arrow took it cleanly through the breast. Xanthippus said nothing as Cimon dashed over with a shout, tossing the bird to his companion to be plucked and cleaned. Xanthippus forced himself to smile, though he felt only exasperation.

The world was in ruins, his homes burned to ash, and he was there, playing games and politics.

'As I said before, Cimon, I have a little meat and bread in my pack. I am going to bury the family here.'

Xanthippus turned to Relas, already snatching feathers in handfuls from the bird.

'You,' Xanthippus said. 'And you, Onesimos. Both of you help me dig the graves.'

To his irritation, Relas looked first to Cimon, but received a nod. The half-plucked bird was left on the packs by the horses. Onesimos sought out the farmer's tools, sensing Xanthippus' disapproval and keeping his head down. Cimon frowned and took a moment to look into the house. That glance stole away anything but a sense of grim duty. He took up the spade he was handed.

They worked hard and well. Before the sun had set completely, three shallow graves were finished in the yard. Xanthippus had put coins into the mouths of the husband, wife and young daughter, before their faces were covered. It was all he could do, though he prayed for them and told them he was sorry they had been so cruelly used. There had been a great deal of blood. As the moon rose, he found he did not want to spend the night inside after all. He lay for a time, looking up at the stars. Cimon stood first watch, wine on his breath and his eyes terrible.

In more normal times, before the Persians had come, envoys of Macedon would have halted by one of the great gates of Athens, waiting for permission to enter the city. That year, all their defences lay in ruins. The Persian army had smashed the stones to rubble. For the Assembly, it was like standing naked in a battle line, without a cloak, without shield or spear.

The king of Macedon and his companions paused at what would have been the boundary to the great city. Alexander could see broken stones stretching into the distance on either side, with the charred remnants of a gate lying by a fallen tower. Beyond, there were houses still, clay-coloured survivors of the great fire, some with new roofs. In the distance, more divine stones rose above the city – the Acropolis, the Areopagus, the Pnyx and the other hills that formed the stage for Athens. All were revealed, a precious robe torn away.

Instead of a wall, a line of hoplites stood across what would have been the main road to the north-west. They waited in place, bronze and flesh, spears ready to repel any invader. It was said that Sparta needed no walls. The men of Athens felt the loss even so.

Aristides strolled out to the horsemen. He wore only a robe and sandals, one shoulder bare. He carried a scroll tucked into his armpit and another in his hand. The Macedonian party dismounted as he approached. He bore no weapons and yet the hoplites had deferred to him. The horsemen exchanged wary glances. The ways of Athenians were known to be peculiar.

'Gentlemen, you find us at a disadvantage,' Aristides said. 'Are you looking for work? We are in need of masons and carpenters ...' he consulted the scroll in his hand, 'and ... potters, yes. If you have any of those skills, I can find you a place. Beyond that, we need no new mouths to feed, at least until spring. I am sorry.'

His gaze lingered for just a moment on the darkest of the three, who wore a neat beard of oiled ringlets and whose fingers shone with gold rings. Aristides waited with eyebrows raised, apparently about to turn away.

The largest of the strangers let his patience vanish. He

tapped two fingers against the heavy lion clasp on his cloak, drawing Aristides' attention to it.

'I am King Alexander of Macedon, ally to the Great King of Persia, personal envoy of General Mardonius, who commands all Persian forces of land and sea. I have come to speak to your Assembly, under formal truce.'

'Can you also make pots?' Aristides asked. 'I cannot tell you how much we need those. They were all smashed, you see. We have kilns running, but without thousands more pots, we cannot store oil or grain or wine.'

Alexander of Macedon blinked slowly.

'Are you . . . *mocking* me, Athenian?' he asked.

He reached for his sword hilt. In response, Aristides smiled and raised his arm. At his back, forty hoplites clashed spears and shields together, suddenly ready to charge. The king of Macedon let his hand fall back naturally enough. He and Aristides weighed one another as he waited for a reply.

'A man who speaks as the slave of Persians requires no mockery of mine,' Aristides said. 'He does it to himself. Come, I will take you to the Assembly. It is almost noon. Your horses, though, must remain here. We need them to pull rubble and beams.'

'My horse is trained for war, not as some beast of burden!' Alexander said, his voice rising in shock.

Aristides shrugged.

'We need them, even so. Your Persian friends killed all the mules and asses. They ate them. We will not mistreat your beasts, except to put a harness on and make them pull. If their treatment troubles you, speak faster to the Assembly!'

Without waiting for their agreement, Aristides gestured over his shoulder. Six of his hoplites came up, all glowering and ready to kill the strangers. The Macedonian group clenched their fists, but there was nothing they could do. Their steeds were taken away, leaving the men somehow reduced.

'What was your name, Majesty?' Aristides asked as he led them through the broken walls and into the streets beyond.

'As I told you: Alexander, king of Macedon,' he replied.

'Friend of Persians,' Aristides added.

'Ally to the Great King,' Alexander corrected, firming his jaw. He glanced at one member of his little group, something Aristides noted. The leader of Macedon seemed painfully aware that every word he said might be reported later.

Without warning, Aristides held up a hand, halting the small group. Cart after cart trundled across ahead of them. Bodies lay on each cart-bed, wrapped and piled like logs. Aristides lowered his head and prayed, his lips moving. After an age, the last of the rickety, creaking transports had passed. Aristides shook his head, looking weary and much older.

'They still wash up every day. We have to collect our people and put them in the ground, before pestilence spreads. Unclaimed, unnamed, unknown to anyone but the gods, most of them. You should come down to the docks before you leave, to watch the widows and children checking the faces of anyone laid out there. You will never see anything more pitiful. They long to see husbands and fathers, even in death. Is that not strange? Though the bodies are so blown and marked now, I would be surprised if their own mothers could truly know them.'

Alexander of Macedon glowered as he walked behind Aristides. On all sides, he saw destruction, the results of fire and men. He understood the bitterness in the one who led him to the Pnyx hill. In that place, walking through the ruins of a once proud city, ally to the king of Persia did not seem quite the boast it had before.

He looked up the hill, to where the Assembly had gathered.

They were still coming in, striding past him, casting curious glances at the strangers walking with Aristides. Alexander firmed his jaw and gestured for Aristides to lead on. He had been given a task by Mardonius. Though he sensed pain and anger and humiliation on every side, he had given his word. *They* had chosen to stand against the hosts of Persia, not him! This was their reward, the proof of his own wisdom in making Macedonia a Persian ally. Alexander had taken gold and offered dust and water to a foreign king. The wisdom of that decision was all around him. Even so, he felt a weight in his stomach as he glanced back, looking over a city burned.

'Why do you sigh, Macedonian?' Aristides asked suddenly.

'The death of a city is a sad thing to witness,' Alexander replied.

'The *death* . . . ?' Aristides repeated in astonishment. '*We* are the city, not wood and stone. We will rebuild. If it falls again, we will rebuild again! A thousand times over. This is sacred ground, Macedonian. Perhaps you do not understand that, knowing only your northern hills and forests. This is the very eye and heart of the world. Come back in a year, or two. You'll see. We have plans for a temple to Athena on the Acropolis that will make the old one look like a stable. The death of a city!' He shook his head and chuckled.

Alexander smiled tightly, but chose not to reply. He had watched corpses trundled along a street below. He had seen burned timbers and wailing children held by their mothers, with no man to protect them. More, he had seen the Persian army that had brought down Athens' walls. There was no hope for these people, though perhaps they did not know it. There was no hope at all.

## 13

Xanthippus wondered if it had been a mistake after all to bring Cimon. The young man was visibly drunk once again, his eyes red and glassy as he rode. Xanthippus suspected the one named Relas had brought skins of wine in his pack. They muttered together in grinning conspiracy, then could be seen staggering whenever they dismounted to empty bladder or bowel. Xanthippus had seen the same kind of half-guilty bravado in his sons when they had been drinking and didn't want him to know. He worried he had brought the wrong man to impress abstemious Spartans. He raised his voice and tried again.

'Cimon! Don't just nod at me. I need to know you have understood.' With an effort, Xanthippus gentled his tone. 'I had experience of Spartans when I lived in Corinth. I know them well enough, better than most. So, I will take the lead. Look to me and make no observations of your own. Do you understand?'

'Of course I understand,' Cimon snapped.

If they had not been approaching a Spartan fortress wall, Xanthippus would have reined in and taken him to task for his anger. It was as dangerous as a drawn sword in that place.

With Spartans watching them, Xanthippus could only ignore the lack of courtesy, his lips a pale line. Xanthippus had spoken as much for the ears of the other two, Relas and Onesimos. They gaped like farmers in the Agora until he cleared his throat. None of them had ever seen the finished Spartan wall, built across the isthmus. It stretched from coast to coast, an hour's march one end to the other – three times the height of a man and strong, Xanthippus could see that. Beyond it, the entire Peloponnese peninsula was hidden from view except as distant mountains – cities of Corinth, Sparta and Argos; Arcadia, ancient home of the god Pan; Elis, where the games at Olympia were held to honour Zeus! All that was cut off from the heartlands that year. It seemed a bitter irony to Xanthippus. He had come from a city without walls, that wanted them, to a wall raised by men who scorned the very idea.

Spartan guards stood on the wall's crest. They had not donned their helmets and carried no shield or spear. Each of them wore the famous red cloak that would wrap him against the night's cold. Some went naked underneath, or wore only a kilt and sandals. Xanthippus endured the insolence of their stares as he dismounted, still a good thirty paces from the wall itself.

The road was well worn there, but there was no sign of any other travellers trying to get through. The closest gate was clearly shut, a solid-looking thing. Xanthippus was wondering how best to approach when they lowered a man down, his foot in a loop of rope. Xanthippus eyed his companions.

'Say nothing, any of you,' he muttered once again. 'They'll be wary with a Persian army in range. Our business lies beyond this wall.'

The Spartan who approached had come prepared for war. Like the others, he wore no helmet, but a belt and sword hung from his hip. Xanthippus could see a second handle jutting from the small of his back, ready to be grabbed. The short, heavy kopis blades were an all-purpose killing tool, much loved by those who knew them. Xanthippus had once seen a Spartan cut down a young pine with one, just hacking at it until the tree fell. It was a fearsome weapon against an enemy. Most men would rather see an honest sword blade drawn than the wicked kopis.

Xanthippus felt himself bristle as the man came into range and halted before him. The Spartans knew their reputation better than anyone. Some of them considered the respect others accorded them as no more than their due. Others delighted in it. To his dismay, Xanthippus thought the officer was one of the latter. The man stood with his hands clasped behind his back, hips rocking slightly forward and back, all while he smiled at them. It was not a pleasant expression. He looked for all the world like a tutor confronted with unruly boys, already enjoying the prospect of the punishment he would mete out. Xanthippus saw the man's gaze linger on the burly figure of Relas. The smile grew wider at whatever he saw in the hoplite. Xanthippus could not look round, but had to endure as the Spartan tilted his head.

'So, lads, what do we have here?' he said. The accent was strange to an Athenian ear, as clipped as their manners. 'What little fish have come into my net today, asking nicely to be allowed through?'

He appeared to be addressing Relas or Onesimos at the rear, but it was Xanthippus who answered.

'I am Xanthippus of Cholargos deme, Acamantis tribe. Archon of Athens. Strategos at Marathon and Salamis. Navarch Eurybiades will vouch for me. The Spartan Cleombrotus will vouch for me. On the orders of the Athenian Assembly, I have been sent with messages to the ephors and kings of Sparta.'

The man's gaze flickered to him, seemingly irritated at being made to look away from Relas. Xanthippus risked a glance back and saw Relas glaring and breathing through his nose like a prize bull. Xanthippus went on quickly, before the fool got them all killed.

*Conn Iggulden*

'My colleague here is Cimon, son to Miltiades, who commanded at Marathon. Grandson to the three-time Olympic champion of chariot-racing, his namesake. Strategos of Salamis.'

Xanthippus caught the Spartan's attention with that. The man looked Cimon over in turn, his mouth twisting as he chewed idly at one lip. The young strategos stared back with red-rimmed eyes. At least Cimon looked like the grandson of an Olympian, Xanthippus thought. The games were held on the Peloponnese every fourth summer, in a truce between all the warring cities and states of Greece. Sparta always sent a team and had a fine history at the games. As Xanthippus had hoped, the man's interest was kindled by the news.

'Cimon . . . the charioteer? The one known as Cimon Coalemos, the fool?' he asked. Despite the name, the sardonic tone had gone from his voice.

'He was not a fool,' Cimon said, looking to Xanthippus. He had clearly been asked a question and he would answer it. 'My father said he was called that because he showed no fear, even when fear was . . . correct.'

'That is what I heard,' the Spartan replied. 'It is an honour to meet his grandson.'

To Xanthippus' surprise, he put out a scarred hand and Cimon took it. For a moment of breathless silence, they both attempted to crush the other's bones to dust, then let go. Xanthippus could see white marks on them both.

'And these two?' the Spartan said. He showed no sign that he had tested his strength against that of Cimon, nor that it had not gone well. 'I need the names of all of you.'

'These men are here as colleagues and servants,' Xanthippus said. He did not look at Relas or Onesimos, who had the good sense to keep his gaze on the ground.

'Are they mutes?' the Spartan asked, stepping close enough

for them to smell sweat and oil, like heat off his skin. He showed his teeth as Relas shook his head.

'I am Relas of the Hippothontis. I was keleustes at the battle of Salamis. Were you there?'

The Spartan slapped him hard across the face with the back of his hand, a gesture of contempt that put a smear of blood on his lip and knocked his head to one side. Relas staggered a step and looked back in astonishment. Xanthippus spoke quickly, his voice a growl.

'We are allies, protected by custom and the oaths of your own king . . .'

He could hardly believe the sheer physical arrogance of the Spartan. The man stood on the balls of his feet, hands ready to lash out again, facing four men.

'Kurios?' Relas said to Xanthippus. 'I am willing, if you will allow me to answer. My mother hit me like that once, when I was just talking.'

As he spoke, the burly man rolled his shoulders and cracked his head back and forth. To Xanthippus' surprise, he saw Cimon dip his head, just enough to be a clear signal of permission. Xanthippus looked again at Relas, seeing his physique and the battered hands. Still, he wondered if the Athenian truly understood the risk.

'No. I would rather pass through the gate and be about the work of the Assembly,' Xanthippus said slowly.

When Relas answered, his voice grated deep enough to recall storms, rumbling in the distance.

'I owe him a reply, kurios.'

The Spartan spoke then, never taking his eyes off Relas.

'I'm always here, son. I can wait for you to come back if you like.' He smiled at Xanthippus. 'You can go through whenever you are ready. We've had word to let you pass. That was before the disrespect of your slave, of course.'

'I am a free man,' Relas said. 'But come, what are words?'

Xanthippus sighed, irritated with both of them.

'I have forbidden it. That is enough,' Xanthippus said.

Relas stood like a statue, breathing long and slow, clearly ready to continue. For a moment, the decision seemed to hang in the balance.

'Open the gate, Spartan,' Xanthippus said. 'Our business is urgent.'

The man squinted at them, shaking his head. His mouth twisted as if they'd offended him.

'It is as I'd heard, then,' the Spartan replied. '*Athenians.*' He said the last like a curse.

Xanthippus let anger drain from him. The man's purpose was suddenly too clear. Victory lay in not giving him what he wanted. Relas seemed to understand it too.

'You move well, for a slave,' the Spartan said. Relas nodded to him.

Xanthippus gestured towards the gate and the guard gave up with a shrug. As they stood before the wall, Xanthippus could hear bars or chains being removed. He saw two men heaving at iron rods above, lifting them clear. At last, the gate swung open and they ducked to pass through it. The arch was low, so each of the four Athenians had to lead the horses with a hand pressing on their heads. The short passage was cramped and cold, with another gate opening onto light beyond. On the other side, they all turned back to see. The wall stretched west and east in a line of stone and solid towers. The Spartans who stood on it seemed worryingly close, easily capable of leaping down. They scowled at men of Athens standing on their land.

The Spartan guard seemed to have lost his bristling anger. Having been denied his contest, he showed only a cold disdain as he pointed down the road.

'Sparta lies three days south, two if your business is urgent. You'll find the ephors on the acropolis. Be respectful, gentlemen. Not everyone you meet will be as patient or as welcoming as I.'

Xanthippus thanked him, but the man showed no more interest. The Spartan made sure the gate and tunnel was secure and trotted up steps to the crest of the wall. He was greeted there by two others. One nudged him in the ribs and said something low, causing him to smile and shake his head. The rest of the guards turned away, watching for threats once more.

Xanthippus looked at Cimon, then Relas, who seemed to have retreated into a sullen anger. All four of them tried to ignore the attention of red-cloaked men in the camp before them. Perhaps two or three hundred Spartans slept on their cloaks in that place, ready to defend the wall. Those men were curious enough to stop their labours and exercise, coming instead to stand close to the road. In the distance, a plume of dust rose behind a runner, naked but for a pair of sandals, carrying news. Xanthippus thought of poor Pheidippides, who had run from Athens to Sparta and back, bringing word of a previous invasion. Four days on the road, with no more than a few hours' sleep. It had been that run, surely, rather than the one from Marathon to Athens, that had cost him his life.

'You showed great restraint, Relas,' Xanthippus said suddenly. He had raised two sons. He knew the importance of a few words in the right place. He waited a few beats before going on. 'Your discipline did you credit. I will not forget.'

Relas nodded without replying, a faint flush spreading.

They mounted up and began to trot, with the setting sun on their shoulder. Xanthippus said nothing when Cimon fished out a wineskin from his pack and passed it around. He refused it himself, however. There were times when Xan-thippus understood young men about as well as he did the Spartans – or the Persians. They were all strange breeds.

Alexander of Macedon was an impressive figure as he stood before the Assembly of Athens. His cloak and armoured tunic did little to hide the breadth of his shoulders or his height. His hair was a paler blond than that of Themistocles, so that it looked like polished bronze or gold in the sunlight.

Some twenty thousand had come to the Pnyx that day, earning the name that meant 'packed in'. Beyond those, the entire city was aware of the presence of Macedonians in their city, all waiting to hear what it might mean. Even building work had ceased, so that silence and a breeze spread across the hill.

'Speak then, Alexander, king of Macedon,' Themistocles said. He sat with Aristides, one knee raised above the seat, his hands casually curled around his shin.

The man looked up to the sky for a moment, choosing his words.

'You'll know by now that I come as an envoy, protected by truce, in peace. Athens and Macedon are not at war.'

Themistocles might have replied, but Aristides reached out and tapped him on the foot that rested on the stone. Themis-tocles subsided reluctantly. The Macedonian observed the exchange and inclined his head in gratitude.

'I have been granted the authority of another, the right to speak with his voice – as a friend. I am a trusted man in the camp of General Mardonius of Persia. More, my honour is known in the court of Xerxes, Great King and holy ruler of the empire of Persia.'

There was a grumble and some uncomfortable shifting in

the seats around him. Too many had lost friends at Salamis to listen patiently to an ally of their enemies praising his name in the very heart of Athens. Themistocles glanced aside to Aristides and rolled his eyes.

The king of Macedon waited for the whispering to cease. He unrolled a scroll of papyrus, the surface crackling as he opened it. His hands were steady, Themistocles noted.

'I am to say this: "Men of Athens, you know one thing of Xerxes, king of kings. You know his word is good. His oath, once given, is cut in stone. I, General Mardonius, say this, his most trusted officer and friend. I speak for him here, as His Majesty King Alexander speaks for me. You Hellenes came to Ionia and sacked cities. You burned Sardis. You know well the reply we made . . ." '

The Macedon king had to halt when too many voices called out over him. He grimaced and waited, but they did not die down until Aristides rose from his seat and looked out across them.

'Let us hear him!' Aristides commanded.

The noise died away. Themistocles had not moved. He watched the foreign king like a hawk, learning all he could from every gesture, every expression and hesitation. Alexander nodded to Aristides, a flush spreading across his face and neck. He began to read once more.

' "King Xerxes will honour any agreement I make in his name. Heed, then, my offer, as if you hear his own voice. As if Xerxes himself stands before you." '

Someone called out a ribald suggestion at that, a suggestion of what they would do if that were true. A ripple of laughter went through the crowd. The Persian who stood with Alexander frowned and glared, biting his lip in anger at the lack of respect. Aristides ignored it. They were Athenians, not statues! He could not damp down all their humour.

*Conn Iggulden*

' "With the authority granted unto me, I say this," ' Alexander went on grimly. ' "There are no terms, or negotiations. I make a single offer. If it is refused, I will begin a war that will result in the destruction of all cities allied with Athens and Sparta. I will raze Greece to ash and bones. Listen well and consider your children. There will be no second chance." '

The king of Macedon paused again, as if he acted in a drama. There was no idle talk at that moment and Aristides was annoyed at the artifice of it. The Macedonian was enjoying his position a little too much. Macedon was a poor place in the north, an envious neighbour. Perhaps that was it. Athens burned was still greater than any of his own cities, if indeed 'city' was not too grand a name for them.

' "If you offer yourselves as vassals, if you offer earth and water as is our custom, accepting Xerxes as your ruler and master of Greece, I will spare you the war that is coming. You will pay taxes to Persia. You will provide hoplites for her imperial armies. You will accept officials from the empire to administer your cities. But in return, your women and children will be spared, your temples will not burn, your gods will remain untouched. Your lives will continue as they were. What does it matter whose face is on your coins? What does it matter who rules you? This is my offer – one I do not need to make. I command a host of hosts, an army unbeaten. Yet I would show mercy – as it has been shown to loyal Hellene states already. There is your proof of our goodwill. I ask only obedience, on behalf of my king. Or war. My answer depends on yours." '

Alexander sighed out a long breath and rolled up the sheet once more. In a louder voice, he spoke.

'I will make this available to you, to read again. I have been told to wait for your answer.'

'And you will wait, because you are a vassal of Persia,' Themistocles said.

The Macedonian king stared coldly at him, but Themistocles had only scorn in his gaze.

It was the man's Persian companion who murmured something at Alexander's shoulder, making him nod.

'Yes, you should listen to your friend there,' Themistocles said. Aristides tapped him once more on the foot. He ignored it. 'Leave your scroll. We'll discuss it when you have gone. Go on, Macedonian. This is a rock for free men only. You are not one of us.'

In answer, the Macedonian king threw the scroll at Themistocles' feet and turned on his heel, striding back down the hill. Aristides picked it up and grunted in irritation.

'What did you gain by that?' Aristides asked.

Themistocles looked surprised.

'Satisfaction. I cannot bear to breathe the same air as that man. Macedon should have stood with us, not kissed the sandals of a foreign king.'

'Do you not see what they did to Athens?' Aristides demanded. 'Perhaps he wished to avoid such a fate for his people. Perhaps Alexander had no ships to take his people to safety.'

Aristides was caught in indecision. He felt he needed to go after the Macedonian party making their way down, yet half the crowd were hanging on his words, looking for leadership.

'He is a slave,' Themistocles said, staring after the king of Macedon. 'He walks like a free man, but that does not change what he is.'

Aristides chose not to continue. He realised he would oppose Themistocles in the debate that would follow, as he had so many times before. It was not as simple as Themistocles appeared to think. The truth had to be teased out in argument and debate. If there was even time, before Themistocles had them all howling for Persian blood! With an exasperated sound, Aristides pressed the scroll into Themistocles' hands and went after the Macedon king. Behind him, he heard Themistocles address the Assembly.

'Why, yes. I *will* read it again, of course! Gather round, lads. Let me tell you what your enemies want.'

# 14

Xanthippus awoke in darkness, his hand snatching at a sword that hung on a hook by his bed. He stifled a groan. If it could be called a bed. He'd thought he had some knowledge of the Spartans from the time he'd spent in Corinth. He had met many of them there, in their distinctive red cloaks. He had never seen them doing business, or discussing the law, philosophy, even military tactics. They had acted as a breed apart, arriving very often at the run, with cloaks rolled and tied on their shoulders. Corinth was just a destination, though some of them frequented gymnasia there.

The city of Sparta itself was not one Xanthippus knew well. He had visited before, in his youth. Perhaps the surprise was that so little had changed. Athens had been rebuilt more than once in his lifetime, before the Persians ever marched into view. Yet Sparta seemed to have been set in amber since he had stood there aged eighteen, with his father and brother.

Xanthippus sat up and swore under his breath. At eighteen, he could have slept in a tree and awoken with nothing more than a stiff cock. At almost fifty years of age, he needed more than a block of wood with a section cut away for the bowl of his skull. He was not sure he had slept at all, spending the night staring at a ceiling, arms folded across his chest, for all the world as if he had died in his sleep.

He could hear Cimon grumbling something, not yet fully awake. The young man's snoring had not helped. Xanthippus remembered startling off his block to it once or twice. Ah, he *had* slept, then! He sat up and opened wooden shutters, slick with varnish under his hands. The stars were still visible outside, though he saw people already up and about. He felt himself flush, his heart beating faster. He would not be shamed by Spartans. It felt at times as if they paraded their virtues in front of others. Part of him suspected he was mistaken, that they simply rose early, ate and drank little – and worked to be masters of war. It was just possible there was no room in them for gentle debate, for politics, for art.

In the pre-dawn gloom, Xanthippus found a large pot and arranged it on a little shelf on the wall, emptying his bladder with some relief. He heard Cimon murmur a question, brought alert by the noise. Xanthippus was just glad Themistocles had not come with him. Aristides might have fitted in well with their Spartan hosts. Themistocles would surely have had them reaching for weapons. Xanthippus sighed as he finished. The gods loved Themistocles, but he seemed to think he had won the battle of Salamis all on his own. If he brought it up one more time to the Assembly, Xanthippus thought they would be breaking pots and arranging his own ostracism. There would be irony!

'Xanthippus?' Cimon asked.

His own pallet was almost as thick as a summer blanket and slightly less scratchy than sleeping on straw. Xanthippus emptied the pot out of the window. He had seen a gutter there the night before, when a single lamp had lit the travelling house.

'I am awake,' he said. 'Rise now, before we have Spartans asking why we slept half the day away.'

He heard Cimon yawning and did the same. Xanthippus dressed quickly and slipped out of the door to knock on the next. There were no locks or bars in the house and he put his head inside, seeing Onesimos and Relas sprawled on the floor. They were still snoring and he had to stamp his foot on the floor to startle them awake.

'Up, both of you. Be alert.'

He went downstairs then, steps creaking on the wood. He saw the fire was indeed lit, with water heating there. A helot barber was already at work, oiling the skin of a guest and wielding a razor with the skill of long practice. Xanthippus considered filling a bowl of hot water and taking it back to his room, but he preferred to be shaved and the man was almost done. There was still no sign of light outside, though the sun rose later every day. He could hear the noise of a city waking, the tramp of feet, voices calling in the distance. Deliveries were being made, food cooked, shops opening. Sparta was a small place compared to Athens, but over a hundred thousand souls lived within its bounds, surrounded by mountains and crossed on one edge by the Eurotas river. Xanthippus wondered how many helots called Sparta home – and how many would travel with the Spartan soldiers, if they ever took the field. Aristides had reported his conversations with Pausanias, the Spartan regent. The news had not been good there. Xanthippus still hoped to persuade the man that honouring his father's oath was the only way Sparta could survive.

As he took a seat and felt strong fingers slather oil over his chin and cheeks, he frowned to himself. One way or the other, they had to have Sparta's army. No one could stand against Persia without them. All he had to do was convince the Spartans it was in their interest to stand against the largest army the world had ever known.

The barber was short, with powerful forearms and a fine, steady hand with a blade. Xanthippus tossed him a silver coin when he was finished. The man blinked and handed it straight back, his gaze on the floor. Xanthippus flushed. In

*Conn Iggulden*

his distraction, he had forgotten helots were not allowed to own anything. He might have paid a slave barber in Athens, perhaps as a contribution to the fellow's savings. He felt a fool. No helot ever dreamed of buying himself free, not in Sparta. They were captives until they died.

Cimon came down in a clatter, his eyes lighting up when he saw the barber. Relas and Onesimos were close behind him, looking around in interest. As Cimon sat and the helot applied oil, there was a growing noise from the street outside and raised voices. Xanthippus was first to the door, looking out.

The acropolis of Sparta lay alongside the city rather than at its heart, as it did in Athens. A stream of people seemed to be heading uphill in that direction. Among them, a dozen horsemen cantered past, red cloaks flying. They expected helots to lurch out of their way or be trampled. Most of them did, though one old woman was buffeted and knocked against a wall. She did not raise her fist or shout after them, as she might have in Athens. Instead, she stood with head bowed, panting in fear and pain.

Cimon had come out with Xanthippus. He looked after the riders as they passed, his face shining with oil.

'What news?' he said.

Xanthippus shook his head.

'Come on,' he said, setting off down the road.

'Is there no food in this place?' Cimon asked at his back. 'I didn't eat last night and I thought there would be something this morning.'

'Not until the first period of work is at an end. That will not be until late morning.'

He gave a quick grin at Cimon's dismay. Relas and Onesimos came out then, falling in alongside as he and Cimon set out, joining the crowds heading to the acropolis.

The four Athenians stayed in a tight group as they climbed, passing hundreds of silent men and almost as many women. Xanthippus kept his gaze from lingering on anyone, though Onesimos whispered and gaped in astonishment, nudging Relas. Free women did walk the streets in Athens, though much more rarely and usually with house guards. These were also rather different from Athenian mothers, being both young and lithe, with earnest expressions. Some wore little more than a single strip of white cloth wrapped and pinned at the shoulder. It hid neither shape nor the gleam of health. Their hair too shone like otter pelts, sparking a memory in Xanthippus. He saw Relas smiling at one woman, seeing only her beauty and not her rising anger.

'If the hair is short, they are married, Relas,' Xanthippus muttered. 'You will ruin everything I am trying to do here, just by speaking to one. Understand? Answer if they talk to you, but otherwise, I do not wish to be accused of corrupting their women.'

'The long-haired ones are unpledged?' Relas replied.

Xanthippus eyed him. The sun had not yet showed itself over the mountains of the east, over Mount Parnon. Yet there was light, a grey and calming gleam before the gold. Relas was grinning shyly at a young Spartan woman jogging along beside them. She did not seem too upset by his attention, Xanthippus noticed.

'Unpledged daughters of Spartan warriors, yes,' Xanthippus reminded. 'Nor am I willing to explain to their fathers why one of my men wandered into the wrong garden!'

Relas dipped his head, flushing at the rebuke. He looked steadily forward as they reached the peak of the acropolis.

Mountains sat around them as if they stood at the centre of a vast bowl. Soldiers in red cloaks were on guard there, while temples opened their doors to reveal lighted lamps within. That golden glow battled the dawn, illuminating the horsemen Xanthippus had seen before. They had dismounted and stood on the highest point, a flat stone, much worn by time. The horses had been led away and they waited as a group.

Xanthippus stood still, his companions settling around him. He found himself in a sea of heads as the crowd thickened and came to rest. He thought he recognised the men on the stone from descriptions by Aristides. The regent Pausanias had to be the one in the centre, deferred to whenever he murmured something and clearly in command. The fellow at his side wore a simple robe and kept his hair unbraided, as wide in the shoulder as the regent. They laughed at something together and Xanthippus nodded. It had to be the soothsayer, Tisamenus. Xanthippus recalled the pentathlon at the Olympics. He had been in the crowd that day, protected by truce. He shook his head. The young Spartans would make their own path in the world. They made him feel old, but the truth was, he had won his battles! He had fought at Marathon on land, Salamis at sea. No man could remain in the bloom of youth for ever. He glanced at Cimon and sighed. Still, it hurt to creak in the mornings. Youth was the great glory of men. He had not wasted his, but it still hurt to know it had gone.

When the acropolis was as packed as the Pnyx, Pausanias raised his hands. Xanthippus half-expected him to call for a speaker, as in the Assembly. He had forgotten the man was regent for the son of Leonidas. In that moment, Pausanias was the battle king of Sparta, with authority to send them to war, or keep them from it. The ephors may have ruled in peacetime, but with a Persian army roaming the land, Pausanias had no limit on his powers at all. It made him a danger and Xanthippus craned to hear every word.

'. . . one of our listeners reached me last night, from Athens. The news is . . . disturbing.'

Xanthippus exchanged a sharp glance with Cimon. The light was growing stronger with every moment. The thought of actually standing on the Spartan acropolis while they discussed news of Athens – and being recognised – was an unpleasant prospect. Xanthippus wondered if he should call out his presence before someone thought they'd caught themselves a spy or a traitor. He felt sweat, or perhaps a trickle of shaving oil, run down his neck as Pausanias went on.

'The Persians have enlisted the support of a small king, out of the north. Alexander of Macedon has gone into Athens to broker a peace with the harlots of their Assembly. He will . . .'

Xanthippus could not stand there and hear Athens defamed. Though his heart raced, he stood tall and called across that place.

'Regent Pausanias! I came as envoy of Athens to answer your concerns. Will you read ill will into that as well?'

The crowd turned to see who dared to speak. For a dozen desperate heartbeats that lasted a mere instant, Xanthippus felt more alone than he had ever done before. Pausanias bent his head and murmured briefly with the soothsayer.

'Come forward, Athenian,' Pausanias ordered after an airless pause.

Xanthippus felt pressure from behind that made it clear he would go, regardless of his will. He heard Cimon growl a response to something, but the small group of Athenians were made to move through the rest, brought to the foot of the speaker's stone, so that they looked up at Pausanias.

'We were to meet at noon,' Xanthippus found himself saying. 'Though I saw the crowds coming here . . .'

*Conn Iggulden*

'It doesn't matter now,' Pausanias said, waving his words away. The man seemed to look out on the world with one raised eyebrow, Xanthippus saw. Aristides had described the expression very well. 'It seems I must travel to Athens this very day, to see what damage has been done. Who would have thought the Persians had the subtlety to turn Athens against us? With such an army, I'd have expected them simply to rest through winter and attack in spring. Yet they spend the cold months plotting and filling the mouths of allies with gold.'

'I . . .' Xanthippus blinked. 'You are travelling to Athens?'

He thought Pausanias might not reply. The man's expression was hard, as if carved of flint.

'I have dealt honourably with your people, Athenian. I met your man Aristides, in Eleusis. He pleaded with me to remember our oaths. Is that not why you are here? Perhaps it is time for Sparta to remind Athens of the same! There will be no peace signed between Persia and Athens!'

As Xanthippus struggled to understand the new information, Pausanias raised his voice to address the crowd once more.

'I will take word to them. While I am gone, my father, Cleombrotus, is in command of all war forces of Sparta, all Spartiates, perioikoi and helots. He stands regent for Pleistarchus, son to Leonidas. Look to King Leotychides, the ephors and the gods. Be vigilant. Obey.'

Men and women knelt, heads bowed across the acropolis, revealing the four Athenians, standing awkwardly. Cimon exchanged a stubborn glance with Xanthippus, pleased to see no give in the other man. With Relas and Onesimos, they endured silent Spartan hostility to stand with their heads unbowed. Cimon shrugged. Pausanias was not his king.

'If you are leaving today, Majesty,' Xanthippus said, 'I shall return with you. My concern was to have you understand why Athens feels we have to fight. Seeing my city will speak more clearly than I ever could.'

Pausanias turned to him with the same raised eyebrow, as if his face had frozen on one side. After a pause long enough for everyone there to know he had not been forced into the decision, he nodded.

'Very well. Fetch your horses. Do your best to keep up. We will not wait for unfit men.'

Pausanias had not been exaggerating, Xanthippus had realised. As kings went, he did not stand on ceremony, or send envoys in his stead. The Spartan regent rode like a man in a race for his life, speaking hardly a word whenever Xanthippus tried to engage him. Pausanias had set out with the sun barely clear of the mountains and then ridden north with a dozen of his personal guard, back up the road to the isthmus. In the small city of Argos, they had been allowed to exchange mounts around noon. Tisamenus had shared twists of dried meat he kept under his saddle, warm from the horse's flesh. The four Athenians ate theirs with relish, though by then starvation made even ancient meat taste glorious.

Back on the road north, Xanthippus settled a piece into his cheek to suck and make last. He noted Pausanias did the same, the Spartan regent looking coldly on as Cimon drew on a wineskin, holding it above his head to get the last drops. They rode hard and for once Xanthippus did not begrudge the young man his comfort.

The night was spent on the side of the road, their horses hobbled. Tisamenus produced another handful of the brown sticks to chew. No fire was lit and it seemed that was all the food or comfort that would be provided before sleep. The animals dozed lightly enough to warn them of wolves or lions. Xanthippus actually found the dusty earth slightly more comfortable than the pitifully thin mattress of the night before. He noted how Pausanias and the Spartans slept wrapped in their cloaks. He knew they were buried in them, in simple plots that bore only a name carved in stone. Their helots were buried without even that, in graves unmarked. The riding party had passed some on the road outside Sparta, simple mounds of earth stretching in rows. Xanthippus had seen a posy of amaranth flowers left on one, dried by the wind.

The riding party reached the wall on the isthmus as the sun was rising again. The Athenians were stiff and ruffled by then, their hair wild. In comparison, the Spartans looked as they always did. They moved well enough as they dismounted and handed over the horses to be checked.

The camp on the Spartan side had turned out when their scouts warned of an armed party approaching. There was no sleepy surprise there, though the sun rose behind them. Pausanias inspected the men and headed into the largest tent.

'Where is he going?' Xanthippus asked Tisamenus.

The soothsayer seemed the most approachable of the Spartan group, perhaps because he was of them but not of their blood. He had not suffered the three stages of the agoge, the brutal education every Spartan boy endured from the age of seven to manhood at twenty-nine. Though Tisamenus was fit and strong, he had not forced his body through agony to perfection every day of his adult life. Many failed and left the city of Sparta. Those who had promised much were allowed to take a wife and father children as peri-oikoi, 'those-who-lived-around'. They were not Spartiates; they could never be part of the elite. Tisamenus occupied some middle ground, almost a unique position. Spartans treated him with respect. Certainly, Pausanias did. Yet he was not one of them, and he could smile where they only glowered.

After a time spent deciding if he should speak, Tisamenus shrugged.

'He visits his father, Cleombrotus, brother to Leonidas,' he said quietly.

One of the other Spartans turned round to glare, but Tisamenus ignored him. He knew his status.

'The one who will rule while Pausanias is with us,' Xanthippus said.

Tisamenus raised his eyebrows at the frowning Spartan until the man looked away.

'Perhaps. He is very ill. It may be that the son of Leonidas is the battle king before we return. Though he is young, there are many who would welcome such a thing.'

'We should not be discussing our affairs in front of strangers,' the Spartan hissed at Tisamenus.

The soothsayer sighed and nodded. He did not speak again and Xanthippus asked no more questions.

Pausanias returned and the party passed through the wall and its gates in short order. On the other side, the Spartans all remounted and readied themselves to ride on. Xanthippus heard Relas clear his throat.

'A moment, kurios, if you will,' he called to Xanthippus.

'What is it?' Xanthippus replied.

Relas did not answer him. He tossed the reins to Cimon and dismounted, walking back to look up at the wall. It was not long before the one they knew from before was lowered down, his foot in a loop of rope.

'What is this delay, Athenian?' Pausanias called.

Xanthippus was a little weary of his high-handed ways by then.

*Conn Iggulden*

'A debt owed, I believe,' he said. He sent a brief prayer that Relas knew what he was doing.

The Spartan wall officer removed his cloak and rolled it, putting it down before he stood to face Relas. The two came together then in a sudden burst of speed. Xanthippus and Cimon winced at the thumping sound of bone on flesh. Both men used their knees and elbows, while Relas scored a great strike with the brow of his head. It left him with a smear of blood across his face, but it knocked the Spartan down.

Relas stood, panting. The exchange had been very brief, an eruption over as quickly as it had begun. He kept his fists raised, however, wary of a rush.

The Spartan scrambled up and rested on one knee. He glanced over at Pausanias, very aware of his audience. In a moment of respite, he wiped blood from his nose and lips, frowning at it. His eye was already swelling shut. Still, anger suffused him. As he rose to his feet, he seemed to have grown larger to Xanthippus' eye.

Relas met him with a flurry of blows. The Athenian took hits on his arms and ducked another, then hooked a cross that caught the Spartan over one ear. The man's legs wobbled at the blow, so that he staggered. Relas followed up, coming forward, finding the head with his fists over and over again, until the Spartan crashed onto his back and lay in the dust, completely senseless, bloody mouth open.

Relas waited until he was sure the man would not rise again and then turned his back on him and remounted. There was blood on his face and hands, Xanthippus saw. He noticed too that Cimon was trying and failing to hide his delight.

Pausanias merely looked disgusted as he dug in his heels and trotted away. It fell to Xanthippus to ease his mount over towards the others of his small group. He saw Cimon clap Relas on the shoulder.

'That was . . . well done, Relas,' Xanthippus murmured. 'You surprised me.'

'He surprised that arrogant whoreson as well,' Cimon said, too loudly.

One of the Spartans still in earshot half-turned at that and Xanthippus grimaced, wondering if Cimon had been drinking already. Surely he had finished the last of it by then?

'If you had not been in exile for the last few years,' Cimon went on, 'you would know Relas is something of a name.'

'I have missed much,' Xanthippus admitted. 'Should I know you?' he addressed the last to Relas himself, who seemed embarrassed.

Cimon answered for him.

'You might if you followed the bouts. He is, after all, the boxing champion of Athens. I never thought I would see him knock a Spartan down! If this damned war is ever over, Relas, you should come back here to challenge at the Olympics. You might have shortened the odds today, but I'd still make a fortune.'

Xanthippus closed his eyes for a time as he rode out after Pausanias, depending on his horse to keep him on the path. He was tired and sore and starving, accompanying a regent already furious with Athenians. Cimon seemed not to care how the Spartans felt about seeing one of their own getting knocked down. Perhaps he was right! They were said to appreciate courage and skill, above all else. They made no pots in Sparta, nor carved wood and stone. Their helots did all that sort of work, for the honour of serving. Xanthippus opened his eyes once more, though he had to squint against the sun's light. Relas and Onesimos rode on either side of him, with Cimon a little way ahead. They did not look exhausted, but sat their mounts well, straight-backed. No, that was not it, Xanthippus realised. They had been cowed before, intimidated by the Spartans. Now they rode as men, as Athenians.

Spartans only made war, or trained to make war. They were mad dogs in comparison to normal men, unstoppable and savage. Xanthippus found watching one of them knocked out by an Athenian had raised his spirits considerably.

## 15

It was impossible for armed horsemen to approach Athens without being spotted. With the city alert to the danger of Persian forces, even the small group from Sparta were tracked and reported as soon as they left the isthmus. Galloping scouts went flat out over the hills before them to give the city as much warning as possible. Xanthippus was proud of the reaction.

As Pausanias led them east, the track swung close to the coast at Eleusis. Fleet galleys patrolled ceaselessly at sea there, watching for enemies and protecting the food supplies that had suddenly become so vital. With more than a little satisfaction, Xanthippus knew signals he had created would be calling ships in from all points. That was part of a plan to stage an immediate evacuation, but it also brought crews home to be part of the Assembly. There were no 'rulers and ruled' in Athens, at least not any longer. The city ordered itself and if it was true men like Themistocles and Aristides could command respect on the Pnyx, so could a hundred others, if they spoke well. The epistates himself held the post only from sunset to sunset, each appointment chosen by lot from those over the age of thirty who put their names forward. It was said anyone could rule in Athens if they wanted, at least for a day.

Towards those broken walls, the Spartan party came, riders covered in dust and sweat. Under moonlight, Aristides himself went out to meet them, close by what had been the Thriasian gate. A hundred and twenty hoplites blocked the road behind him. If anyone saw the ludicrousness of manning a place of entry while walls lay as rubble, the Spartans chose not to comment on it.

Aristides stood in the light of torches, the city at his back studded with the sparks of cooking fires. An odour of meat and mint wafted through the air and Xanthippus wondered if he would ever know hunger like it again. He and Cimon had moved subtly apart from the Spartans as the sun set, choosing to preserve some distance from them as they approached Athens. They had ridden hard all day and covered ground almost as well as the young scouts racing ahead. Pausanias was either oblivious to the exhaustion of his companions, or amused by their suffering. Xanthippus was honestly unsure which it was. The Athenians had realised they would not stop or eat as the day wore on. They'd settled in then to a grim determination not to let the others down. Cimon had seemed to understand without it being said aloud – he regarded everything as a competition, so that was no surprise. Relas and Onesimos had suffered most. Both were used to hours of duty on board ship rather than riding. When Pausanias had allowed a brief respite to empty bladders and pass around skins of watered wine, Onesimos had dismounted and immediately fallen, his legs stiff as boards. No one had laughed. It had been Relas who helped him to his feet and then to mount again, once they had made steam rise from the bushes alongside the trail.

If Aristides was surprised to see the actual regent of Sparta, he showed no sign of it. His sharp gaze picked out Xanthippus and Cimon, his chin dipping a touch as he acknowledged them.

'I give thanks and rejoice to have your presence grace us, Regent Pausanias,' Aristides said.

Xanthippus blinked slowly as he observed a man he

considered incapable of emotional display nonetheless take the hand or kiss each one of their group. Pausanias he kissed on the cheek; Tisamenus, the lips, greeting him also by name. When it came to Xanthippus and Cimon, the Athenian statesman gripped each of them around the back of the neck and kissed them on the side of their heads, almost on the ear. Xanthippus half-expected a whispered message, but there was none.

It was odd how the greeting stole away some of the hostility from the group waiting to enter Athens. Whether Aristides had intended it or not, choosing to welcome them as allies and family meant that the perfect stillness of warriors had no place there and was put aside. Some of the Spartans shuffled as they waited. One yawned and rested his head against his horse's neck as he stood beside the animal. They too had ridden far and fast; they were not made of stone.

'I rejoice to see you so well, Archon Aristides,' Pausanias said.

He had not lost all his stiffness. The eyebrow was still permanently raised and his manner restored formality to his men. Only the soothsayer Tisamenus grinned around him like an urchin.

'And I you, regent. I have looked for you on the hills before this. I told them Spartan honour was not a weak thing.'

Xanthippus observed the tightening mouth of Pausanias as he understood. It seemed Aristides thought he had come to discuss bringing out the army in spring. Or that was the impression Aristides wanted to convey. Xanthippus hid a smile with a bowed head.

'Come, gentlemen, as honoured guests,' Aristides called to them.

He waved his hoplites aside, though Xanthippus was not

the only one to note how they formed up behind. The tramp and jingle of armed men would follow the Spartans right to the heart of the city, it seemed.

Aristides strode ahead and they led their horses after him, passing through the broken walls and taking the road to the Agora. Aristides spoke over his shoulder, his voice raised so that they could all hear.

'The council of Athens has been told of your arrival. There are rooms there, to wash away the dust of the road. I have slaves ready to tend you; water for washing, fruit, fish and wine to sate your appetites. The moon rises. Shall we say two hours?'

'What of the Macedonian?' Pausanias broke in.

Xanthippus watched Aristides frown in confusion. He found he was enjoying the performance.

'King Alexander?' Aristides waited for the Spartan regent to nod. 'He is here, still. He remains in the city. I am surprised to hear word of his presence carried as far as Sparta.'

'You have made no agreement with him, no treaty?' Pausanias asked.

Aristides shook his head. His tone changed subtly, deepening as it lost the artificial rhythms of a host.

'We have not, Pausanias, no. We have made no agreement with an ally of the army that burned Athens, the men who despoiled our temples, who broke our walls and drowned our people.'

The silence that followed was darker and deeper than the night around them. The Spartan regent had the grace to look abashed, though also relieved, Xanthippus could see that. Pausanias had come to prevent an alliance. The anger he saw in Aristides was balm on a wound to him. Xanthippus wondered if Aristides' prickly sense of honour had given away an advantage. Still, some things could not be hidden.

With the moon high above the city, they crossed the open Agora, silent and still. At its edge stood the rebuilt council building, where the tribes of Athens met to administer rulings of the Assembly. Servants led the Spartans to bathing rooms and food laid out for them.

The new bouleuterion building was not shuttered despite the late hour. Oil lamps lit every room there, spilling onto the Agora. Xanthippus thought he could hear the murmur of voices in the main chamber. His people, speaking their souls to the air, ordering the world around them. He wondered how Spartans would fare in front of that audience.

Xanthippus was not surprised to have Aristides approach him, gathering in Cimon with his other arm. Relas and Onesimos waited to one side.

'We have a little time,' Aristides said. 'The Persians have offered peace.' He nodded as Cimon snorted in disgust at the very idea.

'As slaves, perhaps,' Xanthippus said. 'They know nothing of freedom. Was that the Macedonian you mentioned before?'

'King Alexander of Macedon,' Aristides confirmed. 'Sent to us as one we know. A traitor, made to kiss the ground Xerxes walks. You will see him in the council chamber.'

He looked over his shoulder, but there was no sign yet of any of the Spartan group returning. Athenian hoplites remained on guard and they would have reacted to the soldiers of another city creeping around.

'There can be no peace,' Aristides went on, 'not while this Persian army threatens us. I'll test the will of the council, but I cannot imagine they will accept. Themistocles will fill the room with talk of war and vengeance. I may not oppose him! Perhaps the Spartans will understand then that we are in

*Conn Iggulden*

earnest. That is our aim, gentlemen. To bring them out, with us, in the spring.'

'And if they do not come?' Xanthippus said.

'Have you heard they will not?' Aristides said immediately, searching his eyes.

Xanthippus shook his head.

'We had barely one night in Sparta before we were gathered up and drawn back here. This Pausanias keeps his own counsel . . . but he worries me. He knows what we want, what his own father, Cleombrotus, promised as his oath. The brother of Leonidas is very ill, I learned, too weak to see anyone, perhaps close to death.'

'I see. If he dies . . . will that affect the oath he gave?' Aristides muttered. He could hear noises from the antechambers. The Spartans had clearly not wallowed in the pools or dawdled over the food laid out for them. They were already moving and dressing once more.

Xanthippus considered. The truth was complex.

'I think it will, if Pausanias wishes it. Yes. If the regent truly wants to come out and face Persia, it would not matter. Yet I see no great battle lust in him, or none that he has let us see.'

Aristides spat an angry phrase, surprising Xanthippus, who had known him for most of his life and never heard a coarse word. Aristides was the man who had scratched his own name on a piece of pottery when he had been ostracised. His honour and personal discipline were renowned. To hear him swearing was oddly disturbing.

'Perhaps Pausanias can be made to repeat his oath in council,' Aristides said. 'This Persian envoy, Alexander, has been waiting days to hear our reply. Would it hurt us to have the Spartan hear his offer?'

'It might,' Xanthippus said. 'I am surprised you haven't already sent the envoy back to the Persian camp.'

Aristides waved a hand, showing some of the frustration of the previous few days.

'We came close. It is a chance to speak through him to the leader of the Persians, to choose the words this Macedonian will pour into his ear. I have thought long on it, Xanthippus. Having the Spartan regent here has to be an opportunity, one we cannot afford to lose . . . Should we keep them apart? Or let them see one another? Too late, they come.' He took a long breath, squaring his shoulders as he made a decision. 'There is no more time. We'll play this out.'

Pausanias had appeared at the end of a corridor, stepping out of a curtained alcove and striding towards them. The Spartan regent wore a clean robe and sandals and his hair was wet. He looked healthy and yet his arms were marked with white scars. As he approached, it was hard not to take a step back, the instinct of all men in the presence of lions.

Pausanias was the nephew of Leonidas and the current battle king of Sparta. In comparison, Xanthippus felt the grime of the road on his skin, as well as the odours of un-washed sweat and horses still rising from him. He and his companions had given up their chance to eat and bathe in order to speak to Aristides. Xanthippus showed no resent-ment, however. He saw Cimon licking sore lips and shook his head when he felt the young man's eyes flicker over him. There was a war on. Nothing else mattered. Xanthippus would endure a thousand days of thirst and soreness – if it brought Sparta to the field.

'Honoured regent!' Aristides called in greeting, his voice ris-ing to the overjoyed tone from before. He saw the Spartan guards gathering, beginning to crowd around Pausanias. Aris-tides frowned. 'Gentlemen, you are guests, protected by custom and the law. I give you my personal oath, my word. You are protected, on my honour. I have gathered the council of

Athens to listen to what you have to say. There is no need for guards, for swords, not in this place. You are among friends.'

Pausanias stared at him for a moment, then shrugged.

'Tisamenus will accompany me,' he told his men. 'Remain here. Come if I call.'

The message was clear enough to all that heard it. If he roared for them, a dozen Spartan warriors would split the heads of anyone in their way to reach his side. Xanthippus wondered if Aristides had brought enough hoplites to stop them if they did. As the man himself went through to the council chamber, Xanthippus took a moment to knuckle away weariness from his eyes, so that he saw flashes of green. If it came to that, they would already have lost.

Xanthippus stifled a yawn as he entered the hall, seeing every seat was already packed. Themistocles stood on the dais, leaning on a rostrum to address the council. It had been his voice they'd heard, growing louder with every step.

'I welcome Pausanias, regent of Sparta,' Themistocles said immediately, his eyes alive with interest. 'Son to Cleombrotus, nephew to Leonidas, honoured in death. Come, Majesty, address us.'

The one seated on his right had sprung to his feet at the tramp of armed men entering. Alexander of Macedon looked dismayed at the sight of Spartans. The Macedonian king said nothing as he dropped slowly back once more. He swallowed nervously, his throat moving in a spasm.

Pausanias showed no discomfort at entering a room packed with Athenians. They were arrayed before him in half-circles, rising to the rear of the hall like a theatre. When he stood at the central point, his voice carried to all parts of the boule with extraordinary power, a masterpiece of construction. Tisamenus stood at his side, his eyes passing over every face, judging them, seeing who glared or looked away.

The Spartan regent nodded thanks to Themistocles. His eyes rested briefly on the Macedonian, though without particular recognition. Themistocles saw the man's gaze linger on the lion brooch Alexander wore at his shoulder. Pausanias turned from it almost in reluctance to face the council of Athens. He placed his hands on the rostrum and breathed slowly. He had heard of their strange political structures, back in Sparta. The Assembly had seemed a chaotic thing, as it had been described to him. Power without a single ruler, with laws they made up themselves, judgements by common men over noble families? It was a kind of madness. He had seen the burned city all around them. More, he could see new beams overhead and smell pine sap in the air. It was hard not to think of it as a divine judgement on their hubris. Yet they retained some sense of order, even in time of war or famine. The council ruled the city and some like Themistocles had authority over them, even if they were not called king.

That was it, Pausanias was certain. Men were made to be led. Kings were born, then hammered free of imperfections on a forge. Weak lines fell away, so that each generation grew stronger. Pausanias could not help imagining the five ephors at home, men who devoted themselves to the stability of Sparta. They counted their long lives a success if nothing changed at all. The people before him suffered badly in comparison. He smiled at them, but it was the smile of a wolf looking over a pen of lambs on a sunny day.

'You know who I am,' Pausanias began. He made a flick of his fingers, disdaining any other introduction. 'In Sparta, word of this . . . discussion came to me. A scout reached my ear, saying Persia had offered peace to our allies, to Athens. I said such a thing was impossible, but I see that was a mistake. The army that burned this city, that sank our ships and

*Conn Iggulden*

drowned our people, now offers you the hand of friendship. They sent their representative to you, not to me. Yet I stand here as witness, as the eye of Sparta on you. I stand as the judge and guarantor of your honour.'

He turned his head back and forth, making sure they felt his gaze even as they shifted and grumbled at his arrogance. Themistocles stepped forward to answer, but Pausanias raised a hand, his voice ringing out.

'I am aware of your poverty. If that is a weight on one side of the scales, I can remove it. Sparta will pay a stipend to your women over the winter. If you reject the offer of traitors and enemies, I give you my word we will not let you starve.'

The noise had been building in the council chamber as he spoke. Some of those there called out in anger, while hundreds more whispered to friends in a susurration that spilled onto the Agora like the light of lamps. Pausanias frowned at them, unused to the vigour of the response.

'Sit down,' he snapped to one who had risen to jab a finger at him. When movement caught his eye, he saw the hand of Themistocles now rested on the rostrum, tapping the wood. Pausanias turned to him in confusion.

'Regent Pausanias,' Themistocles said, 'we are used to . . . discussing such things. There is no single voice of reply here, not even mine. We will talk through what you have said and then vote on it.'

He glanced over at the Macedonian king, seeing the gleam of sweat on his forehead. That man looked fairly ill at what he had heard. Or perhaps it was just that he realised how little his life was worth in that place, lion brooch or not.

'Should we step down?' Tisamenus said suddenly. 'For you to discuss what you will do?'

He at least seemed to be enjoying himself. Themistocles recognised the man from the description Aristides had given.

Themistocles swept his gaze over five hundred red and angry faces. He chuckled and shook his head.

'I don't think that will be necessary this time. You are the soothsayer who cannot tell the future?'

Tisamenus laughed at that.

'I suppose I am. I know you, kurios. Your name is spoken in Sparta, with respect.'

'I should think it is!' Themistocles said, wide-eyed. 'Considering I saved us all.'

While Themistocles had been speaking to Tisamenus, Aristides had approached. He too laid a hand on the rostrum. Themistocles dropped his and bent his head close over the noise of the crowd, a clamour still swelling as men struggled to be heard.

'Will you speak, Aristides?' Themistocles said. 'What damage will you do, before kings of Macedon and Sparta?' He smiled as he spoke, but there was an edge to it even so.

Aristides sighed.

'I speak for Athens, Themistocles, rather than my own glory.'

'I find my own glory and that of Athens are much the same,' Themistocles replied quickly.

Despite his irritation, he stepped away and gestured for Pausanias to do the same. The crowd saw Aristides standing alone at the rostrum. The noise died slowly, but as more and more heads turned, true silence fell.

*Conn Iggulden*

# 16

Aristides began to speak.

'We have heard the Persian offer . . . Gentlemen, allow me to respond. Are we children, to call out? Raise your hand if you wish to contribute. I will second any one of you who wishes to be heard. There. We will vote, because in Athens, the wisdom of the city does not lie in the judgement of just one man, or half a dozen ephors. In you, in this five hundred, all the ten tribes of Athens are represented. I see Acamantis, Cecropis, Aegeis, Leontis, Oeneis, Antiochis, Aeantis, Erechtheis . . . Pandionis there and Hippothontis. There you are! We do not *represent* the people; we *are* the people. And I will say this. I had intended to take a position against Themistocles . . . not for the first time.'

He waited through a dry chuckle from those who knew them.

'It was my hope to test the proposition, to drink it to the very dregs. Because the survival of our city depends on us making the correct decision here. If we reject the offer before us, if we send this little Macedonian king back to his master with our refusal, they could march against us once more. We have all seen the results of Persians standing in Athens. We know what that means, better than anyone. Now, I will not discuss all we have planned if they return to Attica, not with all the ears in this room. Yet you must understand this: we face destruction, *annihilation*. At such a time, I will not try to rouse you to anger, to cry down the Persian threat, to damn them and dare them to come.'

Despite his words, there was a growl in that room. Themistocles watched in fascination. He knew Aristides only as the driest of speakers. On that night, for the first time, he plucked their strings. Themistocles could feel each note resound in that place. He saw Xanthippus and Cimon were watching in awe as Aristides went on.

'We have heard from the Persians; we have heard too from the Spartans. Show courtesy, gentlemen! Show dignity, as it is taken and earned, not granted to us. *Never* granted! I have stood in this place, with the scent of new wood all around me, where there were ashes – and I have been lectured by a Spartan king, come to tell me my honour!'

Themistocles felt his mouth open. There was silence in that room, without even the tiny movements of men sitting on stone for too long. They had frozen in astonishment to hear Aristides abandon his usual style.

'I know Athenians,' Aristides said, his voice suddenly softer, though more chilling. 'As I know all Hellenes. I know we will not betray our brothers and sisters. The idea is . . . obscene. I do not speak for all those here tonight. I speak with one voice, alone, yet heard. That is our way, our law, our tradition. With that one voice, I say this: I trust in Athens, in our genius, in the labour of our arms, in our ships and the wombs of our women. I trust in our gods: in Athena, in Apollo, in Ares and Poseidon. I may be one voice, but perhaps I speak for more than one when I answer Macedon, when I say, "What happened to you to be so reduced, to come here as a messenger for Persians?" My answer is that we will stand against you, to the last man, to the last woman and child. We will never be your slaves. Never. Tell that to your master, O king.'

A cheer began, but Aristides raised a great shout over it. In all the years, he had never bellowed in a political meeting.

*Conn Iggulden*

Yet Themistocles remembered the man's roar from the field of Marathon. The association caused a cold chill to run down his back.

'And to Sparta, with my lone voice, I say this!' Aristides called over them.

The noise dropped away again as they grinned, their eyes bright in the golden lamplight.

'I say this . . .' he repeated, controlling the exultation that had risen in him. This was what Themistocles loved, he realised. He only told them what they wanted to hear, but it felt . . . glorious.

'I say this. You see our response. You know how we will answer the Persians. We have refused Persian gold. It is not so hard to refuse yours. Put your fears away, regent of Sparta. Though we have given more than anyone, we have yet more to give. We will stand. The question is only whether you will be at our side, or safe behind your wall.'

He turned to Pausanias as he spoke, while the crowd howled and cheered behind him. The Spartan regent looked back with eyes full of anger. Aristides gestured to the rostrum, but it was the king of Macedonia who suddenly stepped forward. It took a moment for the Athenian council to see he stood there, but Alexander gripped the rostrum and remained until the sound died once more.

'I came here from a land at peace,' Alexander said, 'with thriving markets, with city walls. I came as an ally of Persia, my pride intact, though you insult me! I rode past rubble to enter Athens. You poor fools, you have no walls! You *cannot* defend this city, not if you choose to slap away the hand extended to you. I urge you to think again.'

His knuckles whitened on the rostrum as they called out suggestions to him. After a moment he stood back.

'Do as you wish then,' he said to Aristides in disgust.

'That is the heart of freedom, I believe,' Aristides said. 'That choice.'

'You choose an ending,' the king of Macedon said. He shook his head as if in sorrow.

'Perhaps,' Aristides replied. 'But we choose. One day you will understand.'

Aristides turned then to Pausanias and Tisamenus. The soothsayer was wide-eyed and in awe of all he had witnessed.

'Regent Pausanias, we will discuss the offers until dawn. I think then that we will vote on it on the Pnyx, with the whole Assembly of Athens present. You are welcome to attend as witnesses, of course. For once though, I think it will be a formality. Now, I have put rooms aside in the city for you. They are new-built and simple, but perhaps that will not be so strange to men of Sparta.'

He spoke with the noise of the crowd like a clatter of pigeon wings behind him, filling the room. The council hall had been the very first building rebuilt after the fire, the labour of hundreds. It smelled of sawdust, pine, olive oil and sweat.

Pausanias had lost the sense of the room when it had erupted. He was used to silence and discipline, not maniacs all shouting over one another. Yet he recognised the certainty in Aristides, as well as his authority. That had been clear from the moment he had opened his mouth to speak.

'Will you truly decline the funds I offered?' he said at last.

With Alexander of Macedon in red-faced attendance, Pausanias and Tisamenus followed Aristides back out to the rooms and corridors beyond. Behind them, Themistocles and the epistates began to invite speakers. Yet the crash of noise and energy was already dropping in the room. The main event was at an end.

'We will, I am certain,' Aristides said as a door closed be-

*Conn Iggulden*

hind them. 'You understand pride, I think. Of course you do. Sparta saw eight ships sunk at Salamis. We lost the crews of many more than that. Everyone in that room has known grief. So we don't want your silver. We want what was promised, given by your father's word. We want you to summon the entire army of Sparta in spring, to stand with us.'

'I have said we will come out,' Pausanias said. 'When the moment is right, we will be there.'

Aristides fixed him with a gaze.

'That sounds like another evasion, Regent Pausanias. When the moment is *right*? We face an enemy none of us can defeat on our own. Just as we did at Salamis. You don't need me to point out your debts, or the oaths made on your behalf. The only question that matters is the simple one. Will you stand?'

'I have said it,' Pausanias replied. He was clearly furious to be questioned in such a way.

After a moment, Aristides looked suddenly old and weary, exhausted.

'Well, I hope that is enough,' he replied. 'Come, you must be tired. I will show you to your rooms.'

The comforts of a military camp were few and far between, especially in winter. King Alexander and his three companions had ridden hard and far, spending nights by the trail with swords ready to hand. Yet there was no true friendship between them, not when one was Mardonius' own translator, there to eavesdrop on whatever was said to them – or whatever they murmured amongst themselves. Nor had it escaped Alexander's notice that the man had bowed and vanished on entering the Persian camp, heading off to make his report while the Macedonians were reunited with the one they had left behind as hostage. Alexander told himself it did not mean he was distrusted. Mardonius had assured him such things were considered utterly normal, like making obeisance to the king, or eating pistachio nuts. Still, Mardonius had made him wait to be called. The king of Macedon had passed the camp's outer gate in late morning. The sun was low on the hills by the time he was summoned to attend Mardonius. That alone was a mark of disapproval, or so he believed.

Alexander was surprised to find Mardonius talking to three others in his command tent. The general introduced both his second in command, Artabazus, and the commander of the Immortals, Hydarnes. The last was not one Alexander had known before, introduced as Masistius, master of horse.

Artabazus seemed friendly enough on their previous acquaintance, though Alexander could not tell if his easy talk and laughter were real or Persian politeness. Artabazus had a surprising amount of flesh on him, a little tub of a man. The others were as tall and lean as Mardonius himself, with deep seams in their cheeks and eyes that seemed to be completely black. Both Hydarnes and Masistius cast a cold gaze over the Macedonian king. He did not need to ask if the news from Athens had reached them.

'Please, Majesty, you are my guest,' General Mardonius said. 'Sit with me and eat.'

His words were repeated by the translator, who remained standing by the table. Alexander nodded in gratitude, swallowing his nerves and sitting on a bench that wobbled under him. The floor was some sort of dry matting, covering soft ground. He found he had to tense one leg to keep his seat straight. The others took places across from him, while the translator still stood, looming over the table like an ornament. Alexander blinked at the arrangement. It felt as if they had chosen sides, or sat in judgement.

Servants brought food in a dozen small dishes. Alexander recognised figs and spinach greens, as well as spiced hare and goat. He waited through prayers in a language he did not speak. Those were not rendered into Greek, perhaps out of respect for the sacred, he did not know. For the first time in a year or longer, Alexander wondered if he had given up too much for gold and peace.

No. He had seen the burned houses and broken walls of Athens. That was the price of defying these men. A king's first duty was to protect his people against the flood, the fire – and the Persian. Alexander kept his head down as the prayer ended. They ate then, mostly in silence. Artabazus clearly said something amusing about the goat that made Mardonius laugh. Neither of the other two cracked a smile. They ate without obvious relish, as if it was just another chore.

When they had mopped their lips and drunk the wine to the dregs, the same servants entered and whisked all signs of the meal away. Even the table was folded and removed, with one soldier waiting patiently until Alexander understood and rose to his feet. The bench he was sitting on was taken from the room. He felt suddenly vulnerable, facing the Persians on his own. Alexander had to remind himself that he was a trusted ally, his life protected by their honour.

'I am grateful to you, Alexander,' Mardonius began. 'I know how . . . distasteful it must have been to make my offer to ungrateful Athenians. Our friend here has told us how they scorned the peace they might have had,' Mardonius said.

The translator was skilled and spoke in an undertone just a beat behind, so that Alexander could understand almost in the instant. Mardonius saw the Macedonian nod warily in response. He waved a hand as if it was of no concern.

'I do not hold you responsible. Be assured. There is no more to say on that.'

'I did try. I could not move them,' Alexander said.

A little of the hurt he had felt could be heard in his tone. Mardonius reached out and clapped him on the shoulder, almost paternally.

'Some men . . . cannot change,' the general said. 'Will not. Even if you burn their house down.'

Artabazus laughed at that and added something more that the translator did not render into Greek. It seemed the comments of Persian officers would remain private, a distinction that helped Alexander remember he was an outsider in that place. Though he wore a royal brooch on his shoulder, he was still the least of them, in their eyes.

'If I may, general . . . if you truly believed they would not accept your offer, why was I sent, to be humiliated? Why ask at all?'

Mardonius looked up with interest as the translator worked his words into court Persian. The general raised a hand and two servants drifted in with new cups and a jug of wine, dark as blood in that gloom. Even as Alexander had the thought, lamps were lit, illuminating the deepest corners.

'In this land,' Mardonius said softly, 'I speak for King Xerxes, eternal glory to his name and line. For this year alone, I am the voice of the throne of Persia – and that means more than merely commanding a great host. I wonder if you can understand? Artabazus here does not believe Greeks capable of subtlety.'

Artabazus snorted and shrugged, holding out his cup to be filled. Mardonius smiled.

'He thinks they respect a spear-thrust, or a club breaking a skull – but all the rest is just wind.'

'I am, however, a Macedonian,' Alexander said, somewhat stiffly.

Artabazus muttered something that clearly tugged at the corners of Mardonius' mouth. It was not translated. Alexander was really beginning to hate that short bastard.

'Of course!' Mardonius replied. 'My apologies.'

It was obviously insincere. The man and his companions saw no difference between the nations of the west. Alexander wondered if they considered Medes or Lydians just the same as Persians. He decided to keep that question to himself. Men rarely enjoyed having their own hypocrisy exposed.

'My point though, is clear enough,' Mardonius went on. 'If a man loses his house to a storm, of course he will blame the storm. But if the storm says first to him, "Bend the knee to me and I will pass by, I will spare your wife and children" . . .' Mardonius waited for the translator to catch up. 'If the man refuses *then* and loses all he owns, all he loves, who can he blame if not himself? The storm will have torn away all his deceptions. Do you see? He will know he brought it on himself.'

'And you are the storm,' Alexander murmured.

Mardonius nodded so quickly, he wondered if the man had some smattering of Greek. Mardonius had risen in a ferociously competitive culture to stand as the king's right hand. It was worth remembering.

'We *are* the storm, of course. And perhaps his house would always have fallen. But the next man we meet? When I say to him, "Bend the knee," perhaps he will, to spare all he loves. I think . . . this is something you understand.'

Alexander thought of the pride he had witnessed in

Athens, compared to his own. The memory felt like bitterness in his throat. He had traded that pride to stand in that tent, as a trusted man. He looked from Artabazus, who watched with bright eyes and humour, to Hydarnes and Masistius, men dark and apparently hostile to the blond king of Macedon.

'Gentlemen,' Alexander said, 'Persia is a long way away. Let me tell you a prophecy I heard once.'

In the morning, Mardonius had nothing to do while the camp was packed up. He shivered, his teeth chattering. A freezing wind had come out of the north. Squalls of rain made the ground a bog and all tasks twice as hard. The men were pleased enough to be about their business, or so their officers assured him. Mardonius smiled at the sight of one of his sons riding past, in a cloak so sodden it clung like metal, outlining his thighs.

Artabazus was as fine a horseman as Mardonius had ever seen, almost as skilled on horseback as Masistius, who could ride anything with hooves. Yet Masistius looked like a horseman, while Artabazus was somehow both fat and sturdy, a little block of a man. Mardonius had seen him tumbling like an acrobat with some of the young officers, turning full flips in the air. It strengthened joints and bones, so he said. If a horse ever threw him, he would surely bounce and roll, unhurt. The thought made Mardonius smile as the man reined in, curious at the general's odd expression. The rain chose that moment to intensify, determined to pour cold water down both their necks and bow their horses under them.

'We'll be sneezing, or perhaps drowning, if this gets any worse,' Artabazus said by way of greeting.

Mardonius nodded. He hated winter. It was just not a soldier's season.

'We have gathered food enough for a month,' he said. 'I think it will not hurt to remind the Athenians there is a price for their pride.'

'We are the storm,' Artabazus said with a grin. It was the same phrase Mardonius had used to the king of Macedon the night before.

'We are indeed,' Mardonius replied. He waited then, while the rain poured down and the regiments trudged up to form drenched ranks before them.

'What did you think of his prophecy?' Artabazus asked. He had to raise his voice over the hiss and drum of the rain.

Mardonius shrugged.

'I do not believe in prophecies, even if he does.'

'So you will not make him satrap of all Greece? He has been a loyal ally.'

'I imagine that will be King Xerxes' choice,' Mardonius said. 'It will likely be a Persian – you perhaps, Artabazus, who knows?'

'You believe the man's prophecy was wrong, then?' Artabazus pressed.

Mardonius shot a glance at him.

'Who knows, really, about such things? I think if his family is destined to rule all Greece, this is the wrong year . . .' He chuckled aloud. 'Or he is the wrong Alexander of Macedon.'

The army that had formed to march south to Athens was vast. The rainstorm moved across them as it might have crossed a range of hills or a great plain. Winter sun speared behind the clouds as Mardonius turned his horse in place.

'The rain heads south. It is a good omen, I think,' he said. 'We are the storm, Artabazus. Let's remind them of that.'

# 17

The Persian army came south at the pace of a walking man. Two hundred thousand soldiers were in more danger from starvation or accidental injury than any force that might be sent to stop them. Rations were measured out at every stopping point, with each man guarding his personal bowl carefully. They marched on Athens like the rain that went before them: slow, unstoppable and vast.

Athenian scouts came galloping in ahead of the invaders. They risked their necks and half-killed mounts to win every hour they could. Emergency meetings on the Pnyx went as planned, with each member of the Assembly fully aware of what he had to do. Grim-faced, they set about a second evacuation of the city. There would be no one left behind for enemy soldiers to murder or humiliate.

They could not defend Athens, not without walls, not against so many. That at least was not in doubt. Strategoi and archons wasted no time, but set about instituting the emergency plan. Fleet officers were given the work of shepherding families down to the docks. They lined the road to the sea, urging on or carrying terrified women and children.

The council had prepared for the worst from the moment they had returned to burned-out beams and broken gates. Tribe by tribe, families and their slaves had learned where they would go if horns sounded, where they would stand. They could not all rush down to the ships in a panic. It had to be slow.

Themistocles seemed to be everywhere in the crowds at

*Conn Iggulden*

times, reminding them of their duties, calling to mothers to keep their children close. Some still managed to lose themselves, with frantic relatives calling out names. Wailing urchins stood to one side of the road, holding out chubby hands to passers-by.

There were also fights, erupting suddenly as one family objected to being shoved, or men lashed out at one another, caring only for those they loved. Hoplites went in hard then, with clubs or long sticks to lash the crowd. There was no sympathy for those who bled for their impatience, deserved or not. The exodus began in a great stream of men, women and children, tight-lipped and determined.

Bonfires were lit along the coastal hills, kept alight with oil when rain drenched them. Out at sea, patrolling ships saw those points of light and turned immediately for home. Each trierarch, each crew, knew without asking which dock and quay was theirs. It was a plan they had prayed never to deploy, but when word came down, when the enemy sighting had been confirmed, there was no hesitation.

Salamis would be their refuge once again, though it was not the bare place it had been, when women and children had huddled on the dunes. Xanthippus had listened to his wife, as had Themistocles. The result lay in shelters and food stores right across the island. They were unfinished, but they had not expected to need them so soon. The first families began to arrive on packed trireme decks that same morning, stepping ashore and shivering in the wind.

Agariste and her children were among the earliest ones to reach the island, this time accompanied by all the slaves of her household in perfect order, as well as paid servants like Manias and even two stern hoplite guards assigned by her husband. They found her a spot under a long roof, a place resembling a stable, though it was too narrow and roofed in grass so green it was not much protection. Rain was dripping through as they arrived, so that anyone who sat there would surely be miserable. Yet every hour brought hundreds more, then thousands. The people of Athens came down to the port of Piraeus and went quietly onto triremes, enduring mere cold and rain to escape the horrors coming.

Agariste kept Pericles and Eleni close, though Ariphron stood in cloak, helmet, bronze greaves and chestplate. He wore a sword on his hip, painfully aware of it. His shield rested against a pillar of wood, while his dory spear was too tall for that low roof and had to be laid down. As his father still lived and wore the family set, Ariphron wore pieces purchased from three families deep in grief, new widows who needed silver as they glimpsed life without a husband's care.

Agariste could hardly see her son beneath the helmet's shadow. She knew Ariphron was not yet comfortable in the new kit. In more normal times, she would have had the greaves adjusted to fit, the sword's grip remade for his hand, so that it could not be sent spinning away by some jarring blow. At eighteen, her son was unaware of such things, of course. Pericles had walked around him as if admiring a statue. Ariphron clearly thought he looked like a young Heracles, standing guard on his mother and sister with new-found earnestness.

Agariste did not smile at his strutting walk. She only hoped he would not have to draw the sword before the emergency was over. Seated with her hands about her knees and her children murmuring, she was not sure she would get her wish. Some of the faces around them were pale, stunned by the mocking twist of fate that had raised all their hopes, then returned them to the same island. Others seemed to have found refuge in furious anger. They spoke harshly to one

*Conn Iggulden*

another, close to violence, bickering over every piece of space or shelter.

'Where is your father now, Peri?' Agariste asked her younger son.

The boy took it as an opportunity to vanish, of course, going to look for Xanthippus. It seemed an age before Pericles returned, but no one dared approach her in that time. Once more she had space around her children, though she thought it was less her family line and more the hoplites who stood and watched nearby, with iron on their hips. Either way, the crowd knew the protection of her husband stood between them. She hoped they did. Too many scowled at her, as if she was the author of their troubles! As many wept as glared, though she could do nothing for them.

If there were to be furious accusations, even sly spite, it would not be where she could note faces and names, Agariste was half-sure. Weak people always looked for those to blame – and Xanthippus was a name, a senior man. For every oarsman or trierarch who bent the knee in his presence, there would be a dozen wives and mothers who still blamed him for the death of a husband or son. Agariste felt eyes on her, every moment. She was in reach, and they were eaten up with formless anger.

She hoped they understood the significance of the men in bronze at her side. As the shelters filled and were found to be inadequate, thousands more had to sit on the cliffs, jammed together for warmth while the rain fell harder, hissing across the sea. The space around her family and slaves shrank as people shuffled closer, mindless as cattle. On the edges, more than one group came to blows as men tried to make space for their mothers or held up children and shouted for others to let them in. Those who heard pressed their lips pale and were thankful they were out of the wind and wet.

They had all been refugees before, Agariste reminded herself, then returned to something like normal life. She did not know if it was madness to hope for the same, or whether this second blow would break them. Perhaps Athens was truly gone this time. She knew Themistocles talked a grand vision, saying the people were the city, not mere stone or walls. It was hard to see much glory in the shivering crowds on Salamis.

Pericles returned in noise and life, tearing her reverie to rags, skidding on the wet ground as he came to a halt.

'Father is down on the new docks, talking to some of the other strategoi and archons. I listened for a while . . .' He trailed off, clearly recalling the times his mother had told him he would hear nothing good if he eavesdropped on conversations.

Impatiently, Agariste waved him to continue and he grinned at her. He was handsome, she believed. Half the young daughters in Athens knew his name, or so she had heard. She saw the gleam in his eyes that would make him the enemy of their fathers in time, if it hadn't already. Yet there was a sort of innocence in him. At his age, all the grief and rage around just passed him by, if he noticed it at all. In that moment, as his odour of clean sweat and salt washed over her, she envied him. He grinned at her, basking in her love.

'Father said Themistocles organised some sort of search of bags on the docks of the Piraeus. Something to do with a missing cup from the temple of Athena. Then Aristides said he had not heard of a missing cup and Dad said that did not surprise him at all. He said the amount of wealth that had turned up in the search was worth a thousand cups. It will all go to pay the rowers, or something. Confiscated.' Pericles saw his mother was wincing and patting the air with one hand. He dipped his head and lowered his voice to a whisper.

*Conn Iggulden*

'He said something about the Spartans too, but then they saw me and sent me away.'

'What was that about a cup?' his sister Eleni asked.

Agariste shook her head in exasperation. The crowd were desperate for news of any kind. They would all be listening. It would not have surprised her to hear some of the resentment she sensed came from having family treasures taken from them on the docks. If she had known Pericles would speak so loudly, she would have dragged him closer and made him breathe it into her ear. In that too, he was an innocent, gloriously so.

Agariste and Eleni bent closer as Pericles settled himself on the matting, ready to say it all again. Ariphron too came to stand by them, loath to give up his dignity, but caught between duty and desire to hear what was going on. In the end, his discipline won the battle and he kept guard, turning the hollow dark of his helmet on those who clustered too close to his family.

Themistocles looked at the man – no, the archon – whose name would mark the year. He had never regretted bringing Xanthippus back from exile. Xanthippus was made for authority in war, the perfect strategos. Some men thought authority amounted to little more than a good shouting voice and a noble family. Themistocles could have thrown a rock and hit a dozen of those. Yet Xanthippus understood *how* to give orders to others – and the right ones to give. It was a rare skill, which was why Athens only ever appointed ten strategoi in times of war, with a polemarch to command them. The Assembly was a wondrous thing that should not have worked half as well as it did. Yet in battle, on the ground or at sea, men needed to follow orders and trust those who gave them. It was a time for tyranny.

Themistocles realised his particular genius lay in choosing the right men. It meant he was free to keep the whole city in the corner of his eye, to look ahead and plan and plan. Themistocles was beloved of the gods, there could be no doubt about that. Or perhaps he had been blessed by them, given a capacity for hard work and a lively mind. He did not mind which it was. He had saved Athens more than once. He told himself he could do it again, if he could *just* persuade the men before him to break their oaths and undermine their honour.

He looked once more to Xanthippus, remembering how he had commanded at Marathon, eleven years before. Aristides and Cimon stood on the same new docks, impatient. Dozens more gathered around, senior men, though weary; unshaven as the wooden quays they had thrown up in double-quick time. The epistates for the day was on hand, a man of Cecropis tribe. In time of war, wherever *they* stood, the Assembly had convened, that was the simple truth of it. Themistocles breathed and made himself think.

'We can't go on like this,' he said. 'Can we agree that much? They'll burn the city again and I don't know if these people can find the will to rebuild a second time. We've already cut down every tree for a day's march!'

'So we send them out for two days, or three . . .' Aristides said, half out of habit.

Themistocles shook his head.

'To what end? Our one advantage is the fleet, but you know, the Persians have ships still, with their king. Will he be idle? Who knows? If they rebuild and return, we won't be able to take our people to safety. We dealt them a terrible blow in the strait by Salamis, but what if they come back with a fleet in the spring? We'll be exactly where we were

*Conn Iggulden*

when all this started! No, gentlemen, we need to break up this hunting pack. We need to be ruthless.'

'I don't think . . .' Cimon began. He broke off immediately when Xanthippus held up a hand.

Themistocles felt his eyebrows rise. The brash young man had learned respect. Of course he had. If it hadn't been his own idea to send Xanthippus to Sparta, Themistocles might have been annoyed at alliances formed away from his approval. Instead, he congratulated himself privately on making the right choice.

'Let me hear Themistocles,' Xanthippus said.

Cimon nodded and Themistocles shook his head at their serious expressions.

'We are playing for the highest stakes,' he went on. 'Not just our lives and liberty, but everything we are – all we might be. If we *can't* stop them, we lose Athens, Greece, our people. Gone. So when I say this, know that I do not take it lightly.'

'Why are you smiling in that strange way, then?' Aristides said.

'Nerves and weariness,' Themistocles replied, a little sharply. 'To say these words to you three is a little much, even for me.'

He paused then, until at least one of them was ready to take him by the throat and force him to speak.

'Gentlemen, we need to negotiate peace with Persia,' Themistocles said at last, almost in a sigh.

'I swear, I ought to have your tongue pulled out,' Aristides snapped. 'For my own peace of mind. If we didn't *need* you . . . Do you think I have time for this foolishness? By the gods, I . . .'

'Hear him out,' Cimon said firmly.

Aristides blinked, astonished at an order from such a

young man. Themistocles too was surprised to get support from such a source. He wondered how much of Cimon's morning had been spent sucking on a wine-teat.

Cimon shrugged when he saw every eye was on him.

'Well? Themistocles was the one who persuaded Xerxes to split his fleet and then run, wasn't he? If this is another idea *like those ones*, it might be worth hearing. If not, we have lost only a little time.'

'I see your father in you,' Themistocles said. 'And Cimon is right, of course. I have saved Greece more than once. I might yet do it again. Oh, don't snort, Aristides! You argued for the new silver from Laurium to go into the pockets of the people, didn't you, instead of a fleet? Well, that fleet gave us the only chance we had. Who argued for it and saved the lives of every woman and child of Athens? Ah, yes, I remember! And the letters to Xerxes in his tent on the shore? Which genius made him split the fleet? Who sent him running home? Was it . . . I forget, Aristides, can you recall the name of that great hero?'

Aristides stared coldly at a man he detested. Themistocles had never lacked for self-belief, but since the beginning of the war, his confidence had become a thing of bronze, a statue to himself in his own mind.

Themistocles grinned at him, very aware of the opposing forces in his allies. They listened because no one else was offering solutions to the disaster.

'What do we want most?' he asked them. 'Truly?'

'The Persians to leave, or to defeat them,' Cimon replied, when no one else did.

'Exactly . . .' Themistocles replied. 'Though they will not leave, I think, not without some intervention from the gods which we cannot force. We might pray for the death of their king, perhaps. That would surely call these Persians home.

*Conn Iggulden*

Failing that . . . we need Sparta on the field. It is our *only* hope. The events of this morning serve as a reminder, gentlemen. We cannot live in fear. We *cannot* see our city burned, over and over. Nor can we run to Salamis each time, to starve in this poor place. Sooner or later they will bring another fleet back.'

He held up one arm, powerful and tanned. With a sharp movement, he shoved his palm across, as if the whole world might move at his gesture.

'On that side: fear and destruction at their whim, or being vassals to a foreign king. We cannot accept it. So . . . if all that is impossible, ignore it! What is left to us? Only war, to the end, without respite or truce. I stood at Marathon. I walked a deck at Salamis. I will not bend my knee to Persia or any other king. I was born in a free city; I will die a free man. However it comes.'

All lightness and humour had seeped from him. The difference was startling, though he looked older and more weary than he had before. Themistocles shook himself, as if the sea breeze had made him shiver.

'It all becomes simple in the end. If we must go to war, we must have Sparta. The question is only what would bring Sparta out from behind their wall – what would break through their arrogance and self-satisfaction.'

He could not resist looking from man to man to see if they had guessed the answer. Yet the coldness of his previous words still hung in the air like damp. They stared at him, waiting.

'Sparta is safe behind a wall only because Persia does not have a fleet. If we ally with Persia, our fleet could land a Persian army *anywhere* on the Peloponnese – behind their wall. The Spartans could never defend their coast. They would be overwhelmed and defeated in a season.'

'I see . . .' Aristides began. Once more, Cimon interrupted him, the young man's anger spilling out.

'*I* don't. I supported you, Themistocles! You can't truly be suggesting we join Persia to defeat Sparta? If you are, I swear . . .'

'Cimon,' Xanthippus said.

Once again the young man quietened down. Themistocles wondered what had happened on that trip to Sparta to form such a bond between them.

Xanthippus nodded to Cimon, in thanks. Their mutual respect was beginning to grate on Themistocles' nerves.

'I believe Themistocles is suggesting we *appear* to break our word,' Xanthippus said. 'That we only threaten to make an alliance with Persia.' His gaze turned inward for a moment and he nodded. 'That would bring Sparta to the field, as you say, with their own destruction on the line. But it will confirm everything they hate about Athenian politics. They already call us whores, gentlemen. They'll have that view confirmed when we force them out with a threat of our betrayal.'

He glanced at Themistocles then, seeing a man borne down by exhaustion. Xanthippus breathed out slowly.

'We'll be storing up trouble for the future,' he muttered. 'The Spartans won't forget.'

'If we win, they will accept we were right all along,' Themistocles said, 'but honestly, I don't care what they think. Athens was burned, gentlemen. I . . .'

He squinted suddenly, cursing under his breath. A plume of smoke was rising in the distance. Each of them turned to see what had caught his eye and then swore, or muttered prayers. The Persians had entered the city once again. They had come with fire to damage and destroy.

'Whatever we have to do,' Themistocles said softly over the cry of gulls and the noise of the sea washing Salamis. 'We cannot live like this.'

*Conn Iggulden*

Aristides put out his hand and Themistocles took it. One by one the others offered their grip, their personal oath, the gesture spreading through the crowd around them as they sought comfort in the strength of others, a simple grip and release. They sealed a promise of vengeance while the city of Athena burned for a second time.

# 18

A low wail rose from the crowd when they spotted smoke rising over Athens. They knew exactly what it meant. Just the thought of returning once more to the devastation they remembered, to burned buildings and the excrement of soldiers, was enough to cause weeping, sobbing in some. Others swore and shook their fists at an enemy they could not see, calling down the wrath of the gods on Persian heads and the heads of their children.

In the crowd, one man stood up, glaring around him. Bearded and powerful of frame, he looked like a blacksmith, someone who worked with his hands. He wore a stained leather apron and his shoulders were thick with hair, otherwise bare. Agariste felt her eye drawn to him, then to the man's wife as she sat at his feet. The woman half-rose, holding out her hands, clearly pleading with him to sit back down.

In response, the burly man stepped away from his woman and children, raising his voice to be heard.

'The city burns *again*!' he bellowed over their heads, almost to the sky above. 'My shop, my *home* – everything I have is being trampled by Persians. My savings? They were taken from me on the docks by officials from the council.' He held up a tally stick like a talisman. 'I can redeem my losses when the emergency is over, so they said!'

He snapped it in a sudden furious gesture, tossing the pieces at his feet. As the crowd watched wide-eyed, he spat on the ground, making others who sat nearby shift away from him. More were listening as his voice grew in strength.

'My own people robbing me to poverty, while an army of painted dogs roams Athens once again and laughs? I worked for those coins! I gave blood and sweat for them. It is too much!'

'Sit down!' someone else shouted.

'Come and *make* me,' he roared back, red-faced and spattering flecks of spittle. 'Our archons and strategoi care nothing for us! What do they know of hard work? Of *years* of work, of a man's savings taken from him! They'll take our blood, though, won't they, given meekly like good little lambs? Oh, they'll sacrifice us on the altar of war without hesitating. While they sit in fine houses and drink wine. They must laugh, mustn't they? We give all we have, and what do we get for it?' He pointed over to the black smoke writhing in the distance. '*That*. That's what we get.'

Agariste saw the man's wife and children were calling his name, desperate for him to sit down and stop haranguing the crowd. Agariste actually saw the moment he made his decision. She recognised the same mulish expression from dealing with her own husband, the slight dip of the chin that meant he would meet the world with his head down and his shoulders squared. She wanted to call out in warning, but he was not her man.

'Persia offered us *peace*!' he shouted.

The noise of the crowd fell away at that. His words were no more than they had murmured a thousand times themselves over the previous weeks. Yet it was one thing to whisper it to a wife in the privacy of a marriage bed; another to shout it while a Persian army still burned the city they loved. They were made quiet by his daring, or his madness.

'If we had accepted, would they be setting fires once more? No. I would be in my city, working for my living, with my children safe. Not here, in the bitter wind, without even food or water to fill our bellies, without a fire or a forge to keep us warm. Well, I voted to accept peace, because it doesn't much matter to me who sits in splendour and wears gold. All I ever asked is that they stay out of my way. I don't care if they are Persian, or Athenian! If our Assembly, our council, can't protect us, what good are they? If we have no walls, why should I rebuild my house *again* from rubble?'

To Agariste's shock, there was a noise of approval in the crowd around him. She looked at the stern faces of her two hoplites, her eldest son. They were watching as well, she realised. They all were. She swallowed nervously, hugging her daughter Eleni close. She did not know if she could ask the hoplites to intervene, to silence the man. Were there any rules at all, while a city burned a second time? Women knew war very differently to men. Soldiers and their sons imagined only victories, or glorious deaths on the battlefield. No one ever dreamed of running in terror, or being left a cripple. It was always women who had to make do in the aftermath, who had to make an accommodation and accept new men in their homes and beds.

Since the first invasion, Agariste had seen miserable young wives selling themselves, waiting on the streets for customers as the sun set. Their husbands had all been drowned, so they bartered all they had left that was of value. She bit her lip and waited, though rain dripped on her shoulder and she shivered in the cold.

'I propose an offer, made by the people of Athens,' the blacksmith went on. 'A delegation to go to the general of the Persian forces and say, "We, the Athenians, accept your offer of peace."'

A growl of anger met his words as more and more of the crowd understood what was happening. Agariste saw red faces spluttering indignation, but also some nodding heads

*Conn Iggulden*

and men raising their arms in approval, as they did sometimes on the Pnyx.

'Peace is what they want!' the man said. 'The king of Persia treats his allies with honour, we know that. If we want peace, we have merely to ask.'

A stone hit him on the shoulder, bouncing off. He looked up in surprise, utter shock on his face. In that breathless moment, before he could speak, another was thrown, with all the force of rage. It struck him on the mouth, bloodying his lips and knocking his head to one side. He dropped into a crouch, holding his face. Agariste heard people cry out on his behalf, but at least it was over.

He was a strong man. Though his wife tried to hold him, he shrugged her off and rose once more, blood dribbling right down his face and neck, darkening the front of his leather apron in a slick. He began to speak again, but the sight of the blood released something in the crowd. A group of four men suddenly went for him, darting in together. They had picked up stones, holding them as clubs. He had time to turn to face them as the first one struck, smashing him in the cheek.

His wife shrieked as he fell a second time, but the men did not stand back, or run away in shame. Agariste pressed a hand against her own mouth to stifle sounds as they brought stones down on him, breaking bones. The blacksmith would not rise again, that was clear.

They were panting as they let the stones drop, but there was something unsatisfied in that crowd. Agariste saw Ariphron gathering his courage to go forward. She put out a hand and pinched his bare thigh, halting him.

'Stay,' she hissed at her son. 'They will kill you if you go now. Protect me. Protect your brother and sister.'

She saw Ariphron lose his dark expression as he heard her

words and let the call to action fall away. He nodded and she saw the two hoplites were listening, looking for orders, needing them.

Agariste almost rose to her feet when she saw women gathering. The violence was at an end and the four killers began to move away, their expressions blank, even confused. When a woman picked up one of the fallen stones and bloodied her fingers, Agariste could read her expression. It was bitter as the wind or the sea-cold.

'Traitors,' the woman called, pointing at the man's wife and children.

'No! We said nothing,' the other woman replied.

She dragged her children close, bowing her head over them. Agariste saw many of the women had collected their own rocks, red or brown in the wet. Rain fell still, dripping in silver lines under the long roof. Her breath seemed to catch in her throat. She couldn't breathe, couldn't bear what she was seeing.

The women attacked, falling on the little family, smothering screams behind robes and cowls and dresses, arms rising and falling. The rest of the crowd fell silent in stunned grief. Hands touched mouths, but they did not look away. Those who had called in support of the blacksmith edged apart from anyone who might have heard, keeping their heads down.

When it was over, the women stood back. Little bodies lay sprawled and broken, dusty, surprisingly so, as if they had been tumbled over and over, rolled in blood and earth. The mother and her children were all dead; that was clear from the first glimpse. They stared blankly at the grass roof, lives hammered out into the ground.

A space grew around them as the women slipped into the crowd, dropping red stones as they went, standing under streams of rain to wash the blood off their hands. The silence was a living thing under the thundering rain.

Agariste found herself weeping softly, keening like a child. She held Eleni very close, though she knew the woman had held her own daughter just as tightly. It was a mindless comfort, but she could not speak or think, not then. Pericles stood nearby with his mouth open and his eyes wide. Agariste wished she had managed to turn his head from what he had witnessed, but it was too late for that.

She heard the approach of marching hoplites in the clash of bronze, a sound she knew well from Xanthippus when he trained. Themistocles had brought a dozen armed men, but it was the sight of Xanthippus that wrenched sobs to the surface and had her reaching for her husband. Agariste could not say a word as she clung to him and buried her head in the folds of his cloak.

'Who killed them?' she heard Themistocles demand of the crowd.

No one answered. They had shown what they thought of traitors and that was the end of it. Agariste just wanted to go home, but she knew it wasn't there any longer. Rain struggled against fire in Athens. Perhaps it would put the flames out.

War pushed them all too far, she knew. It stole away all the rules and laws her own uncle had helped create. Or revealed them for what they were, perhaps. Even a city like Athens was an artificial thing, fragile as a pot, where men and women pretended there were no wolves and that justice was real. She could not speak. She clung to Xanthippus and he wrapped his arms around her. After a while, her daughter Eleni nuzzled up under an arm and she too was held, safe.

Agariste sensed Themistocles coming closer when Xanthippus raised his head from where he had bowed, pressing his lips to her hair. She stood apart from her husband then, knowing the kohl had run around her eyes and that she was puffy-faced and wild-looking. She smoothed her dress with her hands, wiping tears in quick, rough gestures as Themistocles stopped before her. His hand fluttered at his side, his usual manner dark at what he had seen.

'It's not their fault,' Themistocles murmured. 'They are afraid and angry, but the fault lies with those who forced us out, who brought war to us. These crimes lie at the feet of Persians, with all the drowned men.'

He spoke to her husband, Agariste saw, though his sweeping gaze took in both her sons. Aristides too had come, wearing a ragged robe. He bowed to her and offered a greeting, as if they met in the Agora on a market day. Yet he was strained and pale, she saw.

Around Agariste, with Xanthippus as the central point, a quorum of the council gathered. It was just a few dozen, but they were grim with purpose. Between them, the senior men represented authority in Athens.

While the rain dripped and drummed on the roof, Themistocles addressed them, his voice lower than usual.

'When the Persians go back to their winter camp, I'll send word to Sparta. An ultimatum. At the same time, Xanthippus, I want you to take the fleet out. Find and sink every Persian ship they still have, wherever they have found refuge. Raid their ports, make them pay at home. Perhaps you can raise enough of a fire there to call their soldiers back.'

Agariste looked up at her husband, seeing only certainty in him as he nodded. Her heart sank. Of course he would be part of it. She had married him for his strength, after all. She saw Pericles and Ariphron were at his shoulder. In that moment, she knew they had been taken from her, that they would be going with him. She thought for an instant that she might be sick. Themistocles was speaking once more, his voice low and clipped.

'For the rest, we follow through. Stay the path. We'll bring Sparta out, even if we have to make an enemy of them.'

Pausanias stood on the acropolis of Sparta, shining with health and sweat. Though he and Tisamenus stood panting at the highest point of the hill, they were surrounded by a great bowl of mountains, peak upon peak, stretching back to infinity, with the spires of Taygetos and Parnon standing above all.

In that early-morning silence, they might have been the only ones alive in the world. The two men had run up the hill, racing one another in that strange lightness of spirit that came with exertion, that could banish all other darknesses. It did not last, but seeped away as they breathed deeply. Though the dawn air was cold, the days were lengthening once more, the darkest months behind. At that height above the city of Sparta, Tisamenus thought he could smell cooking fires, but also green growth, phrygana shrubs and sage, the first hints of spring in the air. The mountains looked bare at such a distance. Yet he knew they teemed with life – with hares, wolves, bears, boars and even lions. There would be frosts to come still, of course – and rains to batter the dust down and stain every wall in Sparta with spattered mud. Yet spring would come. Of all things, that was certain. Darkness ended; the sun always rose again.

'I saw your nephew talking to the ephors and King Leotychides,' Tisamenus said. 'He looked well, a fine young man.'

Pausanias nodded, though his mouth quirked in a way Tisamenus knew well, as if he recalled a bitter taste.

He knew Pausanias was troubled, that he feared the

decision he had been called on to make. Yet he knew too that his friend had all the courage he needed. His uncle had been the battle king of Sparta before he'd marched out to stop the Persian host with just his personal guard and a few thousand lesser men. That act still resonated through the city and its people. A single Spartan had survived his wounds, along with all the rest Leonidas had sent away before the end. The account of the king's stand in the pass at Thermopylae was already a legend, his death a demonstration of Spartan will. Tisamenus shook his head in awe as a memory drifted to him. When the Persian king had demanded the Spartans surrender their weapons, Leonidas had sent only two words in reply: 'Molon labe' – 'come and take them'.

Tisamenus looked at Pausanias, seeing his worry in the shadowed gaze across the distant mountains. His friend bore a weight of responsibility great enough to crush a weaker man. The regent's father had died just a week before, slipping away with one great shout of pain in his sleep, his work done. The wall across the isthmus was long finished, of course, testament to him. Pausanias' father had been the living embodiment of Spartan obedience and quiet strength. He had cast a long shadow over his son.

The funeral of Cleombrotus had been a simple thing, the grave marked with just his name. Pausanias had maintained his dignity, as was expected. Though Tisamenus had a memory of waking to the sounds of weeping, later that night, he had not mentioned it. There were lines their friendship did not cross. Even there, alone and in the morning silence, he would not ask how it felt to be the son of a great man, nephew to a great king.

Pausanias had not answered him, he realised. He was considering a different opening when the Spartan suddenly broke his silence.

*Conn Iggulden*

'Pleistarchus is a fine young man,' Pausanias said. His voice was gentle, almost a breath. 'I sometimes wish he had been born a year earlier. He would not need me then. *He* would be the one to lead us all in war.'

No answer was called for, but Tisamenus replied even so. He was not Spartan, after all. He preferred talk to silence.

'The ephors will never let a son of Leonidas leave Sparta, not before he is counted as a man and has fathered a son. That is what you said. I'm afraid the decision is yours alone, my friend. Is it truly such a burden?'

Pausanias glanced at him, before looking back.

'No. I am glad of it. It frightens me, Tisamenus, how this has been dropped into my lap! A year ago, Sparta had a battle king in Leonidas, as great as any we have known. My father was in good health and I was destined for a life of service, twenty-one to sixty – as a soldier, or perhaps in command of ships. The sea called me, calls me still. Yet in just a season, the lion is dead, my father is dead – and a Persian army sits on our land and mocks us. And who will make the decision? It falls to me! I am filled with wonder, Tisamenus . . . but I am also afraid. This is what I wanted, when I asked you to remain at my side. You will win five great contests – five battles! That was what you were told. When I heard that, I knew they could be my victories. I prayed to Apollo to make it so, Tisamenus.'

Pausanias shook his head, as if he had been stung or some muscle had cramped.

'And now I wonder if my pride will bring us all to destruction. The history of Sparta is long, Tisamenus. We have lived in this valley for more than three hundred years and we have never seen an enemy. Not here. Will I be the one to end that history? What if I bring the army out . . . ?'

He did not breathe aloud the possibility that they might

lose. The gods listened to boasting, all men knew that. It was not wise to speak the worst fears, or even grand dreams that might be twisted into some darker shape. For all they knew, the Fates and Apollo had worked through Pausanias to bring about this exact moment of indecision. Tisamenus could not decide for him. They stood in the crucible of the mountains, with the iron growing red.

'If I refuse the Athenians, will Sparta survive? Will they truly give their ships over to Persia?'

'I cannot say,' Tisamenus murmured.

Pausanias made a sharp gesture, cutting the air with his hand held like a blade.

'They *swore* they would not, but then the Persians returned and burned Athens a second time! Can you imagine? I think I understand their fury well enough! Yet if it drives the Athenians to make peace, we will see their ships landing Persians on our coast in spring. We cannot stand against them both, so what . . . must we be driven to war, like cattle? There are so many Persians, Tisamenus!' The regent looked around him to be certain they were still alone. 'What if we go out . . . and still, all I can do is not enough?'

Tisamenus blinked. His friend was asking for advice, perhaps for the first time. He replied without hesitation, his voice strengthening with every word.

'Sparta has no walls, my friend. You told me that. Your father . . . believed there was a reason to build one, across the isthmus. Perhaps he was right, but in the spring . . . you have said it. You cannot survive an alliance of Athens and Persia. I think . . .'

'I must risk it all,' Pausanias finished before Tisamenus could say it. 'I must take every Spartiate warrior, every peri-oikos who lives around, and march them to war. To avoid a desolation in our absence, I must take every helot in Sparta

*Conn Iggulden*

with us. For the first time in our history, I must march every able man to war against a host so great I do not see how we can possibly win.' His voice fell to a whisper. 'Do you see? I must leave the ephors and the women and children and know there is every chance we will not come back. And I *still* have to do it. I swear, Tisamenus. It is too much.'

'You will not stand alone,' Tisamenus said. 'You will have the hoplites of Athens and Plataea and all the other states. You will see me at your shoulder – and you will give me the victory you denied me at the pentathlon! The triumph I was promised at Delphi! Think of that, Spartan! I am owed.'

Pausanias clapped him on the shoulder, chuckling.

'I will not let you down,' he said, growing serious once more. 'By the gods, I pray I will not let anyone down.'

'Is it settled, then? You have decided?' Tisamenus said.

There was a moment of stillness, but then Pausanias smiled and nodded his head.

'I feel a weight lift from my shoulders, soothsayer.'

'I was never a soothsayer, Pausanias, you know that. Just a man promised five victories by the oracle at Delphi. Just that.'

'It is enough,' Pausanias said.

He was no longer breathing hard and he began to walk back down the hill to the city waiting below. After a while, both men broke into a run, faster and faster, skidding on the stones and risking their necks.

## 19

Aristides stood on a low wall, watching a Spartan army approach Athens. It was hard not to feel a thrill of fear at the sight of those red cloaks in the distance. Few men had ever seen so many Spartiate warriors in one place. It seemed Pausanias had kept his word, his father's oath. The oath of Leonidas, reaching out to them, long past his own death.

Themistocles scrambled up beside him, panting slightly and shading his gaze against the pale afternoon sun. The morning had been warm and dry, the sky the blue of childhood memory. Two months had passed since they'd seen Athens burned a second time. The Assembly had sent a formal ultimatum then, to Sparta. Hard choices had to be made in war – what was true one day might not be true the next. Still, both men were pleased they had not been forced to leave their honour on the pyre of Athens. Word had come at last from Pausanias as regent – that year, battle king of Sparta. It had been accepted by his co-ruler, King Leotychides. No one had expected Leotychides to bring the small group of Spartan ships down the coast, joining them to the allied fleet. Of course, Leotychides had insisted on Xanthippus acknowledging him in command. Themistocles still smiled when he recalled his own struggle with the Spartans in that regard. Xanthippus had hesitated for about as long as a heartbeat before accepting vital crews to add to his forces.

From what Aristides could see, the Spartan kings had to have left only women and children at home. None of the archons of Athens had even been certain Sparta could put so many in the field. He swallowed, a little nervously. No Spartan ever built a wall, he reminded himself, or shaped a pot, or cut wood for the fire. Their helots did every bit of manual labour in Sparta. All the while, Spartiates trained, in skill and fitness, for all the hours of light, from the age of seven to the age of sixty, when they finally laid down their weapons. They had no equal in Greece, Aristides was certain. War was their calling, their single purpose. He did not know if it would be enough.

The wall on which he and Themistocles stood was still little more than a foundation running around Athens. Yet its creation had employed a thousand masons and their teams since the Persians had gone. Those men had been given silver taken from the earth at Laurium, ore refined to pure metal, then cut, shaped and stamped as coins, with images of Athena and Heracles. They spent them in the markets of the city, on whatever scraps came in. Stone by stone, they rebuilt.

Fishing boats went out each morning to feed the people, then again all night, with lamps hanging over the sides to attract curious squid. There were even six merchant ships by then, refitted from damaged galleys. Holds had been created where oarsmen once sat, ready to be filled. That vital little group ran as far south as Crete across the Aegean, bringing meat, wood, tools, vital oil and blessed wine back to the mother city. It gave men like Aristides hope they could eventually restore their fortunes, if they were just left alone. His people endured. If a great storm passed overhead, they came out into the damp new day and sharpened their tools. If there were bodies, they buried the dead and mourned, but they went on. They always had, with just a little more pride than most. In this year, named for Xanthippus as eponymous archon, all they had to do was turn back a Persian host the like of which they had never known.

'They come,' Themistocles said.

Aristides sighed.

'Yes, I see.'

Themistocles glowered at him.

'You would deny me even simple pleasures, Aristides? I am filled with joy. We did it – we brought them out.'

'I hear "we" but I think you mean "I",' Aristides said with a twist of his mouth that was not quite humour. He was still watching the Spartans approach, a sight to inspire dread, fear and awe in roughly equal parts.

Themistocles snorted.

'I do not deny my part in saving the city, Aristides. How could I? Nor do I deny yours. It's just that . . . I did more. If you find a statue to me on your return, don't look surprised. Somewhere on the Acropolis, perhaps. In bronze, or white marble. Perhaps you will find one to you as well. At my feet. Looking up in adoration.'

Aristides glanced over. They had never been friends. In fact, they had detested one another for more years than he could remember. He was beginning to realise, however, that he rather liked the man he disliked so much. Themistocles never missed a chance to needle and annoy him, but they stood on the same side and loved the same things. Perhaps that was all that mattered.

'Are you sure you would not prefer to take our hoplites out?' Aristides said. 'I think I could run the city in your absence. If you wanted.'

Themistocles shook his head.

'The people need someone to love, Aristides. To inspire them, you know. They see me as a father to them. More, I know all the mine crews and the coin setters. There is no time now to introduce you to those.'

Aristides looked at the man he had watched over thirty

years or so, going from a young lion of Athens to one with streaks of silver in the mane. No, he still detested him.

As well as a mocking manner that seemed designed to infuriate a serious man, it was irritating that Themistocles had retained so much of his hair. He still looked strong and vital, while Aristides had gone bald and shaved close what little he had left. He had not thought it would matter, indeed felt a little ashamed of himself, but it did. No man was completely free of vanity, it seemed, not even him. Aristides felt the weight of years, especially when he woke up in the mornings and everything hurt for the first few steps. The prospect of marching to war alongside young Spartans was a cruel one. He set his jaw, feeling the sinews of his neck stand out against the skin. He would do what he had to, no matter the cost. He suspected Themistocles felt the same way, but spent at least as much energy making it look easy. Or perhaps some things truly were easy for him. Aristides saw life as a bitter struggle, and all the more valuable for it. Themistocles saw it . . . He shook his head. Athena alone knew how Themistocles saw it.

Both of them looked over as eight thousand Athenian hoplites marched out of the city, halting on the plain to the west. They gleamed gold in the sun, the light reflecting from wide shields, helmets, spears and greaves. Many were in the flower of their youth and strength. Others had stood at Marathon, eleven years before.

Aristides looked over them in pride. The Assembly had elected him their polemarch. On any other field, in any other year, his eight thousand would have been a fearsome enemy, the envy or terror of all who saw them. That day, though, the hoplites of Athens shaded their eyes to watch Spartans marching, red cloaks whipping back and forth, drawing closer with every step. The Spartans did not carry their shields before them, not while they marched to meet an ally. Those shone on the wings of their ranks, borne by their helot slaves. Aristides could hardly believe the numbers of those.

'In truth, I do not envy you, Themistocles,' Aristides said. 'Run your mines and your coin shops. I'll march with these.'

'I think you do envy me, though,' Themistocles said. 'But who can blame you?'

Aristides ignored him. The Spartan army seemed to grow with every pace, a wide and wider line. For a man who had known battlefields, it was hard not to feel his heart race. It was all very well saying they were there as allies, but just standing while a dust cloud swelled and red-cloaked lines marched at him was enough to make the hair prickle on the back of his neck. He felt his breath come faster, like an old hound hearing a hunting horn.

'I can hardly imagine a force to beat these men,' Aristides said. 'But if I do not return . . .'

'You will,' Themistocles said. 'Who else would want you?'

For the first time, Aristides understood that Themistocles was as nervous as he was, as worried for the future. His bitter humour covered it well. It eased Aristides' spirits to know he was not the only one.

'I meant . . . I still have some land and property, but no heirs. I would like it to be auctioned off, the money to go to playwrights. If the city survives, of course.'

'I didn't know you enjoyed such things,' Themistocles replied.

Aristides shrugged.

'When I feed the poor, they grow hungry again. A good play, though, is a story for the ages. Aeschylus is one I would sponsor. He understands tragedy – and he was with us at Marathon. His brother died there. Trierarchia, Themistocles. It is a noble idea. Ships and plays for the city. Our duty.'

*Conn Iggulden*

'If the city survives,' Themistocles said.

They held one another's gaze then for just a moment.

'Yes,' Aristides said. 'If she survives. We have held nothing back, Themistocles. Nothing. This is the season that decides our fates. I thought it was Marathon, or Salamis, but no. It is this spring.'

'Good luck, then, brother,' Themistocles said.

Aristides blinked, then nodded, taking the hand offered in a brief, dry clasp. Aristides gathered up helmet and spear then, the tools of war resting on the ground by his feet. A slave would carry his sword and shield. He stepped down with just a glance back, heading out to stand with the hoplites.

Xanthippus did his best to conceal his pride as his sons came on board. His daughter Eleni would remain with her mother, rebuilding the estate outside Athens. It seemed wrong just to let that once great house sag into its ashes, waiting on the turn of seasons and some hope of victory. More, the household slaves needed work, or they would surely turn to petty vice and idle spite. The freed slave Manias had to earn his pay, now that he had taken on the role of foreman. Xanthippus knew he would either return to an estate remade, or a wasteland. *If* he returned, he reminded himself quickly. The gods punished pride.

The fleet waiting for him in the strait of Salamis was proof of their intent. Only fishing boats and a few merchant vessels would remain to feed those left behind. Every fighting warship of Greece afloat had come to anchor by Athens. They were not as many as they had been at Salamis, but they were all he had. He had kept no reserve, because in that year there was only one enemy. They would resist. That was what had been agreed between Athens and Sparta and all the rest.

Though Thebes and Macedon and dozens of small states had thrown their lot in with Persia, those who had not would march and stand. It was a single throw of the dice for all they were, all they might ever be.

Xanthippus frowned, looking over the busy port. There were crowds shoving and swirling there, women and children braving the roads to watch their men go out. He could see fear in their faces as they strained and peered. He did not feel it himself. No, he felt exultation. This was right. As Themistocles said, no one keeps a reserve in a fight with a bear. It was all or nothing, for a future as free men or slaves.

The galley rocked gently, though she was tied up on the dock. Xanthippus greeted his two sons formally, taking them by the hand and shoulder, turning them to introduce his crew. His trierarch was Ereius, a veteran of Salamis and one he trusted. The keleustes too came up from his post, standing to attention to greet Pericles and Ariphron. The lads took his big hand awkwardly, though Pericles flashed a grin out of sheer pleasure.

They already knew their father's friend, Epikleos, who would command the force of hoplites on board. Epikleos had been present at both Marathon and Salamis, as well as being the one who had galloped to warn the estate in the invasion. They knew their father trusted him. In his own way, he was a friend to the entire family. Xanthippus watched as Epikleos laughed with the two young men. There were lines on his face that had not been there before the Persians.

Xanthippus found himself rubbing his own cheeks. He was thin and tanned, his skin like leather from so long aboard ship. To be a strategos at sea was a constant grind of labour and orders, but he had discovered he loved it. He enjoyed the routines and rituals, even the privations of poor food and limited water. Such things suited him. Life at sea was hard, but he understood it – and every passing day honed the fleet like a spear blade.

To have his sons on board felt like an indulgence of his authority. As a result, he kept his expression stern for the men, almost thunderous. No other rower or hoplite had his sons alongside him. It would not do to show the private joy he felt.

Xanthippus stood alone at the prow as Pericles and Ariphron were introduced to the free rowers of Athens. Ninety men to a side, they were all family men, giving their labour for the city and the households they loved. Xanthippus had warned Pericles the night before to treat them with respect, but he had no fears on that score. His sons admired strength and endurance, as he had taught them.

'I wonder, Xan, if you will burst with pride,' Epikleos murmured at his side.

Xanthippus deflated, breathing out. He had not known how he looked. Epikleos chuckled.

'Oh, don't worry. The men love you for it. Or would you have them see only the cold commander of the fleet? I believe you would!'

Xanthippus grimaced at that.

'No longer. The Spartan Leotychides is navarch.'

'Of course he is . . .' Epikleos said with a grin. 'Right up to the moment you and he disagree. This is an Athenian fleet, Xan. You have said so many times.'

Xanthippus chose not to answer and only shook his head, ending the subject. He did not think there could be spies in that place. His crew had fought at his side at Salamis and they would never whisper his secrets. They were quite likely to repeat something he said as a boast, however. That sort of thing could wing its way around the fleet in just a day or two, even reaching Spartan ears.

Pericles and Ariphron came up from the hold, making fairly hard going of it, while the keleustes swung up like a Barbary ape. They would learn, Xanthippus thought, a thousand things. Ariphron was a little stiff in his manner, while Pericles looked around him with a sort of delighted expression that made Xanthippus want to check the wine in the hold was secured. At almost seventeen, the boy could have been left with his mother and sister, but he had played his father like a harp. Xanthippus had refused his initial request to accompany Ariphron, then watched as Pericles took the news with perfect dignity and restraint, his grief and loss barely visible. His father had held out for two days, then allowed Agariste to persuade him. The result had irritated Ariphron, who thought it unnecessary, but it meant Xanthippus could share his pleasure with both of them — in the sea, the ship and the crew. He felt drunk almost, on salt air and the glitter of the waves.

He knew dangers lay ahead, but he had trained the fleet in the tactics and signals of war. They had learned to ram, sink and burn well enough. Now they would be sharks, gliding out after Persian ships. It was good to hunt; he was eager for it to begin and sensed the same in the other commanders whenever they met. From captains of Corinth and Megara to the Spartan king himself, they were all Greeks that year. Xanthippus sensed a brotherhood that might even survive the war. They wanted to answer the Persians who had slaughtered and burned and raped their people. Plataea had been sacked, Xanthippus had heard, the valiant little city stripped and burned as the Persians marched through. Its people had run for the hills. Some of them had come to stand with Aristides outside Athens, as they had at Marathon. It was an old alliance, but it was based on one language and the gods. That year, they were one people.

*Conn Iggulden*

Xanthippus recalled the family farm he had passed on his way to Sparta. Cimon, Relas and Onesimos were with him in that very fleet, perhaps recalling the graves they had dug, the dusty earth they had shovelled over pale faces. It was right to hunt the ones who had brought about such things. There was no mercy in Xanthippus. He looked out at ships all around and felt his heart grow light.

The sea was vast, but he knew the Persian fleet would have left a mark wherever they went, wherever they had gathered food or stores. Some ships had gone home with their king, of course. Others would have scattered to the four winds. Yet there had been sightings reported for months, whispers and rumours passed from fishing boat to merchant. Xanthippus knew they were out there still. He hoped they kept watch and were afraid, those Persian captains. They had come for slaughter, after all. There was more work to be done, more blood to be spilt, before he could know peace. Wherever they had found to anchor, rest and repair, Xanthippus would be sailing behind, closer every day. After all, he sailed a Greek sea, not a Persian one.

Ropes were unwound from iron stanchions set into the quayside. Oars rumbled out below, pushing the prow away so that the ship swung. Each man below tested his position for comfort, easing pads of cloth into place, or even rubbing a stone against some new splinter that might gouge their side. There were not many of those. The ship had been sanded and oiled from end to end over weeks of preparation. The small hold in the stern was filled with water casks, beans, salt, dried meat and grain sacks, even fresh fruit that had to be eaten quickly before it perished.

Xanthippus watched the great eye of the prow turn to the open sea. The oarsmen beneath his feet dipped and eased back, one slow stroke, then held the blades straight out. The helmsmen kept the ship in a gentle turn as they came side-on to the port.

On deck, twenty hoplites lined up in full armour. They brought a brazier with them and waited in silence as flame was touched to shavings of cedar. Pale smoke rose. Xanthippus stood with his sons and Epikleos, serious and devout.

On the quayside, priests came through the crowds, bringing a sacrifice for good fortune and success. Xanthippus watched as a black bull was brought forth, tugged on ropes by a dozen sweating labourers. The animal dragged two or three of them at a time as they struggled against its appalling strength. The crowd swayed back from it, fearing it would run mad and trample them.

The priests were experienced men and approached it without obvious fear, though the bull tossed its great head and snorted. Some of them poured water from a heavy jug over its head, while others scattered trails of barley seeds. The bull jerked back from the rattling sound, its eyes wide.

The chief priest cut its throat in that moment, making a single gash with a knife so sharp the bull seemed not even to feel it. Blood poured onto the docks and the animal stood still, lowing mournfully, visibly confused as they chanted and sang. The voices of the crowd rose in a great swell. They sang for Athena, whose city they loved. The verses of that went on longer than the chief priest wished, so that he held his hands high for quiet. He devoted the sacrifice to Athena, then Poseidon for gentle seas, Ares, the god of war, as well as Apollo for the blessed light. A long list of heroes were asked for their blessing, including Heracles, Odysseus and Theseus as seafarers. All three had travelled far across that very ocean, seeking adventures or vengeance, or just looking for a way home.

The bull staggered suddenly and dropped to its knees, still

very much alive. Some of the blood was collected and thrown onto a charcoal brazier to spit and sizzle, carried to the gods on clouds of steam. On board the Athenian flagship, twenty paces offshore, Xanthippus made his own personal vows and prayers. He prayed aloud for Aristides to be victorious, for Themistocles to show wisdom and restraint in running the city. He prayed for one more hour of strength than his enemies. His sons lowered their heads and did the same.

When the priests on the quays raised their hands to signal the sacrifice was at an end, Xanthippus went right to the deck's edge, dropping to one knee. They bowed their heads in return, and in that moment, he was free. Free to hunt.

# 20

As lamps were lit across the camp, Aristides drank cold water, washing the dust of a long march from his throat. The first day had been a little chaotic in places. He had volunteered his men to patrol and keep guard in shifts that night, just to be sure the job was done and done well. He also had scouts out far, competing with a group of Spartan boys and some men of Potidaea from the far north – it was hard to surprise a coalition army. There would be a great deal of confusion and duplication as they learned the tasks ahead. Yet it kept the men busy and he trusted no one as much as his own people, not then.

As they camped that first night, the forces still coming in were practically strangers, despite the common enemy. Different factions sat well apart, or in groups formed from those who knew each other well. Aristides had seen soldiers of Corinth camped alongside those of Sparta and Sicyon, more comfortable with peoples of the Peloponnese. In a similar way, Plataea and Megara sat near the hoplites of Athens. Thebes was the great absence among them. Men from Troezen or the island of Aegina would spit when the name came up. In that year, they declared a special hatred for those who had taken gold in exchange for honour, to serve a Persian king. It had not mattered so much when Persia was a distant empire. The invasion had changed what they would tolerate from their own.

After a long day spent marching north, it was perhaps not too bad a showing, Aristides thought. He was pleased

*Conn Iggulden*

Pausanias had summoned the senior officers and strategoi to drink and eat in his own tent. There was no question who led them, even if Pausanias had not demanded an oath from every senior man. This was not the fleet, where Athens held the balance of power and, when it mattered, every captain acted alone. Sparta had brought ten thousand of its best – and over thirty thousand helots. They were by far the greatest force present. They knew that well enough.

Aristides sighed and rubbed his eyes, feeling weary. He had marched all day alongside younger men. It had not been too hard, but he knew the next day would be worse, when he woke aching. Fighting would be an entirely different challenge again. He looked around him, seeing strained conversation and drooping shoulders. They needed to know one another, to trust those on their own side. In such a disparate group, that would be its own challenge. To his surprise, he found himself wishing Themistocles were there. The man's irrepressible brand of optimism was valuable, for all Aristides found it irritating.

Aristides watched Pausanias laughing at something one of the Corinthians said. They had all brought their own supplies, so that the table groaned under as odd an assortment of dishes as he had ever seen. Aristides saw the Spartans only picked at the food, making it harder for the men around them to fill their creaking stomachs as they wished.

He found himself fascinated by the Spartan forces. They shared nothing of their training and rituals with the rest of the world, as a matter of policy. Those who heard their orders on the field of battle tended to be killed before they could write down those observations. Yet when one like Aristides marched alongside, even for just a day, it was hard not to pick up a few things. Aristides thought he had learned at least as much as anyone in Athens knew. He was certain by then that they organised around units of just thirty-six, eighteen pairs of men, commanded by one officer. He had heard the word 'enomotarch', but was not yet sure if it matched the role. Those small groups fascinated him. He had begun to take note of matching shield bosses, then to count patches on the red cloaks. Once he had learned to look for them, they were suddenly always there. Those tight groups seemed to act almost independently, eating and repairing kit as a group. He felt privileged to see them. The Spartans were masters of war, after all. He might have felt the same in the presence of a great playwright or potter.

He had estimated the number of helots as well, a force that far outnumbered their Spartan masters. Aristides remembered the advice he had given to Tisamenus – to bring them all out with the army rather than leave them behind. He assumed it had been followed. Surely there could not be others still in Sparta! Some of the helots carried shields for the warriors; others, just tools, food, cloaks, anything that might be useful. They loped along behind their masters, fit as deer. Aristides hoped they had courage as well, that they would not break and run when they were asked to attack. The helots would not be allowed to stand apart when battle came, he was certain of that.

It was all a far cry from the Athenian phalanx, the terrible push from behind that crammed them all in and forced them to advance, advance, advance. Aristides shuddered at a memory of Marathon, feeling the hairs on his neck and forearms stand up. Or was it just the night's cold. He told himself it was.

Each of the Hellene groups had different structures and names for their officers. Yet they all carried shield and spear. Even in that, the Athenian dory was the longest. Aristides knew exactly how Themistocles would have commented on that. At times, it surprised Aristides to miss the vulgar old thug.

Around him, Pausanias was ordering cups refilled for a toast. Aristides thought his first impression was still right. Pausanias may have had an eyebrow permanently raised, as if the world could only disappoint him. Yet, Aristides had seen moments of worry in the Spartan. Pausanias had never expected to be regent, especially following one like Leonidas. The death of the battle king had left a hole in their ranks, without a doubt. There were times when Aristides wondered how Pausanias possibly thought he could fill it.

He watched Pausanias rise to his feet, Tisamenus standing with him to face the rest of the strategoi and officers at that rough table on dusty ground. Pausanias kept his 'soothsayer' at his side at all times, like a talisman. Aristides did not mind that. If the man had been promised five victories by Apollo's priestess at Delphi, he might bring them all at least one. It had been years since he had competed in the Olympic pentathlon. He was surely due.

'Gentlemen, officers, Spartans, Hellenes,' Pausanias declaimed, addressing them all. He had a faint flush, Aristides saw, perhaps from the wine. 'Tomorrow we will cross the mountains to the north. I do not know yet if Mardonius has moved his camp, or if he will still be waiting for us there. I have no doubt he will have chosen a place that favours his cavalry. Beyond the personal mounts some of you have brought, along with the ponies used by our scouts, we have no real answer to those. It is my intention to try and avoid open ground where they can be used to sting us with spear, sling-shot and arrow.'

Aristides had expected a simple toast to good fortune. The silence in the room was tense as every man there realised they were hearing battle orders. Pausanias seemed relaxed and confident as he spoke, but the mood had chilled.

'I sent scouts to watch their camp over the winter,' Pausanias went on. 'We have an idea of their numbers at around two hundred thousand, perhaps a little more. Yes, gentlemen, it is a host. We have decided to stand against them even so.'

The Spartan looked around steadily until the sudden whispering died away. Aristides found himself suppressing a smile. He'd thought of Pausanias as an arrogant young man, some way out of his depth. It seemed he could hold the attention of a room, however. If the regent knew the field of war as well, perhaps their situation was not as bleak as it seemed.

Pausanias let his gaze settle on Aristides, holding there for a moment. A frown touched his unlined brow.

'I need our most disciplined phalanx formations on both wings. Sparta will hold the right flank, with the Tegeans and the contingent from Thespiae.'

He raised his cup in acknowledgement of those and they returned the gesture. Pausanias nodded, looking over the rest of the men in that place.

'Corinth and the forces of Arcadia will be our centre,' he said. 'There will be some thirty thousand in formation there, when we include Chalcidians, Leucadians, Eretrians . . .'

He named each group with an ease that pleased and surprised Aristides. He could see Tisamenus was murmuring names, no doubt supplying those Pausanias might have missed, but still, it was an impressive feat. Remembering a man's name could secure his loyalty, Aristides already knew that. He supposed it was much the same with cities. Certainly, he saw men smile as their homes were spoken aloud by the Spartan. They had come to save themselves, of course, but also the peoples around them. To his surprise, Aristides felt a surge of emotion that closed his throat and made his eyes prickle. The wine was clearly stronger than he had realised.

*Conn Iggulden*

'On the left,' Pausanias went on, 'Athens will hold the wing, with Megara and Plataea. They will not be turned, I know that. The ruins of Plataea will be visible tomorrow, gentlemen, as we cross the range of Cithaeron through the high passes. The price of Persia in our land will be clear to all of us, if it was not before. We will stand, we seventy thousand, against three times as many. We will face men of Macedon and of Thebes, alongside Persian, Mede and Indian. Yet I do not fear them, this enemy. They have cavalry we lack and land that suits them, but it is not their land. It is ours. Gentlemen, I would not be anywhere else this evening. Nor would I choose any others to stand with me, at my side. We will destroy this enemy. The gods themselves have promised five victories to my soothsayer, Tisamenus. This battle, close by the ruined city of Plataea, will be the first.'

Pausanias raised his cup again and they all rose stiffly, at first in awed silence. Aristides could not resist glancing around the room, looking for weakness or fear. He saw only determination. Pausanias too was looking across them. Aristides met his gaze and dipped his head in acknowledgement. He saw the regent nod in return.

It was the simplest of things to stand there. They had chosen to. Some of those present would surely be killed, perhaps even all of them. Yet they had come out to face a vast host. Aristides felt his eyes sting. The strength of feeling surprised him.

'There is only one toast before war, gentlemen,' Pausanias said. 'To home.'

'To home,' they echoed as one, and drank.

Xanthippus watched as Pericles swung from a rope tied to a single yard across the mast. The boy was not yet as agile as some of the more experienced crew, but he was learning fast.

Ariphron seemed happier on the deck, though when Pericles needled him, he had shown his younger brother what months more sword practice actually meant. Their sparring had drawn a crowd of cheering hoplites. Pericles had taken being beaten well enough, until Ariphron rapped him across the knuckles with the flat of his blade and made him drop his sword. Ariphron claimed it then as a spoil of war and refused to give it back. Xanthippus had heard the details from Epikleos, but as neither son had asked him to rule on their behalf, he had done nothing.

The fleet led by King Leotychides of Sparta was experienced enough to avoid open sea. No one ever crossed the deep waters of the Aegean, where a storm could spring from nowhere. Instead, like the Argonauts or Odysseus, they rowed and sailed island to island, taking known routes where each destination could be sighted either from on board, or from a mountain climbed on land. Their progress was slow and steady, east from Athens, along the merchant path between the islands of Syros and Tenos, with Mykonos in the distance. Every time they saw lights on shore, or fishing boats busy with their catch, they stopped and paid for news of Persian galleys. For three days, there had just been shrugs and shaking of heads. None of the local people wanted anything to do with hoplites or warships of any kind. Their lives went on, with war as a distant thing. Some of them clearly thought it would bring bad luck even to talk of it. They backed away, refusing to speak to the sailors and officers of the fleet.

Xanthippus watched a fishing boat approach, spotting it as something unusual while it was still some way off. Most small boats veered away whenever they caught sight of oared warships. This one made straight for them. He frowned, wondering if the captain was drunk or asleep. Yet there seemed to be a figure upright in the stern, his hand on a rudder. The wind was gentle enough that day. The entire fleet benefited from the shelter of Mykonos, where the waters had turned an extraordinary blue, paler than usual over white sand.

Pericles too had seen the little craft coming. He slid down a rope, burning his hands and landing hard on the deck. The boy gestured and Xanthippus raised a hand to show he knew. Epikleos came up from the hold and Ariphron came to stand by his father, his expression severe. It was unusual enough for some of the other ships to put down small boats from their sterns, seeking news.

The fishing boat might have passed them by if Epikleos had not waved him in. The trireme crew threw ropes and tied the little vessel on. A small sail came down in folds of salt-stiff cloth and the man himself came on board. He was white-haired and very dark from sea and sun. Wide of shoulder and barefoot, he wore loose clothing secured by a leather belt and clasp. He looked around in something like satisfaction at the sheer size of the warship, nodding his approval.

'Who is the master of this wondrous vessel?' Xanthippus heard him ask.

Pointing hands directed the man to him and Xanthippus found his hand taken in a callused grip rather like a glove.

'I heard you were offering silver for news of Persians,' the man said without preamble.

Xanthippus nodded, amused. He thought it likely the fellow was willing to say whatever he wanted in return for good Athenian drachms. Xanthippus was not expecting sightings then, not truly. The Persian king had taken part of his fleet home to secure his bridge of ships across the Hellespont. The rest had been scattered far and wide in their defeat at

Salamis. Perhaps a few had made their way back to the empire in the months since, while others still roamed like sharks in that sea, raiding and burning. They were the reason for the fleet that had come hunting them. Yet he had no idea how many there were.

The fisherman smelled of sun, wine and fish. There was a warmth to him that was instantly friendly, though whether he could be trusted or not was hard to say. Persian gold could smother Athenian silver easily enough.

'We'll certainly pay for a true sighting,' Xanthippus said slowly. 'Sixty drachms to a loyal Greek.'

The man peered at him, so that Xanthippus could see one of his eyes had a slight cast to it, a milky sheen deep within.

'Yes? Well, fetch out your coins, kurios,' he said. 'I know where they are.'

# 21

There were Persian scouts in the hills. It was an odd experience for Greeks to be observed as they marched – especially for men of Athens, who knew those mountains well. The range marked the boundary of Attica and the beginning of Boeotia, where the city of Thebes had its temples and markets. More, the high passes led down onto the central plains, where vines and barley grew and horsemen could gallop. It made perfect sense that Mardonius had placed his camp there for the winter, a nest of worms deep in the good flesh.

All through the morning, lone figures had appeared ahead and above them, high on the crags and peaks. Some were on horseback, dark-skinned men in turbans and cloaks, well wrapped against the mountain cold. Others watched from spots where only a boy or a goat could stand, judging their numbers before vanishing back down the paths to report.

The allies reached the high passes while the sun was still low, having set off in the dark that morning. The Spartans led the column, with Pausanias and Tisamenus at the spearpoint. Their own runners were out by then, with horns around their necks to call warning if they found hidden men or a trap. Pausanias followed campaign rules for hostile territory. His helots had brought up the heavy gear. Each of the Spartiates now carried his own shield and spear, with a sword on his hip and the wicked kopis scabbard through a belt. For those behind, their cloaks were a swirling mass of red.

Pausanias saw the whiteness of the pass ahead, where the land dropped away and left only a glimpse of bare sky. He did not know what lay beyond and he felt his heart thump. It was not just his first sole command, but the first without Leonidas to make every major decision. He breathed long and slowly, forcing himself to calm. If he marched the army of Sparta to destruction, he would live for ever in infamy, as the man who had lost a nation. The responsibility lay heavily on him and he half-stumbled as he marched. Tisamenus glanced at him, understanding.

'I have walked a long way, Pausanias,' Tisamenus said. 'Perhaps we should run for a time.'

Pausanias glanced at him. He was trembling, as much in excitement as in nerves. There were ears listening all around, perhaps men who would report idle talk at home. He kept his mouth still. He was the regent of Leonidas' son, Pleistarchus! Before the end of the year, that boy would be declared battle king – and Pausanias . . . would be free. Or dead, but no longer regent, no longer first soldier in Sparta.

He swallowed, shifting his grip on his shield. How odd that his throat seemed stiff and swollen! There had been furious discussions between ephors, he knew. No one had failed to understand the stakes of that campaign. If the council of ephors had ordered Pleistarchus to lead, that would have been the end of it. Yet Spartan laws were iron. Until Pleistarchus reached his eighteenth birthday, he could not command men in war. Until he sired a son, he could not leave Laconia. His bloodline was just too precious.

Pausanias murmured a prayer to Apollo, giving thanks for the boy's discipline. There had been pain there, of course, when the ephors told Pleistarchus their decision. It would certainly have hurt the son of Leonidas, already wounded by the death of his father. Yet he had obeyed – the secret rule of 'peitharchia': total obedience, even unto death.

Tisamenus looked across to him, waiting for the word.

*Conn Iggulden*

Pausanias felt a wild urge to break into a sprint and throttled it down, with Leonidas and his son as inspiration. They would be disciplined, but not slow.

'Double speed,' Pausanias called to the others.

In reply, helmets were shoved down over topknots and ropes of hair. His men looked out from golden bronze, expressionless and cold as the mountains. The ranks behind them surged on immediately, the noise echoing. They clashed shields and spears, ready to attack at the order of Pausanias. He lengthened his gait, drawing in the cool breeze, passing through the shadow of limestone cliffs. Tisamenus kept pace easily. He bore no shield, only a long spear and a grey-blue cloak that flew out behind him. Ten thousand Spartiates and perioikoi moved smoothly to a faster pace, as they did every day in training. They ran without hard breathing, just stretching out, loosening. They would endure, as long as he asked. Pausanias felt his worry fall away. He gave a great shout, that came back from the hills. They came through the high pass, with the glare of the sun beyond.

Far at the rear, Aristides could see only a sudden surge of movement. He too had noted the Persian scouts set to watch them. Yet there had been no call to arms, no horns blown. It seemed the Spartans were just reacting to being hemmed in, opening a gap between themselves and those behind. The Athenian watched the space appear as the Spartans poured over the pass. The way was wide enough there, the land worn away by merchants and shepherds. The plains lay beyond and, perhaps, an ending. Aristides felt the eyes of his officers on him. He sighed and said a prayer to the deities of that high place. Thales of Miletus had written once that the world was full of gods. On such a day, high above the plains, it felt true.

'Match their speed, in formation,' Aristides ordered.

His knees protested, but at least it was in silence. His eight thousand grinned as they doubled the pace, spears high so as not to entangle the legs of those around. The air was still cold. Some of them shivered, but they were eager enough. None of them had ever dreamed of marching with Sparta against an enemy. For all the horror and blood that might lie ahead, they were in fine spirits that day.

The Spartans went through and found a great plain ahead. In the distance, even the host of Persian forces was dwarfed by the scale of the land itself. The entire army under Mardonius was arrayed before their camp. With air as clear as glass, Pausanias halted his panting men. The shine faded from his blood, stealing the lightness in him. He looked back to the shadowy pass, where the sun never reached and the air was always cold. The helots and his allies were still coming through. He gave orders for his Spartans to stand aside on the northern flanks of Mount Cithaeron. The sun was warm on the earth. He knew they were at least a day from the enemy, yet it felt as if he could reach out and crush them between finger and thumb.

Far out on the plain, Pausanias saw dust plumes of scouts running back to report, still far off from their master and the camp. Regiments of horsemen trotted in formation down below, around what looked like a new city built in the wilderness. He knew the Persians would understand he had come out. Pausanias just hoped his force did not seem quite so small when viewed from the plain.

His people were exposed under the sun. Without food or water at that height, they could not remain on the mountainside for long. Yet Pausanias felt his heart beat faster, his frown deepening. If he went down to the plain, the Persians

*Conn Iggulden*

would use the horsemen he did not have. If he waited, his people would be gasping like crows in just a couple of days. Even with the supplies his helots had brought, there would be no living off the land there, not after a winter with every living thing going into the mouths of Persians.

'So . . . shall we go down and cut his head off?' Tisamenus said.

Pausanias found himself chuckling. The suggestion broke through his sense of being overwhelmed and he clapped his hand on the soothsayer's shoulder.

'Mardonius will wait another day. We'll need to find a good place to camp on the mountain, some lower ridge where we won't roll down in our sleep. One thing is certain, they can't climb to meet us. I wish they would! We will decide where and when to bring them to battle. For now, let these Persian bastards wait.'

Tisamenus saw confidence blooming in his friend. For the first time in as long as he could remember, the perpetually raised eyebrow had settled back. It reflected his own confidence in a man who had trained in tactics for his entire life. Leonidas was Pausanias' uncle, after all. Faced with battlefield decisions, the nerves from before had simply vanished.

Pausanias turned to the Spartiate officers. He gave orders for them to tally the stores available to the column, as well as designating helots to seek out any spring or source of water in the hills around. He sent the rest further down the slopes to locate flat parts for them to sleep, wrapped in their cloaks. Finally, he summoned the leaders to attend him as they ate that evening. Order had been restored in his life. He stared down at an implacable enemy, three times the number of his own forces, armed with horsemen and bows and Persian Immortals just itching for a chance to repay their humiliation at Thermopylae. One way or another, fate had taken his hand and turned him towards that plain, near Plataea.

Xanthippus worked the rudder of the little boat while Pericles doused the sail in water from a leather bucket. The sun was hot, the wind no more than a breath. In the perfect stillness, Xanthippus wanted to laugh at the ludicrousness of their position. They were barely eight days out of Athens. They had expected to spend weeks or even months searching the Aegean for sight or sound of Persian ships, taking them in twos or threes, following every rumour and false sighting, though it cost them labour and injury and precious supplies. He frowned at that thought. Of the hundred and sixty ships he had gathered as vengeance on Persian shipping, two had sunk. One had struck an unmarked rock and gone down as if determined to sail right to the seabed. Only six men had been recovered from that. The other had sprung a leak their carpenter could not patch. The ship had gone down slowly enough for the crew to be taken off, though at the end they'd waded across a deck barely on the surface, bringing back ugly memories of Salamis.

Xanthippus had kept a grim countenance in those passing days, though part of him took joy in the simple work. The men rowed, but not to exhaustion. They landed at every island they sighted, asking questions and purchasing whatever supplies they needed. In the evenings, he and his sons dined on board, or joined the Spartan navarch, King Leotychides. To Xanthippus' surprise, he found the Spartan good company, a teller of tales that often ended with Pericles blowing wine back through his nose and having to have his back thumped. If they had not been at war against a terrible enemy, it would have been idyllic, almost embarrassingly so. Xanthippus had filled every hour with signal training and manoeuvres,

*Conn Iggulden*

repeating actions over and over until he was certain the allies would perform well under pressure. That was the entire purpose of such work, so that men kept moving when ships crunched alongside and blood spattered the decks.

In that, the Spartan king had been content to let him lead. Xanthippus had expected the same sort of prickly authority he had known from Eurybiades at Salamis, but it seemed the Spartan civilian king was too certain of himself to feel any insult. As soon as Leotychides had understood how experienced Xanthippus truly was, he stood back and waved him on. It was a joy to encounter someone so used to command they could actually trust another to act for them. In that, the Spartan reminded Xanthippus of Aristides.

If they could catch the Persian fleet at anchor, Xanthippus would pay the fisherman his weight in silver – and it would still be worth it. He could only clench the steering bar in silent hope at that thought. Pericles turned the little sail this way and that, working it almost like another rudder as he sought out wind. The boy was at home on the water, in a way that pleased his father. Competence was all a man asked of his sons; it was a pleasure, almost a wonder, to see it grow, to know he could doze across the thwarts and let his sons guide the little boat.

Pericles looked up from his frowning gaze across the sea, watching for rough patches where some breeze still blew. As they rounded a spit of land, his father saw the boy's face lighten in amazement. As he too looked up, Xanthippus held up a hand to stop him calling out.

'I see them,' Xanthippus murmured. He made himself breathe slowly, while his heart hammered. 'Now, lads, take us back, gentle as you can. I'll put a net down and we'll drag it for a time. Who knows, we might even fetch a few fish back with us.'

The Persians had a measurement they called a 'parasang', some thirty stades or so. The fleet anchored at Samos lay just three or four off parasangs off their bow, as best as Xanthippus could judge. It was perhaps as far as a man might walk in a morning.

Xanthippus had brought his little boat out from the lee of the island of Icaria. He knew Icarus had fallen into that very sea, escaping his prison in a different age. Xanthippus and his sons had sailed that shore all day, following the fisherman's description, keeping another island on their right shoulders, a place Xanthippus thought was Fourni. The sea was sheltered there, the waves gentle, which was a relief in such a little boat.

A great fleet sheltered off Samos, there was no doubt about that. Xanthippus had glimpsed a host of masts, slender as hairs at that distance, too far off to count. It could only be the Persian ships, anchored in safe waters on the island coast, close by the mainland. They thought they were too far from Athens for anyone to seek them out. He wondered if they were afraid to return home after losing at Salamis, or whether they had just sought shelter for the winter, as soon as they'd found a safe harbour. If that last was true, they might be heading out any day. He felt his excitement build.

Pericles put down a net, trawling it through the water. The waters lapped softly, making a gentle sound. It was a perfect moment, with his sons on a boat. Xanthippus felt his patience unravel.

'Oh, pull it up, Peri. There's no one close enough to see us. I want to get back. Turn us about and head west. Whistle me up a breeze, Ariphron! We'll bring the fleet back with us. By Athena, we've found them!'

Pericles heaved folds of wet netting into the little boat. To his pleasure, there was a big fish tangled in it, fighting the strings. Pericles was looking at it in wonder when Ariphron took a wooden bar and smashed at it, scattering blood and scales until the fish was dead.

'Did you have to do that?' Pericles asked his brother.

Ariphron looked at him.

'Yes,' he said.

The setting sun was warm as they headed back to the allied fleet, the news confirmed. Xanthippus clapped both sons on the shoulder, pounding their backs in delight as wind found them, filling the little sail. Their speed increased, the boat skimming across a dark blue sea.

# PART THREE

'On me the tempest falls.'

– Aeschylus, *Prometheus Bound*

# 22

Aristides watched the Persian horsemen. The sun was rising, the day about to begin. In panelled coats, they shone in the pale rose light, milling, laughing, talking to friends. They reminded him of wasps. The evening before, they had raced in at extraordinary speed, launched spears or shot arrows, then vanished in a plume of their own dust. It might have seemed great sport, if they hadn't left Greek bodies in their wake.

His hoplites had to have water, that was just the truth of it. The mountains were dry for a day's march in any direction. Seventy thousand hoplites and half as many helots needed a vast and constant supply – and water was appallingly heavy. It was simply impossible to send men to carry enough for those who waited and guarded the mountain flanks. By the time they made their way back, they too were parched and gasping. For Aristides, it was like trying to fill a bucket with a hole in the bottom. Despite all their efforts, there was never enough.

There was a stream that crossed part of the foothills, not far from the base of the mountain. It was a poor, meandering thing, but still a vital source of life. There were even a few thin trees clinging to existence on its banks. Each evening and morning, Aristides organised a raiding party to replenish their supplies. Whenever he did, the Persian master of horse would bring his men up from the plain to mill and swarm, looking for the perfect moment to attack. It was hard to know if the man truly wished to deny them water, or whether he only wanted to kill a few Greeks, to blood his young warriors.

Higher on the slopes of the mountains behind, Pausanias and his Spartans had found a place to observe the enemy. Their favoured spot was a natural ridge, overlooked on one edge by a boulder that was its own moss-furred peak. It was dry and level enough to let men lay out their cloaks to sleep. The rest of the allied force spread across the mountainside in smaller pockets, clinging like bird nests, wherever there was room.

While Pausanias made battle plans, they waited, watching food and water dwindle. In such a harsh place, the officers had already cut rations of beans and grain mush in half. There was enough still for a week, but they had not crossed the mountains with a huge baggage train. Without secure lines back to a city, there was a real danger of them becoming too weak to fight. Pausanias had sent scouts back across the mountain passes, of course, but they had not yet returned. If those men drove pigs or goats before them, they all knew it would be many days before they saw them again.

Aristides never took his eye off the watching horsemen. That force of riders had taken to shrieking as they came, as if it were all some sort of game. He supposed it was, to them. They did not fight for hearth and home as he did, for water and survival. As far as he understood them at all, they had come because their king had ordered them to war. They fought because obedience was the only possible response.

He wondered, though, if the horsemen were not a cut above the common soldiers of Lydia or Egypt. Their fine coats had jewels glittering in the stitching. He did not know yet if they were well trained or merely gaudy – nor was he much of a judge, at least when it came to horses and those who rode them.

*Conn Iggulden*

They seemed bold enough. One or two had spent the morning trotting right up to the edge of the mountain slope, pointing to their camp, beckoning the Greeks to battle. They were having a fine old time with an enemy perched out of reach. Yet there was no sense of tension in the Spartan ranks higher up. Aristides had clambered up to the ridge to gauge the mood there and found only order and determination. Despite the lack of food and water, that had been reassuring.

Half his Athenians seemed to have expected a Spartan battle king to march straight at the enemy, as if war were simply a matter of two lines lining up and hacking men to death until a few remained. Instead, Pausanias tied up the entire Persian force by his presence, all facing his way, waiting and watching for him to make his move. Aristides wondered if any of the Persians had slept at all for the previous few nights. They expected an attack: in darkness, at dawn or at sunset. They had no way of telling when or how it would come. He hoped it wore on them. A small voice he would not speak aloud hoped too that Pausanias knew what he was doing.

'I see their officer,' said the man at his side. 'Is that the one you meant? In that strange helmet, like a piece of pottery?'

Aristides did not turn to the speaker, nor the dozen archers who crouched out of sight in a cleft of the land. He nodded, slowly.

'That is the one. I don't know his name, but he commanded their horsemen yesterday – and he comes closer each day. You'll have one chance. I doubt he will risk his neck again.'

He glanced over the little group waiting with bows strung. None of them were Athenian. He had called for the best, for volunteers. These were the ones who had trotted over, now hidden in the midst of the small force of hoplites he had brought down to the foothills.

The ritual was the same each morning and evening, or had been to that point. Aristides would send out sixty or seventy young lads without armour, bearing empty skins to fill them from the stream. When they were full, each of them struggled to run back. Their safety lay in ten times as many hoplites standing guard a little further up the slope, ready to charge down and defend them.

Out on the dawn plain, Persian horsemen swirled and circled, hundreds of them, looking to hurt, to damage. They raised a huge plume of pale dust, wafting high over the plain. Aristides strained his eyes, trying to learn their signals. He knew they would come.

On the first day, they had merely watched, as if they observed a truce or accepted rules in war. On the second evening, they had suddenly rushed in, killing a dozen men in the water before the hoplites shield-rushed them, driving them back. Persian soldiers had patrolled the banks all night to deny them another chance then, tramping back and forth. There was malice there, as well as understanding. Soldiers needed water in a dry land. The Persians tormented the Greeks with what they had to have.

No one knew what the Persian master of horse would order that morning, but the situation was becoming desperate. The Greeks had endured the slow movement of the sun over exposed ground all the previous day. They had sweated in that heat. Each waterskin had been tallied, each swallow counted. To a man they had grown darker, dry and sore, their lips cracking. They would be desperate in a day or two – and then mistakes would be made.

Aristides looked back to his hoplites, waiting in patient ranks of bronze. They knew the stakes.

*Conn Iggulden*

'Brothers – gentlemen of Athens!' he called to them. 'It is time. When I give the word, you will advance in good order, locking shields. Our water-bearers will go in behind the safety of our lines, filling skins as fast as they can. You will then wait for my signal – there will be no retreat before you hear my order.'

He looked over to the Persian horsemen, their movements subtly increasing in speed and sharpness. The wasps knew their moment was coming; they could sense it. There had to be a thousand of them, more than before. Aristides could see their leader on a monstrous black stallion, turning the beast on a tight rein. They had grown confident, enjoying the snare the Greeks had made for themselves.

'You will have to endure spear and arrow,' Aristides said. He shrugged. 'Keep low and remember your shield drills. If they come too close, you may be tempted to advance and cut those colourful whores down. You will not! They test us, test our resolve, that is all. You'll get your chance when we advance with the main force, not some pointless little action here. Your task today is simply to secure water for tomorrow. That is all.'

He glanced at the archers, still crouching in the cleft of land.

'You lads. Stay behind my men, out of sight. You have all marked the one we want. Wait on my order, if he comes close.'

They nodded. Five were from Corinth, with a Megaran and four Aeginetans, a dour little group who muttered Greek in a thick dialect of their own. They seemed to understand him, however, looking out with burning eyes on the enemies of their people.

The sun was rising in the east, as if the horizon had burst into flame. As the light grew, Aristides looked across the plain, seeking any sign of some greater force readying itself to ambush him. The dust rising made it hard to see their main camp. He had his own reserves ready to come running, but it would be to help him retreat in good order. He would not be drawn into a major battle, not without a plan of action. No, this morning was just two fighters, testing one another's resolve and courage. A few deaths here and there, a little blood splashed on the ground. Pausanias would be watching, learning all he could. Perhaps the Persian general would be as well.

Aristides muttered a private prayer to Athena. She too had to be watching her children: her love felt in the dawn shadows and warm air. All eyes were on Aristides as he raised his hand overhead and dropped it sharply. With that simple gesture, he sent his people into danger.

Xanthippus glanced at the rising sun, frowning at the amount of time it had taken to bring the fleet around the island of Samos. He'd wanted to have his ships in place to blockade the Persians by dawn, but progress had been slow. Though the moon had been near full, individual crews took a dim view of rowing in the dark, where hidden rocks could rip their hulls out. Worse, the wind had strengthened, blowing against them and forcing a snail's pace. Half his ships had ceased all progress to block up their sides with leather sheets and oar-gaskets. If it had not been for the sheer sorcery of oared craft moving against the gale, Xanthippus might have longed for merchant ships, with higher sides and larger sails. Yet for all the constant threat and risk, triremes were still daggers of the sea, a wonder of the world.

They had not approached unobserved. He had seen the first bonfire lit on the highest point of Samos while they were still some way off. It was hard not to smile at the thought of panic in the Persian crews as they saw that light. *They* had been hunters once, when they'd come down a different coast on the other side of the Aegean, with their king and an army greater than nations. After their defeat at Salamis, they had gone to lick their wounds, hiding themselves across a hostile sea – and the Greeks had come out, seeking them, ready to finish the work. Xanthippus smiled. It would be a good day.

With the sun rising in the east, the whole island of Samos was made an extraordinary yellow-gold, the coast of Ionia still in shadow. Xanthippus looked for the masts he had seen before, but they were gone. He felt a moment of panic. In the few hours they'd been given, they had moved from the island itself to the shore of that vast Persian coast. They'd beached all their ships. He swallowed a knot in his throat.

The Greek fleet had blocked both ends of the strait between Samos and the mainland. The symmetry of that was not lost on Xanthippus, as it had been exactly what the Persians had tried to do to them at Salamis the year before. King Leotychides of Sparta came from the south with sixty ships. He may have been the civilian king of Sparta, but he had still been raised a warrior and soldier. He could follow a battle plan, on land or sea.

Xanthippus felt anger swell. All morning, he'd had the sense of drawing a net against the Persians, one they could not possibly escape. Yet rather than face him, they'd simply crossed to the mainland, where the mountain of Mycale loomed. Their shore, not his – and a task suddenly much harder than a sea battle he'd been certain he could win.

The strait was deep under his keel. He found his half of the fleet approaching ships of Sparta and Corinth as if they faced one another in battle. Xanthippus called to his keleustes and heard the order repeated below. The hiss of waves faded and the way came off the ship. The Greek fleet slowed, sweeping the waters still. His net of ships was silent for a moment, the wind just a breeze.

The Persian warships were still emptying their men onto the land, even as he watched. They had not had too long a warning, then. Crews and soldiers could be seen like ants, trotting inland, heading away from the Greek threat. He saw the glint of armour and pointless gestures of defiance.

In a way, it was a compliment to him. The Persians had met the Greeks at sea and clearly had no desire to repeat the experience. As soon as his fleet had been sighted, they had run to safety.

Cimon was too far off for Xanthippus to see his reaction. It was hard not to think of the younger man's father, Miltiades. He had pursued Persians ashore and been ambushed. It had cost Miltiades his fame, his freedom and in the end, his life, dead of wound-fever in an Athenian cell. Xanthippus had played a part in that. He felt acid in his throat. Fate had a way of twisting a man's life. He had come prepared for a sea war. The thought of having to march into a hostile land made him clench his jaw. He cleared his throat, a sound more of anger than necessity.

His son Ariphron turned to him in question, expecting his father to know exactly what to do, as he always did. Xanthippus smiled tightly for him. They had passed into the shadow of Samos, with the cliff of the mainland making the air cold. Yet he had been given a task. He would finish it, however hard it became.

'Signal King Leotychides,' he called. 'Have my boat readied. All senior officers are to attend the navarch on his flagship.'

Xanthippus forced a pleasant expression as his friend Epikleos approached. The role of a captain was never a private one, but the decisions were his alone. Still, he nodded at

*Conn Iggulden*

the worry he saw in a man who had known him for years, who had stood with him at Marathon.

'We could burn those ships easily enough,' Epikleos said. 'Just a few arrows soaked in pitch and we'd have the entire fleet alight. That would make the point.'

'Experienced crews can build new ships,' Xanthippus said grimly. 'No, we'll be landing. We came here to punish them, to make sure they never return to Greece. There is only one way to be sure of that.'

Epikleos understood and bowed his head.

'We'll land hoplites, then. I believe I am the senior officer.'

Xanthippus looked at one who had stayed with him over a lifetime, loyal and true.

'Not today. I will be with you, Epikleos. I'll be in command.'

His friend nodded. Together they looked over the shore.

Cavalry terrified standing men. A unit of horsemen could build up to a gallop on one side of a battlefield, then whip past stationary ranks like a thunderbolt, with no time for them to react or pull back. Aristides hated them with the fervour of any hoplite. He still stood in line with the rest, three ranks deep, levelling spears in a forest of thorns. The horses could not break through, for which he was grateful. The sheer weight of armoured man and beast made that a terrifying thought. He did not think the animals could be made to charge a wall of shields, but if they could, the spear-points stood out to kill.

He drew in a huge breath and made his voice a thing of brass, carrying across the field.

'And *hold*! There. Very good. The Spartans are judging us this evening, never mind the Persians. Hold this line. Keep your shields high and locked. Spears ready if they charge. Ground the butts and put a foot on them. Let our lads fetch the water we all need.'

He stopped. He did not have the easy way with them that Themistocles had, he knew that. Yet he thought they understood one another well enough. Soldiers liked simple tasks, without ornament.

The Persian horsemen dug in their heels and came on, accelerating with sickening speed. Aristides looked over his shoulder to where his little group of archers rested on one knee, hidden by the shield line.

'Are you ready?'

'You'll have to let us know the moment,' one of them called. 'I can't see.'

'Then they can't see you,' Aristides replied. 'Very well. On my command, rise and hit the Persian officer you marked before. Black stallion.' He considered the dust that was already choking, the air thick with it. 'If you can't spot him, look to me. I'll point him out.'

Ahead of them, a thousand horsemen raced in, trying to make the Greeks break and run. If they did, they would be slaughtered. Aristides felt the ground trembling. His hoplites would hold that place, neither advancing or retreating. Of course, it meant the Persians were free to swing in, throwing spears with terrible force and then arcing back out again. Aristides watched them come for the first pass, his expression dark. He could see the officer he had noted before. The man gestured this way and that, revealing himself by his commands. Whoever he was, he was lean and black-bearded. His horse stood a hand higher than the rest, a magnificent animal. Aristides pointed it out to the archers peering through their own ranks at the enemy.

'Here they *come*,' someone shouted in the lines. One of

those fools who could not remain silent. Aristides found quite a few of the men made ridiculous comments as they marched towards an enemy. He'd heard it all at Marathon, years before: pointless jokes and crude descriptions that made those around them either grin or swear or roll their eyes. Men dealt with fear in different ways. It did not matter, as long as they followed orders and held the ground.

He watched the leading horsemen get closer and closer, testing their own nerve as they risked being impaled on the spear-points. His men had the butts known as lizard-killers hard into the dirt, with a foot pressing down. It meant they crouched beneath their shields, like bronze apes.

Aristides swallowed. They were confident, the Persians. He could hear them whooping and yelling as they had before, driving one another on. They dragged dust from the dry ground as they came, so that it seemed to rise with them. He kept his eye on the one he had marked as their officer. Aristides asked for a blessing from Odysseus, if the man's shade watched. He had no idea if the archers he'd gathered had half the skill of the old king of Ithaca.

At the last moment, dangerously close, the Persian horsemen swung left along his lines. The spears they threw crashed into hoplon shields with appalling force. Some bounced clear overhead in the impact and shot past. Others punched through the skin of bronze and even the wood beneath, standing out. The sound was a clatter, with cries of pain and gasping breath, all smothered under the thunder of hooves, of animals and men too close together and moving at frightening speed.

'There! Up, archers,' Aristides roared over the noise. 'Where I point! Quick now. Loose!'

He saw the master of horse on his black stallion. The man was carrying a spear high, his right arm raised, balanced and watchful as he picked his spot. Not for him the wild throws of younger warriors. Aristides felt time slow as the man seemed to look him over, not a dozen paces away. He swore he could see the Persian's eyes narrow. It was the mastery of a great athlete, that beat of extra time others can never know. Aristides and Masistius of Persia looked at one another in the midst of a galloping line passing by.

The archers stood, drew and released as if Odysseus himself guided their shots. Aristides saw black marks appear like thorns in the man's flesh. One struck him in the bicep, making him lurch. Another took him in the neck. His hand let slip the reins and he fell, a great howl of dismay sounding amongst his riders.

The archers drew and loosed again and again, showing their teeth in excitement at having targets so close. The bows were powerful and they were fresh and filled with nervous strength. Shaft after shaft hammered through Persian horsemen, so that thirty or more lay still or dragging themselves away in just moments. The great charge swept on, but the rattle of spears and arrows died away. Only three Athenians had been killed. Aristides looked back and saw his water-carriers hobbling back with full skins, bowed down under the weight. It was good enough.

'Six of you, with me,' he said, striding forward.

The riders were already massing for another charge. They looked wounded, as if he had not played the game by the rules they had all agreed. He wanted to laugh at their angry expressions. They had come to Greece and burned Athens. This was owed.

He walked just a little way, past the still-kicking hooves of the great black horse. It too had a shaft in its neck. Aristides did not think it would survive. Its master was certainly dead.

*Conn Iggulden*

Aristides had considered cutting his throat to make sure, but the Persian stared upwards, already still.

Horns sounded behind and above him. Recall. Aristides paused only to glance up at the ranks of red-cloaked Spartans on the mountain, before he was snapping out orders and directing his men back into the foothills. In the excitement of a small victory, he had almost forgotten his own warnings. This was not the battle. This was just a skirmish, a test of will. Of course, those who fell died just as hard. He was glad it had not been him.

'Back now, gentlemen. Well done. Archers? You were superb.'

He did not know if Themistocles would have said something more moving, to make them blush or weep. They seemed pleased enough. As they scrambled up the loose scree, leaving the plain behind, they held their heads high.

Aristides paused halfway up. He was panting, but so were many of the younger men, so he did not let that worry him. He could see the Persian riders had coalesced around the main camp, like a clot of blood in a beef joint. They had collected the bodies of their own, which pleased him. The dead should never be left, nor despoiled. The enemy were not animals, but civilised men. It did not make him hate them less.

As he began to turn away, he caught sight of something moving far off, too far for the Persians below to have seen. Aristides shaded his eyes and squinted. He felt his heart sink when he understood.

A snake of carts was making its way towards their position down on the plain. He did not know if it had been summoned by Pausanias, or was the gift of some community wishing to send food and water to the Greeks. It had to be for them. The Persians had no outposts, no cities that would gather for them, not that year. Unless it was from Thebes. That was almost a worse prospect. If that were the case, it became his duty to intercept their line of supply. It could be the difference between victory and forcing a Persian surrender as they starved. Either way, Aristides knew he had to move against it.

No one down on the plain was aware of the supply caravan, not yet. He had an hour, no more than that. Aristides breathed out, thinking. The helots stood between him and the ridge where Pausanias kept watch. They could carry back whatever food had been brought. He swallowed, suddenly feeling sick. The Persians would react, of course. Stung by the action at the stream, they would surely attack if he came out again. He felt his heart thumping, knowing he had to make a decision in just moments. They needed food and wine to survive, but his instincts cried out against another raid so soon after the last. Yet what if the Persians did come out? That would put them on the plain, with Pausanias and the Spartans on their flank.

Aristides bit the edge of his thumb, his mind racing. What would Themistocles do? No, that answer was clear enough. He would take the risk.

# 23

Aristides was still composing a message for Pausanias when the Spartan appeared, scrambling down the slope from the higher points. The regent was not the sort to wait for news, not when he could see something was happening. Aristides saw the man's famous soothsayer was coming down as well, picking his way with more care.

Pausanias was breathing lightly as he came to rest. Aristides nodded to him.

'Why have you halted?' Pausanias said. 'I sent you no new orders. The water has been collected.'

He seemed to glare and Aristides raised his own eyebrow to match the Spartan. Did the man actually think he had come down to rebuke him?

'Regent Pausanias. Look east and you will see a long caravan of carts, heading this way. The Persians haven't spotted it yet, but they will, any moment.'

He waited a beat, just long enough for Pausanias to squint against the rising sun. That dawn glare would help to hide the caravan from those on the plain, but Aristides was pleased to see the Spartan nod.

'My supply line is through the mountains behind us – land we control. I do not know who sent this one . . .' Pausanias trailed off, thinking.

Aristides cut the air with his palm, suddenly impatient.

'If it is one of theirs, we should deny it to them. I think, though, it has to be for us. Some gift from Plataea, or Leuctra.'

'Plataea was sacked . . .' Pausanias murmured. He shaded his eyes.

Aristides waited. The younger man wanted to command. This was his opportunity. Yet for all his training, a new situation could make any man pause. Aristides stood still, breathing slowly, waiting for the Spartan to catch up with his plan.

'It could be a ruse, a false trail to draw us off the mountain,' Pausanias said.

Aristides blinked slowly. He had considered that, but he paused as if it was a new thought. After a moment, he shook his head.

'It would be the first, from them. The Persians brought a hammer to Greece, not a dagger. I have not seen much sign of subtlety. Of course, it is always possible . . .'

He made himself trail off, hating the seed of doubt that had grown in him. Aristides had spoken confidently, sensing the Spartan needed to be persuaded. Of course, if he was wrong, it would be a Persian masterstroke.

Life or death, success or failure. Command was a lonely business, when so much rode on the outcome. The thought made the morning air seem chill. Aristides could smell his own sweat as he stood there and waited for a decision. No part of their army would move without Pausanias giving the order. That was the reality of standing with Sparta. Aristides accepted it as a fair price.

Tisamenus reached them then, the soothsayer breathing hard and skidding the last steps on loose earth. That part of the slope was steep, so that all three men stood at a sharp angle to the ground. Word of the sighting was spreading amongst those on the mountain. Hoplites waited for orders around them, their lives in the hands of a few.

'The caravan there, on the plain . . .' Pausanias said, stalling for time.

Aristides felt his patience fray. He was twice the age of the Spartan regent. Everything hurt that morning, but he would not miss an opportunity in idle conversation! If it was food and water, they had to secure those carts. He cleared his throat, but Pausanias spoke before he could. The Spartan had made his decision.

'Take your hoplites, Aristides, all eight thousand. I will remain. If the Persians move against you, they'll know I will hit them in the flank.'

Aristides dipped his head in acknowledgement. Every passing moment was one they might need.

'They have so many men, they could send twenty thousand after me and still be ready for you as you come down.'

'No one is ever ready for us,' Pausanias said softly. 'How many do you want?'

'Your helots are the only ones close enough to go right now. Send, what, thirty thousand with me? The Persians would have to split their army to attack so many. If they do that, you can take them in the flank. If they fear trickery and stay in their camp, we will secure the caravan.'

Pausanias hesitated. Aristides could see a change in him, a sudden pressure. He lowered his head a touch and the gaze he turned on Aristides made the older man want to take a step back. Whatever caused the peculiar tension passed like a breeze.

'Very well, Athenian,' Pausanias said. It was an odd form of address. 'But my helots are not soldiers. You will not make them so. They have some blades and spears . . . they'll act the part if I order it. Just . . .' His expression twisted as if he had eaten something sour, as if he didn't want to speak the words.

'They are like children, Aristides. Don't ... get them all killed.'

Aristides felt his eyes widen. He recalled an old tale of Ares and Aphrodite. Those gods had made a son together. The child, that joining of war and love, had been named Phobos – fear. Aristides wondered how many others had learned as much of Spartan society and then lost their life before they could tell anyone. The thought made him swallow, his throat dry.

'We are agreed, then?' Aristides said.

He needed the formal command. Pausanias dipped his head.

'Secure the caravan – bring it back or burn it. Take your hoplites ... and the helots. Apollo guard and bless you, Aristides.'

They clasped hands briefly and then Aristides changed his manner, raising his voice to snap orders as if the Spartan regent was already back with his men.

'Helots! To me. By order of Pausanias. Follow me down to the plain.'

He was not surprised at how fast they rose and followed him, gathering weapons and tools. They had been born to slavery, over a hundred generations. It was all they knew.

His hoplites were as quick to move. They reversed their path through the foothills, with the helots coming down in a flood behind them. The sheer number was comforting in the face of the Persian host. Aristides saw enemy horsemen beginning to mount in response to the movement, ready for whatever was happening. He wondered if they would be lost without their officer. He hoped so. If they chose to threaten his fledgling army, he could not do much to stop them. They could even carry news that the helots were not elite soldiers. He could not help that, for all he longed for a force of cavalry

*Conn Iggulden*

to run them off, even to raise choking dust around his men so that they were obscured.

His hoplites fell into ranks as they came down to the plain. Spears were held upright on the march, with shields on their backs, ready to be thrown round on a simple strap and grasped with the left arm. Aristides felt pride in their manner, then frowned. In comparison, the helots looked ragged.

'Dress those lines!' he roared to his own men. 'Lochagoi to me!'

He waited as around a hundred officers received the order and came trotting out of the ranks. Aristides held position almost at the rear as they came close enough to hear his orders.

'Gentlemen, these helots need officers. Your own men will survive without you for a time. I want shield lines ready on the flanks if the Persian cavalry come too close. For these others ... give me respectable-looking marching ranks, with as many spears as we can bring to bear. Clear? Good, move!'

He settled back. They were not fools or children, those men. As tempting as it was to try and nurse them through every step and order, he knew he would only end up exhausting himself. Better to stare over their heads and seem to see all, while they sweated and cursed to make the helots look like a real army and not just farmers at a country fair, out for a stroll.

Aristides looked over his shoulder, watching the visible consternation in the Persian forces. They had no idea yet what was going on. Orders would be flying, officers called from their tents behind the encampment walls. He grinned at the thought. With just a little luck, the dust raised by his men would obscure the actual caravan completely, so that the Persians never learned why a large contingent of Greeks had suddenly marched away to the east.

He felt his neck ache as he tried to keep the enemy in sight, but helots were trudging through his wake, raising their own dust. Aristides shook his head at the way they ambled along. It was a shame the Spartans hadn't trained them as soldiers, though he supposed he understood why they had not. If Tisamenus had spoken the truth, the last thing any Spartan would want was a force of trained men looking after crops and nursing Spartan babies. They looked fit, though, he noted. They may not have understood what they were being asked to do, but they were not panting and puffing either. It didn't make them soldiers.

Aristides wondered if the Persians would even come out. With Sparta perched on the hillside like a hawk ready to fall on them, they'd suspect a trap from the first moments. What commander would split his force, when his main advantage lay in greater numbers? They had done it at Salamis, through overconfidence. He doubted they would make the same mistake again.

Aristides nodded sourly when he saw only a part of their cavalry set out, raising dust and blurring as they came. Of course, those young noblemen would be lusting for vengeance. No doubt they would report back as well, so that the Persian general could decide what to do.

Ahead of them, not an hour's march away, the caravan would be trundling closer. Down on the plain, Aristides had lost sight of it. All he could do was aim his men in the right direction and pray silently that it was not all some trap of the Persians, sprung at exactly the right moment to bring them all to ruin.

*Conn Iggulden*

# 24

Xanthippus stood at the prow as his warship was driven onto the beach at full speed. He held on as the entire ship trembled under him, the keel skimming through ripples of sand, then settling, coming to rest in a groan of timbers. All around, hoplites of Greece were wading in from boats or climbing down from the sides of their own ships, helpless as whales on land. In the rush and clatter of armoured men, Xanthippus set foot on Persian soil for the first time in years. He thought he felt the ground shake beneath his tread, but it was just the time he'd spent at sea.

The hoplites formed up away from the beach, the great granite mount casting shade over them. The Spartan king waded through the shallows, having jumped from a small boat. Bronze would not be touched by salt water, but all soldiers winced at the thought of iron swords in the sea. Every hilt and blade would have to be taken apart, cleaned and re-oiled when they were done. Some would be ruined even so.

One by one, the beached ships had ropes tied on and taken out to the rest of the fleet. They were not staying alongside the Persian hulls, where they were vulnerable. The ropes were tied to bronze rings on the sterns of those still floating in the strait. The rowers there dipped oars and dragged them back a little at a time. It was a perilous business, though the sea was calm and each one righted itself as it found deeper water and swam. Xanthippus gave private thanks for that.

His son Pericles stood on the sand, holding shield and spear, but lost in that place. Xanthippus swallowed a lump of fear in his throat at the sight of him. He was too young to be on that coast.

'Peri, come over here,' Xanthippus ordered.

He clenched his jaw, feeling the muscles move beneath the skin. There were men of Athens all around, close enough to listen as they checked their weapons and equipment. They knew he would ask them to march towards death and injury, something he would do himself. His authority was absolute in the presence of the enemy, but they were hard men. They would despise him if he sent his son back. He felt his teeth creak and grind. He wished Pericles had stayed on board, as he had been told to.

'I would like to carry a spear for Ariphron,' Pericles said clearly.

His younger son had his jaw jutting and his lips folded in, a mulish expression Xanthippus knew very well. At least the boy had chosen to challenge him in the open. He was wide enough across the shoulders to pass for a hoplite. It would not have been impossible for him to sneak in amongst the men. There would have been no helmet and shield for him of course, even if the hoplites had allowed it. They all knew one another; it was part of their bond in battle, that friends and tribes marched alongside in the phalanx. No stranger could stand amongst them without them knowing. No, Xanthippus realised, Pericles had no choice. The boy waited, defiant, terrified he would be sent back.

Xanthippus looked to Ariphron, waiting in full armour on the beach, white sand spattered to the thigh. His older son was watching him, trusting his decision. Presumably, Pericles had asked him first, or Ariphron would have sent his brother back himself. Both sons waited for their father's word.

Xanthippus felt a great shudder of nerves for them, his

stomach twisting beneath his breastplate. Yet pride swelled there too, that he stood with his sons, boys he had once thrown high into the air. Before exile, before invasion, before war. Xanthippus had felt his life change, the very moment Agariste had first handed Ariphron to his arms. In that single beat of time, he had shifted, from being a son to being a father. It came with fear as well as joy. He knew in his heart he could not protect them from life's perils – or that if he did, he would ruin them. Still, he felt fresh sweat trickle in his armpits.

Spartans would have understood, he thought. Xanthippus had once heard life described as a swallow coming in through a window, dipping through a sunlit room, then out once more into the dark. If that truly was existence, *whatever lay beyond*, nothing in the world could matter more than raising a son. Nothing. The Spartans were said to have a great 'contempt for pleasure', that they saw only what was important. He did not know about that. It seemed a bleak existence. Yet to see Ariphron standing strong and healthy in helmet and greaves, to see Pericles with a shield on his back and a spear in his hand, was a glory Xanthippus did not think he could have explained to another. Still, he felt one finger pick at the nail of his thumb, worrying the skin until it bled.

'*Please*, father,' Pericles murmured. Ariphron nodded too, giving permission.

Xanthippus breathed out, dipping his head.

'Very well. Stay close behind Ariphron, Pericles. Watch his back in the phalanx.'

He saw tears glitter in his youngest son's eyes as he spoke, hardly able to believe he had not been sent back to the ships. The boy grinned like the sun rising and Xanthippus saw Ariphron slap Pericles on the shield across his shoulders, making it ring. His boys laughed together and Xanthippus felt sick, already regretting it. The men of Athens nodded to him when he met their gaze, approving his choice. Pericles was a popular lad with the crew.

The phalanx formed on the beach, eight ranks deep and dense with men. Their expressions darkened as they formed up, sensing bloody work ahead and old memories mingling. Epikleos had gathered the hoplites of Athens and half a dozen small states. Xanthippus had not observed his friend establishing who was senior there. One of Cimon's lochagoi officers seemed to have a swollen cheek and split lip, but Epikleos and Cimon were both inspecting the lines peaceably enough as Leotychides approached their position.

The king of Sparta walked well over sand, Xanthippus noted. He smiled at the thought that all men judge another's fitness for battle, as they meet, and every moment after that. That subtle assessment might have been wasted on a summer evening in Athens. There though, on a hostile coast, it pleased him to see King Leotychides like a great cat, in perfect balance. The Spartan wore a long red cloak and a bronze helmet with a white plume. Beyond that, only a leather cord crossed his thigh, with sandals, greaves, shield and spear in hand. The hair at his head, chest and penis was iron grey, in tight curls. Though he must have been in his sixties, Leotychides looked supremely fit. Xanthippus bowed his head to one of royal rank.

'I see no more than six thousand men here, Xanthippus,' King Leotychides said. 'With so many empty ships, the Persians must have landed many more.'

'Most are just oarsmen,' Epikleos said.

The Spartan king flickered a glance in his direction, judging him. After a moment, he inclined his head.

'Even so. *Our* oarsmen remain aboard.'

Xanthippus waited a beat. The hoplites were silent, stretching away in ranks that included his own sons. He had not held anything back. It occurred to him that this was a man who had dealt with Leonidas for decades, the great battle king of Sparta. For all his personal strength, Leotychides was not used to making decisions of war, the ones that could not be recalled, that led to life or death. It was an interesting insight and Xanthippus gentled his tone as he replied.

'Majesty, the ones who stand with us are all veteran hoplites, the best of Greece – armed and armoured. I would wager any one of them against a dozen oarsmen with clubs or daggers. Trained men go through untrained, as lions against dogs. Your own bodyguard of three hundred will show the way in that, I am sure.'

The king dipped his head, accepting the point as Xanthippus continued.

'Our oarsmen are fit, but untrained. They would be like lambs to Persian soldiers, just as their oarsmen will be to us.'

He paused, wanting the Spartan to know how seriously he took the position.

'I would prefer, Majesty, to keep the fleet manned, not risk our crews in this sort of work. However, I accept your command,' Xanthippus said. 'If it is your wish, I will disembark ten thousand more to march with us. They do have knives, after all.'

The Spartan king waved a hand.

'No, the point is well made, Xanthippus. I am grateful for your consideration. Very well. I imagine these men will rise to the task. The right flank is mine, of course. You'll hold the left?'

It was as much question as order and Xanthippus nodded.

'If you wish it, yes. With your permission, Epikleos and . . .' he waited for Cimon to nod, 'Cimon here will command the centre. I have taken the liberty of sending runners further inland to seek out the enemy. They cannot hide so many from us.'

'Perhaps they have . . . run away,' Leotychides said.

Xanthippus nodded. It actually was possible – the Persians had abandoned their ships, after all. Yet he thought of the ambush poor Miltiades had sprung years before. Cimon looked bleak as he surveyed the rising land ahead. From where they stood, it was impossible to say what lay behind the treeline. For Miltiades, it had been an overwhelming force of Persians and the end of all his hopes.

Xanthippus spoke as if he made an oath.

'Then they should keep running, Majesty. It is my intention to make an ending here. As soon as our own ships are clear, I will . . . with your permission . . . fire their ships. There will be no way back to sea, not for them.'

'Very well. Carry on,' Leotychides said.

Xanthippus bowed to him, the gesture copied by Cimon and Epikleos. The four men clasped hands briefly, testing one another and finding something to reassure. When Leotychides reached his Spartans on the right wing, he raised a hand, ready to give the order.

One of the scouts was coming back in at a sprint. Xanthippus held up a palm to the Spartan. He waited for the lad to get his breath back and bent a head to listen.

'They are . . . just inland, formed up and waiting for us. Fifteen or twenty thousand. No horsemen . . .'

Xanthippus nodded. They could have run, but he had not expected them to. A memory came to him suddenly, of a fight when he was young. He'd chased a lad through half a dozen streets in Athens, until the boy had reached his own home and touched his foot to the threshold. Though he had run before, the lad had turned then, choosing to face his fate. Xanthippus had seen his resolve – and somehow admired it. As the boy's mother bustled up, he'd let him have the day, retreating with laughter and shouts. They had been boys then. It was different now.

He sent the runner over to Leotychides, another to Cimon and Epikleos. After what seemed an age, they had all heard and raised their hands, signalling they were ready to move. Xanthippus drew in a massive breath.

'Enemy in range! Shields ready! Spears ready . . . Forward!'

He let the first two ranks pass him before he eased into the third, beside Ariphron. Xanthippus glanced back to where Pericles walked in his brother's shadow, standing tall despite the weight of the shield and a spear in each hand.

Hoplites of a dozen cities lurched forward with them, each rank pulling down helmets of felt or bronze, raising spears high where they would not foul the legs of those ahead. Those men gleamed in the sunlight as they crested the dunes and passed through the first trees. Behind them, smoking lines flew from Greek ships to land amongst the Persian fleet. It was not long before they were all aflame, a conflagration that spread and roared, high and dark enough to be seen in Greece, or so they hoped. That fleet would not go to sea again, to threaten and kill. Persia had come for war. This was the ending they had earned.

# 25

Aristides forced a hard pace to reach the caravan of carts dawdling across the plain. The Persian cavalry had grown bolder. Over the course of just an hour in their wake, they'd ridden dangerously close. They were met by Athenian lines on the edges, but there was chaos there as well as order. His hoplites could not easily shield helots and still raise spears in formation.

The reward for their tormentors was a blood trail. For every barrage of spears clattering off shields or helmets, for every arrow that missed, at least one Greek would shout in pain and stagger, falling behind. Some fell and lay still. Others took a wound that meant they could not keep up with their friends. Those men called farewells and turned alone to face the enemy.

The horsemen had returned in giddy excitement the first time that happened. Too eager, they circled back, jumping down with swords drawn to kill the wounded man. They had forgotten he might still be dangerous. While his mates cheered, the hoplite cut two of them down before a third took his legs out from under him. They tore his armour and shield from his body then and held them up, jabbing the air in triumph as the Greeks marched on.

The dust helped. Thirty thousand helots kicked up a boiling, shifting wall of it, pale gold and pink as it smeared past the sun. Even as he coughed and blinked grit from his eyes, Aristides was grateful for the run of dry days. Of course, it meant he and the others marched with mouths like sand. His quickly gathered army carried only a few of the skins he had filled at the stream, the water now mixed with wine for vigour. It was never enough. As they kicked and stamped on dusty earth, they lost sight of the Persian camp dwindling behind them. At times it felt as if the land itself was their protection. Aristides hoped it was true.

The caravan master gaped in shock as an army seemed to appear out of a dust storm, like a desert djinn. Faced with that host, the man halted his mules and dismounted to kneel. Aristides came forward, dragging him to his feet.

'Where are you from?' Aristides demanded.

'The town of L-Leuctra, kurios . . . We have brought offerings for sacrifice against the Persians. Meat and wine for the men. Kurios, this poor caravan is all we could raise for you, b-but it . . .'

'Get it moving again,' Aristides snapped. 'Stay close to us and you *might* reach safety. Fall behind and I will burn these carts and leave you for the enemy.'

Aristides had been peering into the distance, watching for the Persian outriders, even as the caravan master stammered his explanations. The Persians had finally ridden right round the Greek force, using their speed and range, hungry for more damage. The dust was already settling around the standing ranks, revealing them.

Aristides was close enough to see the first consternation, the pointing arms. The Persians turned their mounts in place, shouting to one another, staring at the Greek force. The helots did not look like hoplites, not up close. Though some carried spears and shields, most stood with just a knife or some sort of cudgel. They wore no greaves, no bronze helmets. A few had caps of felt or dogskin, with wide belts over tunics and bare legs.

From a distance, they had seemed a huge force, an army of

great strength. Yet the horsemen had finally come close enough to really see them. Aristides winced as a great cry went up. The hunt was on and this time he was the prey. With no way to respond, he could only watch as hundreds of riders began galloping back towards their camp. How would General Mardonius of Persia respond? The man still had the threat of Spartan forces on his flank, ready to gut him as he came out. Yet he was in command of two hundred thousand, more. He would surely fear no force of men.

Aristides turned with the caravan as it was swallowed into the mass of helots. They turned to follow the hoplites who had become the vanguard, taking the lead as they headed back. The slaves looked determined enough, Aristides thought. Around him, helots held knives in clenched fists and marched with heads high. He wondered what it would be like to grow to manhood alongside Spartans, to know that no matter how strong you became, no matter how fit or skilled, you would always be a child to those who owned you. He shuddered at the thought. To make a child of a grown man was a hard thing, even if it was done from love.

The Persian cavalry had vanished back, carrying tales to their master. Only a few remained to observe the hoplites and their strange companions. Their spears had all been thrown and those young men could only glare and sneer. Aristides jogged through to the fore, where his hoplites marched in ranks four deep, a bronze skin across the face of the helots. He kept pace with the front rank of those, observing his men just ahead. His Athenians made a grand show as they marched, spears flashing, bronze gleaming gold. He was proud of them.

Aristides felt his stomach drop away as a thought struck. He did not know if he was marching to battle in that very moment – and if he was, whether the helots would stand, or

*Conn Iggulden*

break and run at the first battle shout. Could he ever understand such men? They had been born to slavery. They were
only there because Pausanias did not want to leave so many
at home in Sparta! As Aristides strode along with them, he
wondered if they had anything like officers among their
number. It was the natural estate of men to raise one or two
to lead the rest. Did that apply to those who lived as slaves?
He looked at the closest one, just a couple of paces away. The
helot was a short, hairy fellow, with black eyes and a nose
like a blade.

'Can you fight at all? You helots?' Aristides called to him.

The man ducked his head when he understood he was
being addressed, the reaction of an oft-beaten dog. Aristides
tried again.

'If the Persians come, will your people stand? Should I
send you back to your masters on the slopes? You have just a
few shields and spears.'

The sullen helot still didn't reply. Aristides reached to take
him by the arm and the man shook him off and moved
sharply away, vanishing amongst his people.

'Why *should* we stand?' another of them said suddenly.

He was younger, with scarred hands and a deeply puck-
ered muscle on his thigh that spoke of old wounds, badly
healed. He limped, Aristides saw, giving him a rolling gait.

'Are the Persians our enemy?' the man said. 'Why? What
have they ever done to us?'

'They will water this dry ground with your blood if you
run,' Aristides said curtly. 'There is that.'

'You'd have us fight without shields? For you, is it? For the
Spartiates?'

Aristides regarded him for a time. On another day, he
might have enjoyed debating the point, perhaps on the Pnyx
hill, with Themistocles, Xanthippus and Cimon all there to

make their observations. Yet in that place, hoplite and helot marched towards a vast and hostile enemy camp, already roused against them. He had no patience to build an argument of force and persuasion. War took everything he loved, he realised. Everything that made life worthwhile. Anger surged in him, sharpening his thoughts.

'Have you ever left the Peloponnese before?' Aristides called, raising his voice to carry to as many as he could reach.

'It is forbidden, in normal times,' the young man replied with a shrug. He looked away, ashamed of his own estate and position in the world. He was addressing a free man of Athens and he could not meet his eye.

Aristides shook his head.

'Tell me then, when will you ever get a chance like this again? If you will not fight for Sparta, fight for Athens! We freed the slaves who took up arms at Salamis. Think of that, today.'

He felt hundreds turn their heads to watch him and swallowed down on shame. Sparta would never free these men, no matter what they did. Freedom was not something they had ever been offered before, even as an idea. Themistocles would have understood, he thought. These were simple men, but he needed them to hold, whatever it took. Even if he had to give them false hope. It was hard to return the awed stares, but he did it.

Ahead of them, Aristides saw a dark line swelling across the land. Dust rose with it, a storm that climbed higher with every step. He swallowed a knot of fear in his throat. The Persians were coming out. His hoplites were just a thin gold line. He suddenly knew he would see them slaughtered, lose his own life, all for a caravan of food. His mind raced. Formation was the key. He had to get it right. He had to . . .

*Conn Iggulden*

A hand touched his arm. It was the older of the two helots, the one who had moved away when he'd first spoken.

'Sparta does not free helots,' the man said gruffly. 'Never. There is no hope for us.'

Aristides opened his mouth, but he could not deny it. He could not. When he said nothing, the man nodded, a little sadly.

'Is it true, though, what you said? Did Athens really free her slaves? We never heard that.'

'Archon Xanthippus gave his personal oath. Anyone who fought or rowed for us that day was freed. Even one of his personal slaves was freed, as I heard it.'

Aristides knew Themistocles would have found words to manipulate the man. He searched for them, but the helot reached out and patted him on the arm once more, silencing him.

'Every year they make a great hunt,' the man said, 'to keep our numbers down.'

A growl went up from those who listened all around. The memory was hard in them as the man continued.

'Their young warriors blood themselves on us, chasing us through the streets and hills. They beat us and cut us if we even look at them, did you know that? Or they force us to drink too much wine and make us dance for their amusement. We are *never* freed. Yet . . . some of us will be free today, I think,' the man said. 'My name is Polyemus. Perhaps I will see Athens one day. I would like that.'

The man smiled, but it was a strange, bitter expression. He clapped Aristides on the shoulder, then looked left and right, as if he waited for something. All around, helots were muttering, talking amongst themselves. Aristides had heard them before and not understood they were discussing what to do. The sound was like the sea, or the wind in a stand of trees. Without warning, one of them raised his voice to a parade-ground bellow.

'Helots! We who are forgotten! We who are dogs! We who are *many*! With Sparta watching, shall we remind them?'

A slow roar built, a growl without words that had Aristides turning his head back and forth. These were angry men, or perhaps just men. If they even knew he still watched, in moments they had forgotten him. They talked only to themselves. Another one of them howled like a wolf. He was answered by a thousand throats and as it died back, the sound was mournful, almost unbearable.

'There is only one freedom for us,' still another called over their heads, 'in choosing to stand, in choosing to die. If we say it is so, it is so. We who are forgotten! We who are dogs! We who are many!'

It was taken up as a chant, by thousands, spreading all around them. Aristides had not thought of them at all as he marched out. They had been there like a wall, to make the Persians hesitate. He felt his heart leap as he understood they would fight, with teeth and fists if they had to. They would remind the Spartans they were many, and that they were men. He wondered if Pausanias would still love them then.

Ahead, closer with every pace, the Persian infantry was coming to meet them. Aristides swallowed fear when he saw more men on the field than he had ever seen. They wore panelled coats and carried shields of wicker. They were Mede, Egyptian, Ethiop and Persian trueblood, an ocean wave of soldiers, ready to crash down and drown them all.

Aristides sent a prayer to Athena. He would meet them, with his hoplites out in front of helots, as a bronze spear-tip. He would have to spread them thin to prevent the Persian front curving around like a bull's horns. Even then, he did not think it would be enough. They were the horizon.

*Conn Iggulden*

Two ranks deep would be pierced in a thousand places, overwhelmed. Yet it was all he could do. He sucked in air to give the order and felt his mouth sag as the helots around him suddenly doubled their pace and surged out. His Athenians could not stop them. They were like a flood. The officers he had lent them were left behind, revealed and marching alone.

Aristides felt fear surge. The helots would surely be slaughtered. Yet he did not think they would come back if he ordered them. He watched the enemy line grow and prayed Pausanias was watching and bringing down the main forces. His throat was like parchment, his lips cracking. It was too late to drink. The battle was upon them, whether they wanted it or not.

## 26

Mardonius was moving, his horse fighting a rein like a bar of brass along its neck. Along with its rider, the beast sensed rising excitement. Mardonius had watched a massive force heading away that morning and suspected a trap from the first moments. The Greeks were cunning bastards; he had learned that much from his own allies. Still, he had failed to see at first what they'd done. It was not a false trail to draw him off. The ruse had been in *who* they were – slaves, marching like soldiers. Alongside a few hoplites of Athens to make them look more fearsome than they could ever be.

His cavalry swirled around his centre, leaderless without Masistius, master of horse. Mardonius felt that loss with them as he moved out with regiments of infantry. When he reined in again, he was a rock in a vast sea, with men flowing past on all sides. Mardonius commanded the centre, Artaba-zus the left, while Hydarnes of the Immortals and the Thebans kept the right wing. Hydarnes had demanded that honour. His Immortals longed to face the red-cloaked Spartans, desperate to avenge their losses at Thermopylae. They would restore their reputation only over Spartan dead.

Mardonius stared up at the mountainside, where Greek forces were suddenly moving in glitters of silver and gold, sliding with him along the ridges, surging ahead of his army as they made their way down to the plain. He showed his teeth. Battle could not be avoided now, he was certain. He was the tempest and they were being drawn in. Piece by piece, city by city, called to judgement.

*Conn Iggulden*

Against the vastness of the mountains, they seemed almost to be children's toys, shining like glass. Mardonius breathed dust, felt it dry his lips. His army was the gale, the desert wind! Even the Spartans were made small against them. Mardonius saw their red cloaks for a time, until they reached the plain and formed up as part of a greater host. He nodded sharply, pleased. They had come down from the heights, just as he'd hoped. He'd moved against their slaves – and they had been forced to respond. Mardonius lost sight of them as dust thickened in a great cloud. He filled his lungs even so, tasting it.

The Persian general gave a war shout, a triumphant bellow that cracked across the regiments. His one fear had been that the Spartans might tear into his flank as he went for the Athenian force on the plain. He cared little for slaves who marched like soldiers! His men could march through those and hardly slow down. No, it had been Athens and Sparta who had defied Kings Darius and Xerxes. They were the foundation stones of the rebellion, who led all the rest. The other Greeks would fall when the men of those cities lay broken, he was certain.

As he moved forward, the last of the Greeks came down to the plain. Dust rushed and grew like a great tree ahead, making it hard to see. Mardonius felt his heart swell with pride as one of his own sons cantered past. They were men of empire, a good bloodline. King Xerxes had promised him a city of his very own once he had brought Greece to heel. Mardonius shook his head in wonder as he recalled the offer. Perhaps one of his sons would rule there after him, a dynasty begun on this very day. It was a golden thought.

Ahead of him, his foot regiments blew horns to attack. The ranks of Greek slaves were swallowed up in their own dust as both sides rushed at one another. His heart raced faster and faster as spears flew, blows were struck and the first men died. This was the weapon he had come to wield. The Greeks had met him on a dry plain and he was pleased.

The wonder was that they did not break in the first moments. As the dust swelled thicker around them, Aristides saw helots surge forward, smashing against armoured lines. He had a sudden flash of awe as he saw hundreds punch through like trident tines, killing in a frenzy. How many had practised Spartan drills and stances in the darkness of their sleeping rooms, learning in the shadows? They knew the Spartans valued courage and skill more than anything else in the world. Perhaps some of them had sought to steal just a little for themselves. Or perhaps it was just because they did not fear death.

The helots had no armour. Before the rolling dust clouds caught up and swallowed them all, Aristides saw them running with blood, still punching knives into throats and thighs, anything they could reach. They were cut down by the hundred from the first moments, killed by dark men in panelled coats. They were spitted on spears and hacked down with longer blades. Yet they did not break, those who were first in. They gave their lives in violent answer, as they had never been allowed to before.

The dust brought its own sort of fear, to those who fought in it. The scraping, kicking steps of tens of thousands coated them all, so that it settled on blinking eyes and made the sun a dim brightness. Aristides felt his vision reduce to thirty or forty men on all sides. It was like being trapped in mist, so that he marched in a ring of clear air, and all else beyond was like a terrible dream.

The clamour of metal and pain was appalling, a noise so great it seemed to batter his face and chest. Men screamed on all sides and he was instantly back in every battle he had ever known, afraid and angry, just wanting to survive, to break those who made him feel that way. He marched with the hoplite line and ahead of him, helots died like lambs. He did not think he could have stood before Persian infantry without shield or armour, with no more than a club or an eating knife. Yet they did – and they died for that wild courage. He hoped it was a kind of freedom in the end.

It was hard to judge time in the dust storm. Aristides had lost sight of the battlefield and where the main force was. He knew he should be angling towards them, to join up with Sparta and Corinth and all the rest. Yet in the chaos and confusion, lines pressed forward and turned, so that it was hard to say where he should go. He hated it, the confusion. It meant it stole away the leader he might have been and made him just a man in line, with spear and shield like any other. Aristides strode forward in tight formation, over the broken bodies of helots.

When they finally gave way, it was with a great cry of despair, so that he felt his heart break for them. The helots had run onto the swords and spears of Persians by the thousand and given their lives. Perhaps the bravest of them had all been killed, or perhaps they had been ground down in pain and blood, until there was no will left to stand. It was his worst fear, suddenly upon him. As they broke, they could sweep his hoplites aside. His Athenians would stand against a Persian line, but they could not cut down helots trying to push through, panting and bloodied.

Aristides bellowed for his men to hold the shield line, but it was impossible. What had felt like a battle became a rout in moments. Helots pushed past him, wild-eyed, making him stumble and almost fall. The Athenians felt their panic and, in that terrible chaos and blindness, they too began to edge back from an implacable and countless enemy. They could not win, not that day. Death stood with them. The last of the helots went through, but the panic and chaos were still spreading. Aristides could not stop the enemy sensing weakness and rushing forward.

'Phalanx! Form phalanx! Eight ranks!' he roared across his people. 'By Athena, come in! *Shield* lines! Lock shields!'

His people stared into the merciless faces of Persians and they were afraid. He heard rather than saw his men try to form eight ranks deep in that place. With the helots in full rout, there was no need to make a wide line. The phalanx could still bristle with spears and keep them alive. He prayed for that.

Aristides wrenched his head round as a great howl came from his left. He realised he had been turned in the fighting. The damned dust made it almost impossible to know where he was on the plain. Yet he heard Persian horns sound and knew with a sick certainty that his hoplites had been swallowed up in the great host. Where was Pausanias? The helots had all run, their miracle drained away. The caravan had bolted somewhere, the animals spooked by the smell of blood and the sounds of war. Aristides rubbed sweat from his eyes. He needed reinforcements or he was done. Every time the dust moved, he peered for some glimpse of red cloaks. All he could see were his own men in bronze, spears quivering, surrounded by the enemy.

*Conn Iggulden*

# 27

Xanthippus was sweating by the time he clambered up the dunes. The Persians waited just a little way beyond. They had not run. Instead, the crews and soldiers of sixty ships had lined up in rough ranks, on flat ground. A breeze blew from where they stood, carrying an odour of spices and memory. Xanthippus found himself thinking of Marathon, eleven years and a lifetime before. He had been younger then, certain of his own strength. Still, there was no doubt in him. He had followed the Persians home to make sure they never came again. Their fleet burned at his back, so that he marched as if out of an inferno. His hoplites may have been few, but they were armoured and trained men. The king of Sparta was there with them, as well as Greeks from all the cities that had refused to bow, to give water and earth.

He looked left and right, seeing a solid phalanx. Ahead, Xanthippus heard Persian officers snap commands. Arrows began to rise slowly from their lines, so very slowly! Like flowers opening. Xanthippus called his orders not just to hoplites of Athens, but for all those who marched with him. Hellenes and sons, all.

'Shields high . . . wait for it! Lock shields!'

Across his marching ranks, golden eyes were made to overlap like scales. Arrows rattled like hail, but there were no gaps, no sudden cries wrenched in pain. The hoplites growled as they brought the shields back down. Some of them used swords to cut shafts that quivered there. Others left them as trophies. The hoplites were breathing hard, ready to begin the worst labour of their lives, the task that would leave even the fittest red as clay. There was nothing like killing in line to break a man, to make his muscles so weak he could hardly lift his arm. Half the ones who died in battle did so because they were no longer able to stop a blow. Xanthippus sent a prayer to Apollo's son, Asclepius, god of health. He asked for blessings too from Ares, who always stood where men shed blood. The god of war would be on that field by the sea, with a mountain overlooking all. Death would stand on his right shoulder. Perhaps one of the Moirai would be with him in her white robe, ready with her shears to cut the threads of life. The Athenian shuddered at the thought of that gaze falling on him.

Xanthippus glanced at Ariphron, his son. The spike of fear he felt would not find an echo in the younger man, of course. It was for fathers to worry, not their sons. He felt his gaze drawn further once again. None of his men returned his stare at first. All their attention was on the enemy. Yet they sensed his eye on them, intruding on their concentration. One, two, then dozens turned to see who watched. When they understood it was Xanthippus, they bowed their heads. Some smiled, showing him confidence. They were men of bronze; hoplites of gold. The Persians had the numbers, but they were poor soldiers. The Greeks were the hunters, the hounds. They had brought their stag to bay and they were ready to finish the work.

Another flight of arrows sprang up, lower in its arc. Xanthippus roared the order, but it was hardly needed. The men locked shields again and did not slow. One swore, with an arrow through his wrist. As Xanthippus watched, the man wrapped a strip of cloth around the wound, then bound his hand to the grip of the shield, pulling it tight with one end held in his teeth. One of his companions leaned in, mutter-

*Conn Iggulden*

ing words of support. Many of them were fathers. They knew what to say. In those moments, it was not kindness but rough humour and mockery that worked best. They would allow no weakness, not when the enemy swarmed before them.

Xanthippus lowered his own shield. It had been hard not to protect his son when the arrows flew. Yet a thousand days of drill had made iron instincts in him. He marched forward with his people, readying the dory spear in his hand. Half again as tall as a man, it was a fearsome thing. In tight formation, with the weight of hoplite ranks behind, the spears were terrifying.

The Persians shifted glassily as he marched on them. There would be no feints, no manoeuvres. No flanks or reinforcements, just the pressure forward, the push of the phalanx. Those behind shoved and heaved, step by step; those in front stabbed and pulled back and stabbed again. They could not stop, nor rest with that terrible tide behind. They would go through the enemy, or they would die.

'Stay close to me, Ariphron,' Xanthippus said.

He saw his oldest son dip his head, trusting his judgement as he always had. More so than Pericles. Ariphron had understood from a young age that his father was respected, that Xanthippus knew what he was doing. Almost as an effort of will, Ariphron had chosen to listen and learn, to become a man through his father's example. That path had led them to this place, marching alongside one another. Ariphron had to be tested in the fields of his day, to cut his own path. Xanthippus felt his chest swell.

More waves of arrows came as they closed to sixty paces. Persian archers were happier at that range, so that they shot and shot, emptying quivers they had hoarded like gold before. Arrows clattered and broke as they struck bronze. Xanthippus felt his head rocked back as one struck his helmet and whirred away, too fast to see. His shield took blows as if some boxer thumped fists into it, but no iron heads sprang through to pierce his hands. The hail of shafts fell to be crunched underfoot in a shifting mass.

Xanthippus could see the archers falling back as they found no more in their quivers. He remembered them from Marathon. He remembered too how they had died in the shallows, making the sea red.

'Front ranks! Spears ready!' he roared to his men.

All along the line, his people lowered the great lengths of Macedonian ash. Some were older than the men who bore them, but cared for, oiled, sanded, the heads kept free of rust. They glittered silver as they came down, the wide leaf blades too thick to bend, strong enough to pierce armour and keep an edge.

Some of the Persians threw their own spears, short and vicious things. A few found a mark in the Greek lines, but the rest seemed to vanish in the flood of gold. Forty paces. Xanthippus was leaving it late, he knew. Epikleos was pointing at him, summoning the order. Over on his right, King Leotychides of Sparta had pulled down his helmet. His red-cloaks drove forward, edging ahead of the rest of the line in their eagerness. Xanthippus could see it all, perfectly clear, as if the moment was carved in glaze. He felt his bladder ache in fear that his own death had come, that the shears were snipping him out of life.

The moment passed. Sound roared back from thousands of throats, calling defiance or anger, or driving themselves to feel no pain. At ten paces, the Persians were a wall, solid on the earth. Xanthippus pulled in a great breath and bellowed across the field.

'Strike! Spears! Strike!'

His front ranks lunged in a sudden rush, like javelin

*Conn Iggulden*

throwers at Olympia, the last three paces long, arms punching forward, driving dory spears into Persian armour. As one, they plunged in and came back red, then in again. Each time, the phalanx ranks gave a great shout. The shield of the man next to them was their protection, but the spears were their teeth. Some of the factions jabbed the length forward with each step, loping in like leopards. Others kept their right thigh forward and shuffled with every lunge, so that dust rose in a thickening cloud.

The Persians crumpled ahead of them. Though some raised spears of their own, they could not match the length. Those first ranks fell before they took a single life, each thrust of the dory spears cutting through shields and panelled armour, then pulled back. Before they could respond, the things licked out again with that awful grunt, over and over.

The Persians panicked when they saw no weakness. The phalanx formation was an armoured skin, gleaming in the sun. Brave men died like children before it, while on the Greek side, the ranks behind began their great heave forward, growling like a sea storm. There was no way to stop the advance, not once it had begun. They would go through, or they would be made wheat against a stone.

Xanthippus pressed forward. Ahead of him, some part of the Persian line fought with rare skill. He had no fear of their factions and regiments, except for the Immortals – and they were not there. Yet these men wore panelled kilts and breastplates. They carried short, stabbing swords and had good shields of their own. There were no more than a hundred of them in that part of the line, but they cut through his front ranks and suddenly he faced younger, fitter men.

He stabbed one right through the thigh with his spear, making him groan. Xanthippus yanked hard, but the head was stuck. Already the Persian was hacking at the wooden length that ended in him. Xanthippus swore and reached for his sword. The leaf blade was made to come free, but sometimes it stuck even so, held in flesh like a lover. Too many men had lost their lives trying to pull it out.

He drew his sword and kept his shield high and wide, protecting the man standing to his left. Xanthippus saw Ariphron stood to his right. His spear had gone and Xanthippus saw him block a swinging blade on his shield before he too drew his sword. Xanthippus felt sweat flood down, stinging his eyes. He could hardly see or breathe, just barely reacting in time to a man half his age, hammering blow after blow. He was so fast! The man's sword seemed alive as he blocked it again and again. Instinct saved his life more than once, though he knew he had been cut. Xanthippus felt the wound as coldness and could only pray it wasn't serious enough to steal away his strength and his place alongside his son.

The man on Xanthippus' left fell, his neck gashed almost through under his helmet. Two more filled the gap and drove into Persians with fresh spears, killing one and wounding another, so that he cried out and was cut down in turn by Ariphron. Xanthippus found himself fighting for breath, his vision growing light and his heart beating hard enough to hurt. He could *not* die, he could not! Yet the ones he fought seemed not to grow weary in their youth. They battered at him in a frenzy, as if they thought to bring an old tree down. He could feel his strength vanishing. There was no rest, no chance to catch his breath.

Ariphron saw his father's shield sag. With a shout of fury, he tried to edge closer, but the Persians sensed the collapse coming and increased their efforts. They knew the plume Xanthippus wore, and the lion shield he carried, already bright with strips and curls of gold. They had cut the old oak down to its last wedge and they were determined to watch it fall.

Xanthippus felt his leg go and sagged to one knee. He did not know if it was a wound or his heart giving out. The young man facing him wasted strength trying to batter the shield he held up, rather than just heaving it aside. More spears gathered on his left and right as the phalanx pressed forward, mindless in its roar. Xanthippus heard Pericles call in fear.

The sound drew him up, like a thread around his heart, so that he could somehow stand again. He breathed, trying to stay alive long enough for strength to find him. He just needed a few moments. Pericles gave a great howl then and Xanthippus risked a glance across as he ducked beneath his shield in the hoplite crouch. The man pounding at him would see only the helmet, shield and greaves in bronze, with no flesh. Yet each blow rang and sapped his strength.

Pericles had not shouted for his father. Xanthippus suddenly understood, his confusion clearing. He saw Ariphron clutching his side and breathing badly. Something had beaten his defence and hurt him.

Xanthippus felt a flash of cold as his son staggered. Blood sheeted from the wound and of course the enemy did not let him recover. They pressed in, made bold by the hesitation they sensed in that line.

Xanthippus was forced to defend himself or die. He had carried a sword, spear and shield for thirty years and his instincts surged back, though he felt grief twist his face. For a time, he fought mindlessly. His arms worked as if they were made of iron, heavy, sodden things that rose and fell and stabbed and pulled back. The Persian he faced dropped when Xanthippus cut him in the groin, severing the great artery there. Blood rushed out with the man's life and the next slipped and fell, so that Xanthippus killed him on the ground, a savage downwards blow that pinned him to the earth.

Along the lines, only that small group had held. On the right flank, Spartans had torn into Persian ranks. King Leotychides and his guard had gone through and over them at a fast walk, red cloaks flying as they covered the distance. The rest broke like a summer squall, turning their backs on Greeks and struggling to get away, to save their lives. The fear spread like plague amongst them, with eyes rolling and men calling out frustration in one breath. In just moments, the will to stand and fight had crumbled to dust.

Xanthippus could not pursue them. He tapped his thigh and looked in confusion at the bright blood on his hand. He had taken a wound and it still ran. Yet there was no pain at all. It was oddly discomforting. The ranks around him pushed on, with all those who had not exchanged a blow trying to get a taste before they were told to stop. The sight of Persians in full retreat was like strong drink in their blood and they laughed as they picked up speed. Some of them looked over in awe to those who had fallen. Yet they were young men and their prey was running. It seemed like just moments before they were past and Xanthippus panted alone with his two sons.

Ariphron was pale as he sank to one knee. He seemed to bow to his father as he sat there, hunched over his wound. Xanthippus dropped down beside him. With sharp tugs and cuts, he tore a strip of cloth from his tunic. The rule had always been to tend your own wounds first, before others. Yet he could not watch Ariphron bleed and do nothing. He cursed as his fingers fumbled. The end would not come free and he picked up the sword once more.

Epikleos came across the field. Cimon had gone on, but when Xanthippus looked up, he was grateful his friend was there. The battle had moved on ahead, with the Persians in full flight. Only a few hundred Greeks remained around them, to cut throats. Some on both sides preferred a quick end. The Persians were not given a choice.

With a neat movement, Epikleos took the strip of cloth. Though Xanthippus tried to protest, he knotted it around the leg. Xanthippus looked blearily at it, blinking as the blood flow slowed.

'It will need to be cleaned properly, in wine and honey, then stitched,' Epikleos said, as if to a child. 'It's deep, but with a little luck and care, it will be just one more scar by next year.'

Xanthippus looked at him, but the world swam and he could not speak. He tried to turn Epikleos away from him towards his sons. He could see Pericles was wrapping another strip around Ariphron. His youngest son moved like a bird, with quick, shaking hands. He had no expertise, no knowledge. In his helplessness, all he could do was rip up his tunic, wrap and press. The boy sat with blood smeared across his face, where he had wiped sweat. Pericles' eyes were huge with panic as darkness poured through the pad of cloth.

With a grunt of pain, Ariphron rolled onto his back, looking up at the sky. Xanthippus felt the world steady around him. He breathed in short gasps and rose to limp a single step towards his son. He lowered himself onto one knee at Ariphron's side. His own wound was just a trickle of bright red, though he saw dirt in it. Yet he could not think of his own pain, the strange daze that had stolen his wits along with his blood. He thought of Miltiades years before, who had died of a wound just like his.

'Let me have a look,' Epikleos said gently to Pericles.

The boy leaned back and Epikleos examined the spot along Ariphron's ribs. He had known Ariphron all his life, Xanthippus realised. He too had carried him on his shoulders and run around the back field. When Xanthippus had been exiled for seven years, it had been Epikleos who'd become a second father to the boys.

They accepted him, Xanthippus saw. Both Ariphron and Pericles looked to Epikleos in trust as he examined the wound. Yet there was a great sadness in his eyes, despite their hope. Xanthippus saw it when Epikleos turned to him and gave a tiny shake of the head. It felt like a betrayal and his strength surged. Xanthippus scrambled forward and lifted Ariphron, pulling him onto his lap.

'No,' Xanthippus said, suddenly hoarse. 'You will not go.'

As he sat there, he could feel blood still coming, a warmth that was spreading across his lap.

'I am sorry,' Ariphron murmured. He saw the tears in his father's eyes and fear bloomed in him. 'Is it bad?'

Xanthippus could not speak. It was not such a great wound, but it was as deep as a sword-thrust and it had slipped between his son's ribs. Blood rushed from him, unceasing.

'It is not too bad,' he said. 'We'll wait until it stops bleeding and then get you back to the ships.'

Ariphron relaxed, though Pericles had seen the exchange between Epikleos and his father. His mouth was open as he looked back and forth, his eyes shining.

'I am . . . very proud of you,' Xanthippus said. 'I do not say that enough, but it has always been true. Do you know that?'

'I know,' Ariphron said. 'I have always known.'

He grew still as he understood. Xanthippus saw him sigh and accept it. Awareness stole through him, creeping. They could not pretend it was just a wound, not any longer.

*Conn Iggulden*

'I did everything right,' Ariphron said. His eyes were dark and Xanthippus was not sure the young man could even see him any longer. 'I tried so hard to be a man you could admire.'

'You are! You are twice the man I am, I swear it. You remind me of my father, Ari. You have earned honour.' Xanthippus felt his own will coalesce, though his voice shook like a child's. 'Know this, beloved boy. We will see each other again. I swear it, by all the gods. We will.'

In that moment, Ariphron was gone. His head sagged slightly to the side and Xanthippus felt his weight as he had not before. He slumped over his son as Pericles began to sob. They sat together, with Epikleos, as a knot of grief on the field.

# 28

In the shadow of Mount Cithaeron, Mardonius felt the land reach down deep into his lungs and choke him. It was an unfortunate thought. He was the one who had called two hundred thousand soldiers a great storm – and that was true, but a storm of dust and earth until the air itself tasted of metal. Though he rode a fine Persian stallion, Mardonius could barely see a hundred paces either side before clouds swirled across his vision. In glimpses, he saw his army surging out, heading to crush their enemies at last. On the wings, somewhere further, his cavalry would surely be riding. He could no longer see them.

Mardonius looked for his Immortals. Hydarnes would be in command there. The danger was he would be too rash, that his Immortals would be made fools by their courage. Yet such anger could be harnessed. Mardonius had given them a chance to win back all their honour. Hydarnes had promised he would wear a red cloak tomorrow, that he would make it the official uniform of the Immortals in recognition of this victory. Mardonius set his jaw, squinting against the dust. He did not like vainglory. Trophies had to be won before they could be enjoyed.

Messengers kept pace with him, trotting their wiry ponies just a length behind. Yet he had no new orders to give, not then. A good commander brought his men to the field when it was the right time, when the enemy was weakest. That he had surely done. Yet his regiments had their own officers. They knew who the enemy were.

*Conn Iggulden*

The thought made him glance to where the Thebans marched on his right. They wore the same bronze greaves and helmets of the Greeks, though their spears were shorter than the ones the Athenians bore. They carried no banners, no long streamers as some of his regiments did. They looked just like the enemy. He wondered if they would stand or run when the time came.

King Darius had trusted those Greeks that came over to him, just as he had trusted Medes and Lydians, Egyptians, or mountain men of India. Xerxes had done the same, accepting strange tongues and foreign blood out of love for his father. Mardonius felt his teeth creak as he clenched and unclenched his jaw. He would not lose a battle for some childish belief in the honour of his allies. He had Persian regiments ready to step in if his Greeks failed him.

He felt himself sweating copiously, suffering with the old madness of command. Had he thought of *everything*? Was there a detail he had overlooked? He prayed it was not so.

He had seen through the first ruse, when tens of thousands marched away. There was a bird at home in Persia that trailed its wing on the ground to draw predators from its nest. Rats sometimes chased the little things, but when foxes saw it calling in distress, they had learned to search for eggs.

Everything had changed when his cavalry had risked their necks, going close enough to really see the Greeks. They were certainly many, but they were armed like fishermen and farmers, without the bronze that made a hoplite so hard to bring down. Mardonius had seen his chance – and the danger of being flanked, with all the Greeks watching like wolves on the mountain.

The general gave a grunt. His was not a peasant army, but trained and disciplined men of forty nations. He had been intending to set a hundred thousand to hold that edge, while he went out to slaughter the rest. Yet the moment he had moved, the Spartans and their allies had come racing down the slopes! Mardonius had thought they would surely attack him, but instead they had pressed ahead of his marching ranks. As the dust thickened, he had lost sight of them, but he had learned something vital. The Spartans valued the men who faced him. Enough to risk everything to get out onto the plain, to give up whatever advantage they had held on the heights.

He'd seen his infantry meet the enemy in a great crash that resounded like a bell rung. Mardonius had gone forward then, keeping discipline, dressing his lines. His men slaughtered those Greeks without armour, killing hundreds every time he breathed, faster and faster.

Dust had swallowed friend and enemy, smothering individual acts of valour. Instead, the battle was revealed in the bodies he reached, lines and patches of them, draining into the earth. They appeared out of the swirling fogs, revealed by his steps as if summoned. It was a chilling thought. Many of them still cried in pain, panting away their last. Some writhed, turning and clutching, reminding him of crabs he had caught as a child.

There were few in Persian coats. He had blooded his army without great cost, raising their spirits. Around him, his people marched with heads held up and weapons high, seeking out the enemy in the haze.

Mardonius had known fogs and autumn mists at home. He jerked his head, craning to hear as new fighting broke out on his left. The wind could carry sounds in strange ways, he knew. He whistled for one of his messengers to attend him. The young rider who came was little older than a boy, red-eyed and stained in dust and sweat. He touched a hand to eyes and lips and bowed in the saddle. Mardonius had intended to send part of the centre out to support the left. As

*Conn Iggulden*

he began to speak, the dust cleared ahead and he could see further. Words died in his throat.

Out of the pale storm, standing lines appeared, emerging like a rock from a shining sea. They carried round shields of golden bronze, with helmets and spears. They wore red cloaks. Mardonius tried to swallow, but his mouth was too dry. He had seen the destruction three hundred of them had wrought. These stood still as stones on the dry ground, but thousands upon thousands of them. They had not run from his approach. Nor had they tried to hit his flank, as he had expected. No, they had raced out ahead of his army and planted themselves in his path, waiting calmly for him to reach them. Dust swirled back in, but he had seen them and he could still make out their shape. They were there, like ghosts, waiting.

Mardonius heard some regiment give a great howl on his right. They had the smell of blood in their nostrils, the enemy sighted. He echoed it, banishing his fear. Suddenly, the entire Persian army was bellowing, a sound to fill the world. Arrows flashed out in vast, clattering volleys that whipped through the dust, making it swirl. He saw the golden ripple as the Spartans raised shields, but they did not fall. Mardonius felt the first whisper of helplessness. He had seen one Spartan king stand against archers, soldiers, the elite. They made other men feel weak and that was half the battle. He strangled the doubts in him. The God of Light would hear the prayers of his men.

Mardonius raised and dropped his hand, sending them all in. There would be other Greeks out there, he knew. He did not fear those. No, he feared the red-cloaked devils who fought so calmly, with faces set, who made his men choke on their own blood.

Mardonius went forward with the rest, drawing his sword as the pace increased. The dust thickened, making the

Spartans appear and disappear as it swirled. Yet they stood still, waiting for the sea to crash over them.

At twenty paces, his regiments broke into a charge, roaring. Mardonius watched the front ranks reach the Spartan spears. Those first, brave men did not fare well. They lunged and knocked iron leaves aside, trying to slip past the points. The leaf-shaped heads broke coats and shields, finding flesh. Mardonius could hear barrel-chested Spartan officers chanting time with the thrusts. Their voices were perfectly calm, sounding over and over like a training ritual. The spears were long and they had weight and strength behind each blow. The wounds they made tore men from life and left them standing, dead on their feet.

The Spartans held well against that vast charge. They did not seem to panic when the Persian advance went around them, swallowing them on all sides. Mardonius had been taught that no army could fight surrounded. It terrified men to have an enemy on more than one side, never mind behind them, flanked and battered to the fore. Yet the Spartans kept formation and Mardonius could only recall the determination he had witnessed at Thermopylae. They had not given up then, despite appalling odds. He felt a cold hand touch his stomach, a sense of illness. No. He still had the Immortals.

He sent his messenger through the dust storm to bring Hydarnes in. The lad raced away, cursing those in his path. Some time passed and a bass roar went up, confirming they were coming. Mardonius grinned then.

The empire did not lose, not in the end. God knew, they had experienced disasters before, but they were the tide. They came in, regardless, carried on gold or blood, or fear, it did not matter much which it was. They still came in.

He let himself be carried closer to the Spartan square, drawn to the noise of clashing death, of metal and flesh and

pain. Movement flashed away in the madness, like a spinning top of gold and red, drawing the eye in horrible
fascination. He nudged his horse closer still, and in that
moment understood he had come too close. One of the
Spartans looked up to see which horseman had drifted in on
the flood. That man recognised the armour and helmet of a
senior officer and pointed. Mardonius could not pull back, not
when his men were being killed on all sides. If he turned, they
would think he had lost his nerve. They would run.

The Spartans were terrifying. He found himself utterly still,
frozen as more and more looked at him. He did not see the
spear thrown, twenty paces along the line. It flew hard and
fast, taking him between helmet and breastplate, in the hollow
of his collarbone. A dozen others flew wide of him, but it only
took one. Mardonius fell, slipping to the ground with his
throat ruined. His eyes were wide in horror and panic as he
scrambled to his feet, heaving for breath with one hand clutching his neck. He could feel his pulses beating and he couldn't
speak. He turned as the Immortals came jingling through
their own people, moving faster and faster as they sighted red
cloaks. Mardonius gave thanks. He stood with one hand on
his horse's saddle-pommel and the other keeping him alive.

The Spartans knew the white-coated Immortals and what
they meant. Somehow, they turned the vast square to face
the ranks charging them. As they came together, Mardonius
felt hope slowly shrivel and die. The Spartans blocked and
stabbed with their spears, like a dance. They shifted subtly
away from blows, so that the strength of better men was
wasted. They were hard to hit, but they knew their own tools.
They tore through the Immortals just as fast as the Persians
could come on. There was barely time for each rank of white-
coated men to understand the threat before they were cut
and speared and knocked down.

When the spears broke, the Spartans drew swords and the killing was worse. They did not seem to tire as ordinary men did. Mardonius watched a great churn of his Immortals as rank after rank was slaughtered. His entire army spun around them and yet they could not break the Spartan square. There was fighting off somewhere else, but this was the heart of the battle, as he had always known it would be.

He had not brought enough men. Mardonius watched Hydarnes himself attempt to smash their line with his horse. The general was spitted on thrown spears, with two more grounded and held up for the horse to run onto. The animal screamed, or Hydarnes did, Mardonius was not sure. He watched and waited for an age, while his army milled and panicked and fought and ran around him. One by one, senior officers died. When Mardonius understood they could *not* break the Spartans, that the day would be theirs, when he could not stand the despair a moment longer, he pulled his hand away from the flesh of his throat and slid to the ground.

The Persian regiments knew the favour of God had passed from them. It had been bad enough losing Masistius, the master of horse, then Hydarnes of the Immortals. When Mardonius slumped, he took their will to fight. As dust coated their throats and made them strain for just one clean breath, they lost the battle madness that had carried them through a dozen lands and across the sea.

Mardonius looked up at faces looming over him. His people. They had come a long way to be in that place. They had burned a great city twice and yet its people somehow still took up arms against them. Other countries had always known when to lie down, when to give up. It seemed no one had told the Greeks. Though it was madness, perhaps it was its own strength as well. He did not blink when dust began to settle across his eyes.

# 29

The air smelled of fire, of char and blood. Xanthippus could smell it on his skin as he stood in a city square and looked down at the governor, kneeling before him. The man still wore his sleeping robe, spattered with blood from his lips and nose. Smoke rose in the south, where Xanthippus had been the evening before. His ships waited for him, in sight of the town, but no longer with those of Sparta and Corinth. Those allies had not understood how important it was to make a mark Persia would never forget. He had come to that place to do more than just burn a fleet! Those black ribs were all behind him, far to the south. He had whipped his people on to find and break the fabled bridge of ships, but that too was gone. Stolen from him. Nothing more than a few piers remained, with driftwood all along the Hellespont shore.

Xanthippus had thought he might feel some easing of his pain if he could have seen that bridge burn. Yet it had been broken, just a thread snapped by storms. The Great King had passed through months before. Xerxes had returned to his palaces and gardens, an empire away from that coast. He would forget them there, Xanthippus knew. If they allowed him to.

King Leotychides of Sparta had seemed to think their work was at an end. Xanthippus had explained at length why it was not. The man had looked at him strangely then and taken his hand in a firm grip, kissing him on both cheeks. His ships had been gone in the morning. Those of Corinth and half a dozen others had rowed away with them.

Xanthippus shook his head at the thought. He did not need allies who looked to Sparta for leadership. He had come to that coast to bring vengeance, for all the Persians had done, for their arrogance, for the murders and rapes and the slaves they had taken. He had seen too many bodies. There were times when he thought he would never sleep again without rising up in the dark, sweating and thrashing.

The governor who knelt on stones with his hands bound in his lap spoke perfect Greek, as so many did on that Ionian coast of empire. They were the descendants of Hellenes, after all, just one or two generations back. The children of men and women who had come to that place to grow crops and build new lives, to seed cities like Athens. Instead of freedom, they had been gathered into the Persian realm.

Xanthippus saw the man was weeping. He bent down to stare at him. The governor's face crumpled.

'Please, kurios. Let my son live. Let me swear allegiance to you, to Greece. Whatever you want. Just let my boy go. He has done nothing.'

Xanthippus looked around. There was blood on the street, bright red. He had chosen to make an example of this town, one that might reach the ears of the emperor himself, as Xanthippus himself could not. The empire was vast, with too many men under arms to march to its heart. Instead, he had burned that coast, a host of villages and towns. He had let free Greeks run before the flames grew too fierce, but when he found Persian tax collectors or their officials cowering from him, he had hanged them in the town squares.

Xanthippus could not remember when he had last known peace. His eyes were red as he looked over the kneeling crowd. They trembled with bowed heads, awaiting their fate.

'You people,' Xanthippus said. 'You welcome Persians into your homes, raising their children as your own. You forget our gods, our tongue. You pay taxes to a foreign king and you forget who you are, who you were . . .' He trailed off, skirting a pit of grief so vast he dared not look into it.

'Please, kurios. Archon . . .' the governor said. 'Let my son go. He is innocent. Will you take payment for his life? I have twenty talents in silver, all I own. I will show you where, kurios. Please.'

Xanthippus shook his head.

'You cannot buy me. You cannot buy his life . . .'

'Father . . .'

Xanthippus jerked around at the sound. Pericles stood there and Xanthippus felt rage suffuse him, darkening his skin.

'I told you to remain with the ships!' he shouted. He grabbed the young man and wrenched at him, his fist twisting the cloth of his tunic. 'How many times will you disobey me?'

'It is *enough*!' Pericles replied. 'Ariphron is gone. Let's just go home.'

'To ashes?' Xanthippus said harshly. 'To a burned city? No, I will make a mark these people will never forget. Take up his son.'

The governor wailed in fear and grief as Epikleos stepped forward. The hoplite officer stood in full armour, wrapped in bronze. His expression was stern and yet worried for his friend.

'Xan . . .' he said. 'There is no need . . .'

'My order is to nail his son to a tree, Epikleos,' Xanthippus said. 'As an example to them all. Then to execute this Persian governor. If you cannot carry it out, relieve yourself of duty and return to the ship.'

'*Please*, kurios!' the governor said. 'Take me, not my son!' He sagged as if he had been knocked out, his head hanging.

'If I refuse an order, my life is over when we return,'

Epikleos said softly. 'If you are my friend, Xanthippus, you will not make me choose.'

He saw nothing but madness in Xanthippus. Though he understood it, he shuddered.

'Order me instead to take Pericles back to the ship, Xan. If you have ever called me a friend, grant me that.'

Xanthippus looked back at Pericles, who wept as he stood there, staring at the son of the governor. The boy was no more than eight or ten years old and he was terrified.

'Very well,' Xanthippus grated. 'Take Pericles back to the ship.'

'Come with us,' Pericles said. 'Leave this behind, father, please.'

'That's enough,' Epikleos said roughly.

He took a firm grip on Pericles' arm and did not look back as he half-dragged him out of the town square. The sea was very blue as they walked away from the sounds of fear and weeping.

'Why?' Pericles said. 'Why is he like this? It won't bring Ariphron back.'

'He is lost,' Epikleos said. 'Or broken. Part of him will remain here, Pericles, with your brother. I am sorry. Your father has been my friend since I was just a boy. I have seen him suffer, in battle, in exile. He has endured great loss. Yet I have never known him to be cruel. I . . . never thought I would see it in him.'

As the moon rose that night, Xanthippus returned to the ships of Athens and her allies. Only the triremes of the Peloponnese had gone; those who remained were still many. He came on board the flagship and removed all his armour to stand naked on the deck. Buckets were dipped into the sea on ropes and handed to him, over and over under the moonlight. He washed away soot and blood and sweat as best he could, rubbing his skin raw with a pumice stone and oil. When he was clean, Epikleos brought him a tunic, sandals and a cloak against the night's cold. Xanthippus wrapped himself in them and lay down on the deck to sleep. All around him were the pupae of his men, awake and grim-faced as they stared at the stars overhead.

Epikleos knelt by the archon and strategos of Athens.

'Your son was . . . grieving for a time. I told him you would heal and be his father once again.'

'I am,' Xanthippus said.

Silence slipped between them like a knife and remained. After a long time, Xanthippus murmured on the edge of sleep.

'I killed that man's son.' He began to sob softly. 'I left the father alive to feel the way I feel.'

'I am . . . sorry to hear that,' Epikleos said, with a sigh.

He had held out hope that Xanthippus might have turned from his rage at the last moment. It was one thing to kill men in battle, when it had to be done. Executing a child in spite and rage was a wound that cried out to the gods. Xanthippus knew it.

'If I could have the day again, if I could go back and change it . . .'

'I know, Xan. I know,' Epikleos said. It was the cry of all weak men and he had not expected it from his oldest friend. Rather than reply, he rose, leaving Xanthippus to choke out his grief into the folds of the cloak, the sounds muffled and terrible. The storm would pass, he knew. Or at least, it would lose its edge, the terrible sharpness of the first cut. Wounds scarred in time, but the skin was never stronger than before.

Epikleos stood at the prow for a time. He could smell smoke on the air, but the ships had turned at anchor and faced west. Athens lay over the horizon. For all he knew, it was in ruins once again, with a Persian army victorious. He prayed for Aristides and their allies, that they had come through.

Aristides felt old, with every cut and wrenched limb making itself known. He had marched and fought since the first hours of the day. He had seen helots slaughtered like lambs. His own Athenians had been surrounded, battered back and back in a great sea of the enemy. Yet at the very heart, Pausanias and the Spartans had stood. They had been a golden stone in the flood – and the Persians had broken against them. Aristides thought he would not forget that, not if he lived for another fifty years.

There had been no respite when the Persians tried to retreat to their camp. Pausanias had given orders to pursue, close on their heels. No rallying point would be allowed for them that year, no refuge. They had come to Greece with trumpets sounding; they would not be allowed to go home on their own terms. Aristides had dipped his head with the rest, putting aside all mercy.

There was a slick of blood down his front that had already dried brown. He had held one man while two of his hoplites stabbed the fellow. He had not died well, that one. Some did, to their credit, though they were just as dead in the end. It was grim work and the Greeks were all exhausted as the sun reached the horizon. Even the long summer day was not enough. The slaughter was terrible and men just sat and knelt when they could not go on, panting in pain, swords slipping from numb hands.

Pausanias called for torches to be lit, standing in the centre of the Persian camp. His soothsayer Tisamenus stood at his side and Pausanias clapped him on the back at intervals, delighted. He had his first contest, his victory.

The camp was vast and empty around them, though Persian tents were being searched in all directions. In theory, it was to look for men hiding, but half the Greeks seemed to be adorned in gold. Only the Spartans stood apart, as they didn't use coins. Their scorn did not seem to dampen the enthusiasm of their allies, however.

Aristides had to identify himself twice to Spartan officers before he was allowed through. He imagined he did not look much like the man he had been that morning. His skin was thick with dust and he was filthy with the blood of others, wiped with oil and muck across his face. Still, he represented Athens in that camp. More importantly, it would not do to let Pausanias claim it as a victory for Sparta alone.

By the time he was let through, he discovered he was not the only leader to have gathered there. It rankled just a little that Pausanias had become the centre, but Aristides knew he had earned it.

'I give thanks to the gods for the victory,' Aristides said.

Pausanias turned to see who spoke and smiled.

'We were blessed indeed,' he said. The man was too pious to put himself before the honour due, but Aristides could see his pride.

'Regent Pausanias,' he said formally, 'it was the honour of Athens to fight alongside you. I hope it will be the beginning of a great friendship. I honour our allies. Alone, we could not prevail. Together, we broke an empire.'

Pausanias did not seem to find those words quite to his liking. His eyebrow raised a little higher and his smile vanished.

'I do not believe Sparta would have sent me out if those in

Athens had not threatened to stand with the very enemy we defeated. Think on that, if you have a moment for reflection.'

Aristides blinked at the anger in the younger man. He supposed it was one way to look at it, but he could not allow the Spartan to define the terms, not when the new day would bring a world without an enemy in Greece.

'Had you come out, Regent Pausanias, before Athens burned for a second time, we would not have been made homeless and desperate. Still, I learned the greatness of Sparta today. I hope you saw as much of my people.'

'I'm sorry, I did not see you fight,' Pausanias said. He eyed the bloodstained, exhausted Athenian standing before him, choosing his words carefully. 'Though I do not doubt your valour.' He might have left it at that, but some impulse made him speak again before Aristides could reply. 'I asked you, though, not to make my helots think they could fight. I am told they stood against a Persian war line. They were cut down in their thousands. I will have the numbers for you in the morning, but it was a heavy price to pay.'

Aristides realised it was the wrong time and place for reconciliation. He recalled the old law, that men should not discuss a battle until they have slept and eaten – and slept again. Tempers ran too high in the immediate aftermath. Blood seethed and men spoke rashly, even to their allies. He bowed deeply to the Spartan regent, including Tisamenus in his gesture. The soothsayer returned it, while Pausanias only nodded stiffly.

'It was a great victory,' Aristides said. 'I will withdraw now.'

'You have a city to rebuild,' Tisamenus said.

'Yes,' Aristides said with a smile. 'Yes, that is true. I will make her even greater than she was before.'

With that promise, he left them, seeking his own people in the darkness all around. Bodies hissed and shifted in the night. There would be little chance for sleep as things twitched and creaked around them on the plain. He found his men, and as he approached, one of their number was holding up a wineskin, boasting to his friends.

'I kept this safe the whole battle, just to toast the victory.'

'May I have it?' Aristides asked him.

The man spun round, ready with a retort. When he saw it was Aristides and heard the man's name whispered amongst his friends, he handed it over without hesitation.

'Of course, kurios,' he said.

Aristides thanked him and took it away. He had lochagoi officers to handle the work of settling hoplites down for the night after a victory. They would send messengers back to Themistocles, telling him they had saved Greece.

Slowly, with every joint aching, Aristides climbed the flank of the mountain until he found a place that felt high enough away from the noise of men. He sat himself on a shelf of rock and moss and drank the wine. It was sour stuff, but it warmed him. He thought he would sit there until the sun rose. He had not expected to see another dawn. He leaned back against a rock that still held some of the sun's warmth. After a time, without knowing it, he slept, the wineskin cradled like a child in his arms.

# 30

Xanthippus came home. The news of victory at Plataea had spread across the Aegean – island to island, boat to boat – until it reached his fleet. He had gathered the captains on his deck and drunk the last of the good wine with them. It was a sort of brotherhood, forged in the fleet actions. Pericles had heard his father and Epikleos talking about it afterwards in a sort of drunken wonder. Even without the ships of the Peloponnese, those captains represented thirty states and cities between them, led by Athens. They had all been alone, before the war. That night, some of them had seen a nation, for the first time.

With the port of Athens in sight, Pericles watched his father going to the prow, curling his arm around the keel beam while their ram crested the waves. Xanthippus' expression was dark, under lowered brows. At the same time, his rowers made a fine show of the approach, oars rising and falling in perfect unison.

The people were already gathering in the port of Piraeus, running down from the city as news spread, ready to welcome the fleet home. They carried branches of red amaranth and waved their arms, cheering along the green hills as the ships rowed by, then racing to the port in desperate hope and joy, where they might see husbands, brothers, sons. The day was warm, the sky clear. Some of the men waved in reply, overcome at the sight of their own people, freed at last from fear. The shadow of the Persian invasion had hung over them for years. The people of Athens had lived with that threat every day. They had seen their fleet driven back in the first battles, the sacred city burned twice, every woman and child forced out as refugees. They had nothing – and they would take it up and rebuild once more.

Xanthippus stood like a knot, out of place as his ships came in and began to disembark their crews. The Piraeus had a dozen massive quays in stone, so that he did not have to wait, but came straight in to be tied on. The crowd cheered like madmen when they saw who it was, calling his name over and over. They brought a plank bridge, but Xanthippus ignored them. Pericles watched as his father jumped down to the dock, standing to balance for a moment as it swayed under him. He saw his father bend and kiss the ground then, patting it like the dog whose gravestone still marked the coast of Salamis.

Some of the crowd came forward to try and touch him, to embrace the man who had saved them at Salamis, then taken the fight to the Persians. In the months he had been away, word had come of his exploits, his sacking of the coast. They lived in a city that had been twice burned, that still smelled of ash when it rained. There were few who had not prayed for him and blessed his name.

Xanthippus turned from those beating his back in joy. A woman tried to press his hand to her cheek and he snatched it away, making her stumble. Epikleos stepped off then beside him, whistling to the hoplites. They surrounded the archon, giving him room to breathe. That year had been named for Xanthippus. It did not mean the crowd owned him.

Pericles gathered his brother's shield and armour in a sack, heaving it onto his shoulder. It was a huge weight and he did not relish the idea of carrying it all the way through the city to the estate. He would do it, however. Though he saw

Xanthippus looking across the faces, searching, his mother was not there in the crowd. Pericles knew she had been told. As a privilege of the navarch of Athens, a ship had been dispatched weeks before with the news. Pericles did not know what her absence meant.

With the honour guard tight around his father, Pericles fell into their wake, barely protected from the cheering crowd. After so long on board a silent ship, with nothing but the sound of the waves, it was confusing, even frightening, to be among people once more, people who did not understand orders and discipline. They kept pressing in and Pericles worried his father would order the hoplites to draw their swords. Xanthippus' face was thunderous as women or men kept slipping through, reaching for him as though his touch could heal. They wept, some of them, or shrieked, oblivious to his discomfort.

Rowers poured out behind Pericles, taking the opportunity. On land, they too became the cheering crowd, raising their hands and shouting. They began to sing the march of Athena in a thousand voices, the tune barely surviving. A dozen triremes emptied in a great throng, crews simply abandoning their ships. On the water, other officers shouted in anger, seeking out any other spot where they could throw a rope.

Striding ahead of that rising chaos, Xanthippus was the dark heart of the procession. Cold and furious, he was nonetheless their focus, the delight of all those who saw him. Miltiades had come back years before, too wounded to walk. Xanthippus was war-thin and fit. He needed no help. The road to his family estate was to the north-west of the city. The best route there was through the Agora, but that meant he led crowds like on a feast day to the centre of the city, their numbers swelling with every moment.

*Conn Iggulden*

Pericles could only stare as the crowds grew bolder, the press of bodies buffeting him as he struggled under the weight of his brother's kit. It would have been easier to wear the armour than to carry it. He looked around for Ariphron, to tell him . . . and felt the loss once more. It was not possible that his brother was gone, his clever, thoughtful brother who always knew so much. His father had refused to bury Ariphron on Persian land, where a tomb might be despoiled. Instead, they had sewn him in sailcloth and marked a burial spot on Icaria. They would come back for him.

Pericles shifted the sack on his shoulder. He was sweating in the heat and heave of the crowd all around. When Epikleos asked if he wanted help, he shook his head. Epikleos seemed to understand that.

As they reached the Agora, Pericles saw the heart of the city was being rebuilt. The council building was rising once again on scaffolding. The Pnyx hill was the same, of course. The steps had been scrubbed clean and shone whitely in the afternoon sun. Above it all loomed the Acropolis. The foundations had been cleared there, but he knew they would raise temples once again. This was Athena's city, after all. Even the army of Persia had not been able to chain her for long. Pericles felt tears come without warning as he looked around him. They bore so many flowers, his people! They cried out and embraced the sailors and hoplites of the fleet returned. More and more poured into the Agora from all directions and yet his father did not stop, but pushed through, determined to reach the other side. Pericles had to struggle to keep up, but he was not recognised and they let him pass easily enough. It was the strangest thing, but Xanthippus and Epikleos shoved past the outer ring and it was all suddenly behind. The cheering crowds all looked inward and never saw Xanthippus heading away from them, his face set and dark with purpose.

Pericles and Epikleos walked alongside one another as they passed through what had been the Thriasian gate. The ground had been cleared there, with markers for a huge new construction. It filled Pericles with excitement, somehow. They would not just remake Athens as she had been, but higher, greater. Why not? His mind filled with visions of wide streets and courtyards, of great gates and monuments, of soaring temples to reflect the glory of the goddess.

Outside the gate, the ruins of ancient tombs still stretched. The Persians had destroyed them all, breaking them with hammers. Pericles thought first it had been to loot keepsakes and trophies – the weapons and armour of Athenians, perhaps. As he walked through a field of broken tombstones, it seemed too thorough for that. Pieces lay in the road with names carved into them. That seemed the merest spite, just to hurt the ones who had loved the dead. In one place, bodies were being wrapped and reburied, piled on one another with a dozen men working to fill a huge pit. Someone had given an order their families could not, he realised. Pericles thought of Cimon's pain when he heard. His father's corpse would be there, somewhere, among the bones and broken things.

In a few months, or a year, Pericles knew Ariphron would be collected from his burial spot and returned to the family tomb. When it too was remade. He felt a chill at that, but their mother would want a place to come and mourn.

Beyond the city, the road was quiet. Xanthippus still walked as if alone, without looking back. Pericles struggled to keep up and had to shake his head twice when Epikleos held out his hand to take the sack of armour. He felt his own mood darken and grow cold as he approached the estate. When they had left, it had been burned out, deliberately despoiled. Hard laughter had sounded in that place as Persians smashed everything of craft and value. Pericles had not been sure he could live there again, but a new house loomed as they approached, low and wide, with a roof of red tile and wooden posts. It looked a little smaller than he remembered.

The estate wall was not finished, so that Xanthippus just stepped over the boundary to his home. A slave called out in warning and the whole house roused to see who approached without an invitation. Pericles felt his eyes fill as he saw Manias and a dozen others appear, armed with swords and clubs. A pale figure moved in the cloister, and then his mother came out.

Agariste approached slowly at first. Her face was calm and yet she walked faster and faster towards them, as if she could not stop herself. Xanthippus stopped and waited, until she drew to a halt before him, looking up. Pericles wanted to shout for his father to embrace her. Instead, they stood and faced one another. Without warning, Agariste slapped her husband hard across the face. Xanthippus could have stopped the blow. He did not try to.

When he did not respond, she did it again, then a third time. Pericles was weeping and he did not know how long they would have stood there like that if Epikleos had not stepped forward and grabbed Agariste by the arm.

'I'm sorry, Agariste,' Epikleos said. 'Ariphron died bravely and well.'

She snatched her arm from him without looking away from Xanthippus. Instead, her face twisted, but to weep rather than rage. Without replying, she turned and went back into the house.

Xanthippus raised a hand to his cheek, that side of his face already swelling. He nodded grimly, shifting his pack. Pericles took that moment to lay down the sack of armour that had chafed and pinched him all the way from the coast. He supposed the set would be his to wear, unless he inherited his father's. In that moment, he didn't feel worthy of either one.

Eleni came out at a run. She had become a young woman, tall and slim. She held out her hand to her father, embracing him awkwardly. Xanthippus said nothing. The silence was uncomfortable and Pericles shook his head when she looked at him, trying to excuse his father for his coldness. He tried to think what Ariphron would have done in his place. That was not such a bad thing, he thought. His brother could be his example, perhaps for the rest of his life.

Pericles stepped forward and put his arms around his sister.

'I'm sorry . . .' he said. His voice choked and for a time, nothing more came.

His father looked past them both, his gaze taking in the changes to the house.

Epikleos took up the sack Pericles had laid down, hefting the weight easily.

'This will all need to be cleaned, repaired and polished. I'll have your brother's name inscribed on the shield.'

Pericles wiped his eyes as he stood apart from his sister.

'I'll do it,' he said, holding out his hand. 'I don't want to give his armour to anyone else.'

Epikleos hesitated only a moment before he handed it over. Pericles breathed deeply, smelling new wood and oil on the air, new crops sown and growing. His mother must have worked day and night to remake the house for their return. He saw new fence posts on the field where he had learned to ride, not yet joined to one another. It brought him a sense of hope, even in the midst of loss.

'Will you stay here tonight?' Epikleos asked his father.

Xanthippus glanced at the door where his wife had gone inside. He grimaced and nodded.

'I think so. You are welcome of course, Epikleos, as always. Nothing changes that.'

'No . . . I'll find rooms in the city. I'd like to hear the details of the victory from those who were there. I'll buy them drinks – and have a few myself.'

Xanthippus looked at his daughter and Pericles. He ran a tongue over his lower lip. His knee throbbed in time with his heart. He was tired, to the bone. Yet his duty was done. The thought of spending a night with Agariste's grief was a different kind of pain.

'Pericles?' Xanthippus said at last. 'Stay here with your mother and sister. That is an order. I will head back into the city. I'll see you when I return.'

Pericles only bowed his head, not daring to reply. His father's mood had lightened just a touch and he did not want to risk any more anger. The young man was completely exhausted and he welcomed a chance to escape the thunderstorm. Instead, Pericles watched, putting his arm around his sister as the two men walked back to the gate, then onto the road into the city.

'I can't believe Ariphron won't come back,' Eleni said suddenly. 'I wanted him to see the house. I've . . . been doing so much, just to have him look pleased and . . . smile in that way of his. Now he won't . . . I'll never hear his voice again, or see him laugh.'

Pericles shook his head. He could feel his brother's gaze on him.

'He knows,' he said, turning to go inside. 'He's already home. I'm sure he made it here before we did.'

# 31

Xanthippus woke with his son's name on his lips, calling out in panic, then suddenly ashamed. He could not reach Ariphron, could not bring him back. He could not undo one day, one single heartbeat that had gone before. He groaned as he sat up, smelling vomit on him. He had always been a fastidious man and he winced at the stench. Worse than vomit. His bowels had emptied! It happened sometimes, he knew, when a man drank as much wine as he had. Yet it had never happened to him. It had all dried, of course, sticking his clothes to him in the night. He wished briefly that he was still at sea, where he could swim. He needed buckets and a great deal of water, perhaps a river . . . He looked around, trying to work out where he was. Two days had passed since he had set foot in Athens once again, or . . . three, he was no longer sure. He had tried to drink himself to death, but it just kept pouring out and then he would start again. By Athena, he was starving! His head! His leg was like a board, the knee was so stiff. The air seemed to fill with flashes of light whenever he moved.

He was not alone in the room, he realised. A strange man lay in the opposite corner, his tunic pulled up, exposing himself in his slumbers. A woman with curly brown hair in her armpits lay alongside him, snoring like a child. The man had a huge black eye, but Xanthippus had no memory of either of them.

He wanted to call for Epikleos, knowing his friend would never have deserted him. Flashes of memory intruded as Xanthippus heaved himself to his feet, suppressing a cry of pain when he found his leg would hardly bend. It was early morning, judging by the light and the cool air. His stomach creaked and heaved. No! He looked desperately for a place to throw up, but there was no bowl or bucket in the room. He leaned over a long line of yellow bile for a time, then limped out into the sun.

The gymnasium field was not empty at that hour. Some of the men of Athens began each day with a swim, while others sparred or ran round the track before heading to their work. The Persians had cut down the trees and set fires where they could, of course. Those marks were still there, but his people had worked hard and there was at least some sense of order as Xanthippus blinked in the light. It helped a little to hold his head in both hands, his elbows away from him.

The river Ilissus ran not far from where he stood. Xanthippus staggered over to it and walked in, down steps made for the purpose. The water was freezing cold and he groaned as he dipped his head right under the surface. With slow and clumsy movements, he stripped naked and rubbed himself clean. His soiled tunic floated away in the current and he let it go. Little by little, he began to feel more alert. He was not surprised to see Epikleos come out, spotting him and jogging over. His friend held one eye closed as if he could no longer open it.

As Xanthippus came out and stood on the bank to dry, he felt his skin roughen. To his dismay, he had to lean over and retch once more, though there was nothing in him, not even spit. Epikleos looked away. He had dried blood on his face and his nose was swollen, Xanthippus saw. He wondered if he had been the one who fought the stranger in his room.

Slowly, Xanthippus sat down on the muddy bank, not caring how it marked him. He dangled his legs in the water and let grief and guilt rush in, colder even than the river. Epikleos nodded, almost slipping and falling as he too descended the steps and entered the water, dipping his head under for the longest time.

The cold reached through the fog in both of them. Xanthippus had not asked for help, not once. He recalled people laughing at him when he'd fallen, twisting his damned knee. Yet there was a lake of sorrow in him still, deep enough to drown a man. Epikleos had stayed with the archon and navarch, with his friend, trying to keep him safe, never letting him go off on his own. There had been both threats and offers the night before, of course. Xanthippus was the hero of Salamis, returned. He was loved by many, though for some he was also the one who had freed their slaves without compensating them.

Epikleos had remained at his side for other reasons too, knowing his friend's mood could turn darker and darker if he left him alone. Some men never thought of the death of friends and loved ones, or the men they had killed. Xanthippus was not one of those. His dreams were always terrible. Death haunted him, the loss of his son most of all.

The stranger from the room came weaving out then, practically falling into the river, so that he hit the water with a dull smack. Xanthippus could hear a woman's voice calling inside the building. He squinted over the field.

'Is Themistocles around?' he asked. 'This is his place, isn't it? I came here once.' He winced in memory of another evening, so many years before. It was someone else's life.

'I hope so. I don't have any money,' Epikleos said, without opening his eyes.

The stranger was drowning, that was clear. Epikleos seriously considered letting the fool continue to thrash about, then relented, stepping back in and heaving him onto the grass. The man took a huge breath and spluttered. Epikleos pushed at him in disgust and he wandered off.

Xanthippus nodded. Memories of the night before bub-

*Conn Iggulden*

bled to the surface. He remembered wanting to see the one who had arranged his exile, who had taken seven years of his life from him. Had he been going to fight Themistocles? Was that it? Wisps came and went, teasing him. He blamed Themistocles for a great deal. Of course, the war with Persia was over. It was an interesting thought. Whatever truce had existed between them was over as well. There was something else, though, he could sense it.

'I owe him,' Xanthippus said.

Epikleos nodded and shrugged.

'So you said last night, a hundred times. So you told Aristides. Do you not remember? He said you should wait until the Spartan had finished. That there might not be much left for you.'

Xanthippus stared for a long time. His lip stuck out as he searched his recollection in vain.

'What Spartan?' he said at last.

Epikleos looked up at the man he admired above all others. One reason he had stayed so close over the previous days was that Xanthippus kept promising to seek vengeance against Themistocles. It was the sort of threat that got a drunk man killed. Even sober, he did not think Xanthippus could win, not against one who had earned his first coins in a boxing ring. Justice took a distant second place to speed and skill, at least when it came to fists.

He was about to repeat all that again when he saw a red-cloaked figure crossing the field. It came back to both men in the same instant. They'd come to warn Themistocles, climbing out of a three-day stupor to carry the news. It had not been the most successful of plans. Epikleos squinted, one eye pressed shut against a headache he still thought might split his skull into two neat pieces.

'That one?' he said, staggering to his feet.

# 32

Eurybiades had set out from Sparta a week before, on foot. He'd raised a cup of wine to Regent Pausanias and the Spartiates when they had returned home in triumph. Helot women and children had lined up in silence to be told if their husbands and brothers and sons were among the dead. Thousands of those had been left on the plain by Plataea. They would not be given graves. Crows and foxes would tug them apart; the wind would make them bones in the sun. Their women were not allowed to weep, not in that moment of victory. Names of the fallen had been collected by the helots who still lived. As they were recited aloud, the women simply turned and went back to their homes, or returned to work.

A great procession had formed from the centre of the city to the acropolis. Pausanias had knelt there to the son of Leonidas, a public display of fealty that would help to keep him safe when Pleistarchus became battle king. He gave an oath of obedience that was the very soul of their city.

Eurybiades heard Pausanias had asked for a position with the Spartan fleet, far away from politics and power. He would not become an awkward presence for a young king. It was a sensible move for a man who had led the city to the greatest battle victory they had ever known. On one day, on the plain of Plataea, Spartiates and perioikoi had justified their entire regime and all their discipline. The stories were told over and over, every detail recorded without vainglory of any kind.

Eleven years before, Marathon had been a victory for Athens alone, one Sparta had not even reached before the

*Conn Iggulden*

battle was won. The year before, Thermopylae had cost Sparta a great king. The fleet battles of Artemisium and Salamis had been fought by an alliance of Greek states. Yet Plataea had come down to Spartan strength of arms and Spartan will, when they were surrounded and outnumbered. And they had proved their worth.

The war was at an end. That was the news that had brought Eurybiades out, with his cloak and sandals, with his sword and kopis knife. Thebes had been ransacked and punished for their part in betraying the rest, survivors exiled without armour, lash marks across their back and ashes in their hair. Every one of their officers had been left in the dust with the slaughtered Persians. There was little mercy in the victors, not then. Persia had learned a hard lesson in reaching beyond her grasp. So had her allies in Greece.

As he'd walked the road to Athens, Eurybiades had wondered if the Persian empire would even survive. With the loss of both army and fleet, surely there would be other eyes on them, looking for a chance to steal wealth and land, to tear them into forty kingdoms once again? He hoped so.

On arrival, Eurybiades took rooms in the city. A widow seemed pleased to have him there, saying she always slept better with a man in the house than she ever did alone. She washed his travel-stained clothes and cooked for him that night. He wore little and ate less, so there was not much need. She seemed to take pleasure in looking after him even so.

When he ventured out the following dawn, he found prices had risen sharply in Athens, to his disgust. The small store of silver coins he carried had been a gift from his brother. Even an hour in a bathhouse cost him half a day's wage! He had needed to empty his bowels and wash away the dirt and grime of the road, but it was still too much. Paying for food too was unpleasant, so that he glowered at street sellers hawking their wares. No Spartan ever ate at a street kitchen at home. Warriors took their meals in communal halls, with simple bowls and spoons provided for them. It had certainly not improved his mood to buy a skewer of cooked meat, then find it was so delicately spiced it made him want to weep.

The widow had lingered near the door to his room the night before, he'd noticed. They were all whores, in Athens. He'd had to throw the cushions off the bed, then roll his cloak and sleep on the wooden floor. He prayed to Apollo to keep him safe from all their foul temptations.

His fortunes had taken a turn for the worse since his return to Sparta. It seemed news had spread of his authority as navarch being scorned by the Athenians – and Themistocles. His Spartan captains had reported all they had witnessed, but of course they had not troubled to explain the difficulties of his position. Eurybiades had gone from being a respected officer to having his good name in tatters. If there was coin worth having in Sparta, it was reputation – and so Eurybiades knew poverty for the first time in his life.

When he asked for Themistocles, it surprised him to have people offering to buy his drinks. As soon as they saw the red cloak, they were clapping him on the shoulder and calling for wine. For all their lack of honour, they seemed to think of Spartans as allies that year. Eurybiades had lost count of the times he'd been asked if he'd been at Plataea. He had not, of course. That fool Pausanias had left a few senior men behind, to run the city. Eurybiades had been one of those he'd honoured with that responsibility.

He frowned as he walked across the city, following directions to a gymnasium he'd been told Themistocles owned. Eurybiades wondered again if the man might be avoiding him. Twice that morning he had reached a place where

*Conn Iggulden*

crowds still were, only to hear that Themistocles had just left. He had almost encountered him on the Pnyx, but as noon approached, he thought he would surely find him where he ate. A tavern-owner had accepted a silver coin for providing directions.

It was a good thing he was not staying another few days, Eurybiades thought ruefully. His collection of Athenian coins was almost gone. Still, it would be worth it. There was a debt owed, one he would be delighted to settle. It might even remove the sting of being left in disgrace at home while his people won a great victory. He tightened his jaw as he reached the city boundary and strode past the wall, still under construction in places. He felt his mouth twist into a sneer. Spartans needed no walls. What enemy would ever dare challenge the warriors who had defeated Persia? Oh, the Athenians had been present, yes, but if there could ever be a set of scales large enough, Sparta would outweigh all the rest. There was no doubt about *that*.

Eurybiades had tried to explain the concept to a group of working men just that morning. They had offered him water from a ladle and refused to accept a single coin in exchange. All they wanted was his memory of Plataea. They had grown quite cold by the time he had finished explaining. Two of them had even followed him for a time, until he'd shown them his kopis blade and challenged them in the street, flinging back his red cloak. They'd slunk off then, quickly enough! Whores and cowards, all of them. Even to be among them left him feeling less than clean. Well, he'd come to fulfil an obligation. When that was done, he could go home, to retirement and peace.

Eurybiades was not challenged at the entrance of the gymnasium, though two burly slaves bowed to him and another went racing off, no doubt to inform their master. The walk out of the city had loosened Eurybiades up, which was a relief at his age. Still, he wondered if he should use the stone weights or take a lap around the running track. His left hip grew stiff at times, though it could be stretched out. He stood in thought, casting his eye over two men swimming and a dozen others exercising in the morning sun. There was a calm there that soothed his spirits, a place more like a training ground of Sparta than the drunk-houses and fleshpits of the city he had just left. Eurybiades had been taught a fine contempt for pleasure, for the weakness it brought. At times, he almost wished Persia could have swallowed these people up. Yet the fate of Sparta had been entwined with them for a time. Apollo grant it never would be again.

He felt a strange twinge of pleasure when he recognised Themistocles coming out to see him. The man wore a simple belted robe, wiping his mouth on a cloth as he came. Like Eurybiades, he bore no armour, carried no shield. Eurybiades had not come for war, after all, but to repay a disgrace. He was not sure if it was a compliment or insult that Themistocles had appeared unarmed, without even a sword.

'Navarch Eurybiades,' Themistocles said by way of greeting.

The Spartan bowed his head.

'Themistocles,' he said stiffly. 'The war is over. I said I would come.'

'And you are a man of your word,' Themistocles said. To Eurybiades' surprise, the Athenian clapped him on the shoulder like an old friend. 'You have walked far. Are you staying in the city, or did you come straight from home? Please, you are my guest. Take wine with me.'

Eurybiades understood there was no rush to begin. He appreciated a man who showed such a fine lack of fear, with death so close. It was worth rewarding and the truth was, his throat was rather dry. Eurybiades dipped his head.

'That would be welcome, thank you.'

Themistocles signalled his servants and a table was brought out, with two chairs. The sun was bright as they took seats. Eurybiades watched as the wine was poured from a single jug, a beautiful piece in black and brown. Warriors danced or fought on the sides, the work of a master. He found his gaze drawn to it.

Themistocles mixed in a little water from a smaller jug, then took a long draught and smacked his lips.

'There, that is joy. Please drink. I think you know I would not poison a guest, even a Spartan.'

Eurybiades smiled tightly, but with his courage questioned, he drained his cup and held it out for a servant to refill. Warmth and flavour spread through him, making his senses swim.

'Very good. You were always quick with a barb, Themistocles. There are times when I regret what passed between us.'

'I see,' Themistocles said thoughtfully. 'Well, have you considered, at least for a moment, that you might have been in the wrong?'

The Spartan only looked at him and Themistocles shrugged, his hands moving through the air as he spoke.

'We pulled back and back – war at sea was new to all of us, you know that! We'd only had a fleet for a few years and never fought in large formation. The Persians had so many ships, there was no end to them. I think you and I came to the same conclusion, at around the same time. We could not win, not there, not against that fleet. All we could do was fight a rear action to slow them down while we retreated. It was . . . yes, the worst day of the war for me.'

Eurybiades blinked slowly. Themistocles spoke with his eyes distant. Without warning, his gaze snapped back to sharpness, then he grinned and shrugged. This was not a man who worried about old decisions, Eurybiades realised. The past was dead for him. It was possible that Themistocles had no real understanding of why Eurybiades was there, that even then he did not believe only one of them would walk out.

'In that moment of despair and disaster, as navarch,' Themistocles continued grimly, 'you gave an order I could not follow – to pull back the entire fleet, abandoning Athens completely to the Persian army. You told me we could blockade the Peloponnese, where Sparta and Corinth lay, but not *my* wife or *my* children, who would be left for the sport of soldiers.'

The gaze he turned on the Spartan had more than a little anger in it. Eurybiades nodded, as if the point had merit. He had known scorn before. He had seen it in Pausanias, in the ephors of home. Yet he had always acted with discipline and honour.

'It is easy to look back and say what should have been done,' Eurybiades said. 'All you have said is true. I understand it! Of course I do! Am I a block? I fought to save the fleet and win a longer war. I asked for too much – and you took away my command. You made a mockery of it – and of me.'

'Then say I was *right*,' Themistocles said, his voice carrying a hint of a growl. 'Say your order was impossible, that you should never have given it.'

'No, I will not say that. You should have *lost* at Salamis! You know it. Only luck and a fool for a Persian king gave you that victory. You could not have known Xerxes would split his fleet! You should have lost that battle and seen your women and children captured on Salamis! Only merest

*Conn Iggulden*

chance saved you all. No, *I* was right, Athenian! For all it galls you, that is the truth.'

Eurybiades found he was leaning forward on the chair, jabbing the air with his finger. He settled back.

'Either way, you disobeyed my order in time of war. You undermined my command. The way things have fallen, your own people will not bring you to court or execution . . .'

'Not for that,' Themistocles said lightly. 'There are things I've done that they don't like, but not that! I saved the people of Athens, Eurybiades! By my count, half a dozen times! There should be statues in gold to me on every street corner! I should have my life story recited by every child for a thousand years. Instead, they don't know what to do with me. Life goes on and somehow . . . they want to put the war behind them. Or to name a thousand heroes and make me just one.' He waved a hand in frustration. 'And instead of gold and land and statues, I get . . . *you*, determined to avenge a slight so petty, so small, it makes me want to weep. You gave the wrong order, you pompous fool. No one in their right mind could have followed it.'

Eurybiades nodded. He stood up slowly, facing Themistocles. In that instant, Themistocles looked grey, older than before.

'I have come a long way,' Eurybiades said. 'It is time.'

'*Really?*' Themistocles said. He clenched his jaw and stood in turn. 'You won't settle it without one of us dying?' He gestured across the open field. 'There is a boxing ring just thirty paces away. I'll meet you there and buy you a meal after, no matter how it turns out.'

'Spartans don't box,' Eurybiades said stiffly. 'No, I choose the sword. Tell me where to stand and have one of your men bring you a blade. I want to be back on the road home before the day is much older.'

Themistocles nodded to the servants who stood open-mouthed at the exchange. The table and chairs were cleared and the breeze blew harder. One of them went for a blade and came trotting back with it held in his arms.

Themistocles looked around, trying to think what his tactics would be. He saw two men standing naked at the river and recognised Xanthippus and Epikleos. They had arrived so drunk the night before he'd thought they might easily be found dead that morning. It lifted his spirits to see both of them awake. Xanthippus raised a hand to him, tilting his head in question. They would be wondering why he was belting on a sword. He was wondering that himself.

Themistocles swore under his breath when Xanthippus began walking over to him. He did not need an audience, no matter what happened. In fact, he would prefer some things to take place without witnesses. He and Eurybiades were alone on the field, no matter who stood and watched.

'Are you ready?' Eurybiades said. 'I have given you every chance to prepare. Come, draw your sword.'

Themistocles held up a hand. He was sweating; he could feel it start to run down his ribs, like paint on his skin. Eurybiades was around sixty years of age, though as fit as any Spartan could be. To have risen to such a senior role, he had to be one of the most skilled swordsmen in all of Sparta. The man would be blisteringly fast and he would not tire. Themistocles glanced at Eurybiades and saw no weaknesses at all. When the Spartan removed his cloak and folded it, the form beneath appeared to be made of teak. Themistocles felt a cold spot bloom in his stomach. Fear. He thought Eurybiades was a humourless fool and a poor leader of men. That mattered little or nothing when it came to facing him with a sword.

'Themistocles?' Xanthippus called as he approached them. 'What is this?'

He and Epikleos came to a halt facing both men. Xanthippus started in surprise when he recognised the Spartan.

'Eurybiades!'

'Oh yes, a Spartan was looking for you,' Epikleos added, deadpan.

Themistocles chuckled, but Xanthippus glowered as he understood.

'This isn't . . . By the gods, Eurybiades, the war is over! Tell me you haven't come here to duel with an ally.'

Eurybiades flickered a glance at the man addressing him. He recognised Xanthippus easily enough, as well as the tone of one used to authority. He had heard that tone when Regent Pausanias had ordered him to stay behind, surrounded by the tatters of his career. Still, he knew Athenian cunning too well to take his eyes off Themistocles. He would not be surprised by an enemy.

'I don't think our friend Eurybiades is open to reason,' Themistocles said softly.

Xanthippus shook his head.

'He has no right to stand here and threaten you on Athenian land! Eurybiades! Stand down. Remove that sword and give it to me. You are not of a rank to challenge Themistocles, not any longer. Nor do you have authority in Athens!'

Eurybiades kept his gaze on the man he had come to kill. When he spoke, his voice grated with anger.

'This is . . . a prior arrangement. Nor is it your business. I will ask one last time, Themistocles. Draw your sword, or I will kill you even so.'

'That would be dishonourable,' Xanthippus snapped. 'And illegal. I forbid it. If you attack an Athenian, I will have you up before the Assembly, Eurybiades.'

'It is not dishonourable to *me*,' Eurybiades replied, suddenly furious. 'I gave this man notice I would come. He accepted then, when he could sneer and mock me! Well, I have come! Let him draw his weapon now and I will finish it and walk home. Nothing else is your concern.'

'He is right,' Themistocles said softly. Xanthippus turned to him in dismay, but Themistocles held up his hand. 'By his own lights, he is. Very well, Spartan. What is one more life?'

Slowly, Themistocles drew his sword. It was barely longer than his forearm, a blade for chopping bone or flesh. It shone as he turned it under the noon sun. Xanthippus and Epikleos backed away a couple of paces, all too aware of how easy it was to take a wound as others fought.

'Let me escort you both to the Pnyx!' Xanthippus tried again. 'We'll let the courts decide this. Why lose a good man? Over what?'

Themistocles realised he had come to the end of all his arguments, all his persuasions. He could almost feel death rushing down on him. Perhaps all those who faced a Spartan in battle felt the same. It would be quite an advantage.

'Come on then, navarch,' he said. 'Do what you came for.'

Eurybiades nodded once. He stood naked. His hair was iron grey. His pectoral muscles had sagged a little; his skin was like freckled leather in folds and creases. Yet he moved well and Themistocles felt cold spread within.

Both men stretched necks and shoulders as they readied themselves. Themistocles waited for the first attack. He needed to know how fast the Spartan was.

When it came, he almost missed it. Eurybiades had been stepping sideways, as if he walked some invisible ring on the grass. With no warning, he closed the distance in two quick steps and Themistocles was suddenly defending himself. The blades rang together twice and Themistocles hissed as he felt a cut along his ribs. He had barely jerked away from seeing his side opened up.

*Conn Iggulden*

He opened his mouth to speak, but Eurybiades gave him no time, even to assess the wound. The Spartan had not come to duel for points, but to kill a man. Themistocles felt his senses fire as the blades clashed again. He managed to block two blows, though he took another gash on his forearm. Blood dripped in fat drops from his elbow as he held the arm up. It hurt, but his pride hurt worse. He longed for a shield, or some advantage over the vicious bastard cutting him to pieces. His eyes narrowed in thought as Eurybiades came in again. Athenian cunning was the only edge he had.

Quick as thought, Themistocles reached down and dragged fingers through the grass, then held the hand closed. The action had brought Eurybiades in again, so that he had to defend madly. Yet the Spartan had seen him grab whatever it was. When Themistocles opened his left hand at him, Eurybiades ducked away on instinct, expecting dust or a stone. There was nothing – there hadn't been time to pick anything up. Instead, Themistocles stepped forward and hammered a massive left cross against the side of the Spartan's head.

It wasn't perfect. Even as he fell, Eurybiades managed to lash out with his sword, cutting Themistocles deeply in the calf muscle. Yet it landed, an impact with all his weight behind it. In a split second, the Spartan lay dazed and panting, blinking up at the sun. Themistocles lowered his sword to Eurybiades' throat and paused there, looking him in the eye.

'Spartans don't box,' Themistocles reminded him. 'Your life is mine, Eurybiades. Give me your word you will not seek me out again and I will let you live. Surrender to me.'

The Spartan looked to one side, to where his sword had fallen. His eye was already swelling and a great bruise was forming on his face. He sighed.

'No,' he said.

Themistocles nodded once and shoved the blade down, working it back and forth until all noise and movement ceased. When he stood, the blade came up with him, bright red in the sun. He tossed it onto the grass alongside the other.

Xanthippus saw Themistocles was trembling, the reaction to coming so close to his own death.

'We really did come to warn you,' Epikleos said. 'He's been all over the city, dropping your name. Honestly, he's lucky a few of your hoplites didn't kill him.'

'Yes,' Themistocles replied, looking down at the body on his field. 'He's a lucky man.'

He swore then as he saw how much blood was spattering from him. He looked at Xanthippus, seeing no sign of mercy or humour. The strategos had come back from war much darker than he had left. Some always did. Xanthippus was no longer the young man Themistocles had sent into exile, nor even the one who had taken charge of the fleet and devised signals and tactics for Salamis. They were all different men. Themistocles shook his head. His wounds were really hurting. The war was over, but it had taken their youth and all that was good.

# PART FOUR

'I know how men in exile feed on dreams of hope.'

– Aeschylus, *Agamemnon*

# 33

The Assembly that gathered in the pre-dawn light numbered more than twenty thousand, all who could possibly fit on the Pnyx. People of Athens camped on the slopes and all around, drawn by the importance of the war inquiry. Scribes wrote furiously, producing as many pages as they could. They sold for four or five times the normal amount, a bounty compared to before the war.

No women were allowed on the stone benches. They gathered instead across the Agora below. Those who had coins paid slaves or messenger boys to shove through the crowds and then report back whatever they heard. For most, it would be the only chance to hear the personal fate of their husbands, spoken by those who had witnessed their deaths. Sometimes, it was just the name of a ship seen on fire or rammed, or an officer's death confirmed by those who had fought at his side. Families waited for news they could hardly bear to hear. In clusters of sisters, aunts and children, they stood with heads bowed and babies held close, mothers hard-faced and cold to all sympathy. There were thousands of those, drawn from their demes across the city and around, there to hear all they could.

The past was only one part of their concern. When the Assembly gathered in such numbers, the law itself was decided by their vote. In moments, justice was called and abruptly decided, without appeal. For many of those present, it was a chance to weigh the acts of those who had led them – and to decide whether to reward or censure the actions brought into the light. Every court in the heart of Athens was filled with jurors, administered by the council of tribes and chosen by lot. There had been a rush of petitions for the state to return wealth taken during the war. Others were brought before a jury on accusations of theft, rape, murder or giving succour to the enemy in time of war. Those were a grim business. Lesser crimes could be punished with a fine, but the crowd often wanted more. Executions were carried out swiftly. Three men were chained for a night to a beam in the Agora, tormented by passers-by until only bloody wrecks remained.

Another three days had to be set aside to hear disputes over property. Those suits came with a risk, however, as the crowd grew impatient with petty argument. Some of the most complex cases simply lost land they could not divide fairly. Those properties were sold at auction, snapped up by wealthier families.

Neither strategoi nor archons were immune. Over a hundred epistatai were there – each one a man who had ruled Athens for one day of the crisis. They became the keystones of the unfolding history, stepping up in turn to say what they had witnessed and done, sunset to sunset.

Aristides listened to as many of those as he could. He stood close to the speaker's stone to hear them, his ragged old robe wrapped around him. He had to use his elbows when others threatened to push him out, but he would not give up his spot. Xanthippus and Epikleos were present, he noted, with Pericles. Though the young man was not yet a voting member of the Assembly, his father had taken to keeping him close. No one questioned a strategos who had already given his first-born.

Cimon had come, standing with forty young men in good cloaks, officers from his wing of the fleet. He had begun negotiations to refit three older triremes on behalf of the city. He was even learning carpentry, so it was said, taking a spot alongside the master woodworkers of the port and learning from them. He insisted on it, so that he could repair and understand the ships. It gave Aristides hope, somehow.

There were reports still of Persian strongholds, on islands untouched by the war. A new generation would seek them out the following spring, driving them from home waters with fire and the sword. Aristides just hoped the voyages would not become a great drunken debauch. The people of Athens had suffered dark years. They needed new tales to inspire them, as they continued to rebuild. With the blessing of the gods, men like Cimon could write stories to equal the Argonauts or Odysseus, a reminder that the great days were not all behind.

Themistocles was there as well, on the Pnyx hill, at the heart. As Aristides let his gaze drift over the silver-blond head, Themistocles talked in a low voice to the most senior archons, men drawn away from their youthful authority by time and war. They had all attended the proceedings every morning as they stretched into a second and third week, with a new epistates chosen each day to call witnesses and order what votes the Assembly wanted.

Scythian archers were present to glower at the crowd and keep order when tempers frayed. Though they were public slaves and owned in common by the people of Athens, they also had the authority to lay about them with clubs if a riot began. Sixty of them stood at the edge of the Pnyx that day, though only as a threat. The crowd grew unruly at times, either in cheering or muttering in anger. Yet the Scythians no longer needed a rope dipped in red paint to gather unwilling crowds to their duty. Since the Assembly had first announced a great inquiry of all conduct during the war, jurors had gathered before dawn each day, desperate to take part.

The process had some of the trappings of a great trial, though many of the speakers merely added to the public record of events. For all the threat of punishments, it was also a chance to tell what they had seen, to have scribes record clashes and alarms they could hardly believe they had survived. Playwrights too were there, scribbling down the details they liked best, fingers and lips black with charcoal or ink.

On the first day of the previous week, Aristides had been the first archon to be questioned. Formally, he'd placed his fate in the hands of the Assembly, accepting their authority over him. Even the crowds on the slopes had been silent then. After all, the oath he gave that day was from a man who had been sent into exile – and then been called home.

In his dry way, Aristides had described his dealings with Sparta, as well as the entire battle of Plataea and his part in it. He'd endured a spiky interrogation by three of his own officers as to his choices on the battlefield and his recollection of the chaos around the helots at Plataea. The crowd was rapt as he described those last, that slave state within a state, outnumbering their masters. Yet Aristides had remained unruffled, answering each question with his habitual calm, offering details and insights that had the crowd straining for every word. He'd spoken from dawn until evening and at the end, his voice was hoarse. As the sun had touched the horizon, the epistates waved off any more questions. Aristides had been given permission to stand down. By show of hands, the Assembly agreed he should be added to the list of honoured men and held immune from further criticism. There might be greater honours in his future, or at his death, but nothing then, while the city was still being rebuilt.

Xanthippus gave testimony after him, over two days and

*Conn Iggulden*

four sessions. He described the sea battles around Salamis with extraordinary detail and recall, though his style was like a recitation and some people yawned as the sun moved. Xanthippus was questioned over the preparations for the second evacuation on the island Salamis, until he grew flushed and annoyed. At the end of the first day allocated for his testimony, he had to defend himself from families demanding compensation for slaves he had freed. It seemed more than three thousand had accepted his offer, rowing for the fleet in exchange for freedom. Those cases were dismissed as without merit, though it was as much because there were no funds as from any sense of justice. More than once, Xanthippus refused to answer, saying he had no recall of whichever detail they were after. It was more contempt for the questioners than truth, that was clear enough. The epistates of the day had grown flustered at his stubbornness.

'Kurios, have you no words for the families of all those lost?' he'd cried at last. 'Must it be just ships and oars and silver coins spent?'

Xanthippus had lowered his head then, struggling to control his temper, for all the world like a bull facing the knife. He breathed slowly and full while the epistates paled, frowned on by half the crowd. Xanthippus had come back from exile to command a fleet – and he had done so with great skill.

Xanthippus had cleared his throat.

'I count them all in those I love,' he said. His words were repeated in whispers like a breeze across the hill. 'Everyone who stood against the enemy of our people . . .'

He'd fallen silent for a time and the epistates had shifted uncomfortably. They did not know how to move on, not while Xanthippus stared at nothing. As the man had opened his mouth, Xanthippus began to speak again.

'Some gave their lives gladly. They flung them away, with more bravery and sweetness than you could know. Some had what they loved most taken against their will. I have seen sacrifices so great they can never be repaid! Men just like us, who wanted to feel the sun again, who went instead into the dark . . .' His eyes had been terrible, his face very still, as if he had been carved. 'They should have monuments, but they should be remembered as well. Their stories should be told, as I have heard here. Not one of them thought we could ever win! Yet in the face of that certainty, with death looking at them, they picked up spears and shields. Because to do so made them men. It made them fathers and brothers . . . and sons.' His voice had choked off then. When he went on, it was thick with grief. 'The gods bless them, my son Ariphron among them. I was a better man while he lived.'

Epikleos had put a hand on his shoulder and Xanthippus breathed, in and out once more, closing the door on it. That session was brought to an end.

No further grief or emotion had showed in Xanthippus through the following day, when he described his actions along the Ionian coast. He spared no detail of his decisions and all he had done there. In the end, as he'd stepped down, they began to cheer him, the sound spreading across the city, deme to deme, district to district. He'd looked at them in confusion then.

The news that Themistocles would testify only thickened the crowds camping around the Pnyx. Every inn and spare room was already taken in the city, while the man himself was kept under guard in the council building. Aristides came to him there and found him pacing his room. With his appearance booked for the following morning, Themistocles was not quite under arrest. Yet Scythians patrolled the corridors and outside. They had stepped aside for Aristides. In part it was because he had already been marked for praise by the Assembly. Perhaps it also mattered that if they had stopped him, he might have returned with a thousand men – men who had stood with him as hoplites at Plataea. That had been the victory none of them had truly expected. Though it had come in the end in chaos, though the Spartans had been the stone in the flood, the Athenians too had stood their ground – and the largest army in the world had fled from them. If it was Aristides who called, the Scythians knew they would be swept away. That awareness was visible in them as they stood respectfully and asked after his health.

'Come walk with me,' Aristides said to Themistocles when he looked in. 'This room is small enough to be a cell.'

'I told them that when they were rebuilding them,' Themistocles replied. He wore a long tunic to his thighs and an old pair of sandals. He cast only a quick glance behind him before stepping out behind Aristides. 'A man has to be able to pace, to think. These rooms are too small. There was some fool of an architect insisting he could get twenty rooms where there were only a dozen before. And the costs! Truly, I have never seen such sums.'

He fell silent in the corridor that led to the Agora and the open air. The Scythian commander was a burly man with a streak of white in his beard. He had planted himself so neither could pass without him stepping aside. Some conflict was being waged in the Scythian as he looked apologetic, yet did not move.

'I have no orders concerning you, Archon Aristides,' he said.

'You have no orders concerning my friend either,' Aristides replied gently. 'None that are lawful. Step aside, please.'

The man hesitated even then, his hand making sharp little

movements in the air as he tried to weigh opposing authorities. Aristides walked on, forcing him to make a decision. The Scythian had barely time to step aside, his back to the wall. Themistocles could feel the man's frustration, though Aristides seemed utterly unaware. They passed through into the cool night air and Themistocles pulled in deep breaths, desperately relieved to be free once more.

'Did you see that?' he demanded. 'If I cannot walk wherever I please, how am I not a prisoner?'

Aristides shrugged.

'I stayed there when they called me. He is just doing what some epistates told him. Until all these trials and inquiries are formally at an end, he does not want to be held responsible for you vanishing in the night. I imagine the crowd would skin him alive tomorrow morning, if you don't climb the Pnyx.'

Themistocles tilted his head, accepting the point.

'Still, they should be honouring me. Of all men. I saved them, the ungrateful bastards.'

He heard Aristides sigh and rounded on him, stopping him with a hand on his chest.

'Well? Why is that so hard to swallow? They cheered Xanthippus! Did I not persuade them to build the fleet he took out? You argued for silver in their hands! If they had voted for that, Aristides, Persia would rule here and we would all be gone. For that alone . . .'

'That was years ago,' Aristides reminded him. 'The memory of our people is short. They have survived a war since then – evacuation, seeing all they owned burned, losing their loved ones . . .'

Themistocles waved a hand in frustration, walking on. The air was cold and he drew it in, letting it fill him.

'A war we could not have won without me! I tell you,

*Conn Iggulden*

Aristides, they'd better remember it tomorrow. I'll tell them the truth when they question me, with their pursed mouths and sharp little eyes. I'll tell them exactly what I did – and why they should be grateful to me. They should be sending their most beautiful daughters to my door, not setting Scythians to glower at me when I ask for a cup of wine!'

'Be calm, Themistocles,' Aristides said.

He let the other man walk in silence for a time. By night, the Agora was vast and open, with all the street stalls and canopies cleared away. The Acropolis was a block across one part of the sky, so that stars showed around it. It was peaceful enough. There were a few drunks and beggars sleeping here and there, but they would fear violence and were not likely to bother two men walking together.

'I have other concerns for tomorrow,' Aristides said at last.

Themistocles turned to him and, under the moonlight, he looked unutterably weary. For all his bluster, he was worried.

'What have you heard?' Themistocles said.

'There is a growing faction who want to see you censured for taking their possessions on the quays of Piraeus.'

'To pay the rowers,' Themistocles snapped. 'And to pay the slaves *Xanthippus* freed. Or perhaps they would have found the fortune we needed somewhere else, with a Persian army marching on Athens and the mines at Laurium closed!'

'Still, there was some story about a missing cup . . .'

Themistocles waved a hand in frustration.

'Yes. I spread that rumour, to have their bags searched.' He slumped then. 'If I could go back and undo it, I would, in all honesty. It was the idea of a moment and there was no need. I saw a sack of silver coins being taken over to Salamis, held like a lover. I just thought – the rowers could use that. I made a quick decision.'

'It has proven . . . unpopular. In one instant, you angered

every wealthy family in Athens. You made enemies there. It will certainly come up tomorrow. You should prepare yourself to be questioned on that.

'Perhaps I will remind them that without me, they would all be slaves, or already dead. That is a fine answer!'

Aristides rubbed his face, wearily.

'I would not say it like that, Themistocles, if I were you. There is a great deal of anger in the city and nowhere for it to go. Thousands of our people are grieving, or still furious. They lost everything, but who can they blame? The Persians are gone! Life must return to normal, but businesses are ruined, homes are burned, families have been broken apart. They . . . lash about, Themistocles, looking for someone, *anyone*, to punish. I do not want to see you become the object of their frustrations.'

They fell silent again for a time, walking across the empty mouths of streets, right around the edge of the Agora. Above them, the Acropolis blocked the moon, untouched by the petty lives and fears of those below.

'I have given my entire life to this city, to these people,' Themistocles said at last. 'My mother was not Athenian, did you know? She was a little blonde woman from Thrace. She worked her hands raw to earn enough just to buy food when I was a boy. We were not rich, Aristides, from a long line of archons. My father left us when I was just eleven. So as soon as I could stand, I worked. I earned coins boxing and wrestling, training others. I spent all I had with tutors to learn my letters. I *remade* myself, even to the way I speak, so no man could hear me and say "foreigner" or "unschooled". Do you understand? I became a name in this city, a man of wealth and influence, rising step by step. I had a year named for me – and men called me "archon".'

'I recall you used some of that influence to exile those

*Conn Iggulden*

who might have frustrated your plans,' Aristides replied. His eyes were dark as the moon gleamed out once more, following their steps. He saw Themistocles wince in something like guilt or embarrassment. The man waved a heavy hand.

'That really *is* a long time ago,' Themistocles said. 'The crowd can be fickle. I thought I understood them then, Aristides! Life was . . . simpler. And then the Persians came . . . I sometimes think my whole life will be in two parts because of them. All I was before them, all I was after.' He sighed. 'I will stand before the Assembly tomorrow and they will demand answers and explanations for every decision I ever made, when not one of them had the balls to stand at my side! I was *right*, more times than I was wrong. That is all that matters in the end. If I made mistakes – as any man would have done – surely my triumphs outweigh them?'

It was said as a plea and Aristides shrugged as he answered.

'I don't know. I saw a man vote at my ostracism, a man who did not know me, but hated that others called me "Aristides the Just" or "Aristides the Good". He sent me into exile because he hated the honour of my reputation.'

Themistocles looked ill as he listened.

'Truly?' he said. 'Then what hope is there for me?'

Aristides looked on him, frowning.

'You have supporters, those of us who know the part you played in the war. Yet . . .' He hesitated. He owed the man more than false hope. 'There are a thousand petty rumours in the city – lies and truths running together like water in wine. They say you took silver from the mines at Laurium, even during the war. Some complain you used their family tombstones to remake the new Dipylon gate.'

'That last is true!' Themistocles said. 'I used what rubble lay strewn about, the broken stones. Will they hold me responsible for the hammers of Persians?'

'I think some will,' Aristides answered. He shook his head. It was not lost on him that Themistocles had not denied the accusation about funds from the mines. 'I have heard voices saying you have too much power, that you have taken too much upon yourself – before the war and even more so after it.'

The last of the catalogue stopped Themistocles cold.

'Aristides, if there are so many who hate me now, how can I ever get through tomorrow *without* being exiled?'

Aristides blinked in consternation.

'Oh, my friend, I'm sorry. I came to you to be sure you understood. I think they have enough, or close to it. I just wanted to give you time to prepare yourself.'

'*What?*' Themistocles said, gaping at him. 'You're telling me there is no hope? I could recite my honours, starting with Marathon – and Salamis, where I saved us. You know that Spartan Eurybiades came to honour the duel he promised? You see this wound, or this?' He pointed to marks on his ribs and a stitched line on his calf. '*He* knew all I had done, even if my own people don't! I wish I could call him as a witness, to tell them all they owe me. The ungrateful . . . !'

He threw his hands up and limped away from Aristides under the moonlight in a great circle. By the time he returned, he was calmer.

'What do they need, six thousand votes? Perhaps I'll have the fleet rowers kick the pot over.'

'And start another war?' Aristides said. 'No, if you are sent into exile, you'll go, as quietly as I did, as well as Xanthippus did.'

'Ah, that's it, isn't it?' Themistocles said bitterly. 'Of course. You two are delighted to see me brought down with petty accusations, with nothing more than gossip.'

He blew air out in disgust. It was hard to believe his own

words when Aristides watched him in concern. There was no spiteful pleasure in the man. No pleasure of any kind in Xanthippus, not any longer.

Themistocles felt drained, empty and tired as he stood there. He muttered a curse under his breath.

'There is always hope, Aristides. While some of them love me, there is always hope.'

'The last thing in the box Pandora opened,' Aristides said, 'after all the evils of the world came out.'

'Well, that is no comfort *at all*,' Themistocles said, though he forced a grin. 'Come on. I should at least try to sleep. I do not want to miss the great and good of Athens saying what a nasty, wicked man I am.'

He turned his steps back towards the council building, where shadows of Scythians waited.

'See those?' Themistocles muttered.

With an audience, he came alive. He raised his head and put his shoulders back, marching across the Agora under the moonlight, his arms swinging.

'Never let them see they have hurt you,' Themistocles called over his shoulder, his voice echoing.

# 34

Themistocles left the council building at dawn. The streets were already filling by then, with crowds desperate for a good spot on the higher slopes, or even the stone Pnyx benches where they could hear him speak. Themistocles looked fresh and clean, his robe bright in the rose dawn. He was flanked by a hundred of the Scythians, so that he frowned around him, feeling like a prisoner rather than a witness.

'Why do you glower so?' he said to the Scythian captain. 'Are you worried for me?'

The man did not reply and Themistocles cursed under his breath, muttering about short men and their dignity.

Aristides was there, at the foot of the Pnyx hill, with Xanthippus and Cimon. Themistocles raised his eyebrows as he sighted them. There was a slight confusion amongst the Scythians as their officer decided he could not prevent the names of Athens accompanying the man he thought of as his prisoner.

'Come to watch a man condemned?' Themistocles called to them.

In truth, he was grateful to see familiar faces, even there. Aristides eased in beside him, Xanthippus and Cimon just ahead. No one stopped walking, with so many Athenians clambering up the slopes. Themistocles imagined being unable to find a spot at his own trial and grinned. What would they do then, with no one to accuse?

'We came to show support,' Cimon said.

The words hit Themistocles like a punch over his heart. He staggered slightly and tutted to himself.

'The people love me,' he muttered. His voice strengthened as he made the sound carry. 'I saved them all, every man, woman and child of Athens.'

He saw Xanthippus lower his head, his face dark with exertion. He had been fitter, once. They all had.

'It means a great deal to me, lads,' Themistocles said, 'that you're here. I will not forget it. Don't expect me to go quietly, though. If it's to be a trial, I can win it – or if they find me guilty, I can still choose a punishment I can bear. As long as they stop short of a vote to ostracise me.'

'Then show them humility,' Xanthippus murmured. 'That is all they want. Show them you are not untouched by all we have seen.'

Themistocles was silent for a time.

'Would you, Xan? Would you act the penitent for all those who long to see me weep and tear my robe? Shall I rub ashes in my hair and rock back and forth like an old woman? Will that satisfy them?'

He watched a ridge of muscle stand out in Xanthippus' jaw. The man simmered, always walking an edge of rage. He was thinner too, Themistocles noted, with far more grey in his hair. Grief and guilt had aged him badly.

'I agree with Xanthippus,' Aristides said, when it was clear the man himself would not answer. 'All the rest – all these accusations of theft and dishonest dealings – they can be answered. Compensation can be paid. They just want to be heard, these men. Let them see you are one of them and they will love you again.'

Themistocles looked at his friend. Aristides walked in a robe that looked older than any of them. He did not parade his own virtue, which made it hard to dislike him. Even so, Themistocles knew the man judged his weaknesses. Aristides had never let a single coin stick to his fingers. He'd given away whatever he'd once owned to the poor of Athens. Themistocles honestly thought the man was wearing all he had in the world. On a normal day, Cimon walked with his companions all wearing fine cloaks, solely for the purpose of giving them to anyone in rags who asked. Before the war, Xanthippus had married the sort of wealth that went hand in hand with power. They *were* his friends, Themistocles did not doubt it. Yet they had not known poverty, or if they had, it was in the nature of a choice. Themistocles shook his head. Poverty was something forced on a man. If he chose to endure it, if he could cast it off like an old cloak, it was not real. They were all great men in their way, he realised. Yet it seemed they did not understand him. After all they had seen and lived through together, he had not expected to feel an outsider, not in that group. He did, even so.

He found himself panting as the steps grew steep. The crowds were thickening around them. His people, beloved to him. He leaned over, his voice low.

'I don't remember any of you there when I had to fight to eat, or when I wrote my first pages for families who could not. I think you were made by your fathers, all of you. I made *myself* – and that is the difference between us. You can take a loss like the one you describe and I think a part of you would not be touched by it. You could go back to your lives after and it wouldn't be a brand still burning against your skin, not for any of you.' He smiled without humour, like a rictus of pain. 'But it would be for me. So they can do what they want. I won't give them anything. Certainly not whatever dignity I have won for myself. Not a word, not an apology, not a tear. If that means an ostracism, I accept it.'

'Is it worth your life?' Aristides said softly. 'Everything you've worked for?'

'Of *course* it is!' Themistocles said. 'I am an Athenian. I

*Conn Iggulden*

made myself who I am – and I saved us all. After that? Nothing else matters. Not even their gratitude.'

He saw the rest of them exchanging resigned glances as they reached the speaker's stone and spread apart. Themistocles stepped ahead, passing through the Scythians escorting him up.

'That will do, lads,' he called across their heads. 'An honour guard is a fine thing. My mother would be very proud. To your places now, with my thanks. Now, who is epistates today? Which of you fine fellows has won that honour? Is it you, with that extraordinary beard? Step forward and show yourself, then! Let them see you.'

Aristides and Cimon stood together, watching Themistocles light up the crowd. Smiles spread as he spoke. It was his own kind of defiance and it was hard not to love him for it.

'Do you think he can save himself?' Cimon said, his voice very low.

Aristides glanced at him. Over the years, he had watched Cimon grow from a pitiful drunk to a leader of men. The war had revealed him, made him a man his father would have been proud to know.

'I think he has one chance,' Aristides said, 'to throw himself on the mercy of the Assembly. He has chosen instead to give them nothing. It is a . . . brave decision, but, no. The people are angrier than he realises. They want someone to bring down, some great name to blame for their troubles and their losses, for their grief and all those they will not see again. I am not proud of them today, though I believe I understand them.' He thought for a moment and amended his words. 'I believe I understand *us*.'

As he spoke, more and more of the crowd pressed in, until the Scythians had to turn people back, sending them down to the lower slopes. Some of those began to shout, having come so far only to find their way blocked by spear-lengths. The mood changed like a cloud passing over the sun and the smiles around Themistocles vanished.

Themistocles looked over the heaving mass of citizens from the height of the speaker's stone and shook his head like a twitch before he summoned his will and made himself confident and calm. The epistates for that day was indeed the massively bearded Athenian who had raised his hand before. At Themistocles' side, he stepped forward to address the people.

'Be silent now, please. Silence! The Assembly is convened,' the epistates announced. He waited for stillness, though it seemed to take an age. 'Those who are present, will you accept your sacred charge: to act with honour and with justice, in accordance with the laws of Athens and the gods?'

In the past, they had sacrificed a ram and dripped its blood in a great ring around that stone. So many recent sessions and a lack of suitable sacrifices had brought an end to the practice, at least for that year. As one, the crowd bowed their heads and said they would. Aristides and Cimon did the same, with as much right to stand there as any free man. Aristides saw Xanthippus greet his friend Epikleos. The man had brought Xanthippus' younger son. The Scythians had not stopped those, he noticed. He frowned at the thought, while the first witnesses stepped up to the speaker's stone, nervous and proud in roughly equal measure.

The ostracism vote was called for and rejected at the end of the first day. Families who had lost their wealth on the docks of Piraeus led that call, but there were too few hands to force a formal count. Themistocles had nodded once then, relieved. On the second day, the crowd had endured testimony from weeping families whose tombs he had used to make

*Conn Iggulden*

the Dipylon gate. The show of hands was closer then, but still not enough. On the third, they heard every detail of Salamis, from Themistocles and hundreds of officers. Some in the crowd cheered his tale of letters delivered to a Persian king. Others called out that it was all lies.

Both Cimon and Xanthippus were recalled to confirm the testimony of others. Each session of around four hours came to an end with a sudden unrest in the crowd, but no clear result. The fourth day was different. Overseers and workers from the mines at Laurium appeared. They described weight missing, empty sacks, payments made to strangers with no record. Nothing could be proven, but there were glares of suspicion turned on Themistocles. He had been in charge of the mines for crucial months of the war, after all.

He did not deny removing valuables from the bags on the docks, or remaking the city walls, or even keeping vast sums of silver in his own home to pay the rowers. He told them instead that they owed their lives to him. On the fourth day, when the cry went up again for a vote of ostracism, enough hands were raised to begin a formal decision. Many in the crowd looked at each other in disbelief. They had wanted to protest, not bring him down.

Aristides saw the moment come, his stomach clenching so hard it hurt him. He had hoped the calls would fail at the last. It was a dangerous move for those who longed to punish Themistocles. Only one such vote was allowed each year. If it failed, he would be immune – and likely to escape censure of any kind. The previous three days had been bruising, without a doubt, though it was hard to say whether Themistocles had his head above water or not. The Assembly of Athens was not forgiving. They distrusted those in power and Themistocles had shown no remorse for anything he had done in the war.

Aristides thought Themistocles himself was not sure how it would go when he stepped down from the speaker's stone. Eight sessions had left him bruised and bloody, but not without support. The trouble was, there was no second pot in an ostracism. Supporters could not vote for him.

Themistocles looked grim as he walked away from the hill, heading down to the Agora to find something to eat and drink. No one was allowed to address the crowd once a vote to ostracise had been called. Yet it would still be hours until there was a result. Those who stood against him had to find small pieces of pottery and scratch his name into the glaze. Those who had some personal reason could add details, or insults, but only the vote counted. As Themistocles passed through the crowd, a huge urn was brought up, repaired with iron strips and rough mortar holding it together. He winced at the sound of lesser pots being broken for their ostracon pieces, but he did not look back.

Aristides remained behind on the Pnyx. He had attended every session and, though he knew better than to speak in support of Themistocles then, he would still watch the process and make sure there were no double tokens dropped in, or an unreliable count made. He watched Xanthippus head down with Epikleos, but Pericles stayed. Of course, Aristides realised, it was all new and exciting to him. The young man saw only the drama, not the man's fate at the heart of it.

When Pericles approached him, the latest epistates was standing nearby, watching them both in suspicion. Aristides was not allowed to speak on the subject at hand. There was still some time before the formal vote, so he took Pericles by the arm, away from the milling crowd.

'Can't you stop it?' Pericles whispered.

Aristides felt his eyebrows rise. He had assumed a son of Xanthippus would have been one of those who stood against

Themistocles. Serious men tended to misunderstand one who laughed at them − at life. Yet Pericles looked pale with worry. Aristides wondered if his brother Ariphron would have lined up to put a piece in the voting pot.

'Nothing can,' he replied. 'Not once it has been called. I only wish they had been successful on the first day. He'd have had a better chance then. Instead, the people of the Assembly have heard every rumour, charge and accusation, fair or unfair, detail after detail. They built their case well, I have to say. Your father and I were exiled for less.'

'Is that it, then?' Pericles pressed him. 'Tell me what I can do.'

'Why, nothing at all,' Aristides said, making his tone a warning. 'If there was another pot for his supporters, it would overflow. He *has* friends and those who love him, Pericles. That was never in doubt. The ones I fear are those who hate him but do not know him. All they know of Themistocles is what they have heard over these days − witness after witness speaking in anger and grief. They no longer believe a word he says and if they are such fools, I cannot change their minds. The law is simple enough.' He began to quote the line from Cleisthenes, long dead. ' "If the *ekklesia* turn against a man, they may vote to banish him for ten years, regardless of name or station, from Athens and all Attica. There is no defence to the will of the people, no appeal. In this way, we defend ourselves against the rise of tyrants." '

'That is a hard law to love,' Pericles said.

Aristides gripped him by the arm.

'Remember that I stood in this place and heard a judgement from my own people that banished me from Athens. If your father were here, I believe he would say the same. He and I *know* what it means − and yet neither Xanthippus nor I have tried to change that law. It is the very last defence of the common man.'

Pericles shook his head rather than answer. Aristides let his hand fall, waiting to see how the young Athenian would respond. Cimon had impressed him before. He hoped Pericles would as well. It raised his spirits to know they understood what was important – and what was not.

'A vote like this took my father from me for seven years,' Pericles said. He had not enjoyed being grabbed and a flush was still spreading on his face and neck. 'I was just a child. Did they think of me then, when they voted to send a hero of Marathon away? They did not. Lesser men than my father took all their spite and failures and scratched pieces of pottery with his name. They did the same with you. Honestly, I cannot believe you would defend this. Themistocles did more to save these people than anyone! Yet they would send him away? And for what? Using gravestones to make a gate? Searching their bags for silver when they were being saved by his fleet?'

'Our fleet,' Aristides murmured.

He saw the epistates was scowling in their direction and walked a little further away. No speeches were allowed after the vote was called. If he forced the man to act, the Scythians would be sent over. As they walked a dozen paces together, Pericles looked at him in confusion, without understanding.

'What?'

'The fleet was bought by Athenian silver, Pericles. It was rowed and crewed and fought for by Athenians. Themistocles played his part, certainly, giving of his best in service to the city. So did your father and Cimon, to exhaustion. They gave all they had, as did the rowers and the hoplites on deck. But they were not saving the people. The people saved themselves! Understand that and you might realise why so many resent him. Themistocles will not let them be proud of

*Conn Iggulden*

anything they did. How many times has he told them they owe their freedom to him? I swear, that man would wear down a stone with his pride. Well, this is the result!'

'Numbers do not make justice,' Pericles said firmly.

Aristides stood very still.

'No? What else is there? Should we give three votes to rich men? To those who have led others in war?'

'Perhaps they should!' Pericles said, though he flushed, embarrassed by his own temper.

Aristides spoke with absolute calm, teasing out his points. Pericles wanted to roar at him. All the while, a line of Athenians was forming to bring their little pieces of pottery up and toss them in, voting on a man's life.

'If we did that,' Aristides replied, 'how long would it be before our society was remade for war? Like Sparta, perhaps! If only strategoi could vote, we would see an endless war, killing all our young, just to create those men of power. Or is it the rich who should lead us? Your father was not of great wealth before he married your mother, as I heard it. Does wealth grant wisdom, then? Was he a better man after that marriage than before? Perhaps. Some men admit to that.'

He chuckled at his own wit, but Pericles looked stonily at him, unbending. Aristides saw the young man longed for something. It was there in his eyes. He sighed.

'Before your mother's uncle Cleisthenes was given the task of rewriting Athenian laws, the pillars of them came from a great man, Solon. He devoted his prime to writing laws for Athens. His friend Anacharsis mocked him for the years he had given to the task. This Anacharsis was a Scythian. He said laws were like spiderwebs, that they trapped the poor and weak and were torn apart by the strong. That is how it was everywhere else, do you see? Still, Solon laboured on. When he was finished, he presented his code of law to all men of Athens, rich or poor, landowner or not. He then left the city, travelling the world for ten years. He knew his people too well. He knew if he stayed, they would ask him to revise and revise, saying "Ah, but what about when a man marries for a second time?" and so on. He left so they could not change a word.' Aristides shook his head in sadness. 'It didn't save his life's work. In just a few years, men put aside his laws, acknowledging no authority but their own. Who can argue when a man has a hundred soldiers, loyal only to him? Who can stop him taking what he wants?' Aristides sighed. 'When Solon returned to Athens, when he was very old, he put on his hoplite armour and stood outside the house of a tyrant of the city, calling on him to go.'

'And did he go, the tyrant?' Pericles asked, interested despite himself.

'No,' Aristides said. 'They never do. Solon died, aged eighty or so. He was a great thinker and he lived an extraordinary life.'

'He failed, though!' Pericles said, driven to astonishment. 'Everything you just described was a life of failure.'

'Was it?' Aristides said, genuinely surprised. 'I do not think it was. There have always been tyrants. Men like Solon are far rarer. Or your great-uncle Cleisthenes, who created ostracism as a final throw of the dice for his people. You should ask your father, Pericles, how he felt about it. If I know him, Xanthippus would say the same. There is no other authority, except for the gods – and us.'

He thought of Themistocles and smiled, though he did not explain why. He let the thought of Themistocles guide his words.

'If a man tells you to bend the knee because he is a king, spit in his eye, just as we did with Persia. If he tells you he is a learned judge, say to him, "Does that make you noble? Are you beyond error? No, you are . . . *not*." If a man tells you to count his gold and *then* bend your knee, just laugh at him. Where does authority lie in a piece of silver? On which face?'

'You honestly think it lies in this crowd?' Pericles asked. To his credit, he was looking at the people on the Pnyx with fresh eyes, searching for something like nobility in them. He glanced back when Aristides chuckled.

'By Athena, no! Except where the laws grant it to them. Do not mistake me, lad! There is petty vice and spite here, jealousy and corruption. There is weakness and fear. If they all call for justice, I will look for the one who folds his arms and remains silent. I will buy his wine for him with the last coin I have.' He shook his head. 'They are my people, but they are hard to love. No, my point was not that they are better or more noble, but that *no one else* has authority to rule. No one. We are all flawed, Pericles. We are all . . . small men. Cleisthenes knew that, as Solon did. Yet when enough of us stand up, to praise or condemn, we have as much chance of being right as any other code. It does not *make* us right – anything of man is always imperfect. But it is still the better choice, always. Trust the people, Pericles.'

It took many hours to prepare and observe the votes, then to count them. Themistocles climbed the hill once more for the final tally, his pale hair darker where he had bathed and left it loose to dry. He betrayed his tension as he stood there, rubbing one hand over the other, unconscious of the reddening skin. The piles of voting pieces were tallied with chalk on slate, checked over and over and set aside by officials of the council. The sun had set by the time they had counted thousands, though the hill was still packed. When word went round that four thousand had been reached, there was a disturbance further down and voices calling, in alarm or jeering, it was not clear.

The family of Themistocles came through the crowd, a large enough number on their own to have the Scythians bustling over. Yet it was just a group of four young men and five girls, the children of two marriages. Themistocles' second wife came to stand at his side, a slender woman of some beauty, with her hair so tight to her head it gleamed like a piece of silk. There was grumbling from some in the crowd, but there were others, too, still willing to support him. They waited, breathless for the result.

When the count passed six thousand, the count was halted. The remaining piles were pitiful little things. It had been close, with just hundreds in it. Yet the law was clear and certain.

Themistocles embraced his wife and children one by one. Some of those present had cheered the epistates when he announced the vote was carried. Others stood aghast, refusing to believe it. Themistocles inclined his head. He was not meant to speak, even then. The Scythians knew the law well, but even their officer looked stunned.

'The gods bless you all,' Themistocles called to them. 'Thank you. I am free.'

Without another word, even as the Scythians began to growl, he turned with his family and made his way down the hill.

# 35

The house and garden were on the very edge of a wild coast, a day south of the city of Argos on the Peloponnese and outside the influence or power of Athens. It was quiet there, with only the sound of the sea and a few birds calling. Cicadas creaked contentedly in the olive trees, enjoying the noon sun.

There was no road to speak of. At the edge of the property, Cimon dismounted on scrub grass, dropping his reins over an ancient gatepost. He looked around in appreciation, breathing in the smell of the sea. He understood that appeal well enough.

A little way off, the ground sloped away down to a stretch of shingle and blue water, carved out from cliffs and always in shadow. A boat had been dragged up on the shore there, a fisherman's hull with one small mast and a sail folded across a sun-whitened seat. The boat was tied to an iron stake against the chance of some storm carrying it off. Cimon saw nets there too, pegged out to dry in the sun. He could hear chickens somewhere nearer the house. The smallholding had the look of a happy place, well tended, perhaps even loved. He nodded, approvingly.

No one seemed to have noticed his arrival.

'Hello, the house!' Cimon called, then waited, standing at the wall of the property.

It was just a little thing. He could easily have stepped over it, but it marked the world on one side – and the property of Themistocles on the other. Row upon row of vines stretched along one side of the house, the leaves dark green. Cimon was admiring those when the man who watered and pruned them stepped out onto the path. Themistocles wiped his forehead with the back of one hand, putting down a basket already filled with grapes. He did not look pleased to see Cimon standing at his gate. Like a statue, Themistocles stood across his path, sickle in hand.

Cimon waited patiently, without challenge. He knew the household needed time to come alert to the presence of a stranger. The day was hot and he imagined some of the family had been sleeping, or sitting in cool shade inside. He sensed the drowsy place coming alive. More than once, the curls of some young woman appeared in the doorway or at a window on the second floor, only to be pulled back. Themistocles remained on the path, standing between his children and a man he had once called a friend.

Still outside the wall, Cimon held up empty hands, though he wore a sword on his hip and a Spartan kopis jutted very obviously from his belt. He had ridden far and one man alone would always be vulnerable to thieves and slavers. Themistocles weighed his presence for what felt like an age before he gestured for him to come closer. Cimon stepped onto the property, walking stiffly down the path towards the house. He stopped when Themistocles held up a flat palm.

'You are my guest,' Themistocles called to him. 'If you have come to kill me, I ask you to declare yourself.'

As he spoke, two young men who resembled their father came out to stand behind him. They made a formidable wall and Cimon saw both sons were armed and openly hostile. They did not know him. Themistocles looked more relaxed than they did.

'I give you my word,' Cimon said, 'on my father's honour. I am no threat to you or yours.' He held up his empty hands once more. 'I have come to bring you news – from your friends in Athens.'

The mention of the city brought a tightening around Themistocles' eyes, but also a hunger. He had been away from the heart of the world for just a year. Cimon thought it might have felt rather longer in the quiet of grapes growing.

Cimon saw Themistocles make a decision. He felt himself tense as the man murmured something he could not hear to the young men. The result was that they turned back and went inside. Themistocles smiled and beckoned him in.

'Excuse my caution, Cimon. Seeing you . . . I had not expected anyone from Athens to visit me all the way down here.'

Cimon had to duck his head to pass under the lintel. The inside of the house was noticeably cooler, a blessing after the furnace outside. There was no sign of wife or daughters and Cimon guessed they were hidden upstairs. He thought he heard whispered voices there. Only Themistocles and one of his sons remained to watch over him.

'Cimon? This is Diocles, my son. If you hand over your weapons to him, I will be more able to enjoy your company. It is your choice. Will you take a little wine, some cheese and figs? There is a fish stew here that is almost ready.'

His son held out an open hand and Cimon smiled stiffly. Themistocles had been forced to trust him before. He did not enjoy being unarmed with at least three other men. Still, he was a guest. Cimon untied his belt and sword, then put the kopis scabbard on top. Themistocles raised his eyebrows.

'Are you a Spartan now, to carry that thing?'

Cimon shrugged.

'They offered me a role as their man in Athens. They sent it to me as a token of that. After you left.'

Themistocles frowned.

'What did Xanthippus say about that? Or Aristides?'

'Nothing at all, as I did not ask them,' Cimon said with stiff dignity. 'Sparta is our ally, don't forget – as is Argos, that gave you sanctuary. I met some of their people when I travelled there with Xanthippus . . .' He stopped. 'I did not come here to discuss that, Themistocles.'

'Sit then and tell me,' Themistocles said.

He settled his guest in a seat under a heavy wooden table, where he could not easily leap to his feet. Themistocles poured water from a jug, allowing Cimon to wash himself, pressing a clean cloth to his hands and face. When he had removed some of the road dust, Themistocles placed cups on the wood and poured watered wine, while Diocles brought over a platter of goat's cheese, olives and crusty bread. Cimon bowed his head as he and Themistocles prayed to the goddess Demeter, in thanks for her bounty.

Cimon was starving after days on the road with just a little dried meat and fruit. He longed for bread in particular, murmuring appreciation as he sampled everything, then let his host finish the rest. Themistocles pressed him to try more, and in the end they cleared the platter between them. Only when it was all gone did Themistocles settle back, his hands crossed on the table before him. Cimon nodded. Courtesy had been observed.

'Aristides has friends among the Eupatridae, in all the noble families, still,' Cimon said. 'I came at his request. He has confirmed this . . . They are to send men to arrest you, Themistocles.'

'What can they possibly find to accuse me of now?' Themistocles said. 'Is my exile not enough for them?'

Cimon grimaced. He had found a man and a household at

peace and he knew he was like a stone dropped into a still pool. He hated to deliver this news, but there was no choice.

'Some of the landowners still blame you for their losses. There is one named Timodemus who cannot hear your name without growing dark and full of blood.'

'Not that dock search again!' Themistocles snapped.

Cimon waved a hand.

'In part. He says you took personal items from him that you have kept for yourself.' Cimon looked around him, as if expecting to see gold ornaments. He sighed. 'I believe it is more that you used silver from the mines at Laurium to pay the slaves Xanthippus freed. They say that was an illegal act, that they were still slaves at that point.'

Cimon felt himself flush with embarrassment. It sounded more like the hounding of a man rather than justice. He could not return the gaze Themistocles cast on him.

'It sounds like they just want to see me broken,' Themistocles said.

Slowly, Cimon nodded.

'Aristides said something like that. He found me as one he could trust and sent me out to warn you before they came. It will be Scythians – at least a dozen of them, sent to arrest you on behalf of the Assembly.'

'If I go willingly, they will say I broke my own exile . . .' Themistocles muttered, 'which is punishable by death. 'Yet if I fight, they will kill me . . .'

Cimon emptied his cup. There was still dust on his hands, he saw, flecks of it driven into his skin like a slave tattoo. He had ridden like a madman, risking his neck on broken ground to give Themistocles time, to bring news that made him ashamed to be an Athenian.

'There might be hope, still,' Cimon said. 'You have allies.

Aristides will certainly speak for you – and Xanthippus, though he has been ill for months now.'

'No . . .' Themistocles said softly. 'No, I see it now. They owe me too much and so they will always hate me. I cannot even stay here and live at peace. Even that will never be enough for them.'

He seemed to come out of a trance then, his gaze sharpening. His voice lost the dreamlike quality. He reached across and gripped Cimon by the wrist.

'You have my thanks, Cimon. I know your father Miltiades would be proud of the man you have become.'

'You spoke at his funeral,' Cimon said, 'when the world had turned against him. I will always be in your debt for that.'

'And now all the world has turned against me,' Themistocles said grimly.

He rose to his feet and accepted the man's weapons from his son, passing them over.

'How fares Athens?' Themistocles asked suddenly, as if the words had been dragged from him.

'Growing, busy . . . full of life. Aeschylus has written a new play about Marathon. You are in it, of course.'

Themistocles groaned.

'I would have loved to see that. I wonder if I can get a copyist to send me the lines.'

Cimon bowed his head.

'I know him quite well. He'll do it for me, I think, as a favour.' He held up his hand as Themistocles began to protest. 'Please, it would be my honour.'

Themistocles took his hand in real pleasure.

'You have no idea how my heart fills to hear that! I get no plays or poems here, not one – Apollo would consider it a desert, I swear. A man needs more than fish and bread . . .'

*Conn Iggulden*

He tailed off, staring into an unseen distance, clearly considering Cimon's grim news once again. The young man belted on his weapons and stood there, uncertain.

'What will you do now?' Cimon asked, strangely unsatisfied.

'What I must,' Themistocles replied with some firmness. 'As always. I will do what I must, to survive.'

He watched as Cimon walked back to the horse he had left at the gate. The ground was dark in spots, already drying in the sun. The animal had clearly been given water while he was inside, as if by invisible spirits. The animal gleamed, all the sweat dust brushed from its coat. Cimon looked around, but he could see no sign of whoever had done it. Even so, he was grateful. He felt a great weight leave him, perhaps because he had completed the task he had been given, or just because he had passed the weight onto the shoulders of another.

When Cimon was gone, Themistocles returned to the shade and cool of the house. His daughters and sons came down into the main room, filling it with life and sound. His wife Nicomache was there, her eyes bright with tears. Of course, they had heard everything.

'We'll have to leave this place,' she said. 'After all the work we've done.'

'I'm afraid so,' he replied softly, looking round. 'I am sorry. It has been a happy time in my life. But if I run alone, I can't trust the soldiers they send not to hurt you.'

'Where will we go this time?' his youngest son said.

Themistocles ruffled the lad's hair. He had already made his decision, though he was not sure how to say it to them.

'You will accompany your mother to find safe lodgings, in . . . Argos, I think?'

His wife nodded and Themistocles felt relief. The city was

barely a day's ride away and they were not well known there. He looked at his sons and daughters. He had spent more time with them in the previous year than the dozen before that. Though the little house had been crowded, he'd grown quite attached to them all.

'What about you?' his wife asked, knowing him well.

He smiled and pressed his hand against her face. Nicomache needed to be embraced, he could sense it.

'There is one place I might be welcome – a place far out of the reach of all my enemies. I'll go there and see if my name is worth anything. If it suits me, I'll call for you all to come out and join me! If not, I'll wait a year and find you in Argos.'

'What place is out of the reach of your enemies?' one of his daughters said.

It was her mother who replied, her eyes dark with sorrow.

'Persia,' Nicomache replied.

Themistocles nodded.

'Come, all of you,' he said, clapping his hands. The sound was loud in that place, so that some of them jumped. 'Gather anything you cannot bear to lose. Someone put a rope on the two mules . . . go on then! Don't stand there and talk to me! Go!'

In a few moments, he was alone with his wife, mother to around half his children. Nicomache came to his embrace, kissing his cheek and then pressing her head against his chest.

'I'm so sorry,' she murmured. 'They should be raising statues to you, not this.'

'I heard they put one up to Xanthippus!' he said, shaking his head. 'Oh, I should have known they would not just let me go. I made too many mistakes, amidst the moments of extraordinary genius.'

He chuckled to himself, but his eyes were dark. Children

*Conn Iggulden*

were already staggering past, their arms filled with all the things they loved. He touched a hand to his eyes, blinking hard.

'Come, my little ones, my pups! I can't leave until I know you are all safe. Let me see you on the road to Argos and armed like hoplites!' He turned to his wife then, kissing her on the forehead as he spoke in a lower voice. 'Before I go to ask a Persian king for mercy and forgiveness.'

'What if Xerxes kills you?' she asked him.

Themistocles shrugged.

'I expect you will marry again,' he said.

She slapped him on the chest, in love and worry more than real exasperation.

Themistocles found a berth on a merchant ship out of the bay of Argos, heading south. It was a slab-sided, wallowing vessel with a large single sail, as far from the warships he had known as a hammer is from a dagger. Yet it could hold a great cargo and withstand rougher seas than any trireme. Themistocles slept below decks with the crew and a thousand clay amphorae of oil and wine. Rats scrabbled in the deep hold and the air was thick with damp, but at least he was protected from the sea spray and wind. If any of the crew or their captain recognised him, they said nothing. He travelled with little more than a sword, a pouch of silver and a second pair of sandals.

Themistocles had never gone to sea from the Peloponnese before. He dreaded being stopped and searched by an Athenian warship. If one of those ordered his captain to drop sails to be inspected, the man would do so in a heartbeat. Nothing could outrun a trireme on a calm sea.

Themistocles had been careful to choose a merchant ship with a cargo to deliver further east. He had wanted to keep as far from Athenian waters as possible. Yet when the wind freshened and rolled in from the south, the captain turned away from his first course. He crept along the Greek coast, always keeping land in sight. It seemed he was no deep-water sailor. He spent part of each day praying at a little shrine to Poseidon on deck. Themistocles made no comment about that. The city of Argos had been neutral in the war, sending no one. As a veteran, he found the obvious wealth and comfort of their people somehow distasteful. They had been saved by everything Athens and Sparta had done, but had paid no part of the price.

Themistocles looked back to the helmsman as the ship turned. Two of the crew were up the mast, adjusting the heavy pine yard that held the sail. To Themistocles' dawning horror, the captain was clearly heading for the Piraeus, south of Athens.

Themistocles felt a cold hand clutch at him. This was how gods interfered in the lives of men. He didn't know how to protest in a way that would not immediately raise the captain's suspicions, perhaps enough to have him put ashore. Themistocles had rebuilt that port! With thousands of slaves and the labour of free men, he had dredged it deeper and built new docks and berths ready to maintain a fleet of war. Since Salamis, the Piraeus had become a vital centre of trade for a thousand small cities and towns, on islands all over the Aegean. Even as he drew closer, with storm clouds filling the sky behind him, Themistocles found he was proud of the busy crowds, bustling along quays he had helped to design. Three great triremes were being refitted there, the wood shining with new oil. Unfortunately, it was also the one place in the world where Themistocles would be recognised in an instant and hailed by his true name – a name he had not actually given the captain of his ship.

*Conn Iggulden*

He held his stomach, groaning as he crossed the deck and went down to the hold. Merchant captains feared plague as much as anyone else and it was not long before the man himself was told of his passenger's sudden illness and came down to see. Themistocles knew he had to walk a fine line. If there was any sign of fever in him, the captain would turn him out onto the very docks he was trying to avoid. His hand was dry as he held it out. The captain took it warily, but did not recoil from some unnatural heat.

'My men say you have fallen ill,' the man of Argos said.

Themistocles shook his head.

'It is an old wound. I fought at Marathon, in the line. Took a spear in my gut . . .' He shook his head as if the memory was too unpleasant to recall. 'It troubles me still at times, so that I cannot eat. It will pass. Have no fear for me. I'll survive to reach the Ionian coast, just as I paid you for.'

The captain had the grace to look a little embarrassed at that barb.

'I'll have to ask you for more if we are held in port for long. If the storm passes by or not, you still have to be fed and your bucket cleaned. A silver a day was the rate we agreed.'

Themistocles wanted to strangle the man. The only ship out of the bay of Argos that had not been stopping at Athens was at that very moment tying up in the port of Piraeus – and he was *still* being squeezed for more coins. No Athenian would have tried it, he was sure. However, his position was weaker than even the captain imagined. They could have asked for every coin and both spare sandals – and he'd still have been forced to pay.

He groaned for a while, then put a finger between cheek and teeth to pull out a silver drachm. Half a day's wage for a working man. It had the owl of Athena stamped into the metal, he noticed. No doubt the goddess was laughing at him in that moment.

'Here, kurios,' Themistocles said with a wince, handing it over. 'I pray it is enough.'

He seemed to collapse then, his eyes closing. The captain leaned over and pressed a hand to his forehead, but then shrugged.

'For today it is. We'll refill our water and take on fresh food for tonight. Perhaps that will ease your pain. I still have a cargo to collect in Ionia, so we'll be on our way as soon as the storm passes, don't worry about that. I'll get you there.'

The captain patted Themistocles on the shoulder and left him, groaning softly to himself in the gloom below decks.

# 36

Themistocles frowned as they sailed into the bay by the city of Smyrna, on the Ionian coast. It had been founded by Hellenes, a seed blown on the wind across the Aegean. Yet it had not been spared the predations of Xanthippus. Themistocles had sat through the testimony of the man's captains and senior officers, though the reality was always different. Smyrna lay just north of the island of Samos and the battlefield of Mycale. Xanthippus had still been filled with grief when he'd anchored his fleet along that part of the coast. The loss of his son had not been dulled by time or action. The results could still be seen in broken temples and burned properties, not yet rebuilt.

Themistocles shook his head. He doubted he would declare his friendship with Xanthippus in that place. The man had run mad for a while, yet still returned as a hero in Athens. He still had a statue raised on the Acropolis! Themistocles felt his shoulders sag. He would not judge another man for the foolishness of crowds.

He found his nervousness increasing as they eased closer to the docks. Merchant ships could not anchor in the bay, not when there was cargo to unload. They had to make their way in under a scrap of sail, with no more than the helmsman at the stern and the captain at the prow to guide them in. Some of the crew had climbed the mast to hang across the yard there, feet resting on just a slender rope. It seemed to be more for fun than to call down warnings.

Themistocles saw another merchant being towed in by a

six-oared port boat, but his captain waved off the offer of another. With the breeze barely a breath, he brought his ship in. Two of his lads threw heavy ropes to shore crew. Themistocles listened to them creak as they were wound around stanchions and grew taut. The ship steadied and the crew were briefly busy as a hive, then still. They had a day of hard labour ahead of them, unloading the amphorae in the hold. Themistocles would not see it. He swallowed, nervously. There were Persians in the crowd, officials even. Two of them approached the ship, ready to tally the contents and take a bribe, or whatever they called the local tax.

Themistocles had stood in a battle line and fought the sort of men who wore oiled beards and panelled coats to their knees. There were not many of them in the crowd there, but the few he saw were all armed. The hand of Persia clearly still reached as far as the city of Smyrna on their western coast. Themistocles felt his jaw clench as he straightened his shoulders and stood behind another passenger waiting to disembark. A bridge of planking had been attached to the side, so that they could walk down. It creaked against the port with the small movements of the ship, still defiantly alive, though they had bound her.

'Thank you, kurios,' Themistocles called to the captain.

The man barely nodded, already involved in dickering over port fees. Themistocles walked down and felt the world sway for a few paces. He eyed the Persians in conversation with the captain and shook his head. He needed someone more senior if his plan was to have any hope at all. He had only a little money left for bribes, or even food. In that place, with the sun beating hard upon his neck and his throat dry, he felt like a desperate man.

He turned back to the captain, interrupting the negotiations so that all three turned on him with a scowl.

*Conn Iggulden*

'I am sorry, but I have news the port master must hear,' he said.

'Tell me and I will pass it to him,' one of the Persians said immediately.

'It is a personal matter . . . I was told to speak to the most senior Persian officer in this city.'

'How can it be personal, then?' one asked, smiling at his own cleverness.

'In the sense that if he does not help me, it will eventually mean his neck.'

The smile vanished and both officials looked him up and down in suspicion. Themistocles was used to dealing with petty authority. He waited in silence until one of them shrugged, happy to pass on whatever problem he was to someone else.

'If you waste his time, you will regret it. His name is Jaavan and at this time . . .' he glanced at the sun, 'you will find him in warehouses at the far end of this dock. Be polite, Greek. He will have your hand if you displease him.'

'Oh, don't worry about that,' Themistocles said with a smile. 'Better men have tried.'

The officials blinked at that response.

'I hope your stomach is better,' the captain said. With a jerk of his head, he indicated Themistocles should leave.

Themistocles nodded.

'Much better, thank you.'

He bowed his head and left them staring after him.


Themistocles had imagined a quiet place, stacked high with sacks of grain. The reality was the sort of chaos he associated with the Agora of Athens. Piles of goods were held clear of their neighbours by stalls made of wood or just painted lines on the floor. A thousand voices seemed to be calling at the same time, a noise which had grown as he walked the length of the docks and then past a dozen buildings that were no more than a roof and beams at the corners. He heard Persian as well as Greek, but the main tongue seemed to be trade, with prices and offers called at the top of their voices. In fifty paces, he asked directions twice and had to refuse a coat draped across his shoulders. He kept one hand on his sword and the other gripping sandals and a pouch of coins.

The man he was directed to see was surrounded by a dozen Persian scribes, all scribbling records and permissions, or taking money and handing back some system of chits and tokens. Large men stood with swords and spears ready to protect the wealth as it flowed in. Themistocles had not seen so much silver in one place since before the war, and he looked around in interest. An enterprising man could surely find something to buy and sell in such a place, he thought, unless the Persians took too great a part. It confirmed for him that the port and the city were no longer Greek, for all he heard the words of his people shouted all around. That was a sad thought, after all they had done to remain free.

He was stopped by a hand on his chest as he approached the port master.

'What do you want?' a stranger snapped at him.

He had to raise his voice to a shout to be heard.

'I have personal business with the port master. Jaavan, is it? He will want to hear me.'

The stranger gave him a long look, then shrugged.

'Wait here,' he said.

Themistocles watched as the man went to Jaavan on his behalf, whispering into his ear. Persian authority seemed to depend on rings of men around the centre, he realised. He wondered how many more he would have to cross as a supplicant. The thought was unpleasant, but he had come to this place of his own free will and he could not complain or go back, not then.

He saw the port master craning to peer at him, then call him over. Themistocles took a deep breath as he went forward. The guards almost growled as he came close to their master, making clear there would be consequences for any rash act. In the meantime, the bustle and noise of the traders went on at undiminished volume.

'Thank you for seeing me,' Themistocles said. 'Do you speak Greek?'

'I do,' Jaavan replied with a thick accent. 'What is your business?'

'Oh, I am not a trader,' Themistocles began. He felt a hand grip his shoulder then as one of the guards began to draw him away. He spoke faster, even as the port master turned back to his previous concerns. 'I am an archon of Athens! I am Themistocles, who commanded ships at Salamis.'

The hand at his shoulder fell away and Jaavan turned slowly back to him, his mouth opening in astonishment. He was in the man's power, Themistocles thought with a sinking sensation. He wondered if he would even survive the meeting. The strangest part was that he found he was enjoying himself. He had no friends around him, no wife, sons or daughters to protect and keep safe. Yet in that moment, he was the young man he had once been. Humorous, ruthless, quick-witted and trusting in himself to get the job done. It was a heady feeling, as if he'd drunk unwatered wine on an empty stomach. Either way, he could not take the words back. He'd walked right up to the cliff edge and stepped off.

Cimon sat on the stone dock and let his legs hang. He was weary and he wiped a smear of oil across his face, then cursed softly to himself. The ship that loomed over him was unnamed as yet, but he had rebuilt it – rebuilt her. There was no question she was female. A good ship could raise a man's spirits on the breeze, but if he pushed too far, if he upset her, she could turn on him, snuffing out all happiness. He closed his eyes as he sat there, feeling the honest ache of a day's hard work in his legs and shoulders. The sun was setting on the Piraeus and he had worked thick olive oil into every beam and joint and crevice on board, sealing the wood against sea and spray. The shine of the oil faded to dull as it sank in, but the wood would survive a generation of hard use, just as long as the ship was re-oiled every season. Some of the carpenters had suggested an Egyptian varnish, with strange substances like pine sap mixed in to give a harder shell. Oil worked best, though, drawn deep. After all, the people of Athens had chosen their patron for the tree the goddess had planted. Not Poseidon, for the salt sea.

Cimon looked up as Pericles flopped down beside him. Xanthippus' son was just eighteen, but he had worked as hard as anyone to get those ships ready. One of them had been rebuilt right to the keel, with months of hard labour and great ribs lifted out on ropes and pulleys. The result had been all Cimon had hoped. His three captains already knew the way ships could sail and row. They were all veterans of Salamis, after all. Now they knew them to the last joint and nail. As they left Athens behind, Cimon knew he could spend a year or two at sea and not fear. They would draw maps where there were none, or redraw those that were so old they crumbled at the touch.

'We have a dozen oars still to turn,' Pericles said.

He waved a hand at the lathes along the docks, where weary men worked pedals wound about with string, while others stood in line and held iron chisels to the spinning

*Conn Iggulden*

wood. The water was thick with a curd of shavings and oil nearby.

'After that, just the tools, the lathes, the fresh food and . . . the water to bring on board. That's it, I think.'

He looked at Cimon with the admiration of a young man for one he respected. Cimon had insisted on learning the skills of the shipwrights. They'd considered it a fine joke at first, a whim of a wealthy young man and his friends. That attitude had faded as some forty of them turned up at dawn each morning. They completed each task they were given with quiet concentration, Pericles among them. He'd understood it was a test of sorts, that Cimon was watching them to see how well they worked together, how quickly they learned. There are worse ways to select crews. In the end, only two men had been turned away and both of those had been badly injured. Cimon had paid for doctors to tend them and slaves to help their recovery. They had wept even so, denied their places at the last.

'That's all, is it?' Cimon said. He opened his eyes, revealing white lines where the sun had not been able to reach. 'We still have to name the three ships – and select the crews for each one.'

'I imagine you have an idea about that already,' Pericles said.

He was almost certain he would be allowed to go with the rest. Though he was one of the youngest, he was a member of the Assembly, with voting rights. Cimon had made him ask permission from his father, but that had been a formality. Xanthippus didn't care. He didn't seem to care about anything any more. He just sat and drank wine without water, reading or staring into nothing as the days passed. If he was disturbed, his temper was volcanic.

Pericles had lived on board the ship for months, far from

his mother and sister as they tended to his father. His world had become those docks and his place in the crews. When he thought of Xanthippus at all, he tried to think of the man he had been before exile and war, not the man he had become.

Cimon looked across at him, interrupting his thoughts.

'Do you have a favourite ship? If you could choose any of the three?'

Pericles squinted against the setting sun. To one who hadn't crawled over every inch of the ships, the answer might have been that they were all the same, or so close it made no difference. Yet he had known the answer in an instant. The prow above his head stood over a great warship ram, of course. It would be their chief weapon against an enemy at sea. Two eyes were painted down there, almost at the level of the waters that fell back from oiled wood – that would rise to white froth at ram speed. The prows of the other two were clean and polished, the upright beam strong enough for a helmsman to grip as he leaned out. Yet this one was carved in a tracery of lines, an image of a woman coiled about with vines. Pericles had watched the carpenter complete the work, tapping away with mallet and chisel when his long shift was over. The man had not been one of theirs but a craftsman hired out of the city. He had embellished everything he touched in some way or another, adding tiny swirls and flourishes in joints and tracery. The woman who looked out on the dark sea was a siren, perhaps, one men would always follow. For Pericles, she made his choice an easy one.

'This one,' he said. 'She is my favourite.'

Cimon glanced at him and smiled at the honest pleasure he saw there.

He nodded.

'She is. I think so too.'

'And . . . are we strong enough to seek out Persian camps?'

Cimon looked over, judging him. He seemed satisfied.

'They have come back to the coast of Ionia, did you know that? Imperial merchants already trade there, with their . . . stamps and taxes. They have come back like flies.'

Cimon frowned for a moment. Heavy-browed, it made him look thunderous.

'But the sea is ours. The islands are ours. That's what I learned at Salamis, Pericles. Athens owns the sea. There are said to be a dozen islands still infested with them, all along that Ionian coast. Garrisons, watching the sea. Persia uses them as stepping stones, controlling the waters all around. Well, I am a free man of Athens and I say no. Our three ships – our three crews – will smoke them out. The sea is for Athens.'

Cimon looked once again at Pericles, his expression suddenly wary. Once more, whatever he saw seemed to reassure him.

'There is something else. I haven't mentioned it to any of the others . . .'

Pericles inclined his head, wanting to be trusted.

'My father . . .' Cimon began, 'he believed the bones of Theseus were out there still. My hope is to search for them.'

Pericles sat straighter, his mouth opening.

'Do you know where?'

Cimon shook his head.

'I know where to start. He is said to have been killed on the island of Scyros. The legend is that his body was taken away, but my father heard there was an old tomb there, in the hills. He always meant to search for it, but . . . he ran out of time. And here we are, Pericles, with three ships, with hoplites with spear and shield. If there is a Persian garrison on Scyros, I will take the island back for Athens and search every cliff and cave and field.'

He fell silent for a time, staring out at the sea. When he spoke again, his voice was a breath.

'Theseus was a hero of mine. He had a palace on the Acropolis and ruled in Athens as a great king, but he gave up his power to the people. Everything that came later – Solon, Cleisthenes, the Assembly – all began with that first step. A man of power, who saw it all for what it was and stepped aside.'

Pericles smiled at the thought. He knew Cimon wanted to be a hero, like Achilles, Theseus or Heracles. He did not mind that – whoever found the bones of Theseus would be part of his story. He rubbed his hands together, his fingers sticky with oil, sweat and dirt.

'He made a mark,' Pericles said.

Cimon looked at him with more than a little understanding.

'He did,' Cimon said. 'And so will we.'

# 37

Themistocles looked out on the landscape passing by. He had spent time on the Ionian coast in his youth. He hadn't known then how far the land had stretched beyond it. He still flushed to think of the amusement in his hosts when he'd travelled just fourteen days inland and asked if the city of Ancyra was Persepolis, where the Great King of Persia had his seat. They had made him wait there for an age while a caravan was prepared, a serious undertaking. Two dozen carts were drawn by mules and oxen. Eighty guards had been hired to ride alongside and see off any desert tribes who might seek to steal or murder. They carried food and water almost like a great expedition or a fleet going out, as if they would have no opportunity to replenish their stocks. They called Themistocles 'honoured guest' and 'archon' in the Persian accent, but they did not answer his questions. Jaavan of the market passed him into the care of a brother-in-law in Sardis, a gift that had earned him kisses on both cheeks and great respect, as far as Themistocles could make out. It seemed the Athenian was a valuable piece to play, a marker on debts or a chance at greater wealth and higher status. He did not think he was a prisoner, exactly, but there was also no question of him changing his mind and turning back.

The caravan trundled around the edge of a great desert and the days fled as his beard and hair grew long. On the fortieth day, when he could no longer stand looking like a wild man, he asked the barber to oil and curl his beard, plaiting his hair in the Persian style. After that, it sat as a weight on his neck, but itched less.

He lost some days to fever and three to loose bowels, so that he had to halt by the side of the road and groan. Most of that time had passed in a blessed blur, though he lost weight and strength alarmingly. His driver kept offering him fruit from hands as filthy as any Themistocles had ever seen, clearly worried about his precious charge.

By the sixtieth day, Themistocles knew he could no longer find his way back on his own, even if they set him free. A man could have spent a lifetime wandering through the forests and mountains they had crossed. They had passed through an empty world, with just a few herdsmen living lonely lives far away from their fellows. As they'd crossed a shallow river ford, his guards had chased off a young male lion watching them, crashing their swords onto shields and making a great clamour until the beast spooked and ran. Some of them wanted to hunt it down for the pelt, but the caravan master only pointed to Themistocles. There were sullen looks for days after, but he could do nothing about that.

He spent each day in a state of stupor, almost, with nothing to amuse him but looking back over the past. He ate with the others, from bowls he wiped out and handed back. He felt his mind dull over time, like a knife unused, so that he struggled to recall particular words, or the faces of his children. Each time, ten thousand times, he told himself there was no going back. If he had judged wrong, the choice was still made. He found himself muttering entire conversations he wished he'd had, or speaking to his wife as if she stood next to him. The driver of his cart spoke no Greek, nor was he a good teacher of his own tongue. Whenever Themistocles pointed to something and asked the name, the man

*Conn Iggulden*

would just stare at him. He was a miserable old fellow, perhaps overawed at meeting a Greek. Or perhaps he had been
kicked in the head by one of the mules and camels, Themistocles did not know.

By his estimate, it was four months since he had arrived
on the Ionian coast. He had almost given up on ever seeing
the Great King, as if he and the others had been doomed to
wander the hills and deserts until they died, never hearing a
friendly voice again. In the depths of his fever, Themistocles
had begun to think he might have crossed to the plains of
the afterlife. The presence of Persians made that unlikely,
however.

He was smiling to himself about some memory when he
realised the cart no longer rocked like a ship over rough
ground. His senses began to sharpen. They had found a true
road and it led . . . He peered into the distance, seeing houses,
temples, a bridge over a river. A bridge! He felt tears come to
his eyes at just that small sign of civilisation. He was caked in
dust and his own filth. His hair was matted with it, his robe
so dirty it was black. He was as thin as a tanner and about as
noisome. There were people on the road, carrying goods and
glancing at the caravan. He felt strange eyes on him for the
first time in an age. Desperately, he tried to remember all the
things he had told himself not to forget, all the words of
conversations he had practised so many times.

His plans tore to wisps as the caravan halted in the road
and Persian guards came to inspect the strange cargo. There
was much conversation, with only a few words he could
understand. His own name featured, repeated many times.
One of the guards whistled for a horse and mounted up, dig-
ging in his heels and galloping off like a good scout.
Themistocles watched him go, feeling like a ghost returned
to the world.

'Where is this?' he called. 'Where are we?'

A few of the guards actually dropped hands to their sword hilts when they heard his strange words. The caravan master patted the air around them, speaking sternly. He would not let his great prize be killed, Themistocles could understand that much. The brother-in-law had given too much time and wealth to bring him so far.

The street was growing busy, Themistocles saw. He realised there was no wall to this city, that the caravan had simply halted on an outer road, near what looked like a tariff house, or some official building. He supposed a city would not need an outer wall if it was part of an empire. As far as they were from the rest of the world, it was hard to imagine a hostile army ever reaching that place. From what he'd seen, they'd starve first, somewhere in the endless mountain forests.

Slowly, Themistocles eased himself down to stand in the road. His movement drew the immediate attention of a guard. The man pointed at him and barked something, clearly ordering him to stay on the cart. Themistocles blinked at him and stood, yawning. He had come a long way and in that moment, he was more alone than he had ever been. Perhaps it was a strength, he was not sure. Certainly, he felt himself, though weary and thin. He was not the man his wife expected him to be in that place, or even . . . an archon of Athens. He was perhaps his mother's son, still. Shorn of all authority and wealth, he had his wits and his endurance. He only hoped he had not been brought across half the world just to be executed as a gift for the king. The thought of his own appalled expression brought him to sudden laughter, a dry sound that went on and on, like a cough.

There were mountains in the distance, though he had seen so many snow-capped ranges by then that he hardly registered them. Yet he had been brought to a place where people wore good cloth and sandals in the heat of the sun, where just a little way along, a baker held up a loaf to passers-by. Themistocles found the oddest yearning in him, for the presence of others. He considered himself a lion, needing no one beyond his mate. The truth was subtler, after so long on the road. Themistocles needed to talk, to pour out good Greek in a torrent, without worrying he had gone mad. He needed to drink wine that was better than ancient vinegar, to eat fresh food instead of cheese rinds he could have used to patch a sandal. He needed the company of friends. That was simply the truth of it.

The man who came riding up to him was around his own age, though he dismounted without any great stiffness. Themistocles watched warily as the stranger came to stand before him, peering as if he had found a gem in the street.

'You are Themistocles?' the man asked. 'Archon of Athens?'

Themistocles nodded in relief at hearing Greek on another's lips.

The man shook his head in wonder.

'The journey has been hard on you, I see. Forgive my poor Greek. It has been many years since I resided in the west.'

Themistocles held still as the man leaned over and kissed him on each cheek. He was not sure if his status as a stranger or the way he smelled prevented the man kissing his lips.

'My name is Omid Saeed Karroubi. I am . . . now, how would you say it? The satrap? No, the governor of this city. You are my guest, from this moment. When you have bathed and eaten, when you have rested, I will take you to the Great King, the beloved.'

The Persian's eyes were very wide as he spoke, as if he could not quite believe what he was seeing. Themistocles bowed his head. He remembered too late that he should probably have dropped to the ground in obeisance. He had promised himself he would do it for Xerxes, but it was not a pleasant prospect, not for a free Greek. He saw the governor's gaze searching him as if he was something very strange. He supposed he was.

By early evening, Themistocles had been bathed and given new robes and sandals. The governor's slaves worked on him like sculptors, seeking out every scrap of dirt and then cleaning it away with brushes, oils, even tiny ivory picks for the folds of his ears. He was astonished at the muck that had clung to him, turning a huge bath black so that it had to be drained and refilled. His hair was unbound by three young women working in silence, their fingers teasing out each knot and braid. They had drawn combs through the worst of it, making his eyes water until he began to laugh at the silliness of his position. They had smiled with him, but still finished their work with seriousness and purpose.

A barber had come then to cut his hair, dropping thick locks of silver and gold onto a marble floor. Themistocles noted how those were collected up and rolled in cloth, no doubt a rarity in those parts. He refused to have his hair retied in the Persian style, though the barber grew red-faced as he tried to insist, pointing again and again at something beyond the room where they stood. Themistocles had to slap his hands away in the end, so that the man retreated with wounded dignity.

Left alone, Themistocles was about ready to sleep when the governor arrived, looking flustered. The man was actually trembling, Themistocles saw. He felt his exhaustion vanish in a flash of fear. Was he to be dragged out, executed? He clenched his fists as the man babbled in Greek.

'You are clean! Much better, much better. You must come

with me, this moment. Please, this way. The king has asked to see you. I thought it would not be until tomorrow, but His Majesty knows your name! He has sent his seneschal to bring you to him this hour. Quickly!'

Themistocles let himself be swept out of the room. He had a hollow feeling, but at least he was clean once more. If he could find a skin of good wine, he might even enjoy whatever followed. He knew the Persians cultivated vines. Some of their best reds found their way to Athens each year, or at least they had before the war. He smacked his lips, longing for just a taste to dull his fear.

The evening was fading into night as he came outside, finding a group of soldiers standing in the yard of the governor's home, or wherever it was he had been taken. The estate and its gardens lay further into the city, but he had no idea of the layout, or even the size of Persepolis. They left with soldiers taking up positions around him, the studs of their sandals loud on the stone roads.

As he passed through the city, he saw long streets on either side, with traders and passers-by halting at the sight of armed men. Themistocles matched the stride of the governor. The man was sweating already, though the air was growing cooler. Themistocles was grateful for that. There was no sign of the brother-in-law from Sardis, his sullen companion for over three months. Themistocles hoped the man had been sent back without so much as a coin.

He felt his own perspiration start as the guards lit torches, the better to see their way. The streets were dark by then and it seemed most of the city was going to their beds, so that the roads emptied. Or perhaps they just knew better than to get in the way of soldiers. Themistocles swallowed, nervously. He still didn't know if Xerxes would want to see him killed or not. He had never met the young king and his entire judgement of him was from one or two actions in the midst of a war. Themistocles murmured prayers to Athena and then wondered if she could possibly hear him, so far from home.

He passed through gates, each column a building in its own right, looming white in the darkness. Themistocles heard voices calling in challenge and the answers given. His companions did not seem to slow, but loped up a flight of wide steps, then on and on through the night, past layers of guards and through cloisters of green marble. At intervals, part of the group would peel off. Some were replaced by others in a different coat, or no uniform at all. Servants? Members of the royal household? It was all a blur to him. At least Omid . . . He had forgotten the rest of the man's name. At least the governor was still at his side, for all the man looked strained and nervous.

Huge doors opened ahead, timed so that the group would not have to halt or even slow. Light spilled across a stone floor so polished Themistocles could see reflections of their torches in it, like sparks moving. He went through into a hall lined with men and women, all standing perfectly still. He flashed glances to the sides, taking in faces and strange garb as he was made to keep walking. The governor slowed and Themistocles found he was panting. How had he become so unfit?

At the far end, a man rose from a throne of gold and descended a flight of steps. Themistocles understood as the governor whispered a prayer. A moment later, every one of them halted and dropped to their stomachs on the marble. They were in the presence of Xerxes, Great King of Persia.

Themistocles hesitated, then lay down with them. He had sworn he would, though he was grateful Aristides was not there to comment on it. Yet he was far from home and he still hoped for something like mercy.

*Conn Iggulden*

The king approached with another man at his side. Xerxes spoke in Persian and his translator repeated the words.

'Up, please. You may stand. I heard this evening that you had come far to see me,' Xerxes said.

The young king was smiling, but as Themistocles rose, he did not know if it was an expression of innocent joy or some darker delight.

'I could not wait until tomorrow!' Xerxes said. 'You, the man who saved me from destruction! Who offered to surrender the great fleet to me at Salamis. You, the first in Athens! I honour you, Themistocles.'

Themistocles felt his eyes widen as the translator repeated words he had longed to hear. He'd thought to make the same argument in a thousand different ways on his journey into the heart of Persia. All Xerxes knew of him was the two letters he had sent. With the right emphasis, Themistocles had saved the king's life. He felt relief rush through him as if he stood under a mountain stream. He staggered and Xerxes himself reached out, taking him by the arm. The action caused a ripple of astonishment to pass across the hall. The king had touched a Greek, in his own palace. Themistocles hoped it was not some great crime. He was like a child there, until he learned more of the language and customs.

'Majesty,' he said, 'you honour me in your mercy. I have been cast out by my own people. I thought . . . I hoped I would find a place, a welcome in this court.'

Xerxes nodded continuously as the translator repeated the words.

'Of all men, I owe you . . . more than I can say. I will give three cities to you, Themistocles of Athens, to rule as your own. You will have gold, gems, slaves by the tens of thousand. I will make you a satrap of my throne, Athenian, to honour you for all you have done. If I had known just a few more like you, I would not have lost poor Mardonius.'

Themistocles felt tears come to his eyes, unbidden. He had dreamed of just that response, but the reality came crashing down on him. Xerxes had lost so much in Greece. There had been every chance he would have had Themistocles killed and his head returned to Athens. That was the strain Themistocles had lived with for the endless trek into the interior. Having it lifted away left him giddy and light-headed.

'Are you well, Themistocles?' Xerxes asked in concern for him. 'Should I have let you rest?'

'Majesty, I have never been better. I bless you for your generosity and great heart. I only wonder . . . is there wine?'

# 38

Themistocles stared over a city as wide and deep as Sparta, with a green mountain on one side and ten thousand families down in the streets and markets, given to him to own. He had taken an empty palace built on a hillside at the edge, for the view it commanded. It had been empty, but furnished, as if its previous owner had just walked away. Themistocles had not liked to ask about the man who had lived there before. He suspected he knew the answer. Whatever the king gave, the king could also take.

A trio of house slaves brought platters of grapes and cheese, with a jug of wine as good as anything he had known in Athens. Themistocles knew he was drinking too much. He had almost drowned himself in the first weeks, but surfaced somehow, despite all the weight of regret.

There was nothing else to take up his time and the evenings stretched to eternity. The days were pleasantly warm, though it was autumn as he understood it. He had been assured the winter would bring cold. He could not complain, though the dream had soured for him in just a few days. Nothing was what he had hoped it would be.

Xerxes had made him a governor, or a satrap, whatever term he preferred to describe his new estate. The truth was rather different. Though Themistocles had guards, they were not loyal to him. They spoke no Greek and when he learned the right words in Persian, they reacted slowly or not at all, with scorn on their faces. At times, they ignored him completely, standing stiff-faced. Themistocles had not yet tried to dismiss them from their posts, to be replaced by others. He was almost certain they would not go – and the extent of the farce would be revealed.

Even the slaves were both his and not his. They clipped hedges in the gardens, hedges that had been there before him and would no doubt be there when he was gone! They served food and wine easily enough, but without meeting his eye. He felt like a prisoner.

He thought of the treasury he had been shown on his first day. That was a pleasant memory and he smiled at it. The head of his guards had unlocked great iron doors. Themistocles had walked into a room of gold and silver, piled carelessly. It looked like a great fortune, more than he had ever seen before. In that moment, he had found himself wondering how he might get it all back to Athens.

His smile fell away at the memory and he emptied the cup, not noticing as it was filled again. There would be no return home, that much was clear. Every few days, the Great King summoned him to the royal palace, to be paraded before friends and lords and relatives like a curiosity, a bird in a golden cage. The young king's pleasure in him was real enough, Themistocles believed. It was just that he had come to the final house of his life. There would be no more challenges, no triumphs or disasters, ever again. All the years ahead lay in the view and the wine he drank. He grimaced.

'Is it not to your taste, master?' the slave asked.

His translator repeated her words in the dull monotone Themistocles had learned to detest. He had started lessons in Persian, determined to be less helpless among them. Too many of the king's noble friends assumed there was only one language in the world. They asked him questions in their own tongue and looked offended when he had to shrug or look for the scribe who knew Greek.

Themistocles sighed to himself. He had begun to learn their names, but this particular house slave was not one he knew. Themistocles squinted at her.

'It is very good. No, I was just thinking of the past.'

She waited for the words to be repeated in Persian, then nodded politely, retreating. He cursed under his breath. Conversation was impossible in those circumstances. He felt about as alone as he had on the journey there, but without the desperate hope that had kept him going. No one else would have thought of going to Persia, to the very heart of their royal city! He had, though. He was a man who *never* gave up, no matter how things turned against him. That was his gift – and he had won, again and again, because of it.

The great plan had been to remind Xerxes of a debt owed, at least as the king might have seen it. There had been risk, but Themistocles had few friends and nowhere else to turn. If things had gone well, he'd intended to bring his family out as well. He looked around him. The last governor of that city had lived in the same palatial home. No doubt he had learned the names of all his slaves. Perhaps his children had laughed and run in the courtyards and cloisters. Yet the man had been plucked out and made to disappear on a whim of the king. Themistocles wondered how long he would remain a novelty in that court, before someone else caught the king's attention. The thought chilled him. He was a world away from home and he was certain of one thing. For all his new titles and wealth, he could not leave.

He heard someone clear their throat behind him and looked over his shoulder. His seneschal was there, another he had inherited. The fellow seemed to treat the house as if he owned it and Themistocles was just a troublesome guest. That evening, the man stood to attention, so that Themistocles felt his heart sink.

'Satrap Themistocles, your presence is required . . .'

'Yes, at the palace, by the king . . .' Themistocles interrupted, standing up.

He gripped the chair for a moment, aware that he was a little drunk. It had been a few days since Xerxes had last paraded him, that wonder of Athens and the west, believer in democracy and other strange things. No doubt another group of royal relatives and hangers-on had come to see and hear his strange tongue. He sighed. The last group had brought out a dory spear and demanded to be shown how a hoplite used it. It had been . . . He shuddered.

'Your presence . . .' the seneschal began again, his mouth twisting in distaste. He didn't seem to approve of wine.

Themistocles nodded to him, waving his hand and shutting one eye, to be sure he had the right one.

'I am *coming*!' he roared.

He felt suddenly foolish, shouting at servants, but there was no taking it back. He strode out. It didn't matter. The king's palace was a day's ride from the first of his new cities. Xerxes had kept him close – a great honour, as it had been explained to him. Yet it was not freedom. Themistocles found his horse in the courtyard, saddled and ready. It was strange to see the six guards waiting for him, stone-faced in patience. There were no thieves on Persian roads, after all. The king's men had hunted them all down and hanged them.

Themistocles remembered being a happy drunk when he had lived in Athens. Wine had released his love of pranks and song, so that he was more likely to injure himself falling off a table than anyone else. For some reason, the Persian reds brought out melancholy, stealing through him as he rode.

When he reached the king's hall, Themistocles was relieved at first to find no new group of Persians waiting to be

*Conn Iggulden*

entertained by him. The long room was darker than before and empty of the usual crowds, even of the servants who usually waited around the king like ghosts. Only the translator stood at the king's side, like a statue in oiled wood.

Xerxes sat his throne with one bare leg hooked over the arm. When he rose from it, he wobbled. Themistocles bit the inside of his lip rather than risk a smile. The king was at least as drunk as Themistocles had been. The long ride had sobered Themistocles up and he felt more his old self than before. In fact, he was starving. He lowered himself to the floor and pressed his forehead against cool polished stone. He waited a beat, then rose to look up at Xerxes.

The young king wore a kilt of gold strips, with some sort of armoured piece of gold across his shoulders, held by wire or threads. His eyes were glassy as he looked on Themistocles.

'I knew you would come, Themistocles. If I asked you. You are a loyal man,' he said. There was a slight slurring to his words, though not when they were repeated in Greek by his man.

Themistocles bowed in response. He had not seen Xerxes like this before. He suspected the young king was at least as dangerous drunk as he was sober – and Themistocles knew they would not truly be alone. Somewhere in the vast darkness along the edges of that hall, where the torches did not reach, armed men would surely stand. He breathed slowly, trying to be calm.

'I came to see my father in this place,' Xerxes said. Wine spattered as he waved a cup of it. He saw the drops bead like blood on the polished stone and shrugged, waving his other hand. 'I came here, when he was dying, when he asked me to finish the work he had begun.' His face creased in sudden grief, like a child. 'I could not do it. I let him down. I lost Mardonius and his sons. I lost Hydarnes and the Immortals . . . Masistius, master of horse. Hundreds of ships. All gone.'

Themistocles felt cold sweat trickle between his shoulder blades. He could not help glancing at the goblet the king was waving. There was no slave to refill it, he noticed. Could he ask for a cup?

'If not for . . . *you*, I would have lost my own life as well. You, an Athenian.' Xerxes jabbed the air with his hand. 'You warned me to protect the bridge of ships. It fell to a Greek to save me.' He began to laugh, though it might have been sobbing, it was hard to tell. 'Can you believe it?'

Themistocles thought he was not expected to reply. He waited, looking up at intervals. The king was *wildly* drunk, he realised. Young men could reach a stage of 'ecstasis' where the world became simple and they stepped outside themselves. It seemed Xerxes had reached that point – some time before.

'It took my father years to gather an army and a fleet to invade Greece. I tried to finish his work and I . . . could not. I failed. But you know what I didn't have? What my father didn't have?'

Themistocles looked up, his stomach clenching.

Xerxes nodded at him.

'He didn't have you, Themistocles. On the night you came to me, I shouted, "I have Themistocles!" – because you are the key to going back. You are the one I will make my general, who will . . .' he clutched the air, his hand closing as a claw, '*gather* them under one throne and rule . . . as my satrap of all Greece.'

He stared down at Themistocles in triumph.

'Will you take my hand? Will you swear on your gods to lead my armies, Themistocles? Your word . . . saved me once. I know you are loyal – and you know the Greeks better than

*Conn Iggulden*

anyone. You have the . . . cunning I need, the mind. Will you do it?'

Themistocles took a moment to prostrate himself on the ground once more. He felt the cold stone right along the length of his body. He glanced down as he rose, half-expecting to see a shimmering image there in sweat. His smile was wide and his eyes glittered in the torchlight as he replied.

'It would be the greatest honour of my life, Majesty. I will.'

'Swear it on your gods, Themistocles. I know you are a pious man. Swear it on those and I will embrace you as a brother.'

Themistocles laughed.

'It is too great an honour, Majesty, but I swear service to you, fealty to the throne. I swear it on the poet, Apollo, on Ares, the god of war – and on Athena herself. I will lead the armies of Persia back to Greece.'

Xerxes came down the steps, so swiftly Themistocles feared he might fall. To his astonishment, the young king embraced him, smearing his neck with tears and wine.

'I want to hear your plans, Themistocles,' Xerxes said, standing back. Slowly, he kissed the Athenian on the cheeks and then the mouth.

'I will work on it from this moment, Majesty, I swear. I will not sleep until I can return here with a campaign for you. You honour me, Majesty, more than I deserve.'

As the translator repeated the words, Xerxes nodded blearily, his wild enthusiasm flickering as he felt the effects of the wine swell his stomach. It roiled and groaned as he pressed a hand against the bare flesh. He began to climb the steps again, looking for somewhere to vomit.

'Return in . . . three days, Themistocles. I will assemble the most senior men of the army to hear all you have to say. Go with God, Athenian. You are blessed and honoured.'

Themistocles prostrated himself for a third time, then left the long hall, his footsteps echoing behind him.

He arrived back at his palace on a hill later the following day. By the time the sun rose again, Themistocles had been up all night, writing furiously. The results were in a pile on his desk, each one bearing the name of one he loved. Aristides was in that pile, as well as Xanthippus and Cimon. Themistocles had written to his wife and children too, one by one. A little brazier burned by the desk, proof against the night's chill. He had used it to mark each letter with candle wax. Silver coins had been pressed into it, enough to carry each one home.

The night had been blessedly cool, for which he was grateful. He had poured himself a little wine at some point, but melancholy had threatened once again. The cup sat, still full, before him. As the dawn strengthened, he stared out across the valley where his city nestled. There were wisps of cooking fires already rising there, families coming awake and setting about their day. It truly was beautiful. He wished his wife could have seen it, just once.

Themistocles collected the letters and pressed them to his lips, then dropped them, coins and all, into the brazier. They curled and browned as he took up the knife he had laid close by. He drained the cup of wine and placed the blade across his wrist. The sun was rising. It would be a good day. He pulled back hard, cutting deep.

When the house slaves found him, they began to scream, rousing the guards. The seneschal checked the body and shook his head, pale and frightened that he would be held responsible.

The Athenian was dead. The sun had risen and the air was growing warm.

# Historical Note

The philosopher John Stuart Mill once described Plataea as more important to history than the battle of Hastings. Though often overlooked in favour of Thermopylae, or the extraordinary sea battle at Salamis, Plataea was the event that saved Greece – and with it, the idea of democracy. Perhaps it would have arisen somewhere else; perhaps not. It is true that if the alliance of Greek city states had failed there, the Persians would have secured a western empire. If they had done that, there would have been no Rome, a city of barely forty thousand people at the time of the Persian invasion.

History has many fathers, many moments on which the future seems to rest. They may seem inevitable now, but at the time, no one could have known Greece would survive. Athens had been burned and a huge invading army roamed the plains – accompanied by thousands of Greeks who had thrown their lot in with Persia. The Theban hoplites were the most famous of those, but there were also horsemen from Larissa and Pherae – and on the Spartan peninsula of the Peloponnese, the city of Argos remained neutral and sent no one. The influence of Persia was vast, its wealth limitless. After all, the legendary riches of Croesus were just a small part of the Persian treasury.

On the island of Salamis, it is true that Xanthippus' dog tried to follow its master and drowned. We do not know its name. The dog's tomb existed for centuries afterwards, though it is lost today.

At sea, Themistocles, Xanthippus and Cimon worked together with the factions of their allied fleet to hold the strait against vastly superior forces. It is not far-fetched to say they could not have won without Themistocles sending a message to King Xerxes. The Persian king already had Greek allies at sea and on land. The idea would not have been so strange. The first message was a ruse to split the fleet – a chance to wrench victory from an impossible situation.

With half the Persian fleet rowing around Salamis in a pincer movement, Themistocles sent a second message, in what has to be a stroke of genius. By 'revealing' a threat to the bridge of ships, he panicked Xerxes into packing up his pavilion on the shore and leaving Athens – taking a decent part of the fleet and army back to protect his line of retreat. It is, simply, the ruse that won the war – and Themistocles was responsible. If we include the fact that it was Themistocles who persuaded the Assembly of Athens to build a great fleet in the first place, it is hard to exaggerate the role he played. He is almost single-handedly the man who saved the west. I have always loved moments where history seems to turn on a single life, such as when the Mongolian armies of Tsubodai were brought home from their great trek by the heart attack of a khan. The events around Salamis were of a similar magnitude, or greater still.

I sent Xerxes away on board his flagship, but the historian Herodotus said he left by land, taking a large part of the army with him. That probably explains why a great part of his battered fleet ended up at Samos for repairs. As is often the case, the real history is slower than I would like – and more detailed than I can always fit in. Xerxes departed, yes, but there was time enough for the Athenians to send a messenger to him, asking how he expected to pay for all the damage of his invasion! He cannot be said to have ever really understood the Greeks. In confusion, Xerxes pointed to Mardonius and said they should look for payment from him. He may have meant it as a threat, but Mardonius actually would pay with his life at Plataea.

It is also true that Mardonius was not hell-bent on war, that he first tried to arrange for Athens to surrender with the help of one Alexander of Macedon. (This particular Macedonian king was the ancestor of Alexander the Great.) At this time, Macedonia had become a loyal ally of Persia. Alexander visited Athens as an envoy and put the Persian case.

Note: I wrote a Spartan shaking hands with Cimon at the isthmus of the Peloponnese. There is a modern myth that ancient Greeks and Romans did not shake hands. It may not have been as common, but there are references to shaking hands on greeting that go back to the ninth century BC. The gesture is mentioned in Homer, sealing agreements and as proof of trust, so the meaning seems not to have changed a great deal. It was also carved in images on gravestones from this period in Athens, often as a final handshake between the deceased and a loved one.

When the Spartans heard Mardonius and Alexander of Macedon were making overtures to Athens, they sent a party to Athens to demand an end to negotiations – and offered to pay to support the women of Athens. That scene is reported in Herodotus. The Athenian council was furious at the implication. They formally rejected both the Spartan and the Persian offer – and in reply, Mardonius marched south to sack Athens again. He was a man of his word and his threat had been quite clear. For a second time, the Athenian fleet ferried the people to safety. For a second time, the soldiers of Persia despoiled and destroyed everything the Athenians had been rebuilding. I do not think this is general knowledge, but it is one of the most extraordinary events of the period. Persia sacked Athens, not once, but twice in a few months, in 480/479 BC.

The second sacking was every bit as traumatic as you might imagine. Violence erupted among the refugees as they argued whether to accept the Persian offer. Some were stoned to death, killed by their own. The Athenian strategoi sent messages to Sparta, saying they could not endure another attack. Unless Sparta sallied out in the spring, they would become allies of Persia. Crucially, they threatened to surrender their fleet to Persia – a fleet which could then land anywhere on the Peloponnese peninsula where Sparta lay. If that had happened, there would have been no great flowering of Athenian politics, democracy, art and philosophy beyond that point. None of the great playwrights would have flourished under a dictatorial Persian rule. Between them, over a decade, the Athenian hoplites at Marathon, the crews at Salamis and the Spartans at Plataea all saved Greece.

The main Persian commanders at Plataea were Mardonius; his second, Artabazus; and Masistius, master of horse. There is a question mark over whether Hydarnes, commander of the Immortals, was there. Herodotus mentions him refusing to leave the side of Xerxes, so he might have gone home when the king left. However, the record is a little confusing, as Xerxes seems to have given Hydarnes a role in bringing the army home – and the army remained in Greece.

The battle of Mycale is traditionally said to have occurred on the same day as Plataea. They were hundreds of miles apart, however, so it's impossible to say. Xanthippus was there,

*Conn Iggulden*

with King Leotychides of Sparta in nominal command of the fleet. There is no record of Pericles and his brother Ariphron being present. Without a solid record of where they were, I put them where they might have been. It is somehow surprising that there is no record either of what happened to Ariphron, or even the name of Pericles' sister. They vanish from the record. However, I needed to explain the horror that followed – where Xanthippus is impossibly cruel. Punishment by crucifixion was not uncommon, but is still utterly out of character for the man – the only time in his life something of that sort is recorded. For that reason, it made sense to give him a reason to hate.

The image of the swallow flying from darkness, through a lighted room and out into the dark once more, is from *The Rubáiyát of Omar Khayyám* – an anachronism here, as he lived some fifteen hundred years after Xanthippus. However, the image appeals to me, though I have hopes for whatever lies beyond the room.

Themistocles made a number of errors during the war – though they were trivial in comparison to his achievements. It is true he had the bags of evacuating Athenians searched for valuables as they queued to get to Salamis. In one fell swoop, he confiscated the wealth of every rich family in Athens. He did it to pay the rowers of the fleet, who needed vast sums of wages just when the city was effectively bankrupt. However, it earned Themistocles a huge amount of ill will. It is also true that he used the broken tombs from the city cemetery as rubble for a massive new gate and wall. That seems to have been a classic politician's error – he just didn't realise how badly that would be received. Finally, the man who saved Athens seems to have been unable to stop telling people how much of their freedom they owed to him personally. In a society that had sent 'Aristides the Just' into exile, a man renowned for his integrity and dignity, it should not be a surprise that Themistocles was finally exiled. It is only surprising that it didn't happen until around 472 BC, some years after Plataea. He lived for a while in Argos, on the Peloponnese. Denied the protection of Athens, he was then accused of corruption and threatened with new trials. He decided to flee to Persia. I have compressed those years.

The last part of the story of Themistocles – how he died – is difficult. There is a persistent legend from the period that is as I've described it. Xerxes is said to have welcomed him in delight, crying, 'I have Themistocles! I have Themistocles!' From his point of view, of course, Themistocles was the Athenian who had tried to surrender at Salamis – and given good advice about the bridge of ships that may have saved Xerxes' life. The fact that Xanthippus brought a fleet later on to ravage that coast can only have helped persuade Xerxes that Themistocles had been on his side.

The Persian king gave Themistocles a number of cities as his own. When the boy who had struggled to survive as a child in Athens was finally as rich as any small king, Xerxes is said to have asked him excitedly how he envisioned returning to Athens at the head of an army.

Given the circumstances, it is hard to be certain what happened next. The only records would be Persian and as with all the things of men, they would not record everything that happened, especially if it reflected poorly on the Great King. The legend is that Themistocles took his own life rather than betray his people. We will never know the details, only that he never came home. His was a magnificent life. I doubt I have done it justice. For those who would like to know more of the period, I recommend: *The Histories* by Herodotus, *Daily Life in Greece at the Time of Pericles* by Robert Flaceliere, Plutarch's *Life of Pericles* and *The Spartan Army* by J. F. Lazenby. I'll keep back the name of my favourite source of all until the next book.

Xerxes would not go on to have a long reign. He was killed by his bodyguard and a eunuch around 465 BC. The cultures of Persia and Greece would not overlap again until a Persian prince named Cyrus came looking for an army to defeat his brother – Artaxerxes. That story of ten thousand Greek mercenaries trying to get home is one I told in *The Falcon of Sparta*.

In Greece, as Themistocles passes from the stage, two great cities stand: Sparta and Athens. What follows is a struggle between democracy and kings, with its roots in the uneasy but ultimately successful alliance against Persia. Athens and Sparta fought a common enemy at Artemisium, at Salamis, at Plataea and at Mycale under Xanthippus. When that terrible enemy was finally defeated, they did not need one another any longer. They pulled apart, as hostile as ever. The Spartans turned their gaze inward and went home, but the Athenians didn't. They had seen how well the fleet had worked – stronger together than apart. A nation was born in those ships.

In Athens, a new generation arose: Cimon, son of Miltiades, Aeschylus, the father of tragedy – and Pericles, son of Xanthippus. He would have to guide his people through a conflict as great as any they had known, the city of Athena thrown once again into a crucible. The story that resulted is greater than all that went before.

Conn Iggulden, London